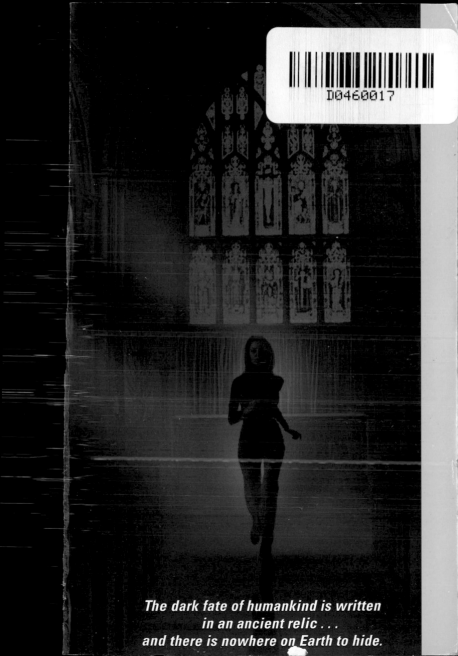

*The dark fate of humankind is written
in an ancient relic . . .
and there is nowhere on Earth to hide.*

By C. S. Graham

THE BABYLONIAN CODEX
THE SOLOMON EFFECT
THE ARCHANGEL PROJECT

C.S.GRAHAM

THE
BABYLONIAN
CODEX

HARPER

An Imprint of HarperCollins*Publishers*

This is a work of fiction. Names, characters, places, and incidents are products of the author's imagination or are used fictitiously and are not to be construed as real. Any resemblance to actual events, locales, organizations, or persons, living or dead, is entirely coincidental.

HARPER

An Imprint of HarperCollins*Publishers*
10 East 53rd Street
New York, New York 10022-5299

Copyright © 2010 by Two Talers LLC
ISBN 978-0-06-168936-9

First Harper mass market printing: December 2010

HarperCollins® and Harper® are registered trademarks of Harper-Collins Publishers.

Printed in the United States of America

Visit Harper paperbacks on the World Wide Web at
www.harpercollins.com

10 9 8 7 6 5 4 3 2 1

For Grady

Many will say to me in that day, "Lord, Lord, have we not prophesied in thy name? And in thy name have cast out devils? And in thy name done many wonderful works?"

And then will I profess unto them, I never knew you; depart from me, ye that work iniquity.

MATTHEW 7:22–23

THE
BABYLONIAN
CODEX

1

Noah Bosch waited in the lee of a small Alpine shop, its steep roof draped with snow, its cold-frosted windowpanes giving glimpses of exquisite crystal figurines that cost more than he earned in a month. A light snow had begun to fall, the temperature plummeting rapidly as the surrounding steep slopes cast the valley into shadow. But despite the cold, Noah was sweating, his throat dry with fear and anticipation as he studied the tanned, supremely confident faces of the men filling the icy streets of the exclusive ski resort.

A convocation of fat cats in the snow. That's what the irreverent called this annual gathering of the obscenely rich and powerful here at the World Economic Forum in Davos. These were the kinds of guys who owned not one but two yachts worth $100 million each, who could drop a couple hundred thousand at a blackjack table in Monte Carlo as if it were so much loose change.

Because to them, it was.

They ruled the world, these men, although no one had elected them. They were the richest of the rich, a superclass of hedge fund managers and international bankers, corporate CEOs and venture capitalists. They came here every year to network and schmooze and set the agendas that would determine the lives—or deaths—of the other six billion inhabitants of the planet.

The official pass dangling around Noah's neck identified him as an outsider, a journalist admitted only to observe and report. But no one needed to read his name tag to know that he wasn't one of these captains of the universe. He was marked by his ratty tan parka; by the clumsily cut brown hair worn a little too long; by the lanky, narrow-chested body of a twenty-something geek without a private gym or the leisure to schedule regular workouts with a personal trainer. A tall, long-legged woman in a cropped mink jacket, her gloved hand tucked into the elbow of a man three times her age, glanced over at Noah, her lips twitching with amused contempt.

Noah ignored her.

The sessions at the Congress Center had finally ended. Narrowing his eyes against the thickening snow, Noah anxiously scanned the growing crowd on the ice-covered Promenade. He was looking for one man: the newly inaugurated vice president of the United States, Bill Hamilton.

Where was he?

He spotted the tall, silver-haired Southerner an instant later. Flanked by two Secret Service men, Hamilton was pausing to read the blackboard easel set up on the sidewalk in front of a fondue restaurant when Noah pushed his way through the crowd toward him.

"Excuse me, Mr. Vice President?"

One of the Vice President's Secret Service agents moved to block him. But Hamilton turned with a politician's ready smile and waved the bodyguards back. He was a handsome man, his face tanned and open, his eyes a brilliant blue. "I know you," said Hamilton with the affable charm that had helped win him the number-two slot on his party's ticket. "You're that journalist—Bosch, isn't it? The one who thinks someone is planning to kill me."

One of the Secret Service agents—a musclebound tank with small dark eyes and a neck as thick as his head—laughed.

Noah set his jaw. "Please, Mr. Hamilton; you've got to listen to me. I don't know how they'll do it, but they plan to make their move *here*, at Davos. And I tell you, this is meant to be just the beginning."

Hamilton's smile was still in place, but the vivid blue eyes had hardened. "Look, Noah— You don't mind if I call you Noah, do you? I appreciate your concern. I really do. But take a look around, son. No place is more secure than Davos. You can't walk half a block without running into a Swiss police check. No one could touch me here."

"Mr. Vice President—"

Hamilton reached out to pat Noah's shoulder. "Son, I don't know who's been jerking your chain, but you can't believe ninety percent of what you hear in this business." He nodded to the restaurant beside them. "Why don't you go sit down, have a nice cup of hot chocolate, and relax?"

"But—"

"Good day, Mr. Bosch."

The Vice President moved on up the snow-filled street, his deep, drawling voice raised in cheerful greeting to a man Noah recognized as a defense contractor from Texas. Noah chewed his lower lip in frustration. Maybe what he needed was to—

Even though he was watching, Noah couldn't understand what happened next. One minute, the Vice President was

striding energetically up the street. Then he went down, and
Noah heard the thump of Hamilton's long, solid body hitting
the ice. A woman let out a soft gasp. Someone shouted, "Is
there a doctor? Get an ambulance. Quickly! *Oh, God.* I think
he's dead!"

A shocked, jabbering crowd of expensively dressed men
and women converged on the fallen man. Over their heads,
the Secret Service agent's dark gaze met Noah's.

Noah felt a chill run up his spine. He took a step back,
then another and another. When he reached the snowy alley
beside the restaurant, Noah turned and ran.

2

Two men walked along the C&O Canal towpath in Georgetown, their shoulders hunched against the brisk wind. The sky was a clear, cold blue reflected in the placid waters of the canal beside them. Neither man was here for the view.

"We're concerned about the appearance of this journalist in Davos," said the younger of the two men, adjusting the sleeves of his soft gray Italian suit so that they lay just so against the cuffs of his crisp, hand-tailored white shirt. "I assume this Mr. Bosch is being taken care of?"

The second man—taller, darker, more heavily muscled than his companion—kept his gaze on the bare branches of the trees before them. His name was Duane Davenport, and as head of the FBI's Criminal Investigative Division he was one of the most powerful men in the Bureau. "We're on it," he said simply.

"You know where he obtained his information?"

"Not yet, but we're working on it."

A tight smile flattened the other man's lips. He had bland, forgettable features and straight, corn-silk-fine hair that had a tendency to fall forward from a receding hairline so that he was always smoothing it back. He swept it away from his face now in a quick, fastidious gesture. "Work faster."

Davenport swallowed a spurt of annoyance and kept his voice even. "You can tell Mr. Carlyle he doesn't need to worry."

"Mr. Carlyle decides what he does and doesn't need to worry about."

The younger man's name was Casper Nordstrom, and for the past ten years he'd served as personal assistant to Leo Carlyle, an international financier who'd taken advantage of the deregulations pushed through back in the eighties to amass billions. Being a personal assistant might not sound very powerful, until you realized that Carlyle made all of his moves through Nordstrom. One whispered suggestion from Nordstrom was enough to send everyone—from senators and congressmen to judges and generals—scrambling to do his bidding. To cross Nordstrom was to cross the powerful, shadowy figure who stood behind him, and that was something few men dared to do.

Duane Davenport cleared his throat. "Everything is under control."

Unlike Nordstrom, who'd been bred in the rarified atmosphere of Andover and Princeton, Davenport had grown up on the streets of Trenton, New Jersey, the son of an out-of-work longshoreman and an alcoholic mother. He'd started out as a cop walking a beat in Trenton, then joined the Bureau as a Special Agent assigned to organized crime while he was still finishing up his law degree at night school. In the twenty-two years since then, he'd risen rapidly through the ranks, and he owed much of that advancement to Leo Carlyle's influence. Carlyle was very good at identifying bold, willing men in everything from politics and the judiciary to law enforcement and the military, and then shepherding them through to positions of power.

"Frankly," said Davenport, pausing to let a slim, auburn-haired woman on a red bicycle zip past them, "I'm more concerned about this Ensign Guinness the Art Crimes Team is bringing in this weekend to work on the antiquities stolen from Iraq."

"You mean the remote viewer?" Nordstrom gave a sharp laugh. "Don't tell me you believe in that hocus-pocus nonsense?"

Davenport watched the bicyclist disappear around the bend. "There is much in God's world we don't understand."

Nordstrom shrugged. "Then eliminate her."

"If I have to, I will. I've detailed one of my men to work with the special agent involved in the project. If Guinness comes up with information that could be dangerous to us, he has orders to take them all out."

Nordstrom glanced at his watch. "The second phase is set to begin in just five days. It's critical that you not let yourself get distracted."

Davenport huffed a soft laugh. "By Ensign October Guinness? Are you kidding? I checked her record. The woman's a real whack job. The Navy gave her a psycho discharge just months into her tour in Iraq. The only reason they brought her back to active duty was because T. J. Beckham insisted on it."

Nordstrom frowned. Until last month's inauguration, T. J. Beckham had been the vice president. Now he was back in Kentucky raising coon dogs. "So she no longer has a sponsor. Why not simply have her called off the case?"

Davenport shook his head. "This isn't an assignment. It's a personal favor to an old friend, through unofficial channels. I might have been able to shut the whole thing down with strong-arm tactics from my end, but now is not a good time to stir up some of the old questions about what happened in Baghdad."

"You think taking out a couple of Navy personnel and an FBI agent isn't going to stir things up?"

Davenport smiled. "I told you, Guinness is a certified whack job. If my man has to eliminate them, he'll fix it so it looks like a classic murder-suicide. Nothing could be simpler."

3

October Guinness was scanning the arrival and departure monitors in the New Orleans airport when she felt a strange sensation steal her breath, leaving her shaky and hot.

She didn't realize her reaction showed on her face until Colonel F. Scott McClintock, who'd driven her to the airport, said, "What is it, Tobie? What's wrong?"

She gave an unsteady laugh and turned away from the bank of monitors, toward the security line. "I don't know. Maybe somebody walked on my grave." Remembering where she was, she cast a quick glance around and lowered her voice. The airport was thick with tourists flying in for the last weekend before Mardi Gras—and locals fleeing the crowds and traffic congestion that meant Carnival in New Orleans. "Can I say that here without getting arrested?"

McClintock smiled. "Last I checked." Standing well over six feet tall, with a thick shock of white hair and a weathered face, the Colonel had spent more than thirty years as a psychologist in Army intelligence. Although officially retired, he still saw VA patients on a volunteer basis. But his main focus was the work he did with Tobie: setting up a small, hush-hush remote viewing program at the Algiers Naval Base, across the river from the French Quarter.

Now, his smile faded slowly as he continued studying her face. "Are you worried about flying?"

"In a jet? No. As long as it's not a helicopter, no problem." Tobie had had a really bad experience with a Kiowa helicopter in Iraq.

He laughed. "I can promise, no helicopters on this assignment."

She was on her way to Washington, D.C., to work on a project for an old friend of the Colonel's at the FBI's Art Crimes Team. The ACT was still trying to track down the thousands of artifacts looted from Iraq's National Museum during the 2003 fall of Baghdad. The expert in charge of the project, Special Agent Elaine Cox, had asked for Tobie's help in locating a dozen or so of the rarest items.

Unfortunately, the Colonel himself had had to back out of the trip at the last minute, thanks to a torn rotator cuff that required immediate surgery. He paused beside Tobie at the end of the security line and said, "I wish I was going with you."

"You focus on getting better. Peter and I work together just fine and you know it."

McClintock's eyes crinkled in a smile. Peter Abrams, McClintock's assistant, had flown up to D.C. the night before and would be taking McClintock's place in the project for the Art Crimes Team. "Yeah, I know it. But I'd still like to be there."

From a TV in the bar beside them came a reporter's lightly accented voice. *"The world is in shock today following the sudden death of United States Vice President Bill Hamil-*

ton. Preliminary reports suggest Hamilton may have hit his head after slipping on the ice, although it is also possible the sixty-two-year-old Vice President may have suffered a heart attack. We're still waiting for an official comment from President Daniel Pizarro, inaugurated just two weeks ago tomorrow. We expect to have that in the next half hour."

McClintock nodded toward the TV set. "That might be what has you unsettled."

Tobie followed his gaze to the screen, where a reporter in a heavy, hooded coat could be seen against a backdrop of steep, snow-covered slopes. And she felt it again, that swift sensation of what she now recognized as disembodied fear. "Maybe," she said softly.

"Listen, Tobie . . . if you think this might be a bad idea, you can still back out. I'll just tell Elaine—"

She jerked her gaze away from the snowy scene. "Are you kidding? We couldn't ask for a better chance to show all the skeptics in D.C. just what remote viewing can accomplish. I wouldn't miss this for anything."

She was almost at the front of the line. McClintock said, "Just . . . be careful, you hear?"

"I'll be fine. I'm going to be sitting in a soundproof room remote viewing a bunch of dusty old artifacts." She pulled her boarding pass out of her carry-on bag and fumbled for her ID. "How dangerous can that be?"

4

"This is the most excitement I've seen at Davos in years. If ever." The United States secretary of state, Forest Quincy, stretched his short legs toward the fire that crackled sedately on the hearth. He held a glass of French Colombard brandy from the Tishbi family cradled in his left hand and one of Leo Carlyle's famous hand-rolled Cuban cigars in the other. As he settled deeper into the tapestry-covered wingback chair, the gray vest of his three-piece Armani suit pulled gently across the soft swell of his stomach. Quincy had a well-deserved reputation for overindulgence in the sins of the flesh.

Leo Carlyle splashed a measure of brandy into his own glass and smiled at his guest. "And to think you almost decided to give the World Economic Forum a pass this year."

Unlike the Secretary, Leo was the kind of man who valued discipline and took pride in his self-control. At just above medium height, he kept his naturally powerful body strong and hard with a carefully honed weight-training regimen. He might be fifty-six years old, but his hair was still thick and dark, as were the heavy brows set straight above his smoky hazel eyes. For some years now he had worn a full beard, as dark as his hair and meticulously trimmed. According to *Forbes*, he was one of the ten richest men in the world.

Leo was proud of that, too.

Quincy glanced up. A balding man in his early sixties with a ruddy complexion and an unusually small nose, he had served as secretary of state for the last eight years. The inauguration of the recently elected president, Daniel Pizarro, just two weeks ago should have changed that. But the new president—a half-Jewish, Latino ob-gyn, for Christ's sake—was a bleeding-heart liberal with all kinds of outdated, sixties-era feel-good bonhomie. Thanks to the idiot's misplaced belief in the virtues of bipartisanship, Quincy was still secretary of state.

It was a situation the new president would not live to regret.

"I didn't know you intended to make your move here," said Quincy. "In Davos, of all places."

"Can you think of a better place?"

Quincy laughed. "No. But you might have warned me."

"The fewer people who know the details of what we're doing, the better."

Quincy worked his jaw back and forth in what Leo recognized as suppressed annoyance. "It's not exactly like I'm a bit player in all this," said the secretary.

Leo set aside the heavy crystal carafe with a soft thump. "I never meant to imply that you are."

It was a lie, of course. Secretary of State Quincy, like former president Randolph before him, was a puppet. A politician selected and groomed by men who managed, financed, and carefully promoted his career for their own ends.

Still faintly smiling, Leo came to settle in the chair on the opposite side of the fireplace. The premier suite at the Belevedere was reserved for him every year at this time, although he did not always choose to attend the Forum. Lately Davos had become overrun by NGOs and self-indulgent, conspicuously philanthropic celebrities who wanted to talk about AIDS and the environment and a host of other liberal time wasters.

Conspiracy theorists the world over loved to tut-tut and shudder at the power of the "Davos men." But the truth was that a conclave like Davos was too large, too diverse, too *open* for its members to ever effectively connive together to rule the world. Their plenary debates were even available on YouTube, of all things, with key quotes going out on Twitter.

But there was still a place in the scheme of things for organizations like the World Economic Forum. If nothing else, they kept the energies of the masses focused and distracted. The real work of determining the fate of the world was done elsewhere, by men like Leo working in select groups of likeminded individuals who kept their meetings closed to the press and their membership rolls a secret. Organizations whose members realized that if they didn't act quickly—and aggressively—their days of God-given, untrammeled economic dominion might soon be brought to an end.

"And the next step?" said Quincy, puffing on his cigar.

Leo raised his brandy to his lips and smiled. "Patience, Forest. The second phase will come at its preordained time."

"And that is—when?"

"Soon. Very soon."

5

Special Agent Elaine Cox of the FBI's elite Art Crimes Team stood at the one-way mirror, a folded sheet of paper clenched in her hand, her gaze fixed on the honey-haired young woman seated at a table on the far side of the glass. Elaine had been an FBI agent for eighteen years. If asked, she'd have said she was hard to impress and almost impossible to amaze. But what she'd witnessed in the last few hours had her blood thrumming with excitement and wonder.

She'd read a lot about remote viewing over the years. From her long friendship with Colonel McClintock, she'd heard about the incredible successes the Army had had with RV before their program imploded back in the nineties. But nothing could compare with being in a controlled environment and actually watching a master remote viewer reach out with her mind and "see" an object hundreds—perhaps even thousands—of miles away. Maybe, just maybe, they'd be able to use the information October was providing to finally track down some of the most precious of the tens of thousands of artifacts still missing from the museums and archaeological sites of Iraq.

A clipped male voice at Elaine's elbow said, "It's all bullshit. You know that, don't you?"

She turned her head to study the wiry, sandy-haired agent beside her. His name was Mark Kowalski and he wasn't part of the Art Crimes Team. He was here as a special representative of Duane Davenport, who'd insisted one of his men be present to observe the remote viewing sessions. On one level, that annoyed the hell out of Elaine. But she was smart enough to realize that putting up with the presence of a skeptic like Kowalski was a small price to pay for Davenport's letting her project go forward. The head of the criminal division was well known for being hostile to anything that even vaguely smacked of what he liked to call "New Age woo-woo idolatry."

She opened the folded paper she'd been holding and held it out. "You call this bullshit? Look at number four on the list."

Kowalski stared at the paper, his nostrils flaring. The sheet contained a list of the twelve items Elaine had selected from among the thousands that had disappeared from Baghdad's National Museum during the U.S. invasion and occupation of Iraq. The loss of Iraq's archaeological treasures was an unforgivable tragedy, not only for the Iraqi people but for all of mankind. As the site of ancient Mesopotamia, Iraq was the cradle of Western civilization. From its rich, fascinating cultures—Sumer, Assyria, Babylonia—had sprung everything from writing and seeder plows to sailboats and the concept of zero. As an American, Elaine felt a profound weight of personal responsibility for what had happened, and she was determined to get as many of the artifacts back as she could.

It hadn't been easy, narrowing the list down to just twelve items. But she only had October for a few days, and Elaine knew she couldn't push the girl too hard. Even with the best viewers, fatigue would set in after a while and the viewer's accuracy would start going down.

Following the protocol suggested by McClintock, the name of each of the selected items had been written on a separate three-by-five-inch card that was then placed in a double, opaque envelope and randomly assigned a four-digit number. When October viewed an object, she was told nothing about the item except the number written on the front of the envelope.

That afternoon, she'd been run against "item number 3524." She'd described a gold dagger with blue stones set into the handle and sheath. Even without looking at her list, Elaine had known immediately what October was "seeing." It was King Meskalamdug's dagger, from the Royal Cemetery of Ur. October had described the item against a backdrop of what sounded very much like the Park Avenue apartment of Aaron Leibowitz, a wealthy, well-known specialist in ancient Middle Eastern art who Elaine had long suspected maintained a secret collection of stolen antiquities.

Of course, October's viewing wouldn't be enough to enable them to arrest Leibowitz or even get a warrant to search his apartment. But now that they knew where to look, Elaine's team could begin gathering the evidence that would, hopefully, enable them to nail the bastard.

"She musta seen the list," said Kowalski.

Elaine tried to tamp down her temper. "You know she didn't."

"She's either seen the list, or she's made a pact with the devil. What we're witnessing here could be some sort of wizardry."

At that, Elaine let out a peal of laughter.

A muscle bunched along Kowalski's prominent jaw. "You think that's funny?"

On the far side of the glass, Peter Abrams, the Naval Intelligence psychologist who worked as McClintock's assistant, cleared his throat and said, "Okay, Tobie; you ready?"

Kowalski said, "Leviticus tells us that a woman who is a medium or a wizard should be—"

Elaine held up her hand in an impatient gesture, silencing him. October and Abrams were in a soundproof chamber, with an audio-video feed to the observation room and the recording equipment it contained. But Elaine didn't want to miss a moment of this next session.

Abrams rested his palm on the opaque envelope lying on the table before him. "Relax now, Tobie. Focus your attention on item number eight nine two one. Describe your perceptions to me."

October sat in a comfortable chair on the far side of the table, a carafe of water, a pad of paper, and pencils within easy reach. She was a small, slim young woman in jeans and a navy pullover, with dark brown eyes and shoulder-length hair she wore pulled back in a clip. She had spent the last ten minutes settling into a meditative state McClintock called the Zone. Now she said, "I get the impression of something smooth. A number of similar items that are smooth and transparent, like glass. Only, they're not glass. Each item is formed of two rectangles of this material, sandwiching something between them. There are many of these glass-like units, each about nine by eleven inches. It's like they're lined up sideways." Reaching for the drawing pad and pencil before her, she began sketching in long, bold strokes. "Like this."

Peter Abrams cleared his throat. "You say something is sandwiched within these glass-like units. Can you describe it?"

October nodded. "Each one is very similar. They're old and flat. I get an impression like sheets of paper. But they're not paper, they're woven. Sort of like cloth, but they're not cloth. They have writing on them."

Elaine was aware of Special Agent Kowalski shifting uneasily beside her. She glanced at him, her earlier sense of elation beginning to ebb. She thought she had a pretty good idea what October was "seeing": an ancient papyrus, once divided into folios and bound into a codex. Invented by the Romans, a codex was an early form of book that replaced the scroll. From Tobie's description, it sounded as if the pages of this codex had now been separated and preserved by mounting each in a double-window mat sandwiched between two sheets of quarter-inch ultraviolet-filtering acrylic.

The problem was, there was no codex on Elaine's list. And because the number written on the envelope—8921—was completely arbitrary, they wouldn't know what artifact Tobie was supposed to be viewing until they opened the envelope.

"Can you read the writing on these woven sheets?" asked Abrams.

"No. It's unfamiliar to me. But I keep getting these flashes of strange images."

"Describe these images."

October shook her head, her brows drawing together. "It's like . . . biblical illustrations. Of the Tower of Babel. The Hanging Gardens of Babylon." Her pencil moved across the paper, but even from this distance Elaine could see that she wasn't sketching walls or gardens. She was drawing a huge, strange cross.

"Maybe back up a bit," suggested Abrams. "Tell us something about the environment."

"I'm inside a room. It's cool. Very dry. Controlled. The lighting is subdued, without windows. It feels like it's a shrine, or a museum. Only, there are no people."

"Can you see anything else in the room?" asked Abrams.

"More glasslike sandwiches of different sizes, held in

their own special cases. A flat surface, like a table. A locked cabinet."

"Anything else?"

"I don't think so."

"Okay. Can you get above the room? Maybe tell us something about the building?"

"I get the impression of rough wood. Very rugged, yet also oddly luxurious." As she spoke, she started a new drawing. "It's like a log cabin, only on a grand scale. Like a lodge."

She barely looked at her work; it was as if the images flowed directly from her mind to the paper. "I don't think it's a building open to the public. I get the impression of a private place, guarded, with many secrets. This is a place where all is not as it seems."

"Can you shift your angle a bit? Tell us something of the surroundings?"

"I get a sense of grass, browned by winter. There are stands of trees, like a forest. Some have bare branches, but most are evergreens." She started a new drawing.

"Here's the main building." Her pencil moved across the page. "The trees are here . . . and here. It's like I'm perched on a slope, looking out over water. A wide expanse of water. I get the feeling of cold. There's a long, straight road nearby. Only, it's not a road. It's paved, but it starts and stops suddenly. There are lights—here, and here." She added them to her sketch. "I think it's a runway, not a road."

Again, Elaine was aware of Kowalski shifting his weight beside her, as if he were uncomfortable.

October said, "Yes, it must be a runway. There are two men standing beside a plane."

"Can you get closer to these men? Maybe tell us something about them?"

"I get the feeling of great power and wealth. Power, and a

dangerous kind of arrogance. It emanates from both men."

Elaine found herself choking down a welling of frustration and disappointment. She knew remote viewing was never one hundred percent accurate; McClintock had warned her of that. She realized now just how lucky they'd been with the first viewing. Not only had October zeroed in on the artifact, but Elaine herself was familiar with the New York apartment October described. But this session . . . this session was a complete miss.

Peter Abrams was saying, "Can you go back to the building at the top of the hill?"

"I can, but . . . . there's something oddly compelling about these men. I'm getting impressions of snow. But although it's cold here, there is no snow on the ground. I keep getting the name 'Noah.'"

"Just the name?"

"Yes."

Elaine was aware of Special Agent Kowalski stiffening beside her. She threw him a quick glance and found him gazing at October with narrowed eyes.

"Tell me more about this snow," said Abrams.

"I get the impression of a deep valley. Something very important is to happen in this snowy place and it's linked to something else that is planned for a different place. An event these men expect to remake the world."

In the small soundproof room, Peter Abrams stared across the table at October. "Did you say, 'remake the world'?"

"That's what they think."

Elaine felt a chill run up her spine. She had no idea what October was targeting, but she nevertheless had no doubt that October had been drawn by one of the artifacts on that list to *something*. Something powerful and frightening.

Anything can be targeted, McClintock had told once her.

*A person, an object, an organization. Anything. Even some-
one's thoughts can be targeted. You just need to have a good
enough remote viewer.*

As if from a long way off, she heard the sound feed of
Abrams's voice, saying, "Describe this event they're planning."

"I keep getting images of a snake. Not a coiled snake, but
a ruby-eyed snake slithering through a swath of green. I get
the feeling of water. Lots of water rushing in, like a flood.
Only, the flood isn't the event, it's—"

Elaine heard a sliding click. She was so focused on the
drama unfolding on the other side of the one-way mirror that
her brain moved slowly, identifying the sound too late as the
rasp of a pistol being racked.

She turned just in time to see Special Agent Mark Kowalski aim his suppressed Glock 26 at her head and fire.

6

"Tell me more about this water you're seeing," Tobie heard Peter Abrams say. "Is it moving, or still?"

She drew a breath and let it out slowly, centered deep in the near dreamlike state of remote viewing. "I get the impression of both," she said. "It's like—" She broke off, her eyes widening as an inexplicable, suffocating terror coursed through her.

Across the table from her, Abrams said, "Stay deep, Tobie. Focus on the target."

Tobie found she was struggling simply to draw a breath. "I'm trying. It's just . . ."

"I understand. But it's important that you hold your focus. Tell us about the water."

"The, uh, water . . ." She closed her eyes and willed herself to sink back into her Zone. "The water—"

The heavy soundproof door on the far side of the room flew open and hit the wall with a crash. A man she recognized as Special Agent Mark Kowalski burst into the room, his big Glock held in a purposeful two-handed grip. Tobie was facing him, the table between her and the door. But she was still drifting in the upper levels of her Zone, her limbs heavy as if in sleep, her reaction times slow.

"What the hell?" demanded Abrams, his chair skittering across the floor as he pushed to his feet. "What's wrong?"

Kowalski's first bullet hit Abrams in the shoulder, his shirt instantly blooming a wet scarlet. Slapping one hand to his bloody shoulder, Abrams staggered backward and went down.

Kowalski pivoted toward him, gun extended.

"No!" screamed Tobie. Thrusting up, she grabbed the carafe of water and hurled it at the shooter just as his finger tightened again.

The carafe hit the FBI agent high on his upper arm then careened off to slam into the wall. The vessel shattered, spraying broken glass and water across the room. Kowalski flung up a crooked elbow to protect his face. Tobie heard the *pop-pop* of two more suppressed rounds. Abrams jerked. Lay still.

Her heart pounding painfully, hands curling reflexively into fists, Tobie scrambled around the table and launched into a flying snap kick. The ball of her foot slammed into the FBI man's tightly clenched jaw. His head whipped around and he let out a grunt.

Landing lightly, she hit him with a roundhouse kick to the side of his head. He dropped to his knees, stunned. But his body was turned in such a way that his gun hand was still sheltered from her.

She whirled and fled through the open door.

Erupting into the deserted corridor, she veered to the left, toward the bank of elevators that lay at the core of the building. With the clatter of her own frantic footsteps echoing loudly in her ears, she tried desperately to remember what she knew about the unfamiliar building complex.

Special Agent Cox had arranged for Tobie to perform her

remote viewings at the offices of a private consulting firm that worked with the FBI. The soundproof room and its adjacent control room lay on the third floor of a multistory building that formed part of an office park of clustered modern high-rises surrounded by acres of rolling lawns and trees. When Tobie arrived earlier that afternoon, the parking lot had been crowded, a steady stream of people going in and out of the offices.

Now it was late, the offices dark, the corridors deserted.

The silent bank of elevators rose before her but she realized she couldn't afford to wait for one. Pushing open the heavy metal fire door to the nearby stairs, she pelted down the bare concrete steps.

Her breath was soughing in and out, her blood pumping so hard she was shaking. She hit the landing for the second floor and kept going, around and around. From up above came the sound of the fire door opening again.

"Oh, shit," she whispered. She remembered seeing a security desk in the lobby, just inside the entrance. There'd been an armed security guard on duty when she arrived.

Please, please still be there, she prayed.

Slapping open the fire door to the ground floor with outstretched hands, she burst into a softly lit lobby of polished marble floors and mirrored walls. Behind a counter near the wide expanse of glass entrance doors sat a plump man in his late fifties, his shiny bald head ringed by tufts of graying hair. He had his feet propped up on the desk before him, an opened bag of potato chips in one hand, his gaze fixed on what looked a clip from *The Colbert Report* running on his laptop.

"There's a man with a gun!" Tobie yelled as she pelted toward the entrance. "He's already killed two people upstairs and he's right behind me!"

"Huh?" The security guard dropped his feet off the desk with a plop, his jaw going slack as he swung toward her.

Tobie heard the fire door burst open behind her. "Either get out your gun or run!" she cried.

The guard lumbered to his feet, one hand groping toward the holster on his belt.

"*Hurry!*" Tobie shouted as she raced past him. Through the row of glass doors she could see wide steps and an access ramp that led down to the darkened parking lot. The vast expanse of asphalt lay nearly empty and gleaming wet beneath sulfurous floodlights. With a shock she realized that at some point during the last few hours the weak winter daylight had faded into night, and it had begun to rain.

She flung open the nearest door and catapulted out into the cold night air just as Kowalski fired off two shots. She heard the security guard make a hideous gurgling sound.

"Oh, God, no," she whispered, then flinched as a pane of heavy safety glass exploded behind her.

"Shit!"

Flying down the concrete steps, she darted sideways into the shadows thrown by a row of shrubs along the building's foundation. Cold raindrops stung her face, beat down on her shoulders as she tore through the night. Throwing a quick glance across the parking lot, she realized there were lights still burning in the windows of the far building.

For one desperate moment she considered running there for help. But then she realized she'd be a easy target crossing the open stretch of asphalt. And even if she made it, Mark Kowalski had already shown he was willing to kill anyone who got in his way. She couldn't put more lives at risk. Her only hope, she realized, was to head for the rolling parklike grounds that stretched beyond the office complex and try to lose herself in the woods.

But when she reached the end of the building, she discovered she'd suddenly run out of shadows. An open expanse of floodlit lawn stretched between her and the trees.

Shit, she thought again.

She could hear Kowalski's quick tread on the steps behind her. Sucking in a deep gasp of icy night air, she pelted across the wet, floodlit grass. With each step, she kept expecting to feel the shattering impact of a bullet ripping through her body. Arms pumping, legs reaching, she was five paces away from the wood. Three. She gave a desperate sprint and felt the dark shelter of the trees close in around her—

Just as a bullet thumped into the thick trunk of an elm beside her shoulder.

She caught her breath on a sob. Swerving first right, then left, she wove in and out of the trees, trying to avoid giving her pursuer an easy line of fire. A rock rolled beneath her foot and she slipped, wrenching her right knee. Wet branches slapped her face, tore at her hair and clothes. Trailing strands of ivy wrapped around her ankles, tripping her. She stumbled out of the underbrush onto a well-groomed jogging trail and had to fight down a nearly irresistible urge to follow it. But the open, predictable course would favor the faster runner, and Tobie knew she was hopelessly outclassed. Her right knee had turned into a white-hot agony, and her lungs ached with every breath.

And the nutcase behind her looked like he ran ten miles a day before breakfast.

Throwing up one arm to protect her face, she crashed into the rain-soaked shrubbery on the far side of the trail. Despite the near freezing temperature, she was drenched with sweat. Each breath was a painful gasp. She could hear Kowalski plowing through the undergrowth behind her. He was gaining on her.

Over the pounding of her own heartbeat she caught the faint hum of traffic punctuated by an angry beeping of horns. She swerved toward the sound and almost missed the small rocky stream at her feet.

She launched into a leap at the last instant, barely clearing it. A few moments later she heard a splash, followed by a clatter and a loud curse. Her heart soared with triumph, but she knew the FBI man's blunder had earned her no more than ten, maybe fifteen seconds of extra breathing space. Then she burst out of a stand of rhododendrons and practically slammed into a six-foot-high chain-link fence that ran along the top of a ten-foot high concrete wall. Below her, at the base of the retaining wall, stretched a six-lane expressway crowded with late rush hour traffic creeping along bumper to bumper. An endless sea of cars extended in both directions, headlights stabbing into the night, taillights reflecting red off the wet blacktop.

"Oh, my God," she whispered, fighting to draw air into her aching lungs. Wiping the mingled sweat and rain from her face with her forearm, she swung first one way, then the other.

The fence continued unbroken as far as she could see.

7

Tobie forced herself to draw a deep, steadying breath, her gaze raking the darkness. She obviously couldn't go around the fence or through it. But maybe she could go *over* it.

Her gaze settled on a big oak growing close enough to the fence that one of its branches hung out over the drop-off. *Could she reach that branch?*

And even if she reached it, how was she going to get down on the other side without killing herself?

The sound of Kowalski crashing through the brush reminded her she had no choice. Leaping up, she grasped one of the oak's lower branches and crabwalked her way up the rough trunk until she could lever her weight onto the limb. There, shaking with fear and exhaustion, she drew in a steadying breath and carefully brought her feet beneath her until she was crouched low on the limb.

She studied the branch that hung over the fence. It jutted out a good two feet higher and something like three feet to her left.

Bracing her weight against the trunk, she eased up into a standing position. Resisting the urge to look down, she leaped toward the next branch. Slipped. Almost fell. Caught her balance.

Shaking badly, she straddled the massive branch as if it were a horse. Then she scooted out until she was directly over the fence. Wrapping her arms around the limb, she eased her weight off the tree.

The rough bark scratched her face, snagged her sweater. She felt blindly with her feet for the top of the fence. The air here was thick with the exhaust fumes of the cars idling on the roadway below. She could feel the heat of their engines roiling up to her. Then the toe of one tennis shoe found the fence. Slid off. Found it again.

Letting go of the tree, she half scrambled, half slid to the top of the retaining wall. She hung there, her fingers twisting painfully in the metal links of the fence, the cement of the wall wet and cold against her body, her legs dangling in space.

Over the purr of an endless sea of idling engines she could hear running feet, approaching fast. She took a deep breath and let go.

She landed hard on the shoulder of the road. The jarring impact tore through her knee, stealing her breath in an explosion of fire. For a moment her leg buckled and she went down, catching herself on her out-flung hands.

She pushed up at once. The car beside her—a late model BMW two-door—was just starting to roll forward. She sprinted across in front of it, one splayed hand thrust out as if she could somehow will the driver not to hit her. She glimpsed a man's pale, startled face staring back at her through a rain-speckled windshield. Then he flashed past.

The driver of the Porsche in the center lane laid on his horn in warning and hit the gas. She swerved to avoid him, running down between the first two lanes of traffic. She was limping badly, her hair hanging in wet, dirty clumps. Her hands were bleeding, her jeans torn. She scanned the slowly moving lines of vehicles, looking for a cop.

Nothing.

The cars around her were beginning to pick up more speed. A guy in a white pickup truck punched down his window and shouted at her, "Are you nuts? Get outta the road!"

She thought about hammering her fists on someone's window and asking for help. But then she threw a quick glance over her shoulder and spotted Kowalski jogging along the side of the road toward her, his gaze sweeping over the traffic. Would he risk shooting her in front of a hundred witnesses?

Are you crazy? she told herself. *He's an FBI agent. He'll just say you're a terrorist.*

She glanced around in despair, hemmed in on both sides. She was as trapped by the lanes of moving traffic as she'd been by the fence.

Narrowing her gaze against the rain, she focused on the silver SUV headed toward her in the center lane. A dozen or so feet separated it from the semi coming up behind it. She tensed, ready. The instant the SUV splashed past, Tobie sprinted across the lane. The semi's massive grill bore down on her, its horn blaring as it thundered past in a sucking whoosh of hot air.

She paused, her hands braced on her knees as she bent over, trembling. She now had two lanes of traffic between herself and the killer. But the traffic was moving faster. She had to get out of there.

Her heart pounding, she eyed the laden car carrier lumbering toward her in the center lane. Loaded with Volkswagens that gleamed white and red and silver in the rain, it had a steel ladder riveted right behind the cab.

As the transport rumbled past, Tobie grabbed the rungs of the ladder. Her feet slipped off the wet bottom rung and for a moment she dangled painfully from her outstretched arms, the pavement rushing dizzily beneath her, the truck's gears grinding as the driver accelerated. Gritting her teeth, she managed to pull herself up and squeezed her body into the narrow space between the back of the cab and the first car.

She crouched there, her breath rasping painfully in her throat as the transport whizzed past the FBI agent. She'd have sworn he stared right at her. But she must have been hidden by the shadows, because he simply turned away, his gaze scanning the lines of cars as they picked up speed.

Gingerly, she eased back on her haunches and squeezed her eyes shut. She was safe.

For now.

Jax Alexander hunkered down in front of his fireplace, a poker in one hand and a glass of fine, aged cognac in the other. He'd just finished a really, really bad week that included being shot at by both Somali pirates and U.S. Special Forces guys, and then almost getting his ass fired by Gordon Chandler, the new head of the CIA, who just happened to hate Jax's guts.

But all was now good. He had a few well-earned days off. The row of candles on the mantel above flickered softly. A vintage recording of Edith Piaf played over the sound system. On the comfortably scuffed brown leather sofa behind him, Kelly Yardley stretched out her impossibly long legs and let out a satisfied sigh. Jax's erratic, secretive lifestyle had a way of destroying his relationships with women. But for a change, things seemed to be working out with Kelly.

"This is just the kind of nasty, cold night for a fire," she said. "A real one, I mean." She drew in a deep breath. "I love the smell of wood smoke. Reminds me of camping as a kid."

Jax shifted the logs, sending a whoosh of flames up the chimney. "You went camping as a kid? I didn't know that."

She laughed. "There's a lot you don't know about me. Not as much as I don't know about you, mind. But—"

She broke off as a loud knock sounded on the front door. Her head turned toward the sound.

Jax ignored it.

The knock came again, then turned into a pounding.

"Aren't you going to answer it?" asked Kelly.

He set aside the poker and pushed to his feet. "No."

The thundering continued.

"I think you ought to answer it."

He bent to give her a long, lingering kiss. "If you insist. I'll be right back."

Still carrying his brandy snifter, Jax wandered into the entry and put one eye to the peephole.

October Guinness stood on his front porch, her hair hanging in wet clumps around her dirty, scratched face. She wasn't wearing a coat. Her jeans and pullover sweater were torn and muddy, and she had her arms wrapped across her chest as if she were cold—or else barely holding herself together. A taxi idled at the curb, its exhaust billowing up in a white cloud of condensation in the misty night.

Jax thrust back the deadbolt and jerked open the door. "October? Jesus Christ! Come in."

She stayed where she was, her voice a low, harsh whisper. "Are you alone?"

"No, but that doesn't matter. What the hell happened? You're soaked."

"I'm sorry, but I didn't know where else to go. They killed Peter and Elaine, too."

Jax didn't have a clue who Peter and Elaine were. He said calmly, "I'll call the police," and tried again to draw her inside.

Still she hung back. "No! No police. Not until I get sorted out in my head what's going on."

"October, you're freezing and in shock. For God's sake, come in."

"I don't want anyone to know I'm here. Do you have a side door?"

"Off the carport. It opens to the kitchen. But—"

"I'll meet you there. Can you pay off the cab? I had to leave my wallet and everything else."

Jax met her wide, frightened brown eyes, and nodded.

8

Duane Davenport stood at the window of his office in the J. Edgar Hoover building, his gaze on the rain-washed expanse of Pennsylvania Avenue below. Night had long since fallen, the streetlamps and traffic lights reflecting off the wet pavement in a frosty blur of white and red and green.

He loved standing here. It was as if he could feel the power and energy of the city pulsating around him. A power that he was helping to shape and control.

Still faintly smiling, he reached for his phone and called his wife, Sarah. She picked up on the second ring.

"Hi, honey," he said, glancing around as Special Agent Laura Brockman came into the room. Brockman paused just inside the door, a file tucked under one arm, her gaze politely averted. Davenport turned back toward the window and said to his wife. "Looks like I'm going to be a while yet. Why don't you go ahead and feed the kids?"

Sarah said, "You want me to wait for you?"

"Nah. I might be late. I'll give you a call when I'm on my way home. Love you."

He put away his phone and turned back to Brockman. "What you got for me?"

She held out the file. "Here's everything we have on Noah Bosch." Brockman was a delicately featured young woman in her early thirties, with long, fine blond hair, killer legs, and gray eyes. In addition to being a crack shot, she had a black belt in judo and a ruthless ambition that scared the hell out of most men. Davenport could think of few worse fates than being married to a woman like her. But there wasn't anyone he'd rather have at his side in an operation. She was without a doubt the finest agent he'd ever worked with— smart, efficient, and relentless.

"Any luck yet finding the asshole?" he asked, leafing through Bosch's file. He paused to study a photo of the journalist's narrow, effete face, and felt his lips purse with distaste. *Typical anti-American sonofabitch*, he thought; the guy probably kept a copy of *Thus Spoke Zarathustra* beside his bed.

"Not yet, sir. It would help if we could involve Interpol."

Davenport looked up. "Negative. The last thing we want is our fingerprints anywhere near the case when Mr. Bosch suffers a fatal accident."

"At least we know he's still someplace in Europe."

Davenport nodded. They'd been watching all the transatlantic flights. "You're monitoring his cell phone?"

"He's obviously pulled the battery. We can't get a signal on him."

"He'll turn up. And when he does, we nail him." Davenport tossed the file on his desk in disgust. "Taking care of Bosch is going to be the easy part. What I want to know is, where the hell did he get his information? Who's his source? We obviously have a leak, and I want it plugged."

"We're working on it, sir. I've got a few leads."

"How hard can it be to—" Davenport broke off as his

phone began to ring. He reached for it. "Davenport here."

Mark Kowalski's voice was tight. "The girl got away."

Warren Patterson braced his hands against the pulpit, his gaze scanning the crowd before him as the strobe lights played over their upturned faces.

The lights were timed to pulse at fifty-five to sixty cycles per minute, which was the rhythm of a slowly beating human heart. The music, likewise, was tied into the same repetitive, carefully calculated beat so that the sound and light worked together to generate a calm, altered state of consciousness. It didn't work on everyone, of course; generally only about 20 to 25 percent of the population. But that was still sixty million people in the U.S. of A. alone.

According to the CIA guys whose reports he'd studied, it was called the alpha state. The CIA had gotten interested in the whole topic years ago, when they'd discovered that people in the alpha state are twenty-five times as suggestible as people operating at normal, or beta, consciousness. A psychologist watching Patterson's congregation would immediately recognize all the external signs of people entering a trance, their muscles relaxing, their eyes dilating, their bodies swaying back and forth.

Patterson watched his audience, too, so he knew exactly when he had them.

The music rose in a crescendo, then stopped.

"Hallelujah!" he shouted.

Five thousand joyous voices bellowed back at him. "Hallelujah!"

He leaned forward, as if imparting a secret. "Do you know what time it is, ladies and gentlemen?" He smiled. "No. Don't look at your watches. I'm not talking about *man's* time. I'm talking about the *Lord's* time. And the Lord tells us that the time has come for us to stop just sitting around, praying to

Him and waiting for Him to come. The time has come when
the people of God must go on the warpath for Him. Make no
mistake about it, our God is a War God. Those who claim to
talk to you in the Lord's name, who talk of peace and good
works, they have it all wrong. They have misled the Lord's
people."

Patterson let a sneering note of contempt color his voice.
"That's right: they have misled you! Jesus is not a Lord of
peace. Jesus is not a lamb. Jesus is a *lion*. Do you know what
a 'host' is? It's an army! God is a warrior! Hallelujah!"

"Hallelujah!"

They were his now. Pumped, ready to fight—and highly
suggestible. It was a talent some people had, just like a talent
for playing the flute or basketball. Patterson's talent was for
controlling people. Once, he had been a used-car salesman.
Now he was the pastor of one of the largest congregations on
the East Coast. Over the past forty years he'd built up a massive worship complex he called Trinity Hills. His television
program was watched by hundreds of millions worldwide.
He had his own university, five houses in three different
countries, two private jets (all tax deductible, since they
were registered to his ministry), an oil refinery in Texas,
and the leases to gold and diamond mines scattered across
Africa. The Lord had smiled upon Warren Patterson. He had
no doubt that he was one of the elect, one of God's "Chosen
Ones."

"The time has come," said Patterson, delivering his words
in the same hypnotic forty-five to sixty beats per minute,
"for God's people to take up the cause of the Warrior God.
Right now, God is calling all of us to serve his mission and
make it ours. And what is our mission? *To retake dominion
over what is rightfully ours!*"

"Hallelujah!" shouted his audience in a frenzy.

Patterson smiled. "Yes, my friends; the time has come for

God's church to listen to what he is really saying. It is time for us to leave behind the old 'Gospel of Salvation' and embrace the 'Gospel of the Kingdom.' God's Kingdom *is* of this world! And God tells us that all men everywhere must be made obedient to His word. Everywhere."

Patterson could see his assistant, Scott Weber, hovering just out of sight of the TV cameras. Scott was an intern from Liberty University. Tall and lanky, with a shock of blond hair and bad skin, he was nerdy and clumsy and naïve. But the kid was hardworking and eager to please, and his dad was the CEO of a major defense contractor. In other words, someone well worth cultivating.

Nodding almost imperceptibly to Scott, Patterson let his voice roll on. "The Bible tells us that for thousand of years now, the Kingdom of Heaven has been coming. Not peacefully. Not by good works. But by the swords of God's warriors. Today, we are called to be God's warriors. You and me. And you know what that means?"

Five thousand faces stared up at him, waiting to be told. To be led.

He said, "It means that the time has come when all men, everywhere, must be made to bow before King Jesus whether they want to or not. And that means ceding God control over every aspect of their lives. To do anything less is worse than a sin. It's *treason*." He held up both hands. "Hallelujah!"

"Hallelujah!"

He could feel it now. They were pumped. Excited. Ripe. At Patterson's sign, a troop of blond, nubile young women dressed like angels floated onto the stage, their sweet voices raised in song. As ushers passed the collection plate, a voice rolled in the background at the same forty-five beats per minute. *"Give to God. Give to God."*

Catching his assistant's eye, Patterson slipped off the stage.

"Well?" he snapped. "Any word?"

"The EPA is saying the refinery violates forty-nine different environmental protection regulations. They won't let it start back up."

Patterson felt an angry rush of heat that left him shaking with rage. "Fucking sons of bitches. Of course it does! It always has. Why the hell should that make a difference now? Do you know how much I'm losing every fucking day that thing is shut down? Who wants a bribe now?"

Scott Weber's nostrils flared on a quick, frightened breath. "The problem is President Pizarro, sir. He's ordered the EPA to institute a new zero-tolerance rule."

"Pizarro," sneered Patterson. "Fucking little wetback shit." He watched the ushers working the crowd. The collection was almost finished. Time to get back onstage. "Call the governor of Texas. He owes me. See what he can do."

"Yes, sir."

Carefully smoothing his silk tie, Patterson leaped back onstage. He raised his arms wide, the paternal smile back on his face as the music came to an end and the haul from the collection plates was tucked away. "Let us pray."

9

"I'm sorry I ruined your evening. Was your girlfriend mad?"

Jax studied the bedraggled woman who sat cross-legged beside his hearth. She'd had a shower and changed into a pair of Jax's sweats and an old Yale sweatshirt that practically swallowed her. Now, her hair slowly drying into soft curls, she had her hands wrapped around a mug of hot chocolate laced with rum.

He said, "Well, I don't think she was exactly happy, but she understands. I told her I had to get back to Langley."

October looked up from blowing on her chocolate. "She knows what you do?"

"She's a smart lady. It didn't take her long to figure it out." He watched October shiver as another chill ran through her. "So you're telling me you don't have a clue why this FBI agent—Kowalski, you said his name was?—suddenly went berserk and started killing everyone in sight?"

"No."

"You're sure he killed Special Agent Cox, too?"

"She was watching the viewing from the control room. If

she'd been alive, I can't believe she wouldn't have tried to interfere."

"Unless she was in on it."

October shook her head and took a long sip of her chocolate. "Something pulled me out of my focus right before Kowalski burst into the room. I think it was the terror Cox experienced just as Kowalski killed her."

Jax went to splash more cognac into his glass. He sipped it a moment in silence then glanced over at her. "You never told me you can sense that kind of stuff."

A hint of color touched her pale cheeks. "I don't think I'm unusual. I think most people would have felt it. The difference is, I've learned to trust the knowledge that comes to me from other sources."

Other sources. Jax cleared his throat. He'd known October for more than six months now. He'd worked with her on two critical assignments. But this whole woo-woo business still made him uncomfortable. It wasn't that he'd never seen remote viewing work, because he had. He knew all about the RV program the Army had run for years up at Fort Meade, and about the extensive research conducted by respected physicists at Stanford Research Institute in California. But despite it all, he still had a hard time believing that remote viewing was real. It was as if he kept hitting a mental disconnect. The entire principle behind RV—the idea that someone could sit quietly in a secluded room and reach out with their mind to touch, feel, smell, even taste an object thousands of miles away—simply flew in the face of everything he'd ever been taught about reality.

Yet he'd seen her do it.

He came to sit in the leather armchair beside the hearth, his forearms resting on his thighs, the cognac cradled in one hand. "Okay," he said. "Let's try to reconstruct this. The Art Crimes Team brought you to D.C. to help track down a dozen or so of the most valuable antiquities stolen from Baghdad during the U.S. invasion." He paused. "Isn't that what you call frontloading?" Any information about a target given to a remote viewer before a viewing was known as frontloading. Too much frontloading could compromise the validity of a viewing.

She shook her head. "Not really. Any time you're dealing with a pool of similar targets, the pattern will quickly become obvious to the viewer anyway."

"So how many targets had you viewed before this guy tried to kill you?"

"Just two. We had a really good session this afternoon, so we decided to go ahead and do another viewing before we stopped for dinner. I was still working the second target when all hell broke loose." She leaned forward. "The thing I don't understand is, if I was the primary target, why didn't Kowalski shoot me first, rather than Peter?"

"It's standard military procedure: if you have two targets, you take out the one who's the biggest threat to the success of your operation first—in this instance, that was Abrams." Jax drained his glass and set it aside. "Could be this Kowalski is in some gazillionaire's pocket. I understand some of the items taken from Iraq are worth tens of millions of dollars each. Altogether, we're talking billions of dollars' worth of loot. I can see some wealthy collector hearing that Cox was bringing in a remote viewer and deciding to shut you up before you could finger him."

She studied him over the rim of her mug. She didn't look convinced. "You think that's what's behind this? Greed?"

"What else could it be?"

Setting aside the chocolate, she pushed up from the floor and began to pace the room, her arms wrapped across her chest. "The second target was some kind of ancient manuscript. I don't know what, exactly. But I got the impression the manuscript isn't valuable only for itself, if you understand what I mean."

"No."

"I mean, the people who have it think it's important because of what it *says*."

"What it says? So what does it say?"

"I don't know. I kept getting a weird collage of religious symbols—crosses and snakes. The Hanging Gardens of Babylon. Even Noah."

"As in Noah and the ark?"

"I'm not sure. I was getting images of a flood, but I don't think it was connected to Noah. Noah had something to do with the snow."

Jax blinked. "Snow?"

She gave a rueful laugh. "I know it sounds like a jumbled mess. The problem is, I was interrupted before I could sort it all out."

"Did you get anything on the location?"

"It was strange . . . like a log cabin, only huge—and very modern inside. I didn't get anything about where it is or who owns it."

"What else did you see?" he asked and then suffered another of those mental disconnects. *I can't believe I just asked that, like I believe in this shit.* And yet, he realized that, at some fundamental level, he did believe that October's talent was real. Even if he couldn't understand it.

She raked her drying hair back from her face with splayed fingers. "I found myself drawn to two men who were standing near a private runway. One was an older man, but still energetic and vital. Quite tall, with white hair and brilliant green eyes. Very attractive, almost charismatic. He's the one who was getting ready to board the jet that was waiting on the runway." She paused. "I think it was a Gulfstream."

"What was the other guy like?"

"Slightly shorter. Very solid build. Dark beard. I think the log cabin place is his."

Jax took a deep drink. "Okay. So what drew you to these guys?"

"I sensed great power and wealth emanating from both of them. And incredible arrogance."

"Men who are powerful and wealthy usually are arrogant," Jax said dryly. "You just described virtually everyone in Washington, D.C., who doesn't live in a ghetto."

She gave a soft laugh, but shook her head. "It's more than that. It's . . . it's like a pathological conviction of righteousness. These people are planning to remake the world." She paused, as if reconsidering. "No, that's not exactly right. They've already planned what they're going to do. Now they're putting their plan into action."

Jax stared at her. "What did you do? Read their minds?"

She gazed back at him silently.

Feeling suddenly hot and uncomfortable, he pushed up from his chair and went to stand on the far side of the room. "Jesus Christ. You're not telling me you read minds, are you? Please tell me you don't read minds."

"No," she said slowly. "Not exactly."

"Then what? *Exactly.*"

A flicker of light and movement drew her gaze to the flat-screen TV mounted on the far wall. He had left the picture on with the sound muted. "It's not like I'm reading people's minds when I remote view them," she said slowly. "It's just that I . . . I feel their emotions. And sometimes they communicate their thoughts to me—particularly if they're obsessing about something."

"I call that reading their minds. Can you do that sort of thing all the time or only during a viewing?"

"Only when I'm doing a viewing," she said glibly. Too glibly. "And even then, it's not like these people's minds are open books to me. I just get flashes. Impressions."

He narrowed his eyes, studying her pale, scratched face. "So what is this plan of theirs?"

She shook her head. "I don't know. Like I said, it was all wrapped up in this weird religious symbolism. But I kept getting images of snow—a snow-covered European-style village that reminded me of the footage they've been showing all day of Davos."

Jax held himself very still. "October? What are you saying?"

She stared at him with wide, dark eyes. "I think these people killed the Vice President."

10

"But that's not possible, October," Jax said gently. "The preliminary results of the autopsy were released about an hour ago. Vice President Hamilton died of a massive heart attack."

"You can provoke a heart attack, can't you? Even in a healthy person? *Can't you?*"

"So that it can't be determined in an autopsy? Not that I know of."

"But it might be possible?"

"Theoretically? I suppose so. But why would anyone want to kill Bill Hamilton? The guy was put on the ticket to woo white Southern voters. President Pizarro is the one with the real power."

"You don't understand. Getting rid of Hamilton was just the beginning. They're planning something else."

"What else?"

"I don't know. It was all such a weird jumble."

Jax found himself torn between an instinctive rejection of everything he was hearing and an uncomfortable awareness of just how right she'd been in the past. He said, "Tell me exactly what you saw."

"It's not anything I can pin down. Sometimes . . . knowledge just comes." She swung toward the door. "We need to get this to the Secret Service, fast. Do you know who—"

"Hang on," he said, catching her arm and pulling her back around. "What do you think you're going to do? Go to the Secret Service and tell them—what? That you got the 'impression' while doing a remote viewing that two men you can't identify are planning to do *something*—you don't know what—just that it involves snakes and crosses and the Hanging Gardens of Babylon?"

She stared back at him, her eyes wide and dark, her voice low. "You don't believe me, do you?"

"I'm not saying that." Jax blew out a long, troubled breath. "The problem is, you have nothing to back up what you're saying, except for a remote viewing session that no one in the government is going to believe is real."

"The Vice President is dead!"

"Yes. But we can't prove the men you saw had anything to do with that. You know your interpretation of what you see is sometimes a little wonky."

"*Wonky?* So if what I saw was so 'wonky,' then why the hell did those men try to kill me?"

"We don't know they did. One specific FBI agent tried to kill you," he corrected. "And right now, as far as the government is concerned, when it comes to what happened tonight, it's your word against his."

She stared at Jax, and he knew she was thinking the same thing he was: that with that psycho discharge in her files, no one would believe a word she said.

"Until we have a better idea who we're dealing with here, I think you need to—"

He realized she was no longer looking at him. "That's her," said October, nodding toward the television. A newsbreak with a photograph of a woman had just flashed across the screen. "Elaine Cox. Turn it up."

Jax scrambled for the remote and took the TV off mute.

"The FBI lost one of its own today," announced a reporter with thick dark hair and striking features. She was standing in front of an office complex ablaze with lights. Police cars and ambulances, their red and blue emergency lights flashing, packed the rain-drenched parking lot around her. *"Special Agent Elaine Cox, an eighteen-year veteran of the Bureau and mother of three was gunned down this evening here at the Warton Office Park in northern Virginia."*

"I didn't know she had kids," said October softly.

"Also killed was Billy Crouch, a security guard employed by Capital Protections. A United States naval officer, whose identity is being withheld, has been rushed to the National Naval Medical Center in Bethesda, where he is listed in critical condition."

"Thank God." October sank down on the sofa. "Peter must still be alive."

"The shootings were reported by FBI Agent Mark Kowalski—"

"That him?" Jax asked as a man with short sandy hair and blunt Slavic features appeared on the screen.

"Yes."

Kowalski had half a dozen microphones stuck in front of him and was giving what appeared to be a mini press conference. "I was gone for maybe twenty minutes, picking up some burgers and fries," he said in a thick Jersey accent. "I'd just come back and was getting out of my car when I heard shots and saw a young woman running away from the building. I called upon her to halt. When she failed to comply, I gave chase."

"Holy shit," said Jax, sinking down beside October.

The camera returned to the newscaster. "The police have yet to release a formal statement, but we do know that the FBI has named this woman as a person of interest." A picture of October filled the screen.

Wordlessly, Jax reached out and squeezed October's hand.

"Naval Ensign October Guinness is twenty-five years old. She has dark blond hair and brown eyes, and is listed as being five feet four and weighing one hundred fifteen pounds. According to unidentified sources—"

"What the hell?" Jax pushed to his feet. "What's this 'unidentified sources' crap?"

"—Ensign Guinness has a history of mental problems and was at one time given a psychiatric discharge from the Navy before being called back to active duty last summer."

Jax glanced down at October. She was staring at the TV, one hand pressed to her mouth.

The newscaster's voice droned on. "Anyone with information about Ensign Guinness's current whereabouts should contact the number on the screen immediately. We'll have an update at ten."

"Son of a bitch," said Jax, zapping off the television. "We've got to get you out of here."

"What?" She shook her head, not understanding. "But . . . why?"

"Because for all we know, the taxi driver who dropped you off at my doorstep is calling his local FBI office even as we speak." Grabbing a gym bag from the entry closet, he moved systematically through the house, tossing in October's wet clothes and assorted other items. "The first thing we need to do is figure out who we're dealing with here."

"How the hell do we do that?"

"By preceding from what we know to what we don't know. And right now, the only thing we know for sure is that the idea of you viewing that list of artifacts was enough of a threat to these guys that they sent someone to watch the viewing—and kill you if you saw something they didn't want you to see."

"I just don't understand what some ancient artifact could possibly have to do with the death of the Vice President."

"We don't know that they're connected. Let's just focus on the artifacts, okay? I want to talk to someone who knows enough about Mesopotamian art and history to decipher all those symbols you were seeing."

She watched him slide a magazine into his Beretta and click it home. "Got someone in mind?"

"As a matter of fact, yes." Jax slipped the gun into its holster and clipped it onto the inside of his waistband at the small of his back. "When was McClintock going in for surgery?"

"Tomorrow."

He tossed her a phone. "Call him. Tell him you're okay and that you're with me. He'll know to keep his mouth shut if anyone comes around asking questions. And tell him he'd better have the Navy mount a twenty-four-hour guard on Peter Abrams."

She caught the phone and stared at him. "You think they might try to kill Peter in the ICU?"

"Right now, Peter Abrams is the only person besides you who knows what really happened tonight." Jax pulled a cream sweater over his head and reached for his peacoat. "They already tried to kill him once. The minute it looks like he might live, whoever is behind this will go after him again."

Jax zipped the gym bag closed and caught her arm. "Come on. Let's go."

11

Daniel Pizarro still felt as if he were living in someone else's house.

He'd been in the White House for two weeks now. His suits hung in the closet. His underwear was tucked into the drawers of a chest that once belonged to Woodrow Wilson. His eight-year-old's drawing of a cat decorated the door of the refrigerator in the family quarters. Yet he still felt as if the house belonged to his predecessor. As if someone might at any moment politely ask Pizarro to leave.

"You'll get used to it," said his visitor, a crusty octogenarian senator with an age-spotted face and arthritis-gnarled hands.

Daniel smiled and went to pour his guest a drink. "How many presidents have you seen come and go in the fifty-odd years you've been in D.C.?"

"You're the eleventh," said Senator Cyrus Savoie without having to stop and count.

Pizarro laughed. "Keep track, do you?"

"Of course."

Pizarro handed the Senator a fresh gin and tonic. "Never had any desire to run for the office yourself?"

"Once or twice," admitted Savoie in the strange, guttural accent of an old-time New Orleanian. "When I was younger. Fortunately, I overcame the urge. Now, I'd just as soon not be president pro tem of the Senate. But that's what happens when you outlive all your colleagues."

Pizarro laughed again and went to settle in the armchair on the opposite side of the fireplace. "It looks so easy from the outside. You know what you want to do. Then you get in here and you realize your hands are tied in ways you never imagined possible."

Savoie took a slow sip of his drink. "Doesn't help, having your vice president drop dead of a heart attack two weeks after the inauguration."

Pizarro scrubbed one hand across his face. "That's the understatement of the year." Bill Hamilton had been the consummate Washington insider, the guy who'd graduated from Yale Law, who'd spent four terms as a U.S. Senator, who knew exactly how the system worked—and didn't work.

Pizarro, on the other hand, was the ultimate outsider. A two-term governor of New Mexico who'd been born just eighteen months after his parents slipped across the border from Mexico, he'd gone to medical school on a scholarship and practiced as an ob-gyn before being pulled into politics almost by accident.

Or at least, that was the popular image, and Daniel had never tried to dispel it. But the truth was that he'd been passionate about politics ever since the day, as a lonely twelve-year-old, he'd learned his mother had hemorrhaged to death after his birth because the local hospital refused to treat her.

"It's not going to be easy, finding someone with the right mix to replace him," said Pizarro.

"You don't want to wait too long," Savoie cautioned. "You're not immortal, Daniel. Your election has stirred up some nasty emotions amongst certain elements. And the last thing this country needs right now is an eighty-five-year-old president."

"You?" Pizarro frowned. "I thought that according to the Constitution, the Speaker of the House is next in the line of succession."

"Theoretically. Except that Marie Barnett has just been named the new Speaker."

"So?"

"Marie was born in Canada, remember? She's ineligible. Which means that if anything happens to you, I'm 'it.' And I'm telling you, I don't want to be president. You need to get yourself a new veep. Fast."

12

"Her name is Dr. Elizabeth Stein," Jax told October as they zipped through the rainy streets in his little black 650i BMW convertible. "She's an expert in ancient Mesopotamian history."

"So how do you know her?"

"She was one of my professors at Yale."

"I still can't believe you majored in history," said October.

Jax laughed. "To be frank, neither could Professor Stein. She was convinced I'd end up in prison. She moved to Georgetown a few years ago when her husband died and she retired. But she's still actively involved in research and consults part-time with the Smithsonian."

He was aware of October studying him with an intense, solemn gaze. "You trust her?"

"Implicitly."

Professor Elizabeth Stein was a startlingly tall, wiry woman with steel gray hair and heavy eyebrows, her skin permanently tanned and weathered by years spent beneath a fierce Middle Eastern sun. Jax had called en route to warn her that he and a friend needed to talk to her about something urgent.

She met him at the door of her Georgetown rowhouse, her arms thrown wide to envelope him in a warm embrace. "Jax. It's been too long," she declared in her trademark Oxbridge accent. "Do come in, quickly. What a frightfully nasty night this is."

Jax hesitated on the steps, a cold mist billowing around him. "You know that friend I told you about? I should probably warn you that she—"

Dr. Stein gazed beyond him, to where October waited just beyond the front gate. "I saw the news. I think I understand why you're here. Tell your friend there's no need to worry."

Chatting pleasantly about the days when Jax had been her student, Dr. Stein bustled them into a warm, gently lit kitchen. In place of the standard built-in cabinets, the kitchen was furnished with an eclectic collection of gently worn pie safes and Hoosier cupboards. She fixed hot tea and loaded down the old round oak table overlooking the dark rear garden with plates of small cakes and scones with jam and cream. Then she pulled out one of the pressed-back chairs, sat with her chin propped in her fists, and leveled him with a fixed gray stare.

"I saw what happened to Elaine Cox. I assume that's why you're here?"

"I didn't kill her," October blurted out, her hands cradling a delicate cup of pink flowered porcelain.

Professor Stein blinked. "Goodness. I never thought you did. But why don't you tell me what did happen?"

October glanced at Jax.

He said, "You knew Special Agent Cox was bringing in a remote viewer to help locate some of the antiquities looted from Iraq?"

"Yes. She contacted experts at a variety of institutions, from the Smithsonian and the University of Chicago to SUNY Stonybrook and the Massachusetts College of Art. We were each asked to draw up a list of what we considered the ten most important items looted from the Iraqi National Museum and Library."

"The National Library?" said October.

Dr. Stein nodded. "The library burned a few days after the fall of Baghdad. It's generally assumed the fire was set to cover up the theft of its most valuable collections, although it could have been more malicious than that. Thousands of irreplaceable texts were lost—everything from illuminated medieval Korans and ancient Arabic copies of Greek and Roman texts to early Bibles."

"Bibles?" said October.

"Mmm. Yes. Most people don't realize that Iraq was one of the most important centers of early Christianity."

Jax said, "Did all these experts Agent Cox contacted know what she was planning to do with their lists?"

"Most thought she was simply endeavoring to refocus the Art Crimes Team's efforts."

October took a slow sip of her tea. "Why did she tell you?"

"Elaine and I have been friends for more than a decade—we've worked together many times. Billions of dollars' worth of artifacts are stolen and traded every year, and the vast majority of them come here, to the United States. I think Elaine knew me well enough to be confident that I wouldn't disparage what she was going to do—or, worse, blab about it to the press."

"You're familiar with remote viewing?" said October in some surprise.

"Yes, actually." A soft smile lit up the professor's eyes. "I understand you're a remarkably talented viewer." The smile faded as she looked from October to Jax. "Don't tell me that's why Elaine was killed. Because someone was afraid of what you might see? Bloody hell."

Jax gave her a quick rundown of the evening's events. At the end, he said, "Do you know what was on the list of twelve items that Agent Cox selected for October to view?"

Dr. Stein blew out a long, troubled breath and shook her head. "I'm afraid not. Elaine kept her final selection quiet—even from me. Part of it, I know, was because she didn't want anyone to be able to claim that October could somehow have known ahead of time what the items were. But I think she was also worried about offending my professional sensibilities—you know, in case items I considered terribly important were left off." Dr. Stein pushed up from her chair and went to put the kettle on for more tea. "How much do you know about the looting of artifacts from Iraq?"

"Not much," said October.

Dr. Stein stood with her arms braced against the kitchen counter. "The history of Iraq stretches back more than eight thousand years. Every time I think about what has happened—what the world has lost . . . I just feel sick. It's difficult to overestimate the debt we all owe to the ancient Iraqis. From the civilizations of the Tigris and Euphrates rivers came the wheel, astronomy, writing—even the concept of cities and government. Hammurabi wrote the world's first law code in Babylon over three and a half thousand years ago. Uruk was the scene of the *Gilgamesh Epic*. Abraham was said to have been born in Ur . . . How can anyone put a price on that kind of heritage? But people do. People who know the cost of everything and the value of nothing."

"How many artifacts were stolen?" October asked hoarsely.

The professor made a harsh sound, deep in her throat. "That's the problem. We don't even have an accurate accounting. The Baghdad museum housed something like one hundred seventy thousand artifacts, everything from exquisite gold ornaments and massive Sumerian statues to small five-thousand-year-old tablets bearing some of the earliest known writing. But the thieves who looted the museum also burned its archives and catalogues, which means that no one knows exactly what is missing."

"But . . . why would they do that?"

It was Jax who answered. "To make it harder to track down the items. And to complicate the Iraqis' efforts to lay claim to any items that are found."

Dr. Stein nodded. "It's not an easy process, reclaiming stolen antiquities across international borders. There's even an organization of big-time collectors and dealers in this country that's working to get the U.S. government to essentially scrap laws like the Cultural Property Implementation Act and the National Stolen Property Act that are designed to stop the trafficking in stolen antiquities. Needless to say, its members are very rich and very powerful."

"That's disgusting," said October.

Jax shrugged. "Money talks."

Dr. Stein nodded. "The situation is made worse by the fact that Iraq was under a crippling embargo for more than a decade before the invasion began. People were starving. Farmers started looting archeological sites for items to sell, just to stay alive. And even when discoveries were turned in to the Department of Antiquities, there was no money to fund research or publish papers."

"So you're saying no one really knows exactly what was taken?"

"Not entirely. The most recent estimates put the number of artifacts still missing from the Baghdad museum at between ten and fifteen thousand items. But that doesn't count what was taken from the National Library, or from provincial museums in places like Basra, or from the unprotected archaeological sites themselves. All together, you're probably looking at hundreds of thousands of artifacts."

"Jesus," whispered October.

"The most infuriating thing about all this is, it didn't need to happen. Once it became obvious the United States government was bent on war, the scholarly world *begged* the British and the American administrations to take active steps to protect Iraq's antiquities."

"You mean, the way we did the oil ministry?" said Jax wryly.

Dr. Stein nodded. "One tank at the museum's gates would have been enough to save it. Just one tank. Instead, U.S. forces drove away the Iraqi soldiers guarding the museum and then left it wide open."

The shrill whistle of the teakettle cut through the stillness. She turned to shut off the gas and pour the boiling water into the waiting teapot.

October said, "Were there any ancient manuscripts at the museum? Or would those have all been at the National Library?"

"I believe the museum had a collection of Torah scrolls, as well as some very early Christian writings."

"Nothing earlier?"

"Not to my knowledge. The ancient Babylonians did use papyrus, just like the Egyptians. But none have survived."

Jax saw October's eyebrows draw together in a frown. If she hadn't "seen" an ancient Babylonian papyrus, then what had she seen?

"My own specialty is cuneiform tablets," said Dr. Stein, bringing the teapot back to the table. "That's why Elaine consulted a variety of scholars with different specialties. She assumed—quite rightly, I suspect—that our selection of the ten most critical missing items would be weighted heavily towards our own specific area of expertise."

Jax smiled. "Was there a manuscript on your list?"

Dr. Stein let out a *humph*. "Are you serious? There wasn't anything on my list under four thousand years old." She fixed her fierce stare on October. "One of the items you viewed was a manuscript?"

"I think so, yes."

"Any idea what it was?"

"No." October reached for a pen and notebook that rested on a nearby counter. "May I?"

"Of course."

"I kept getting impressions of what I think were symbols," said October, sketching rapidly. "A snake. A large expanse of water, like a flood. And this." She drew an object that looked like a strange combination of a cross and a menorah. "Have you seen it before?"

Dr. Stein tilted the notebook toward her. She was silent for a moment. Then she said, "Yes. I have."

13

"It's known as the Cross of St. Thomas," said Dr. Stein, her gaze on October's sketch. "Or sometimes the Nasrani menorah, since it's based on the Jewish menorah. These candles—three on each side—represent God as a burning bush, while the central branch is the cross. The dove at the top is the Holy Spirit."

"But . . ." October frowned. "What does this have to do with Babylon?"

"Legend has it that St. Thomas came to Babylon after leaving Syria, before traveling to India." She traced the outline of the Byzantine-style cross with one finger, her brows drawing together in a frown.

"What is it?" asked Jax, watching her troubled, lined face.

"I don't know if I should—" She broke off, then began again. "I've heard persistent rumors that there was nothing accidental about the looting of the National Museum and Library in Baghdad. That it was in fact the result of a carefully planned project to steal the country's historical treasures."

"What exactly are you saying?"

"I'm saying that the looting was not random. Oh, some of

it was—especially on the second day, when people from the surrounding neighborhoods descended on the smashed galleries with wheelbarrows and carts. But many of those items have since been recovered. The first thieves on the scene knew exactly what they had come for—and they arrived with special equipment to lift and transport the heaviest items. These were men with the skills to open locked vaults—and with the knowledge to focus on the most valuable antiquities. They were there for very specific objects and they knew where to look. It was almost as if they had lists of the most important items—as if dealers and collectors had placed their orders in advance." She paused. "I've even heard reports that a U.S. military armored vehicle stood in front of the gates while the thieves loaded their trucks."

October glanced from the professor to Jax, and back again. "But . . . that's not possible. Is it?"

Professor Stein shook her head. "I don't know what to believe. But I do know that even after the museum authorities alerted the Americans to what was happening, the military made no effort to prevent the objects from leaving Baghdad. Seriously, think about it: some of the missing artifacts were huge. How did the thieves get them out of Iraq, unless they had someone cooperating with them?"

"In other words," said October, "the people who now possess the antiquities on Elaine Cox's list could actually have placed *orders in advance* for them?"

"Essentially, yes."

"Not only that," said Jax, "but whoever was behind the theft has some serious connections in both the United States military and the previous administration."

"Okay," said October, leaning back in her chair, her hands flat on the table. "I think I'm more scared now than I was before."

Later, when Dr. Stein walked with them to the door, she said, "If you like, I can contact some of my colleagues—attempt to reconstruct the list of items Elaine might have chosen."

"*No*," said Jax with more force than he'd intended. He swung to face her. "You can't do or say anything to betray the least interest in what has happened."

As if affronted, Professor Stein drew herself up to her full, considerable height. "If you are by chance concerned that I am incapable of concocting a plausible story should the police become aware of my inquiries—"

Jax laid a hand on her shoulder and said quietly, "It's not the police I'm worried about. Two people are already dead, another is in the ICU, and October here is the object of a massive manhunt. I don't know exactly who we're dealing with, but whoever these people are, they're scary. Promise me you won't do anything."

She stared back at him mulishly.

He gripped her other shoulder. "Dr. Stein, *please*. You can't help us if you're dead. Promise me you won't say anything to anyone about this."

Reluctantly, she nodded.

But Jax was afraid he'd already put her in danger, just by coming here.

"I still don't get it," said October, shivering slightly as they walked back toward where Jax had parked his car. The rain had eased up again, but the night was cold, the streetlights shining through the bare branches of the trees overhead casting long shadows across the wet sidewalks. "What could some ancient Christian manuscript possibly have to do with the assassination of the vice president of the United States?"

"We don't know that Hamilton has anything to do with this," Jax reminded her. "That's your interpretation of what you saw. But Hamilton's death could be just—what's the RV word you use?—imagination overlay."

October's eyes narrowed. *Imagination overlay* was the term used to describe the intrusions that could bleed into a viewing from the viewer's own imagination. It had always been one of the most troublesome aspects of remote viewing: there was simply no way to distinguish between actual information a viewer was accessing about a target versus what was simply coming out of the viewer's own head—supplied by her imagination.

She said, "It wasn't imagination overlay."

"You don't know—" he broke off, his gaze focusing on a sedan cruising slowly down the street toward them, the silhouette of its lightbar marking it as a patrol car. As in so much of Georgetown, the tall, narrow rows of town houses lining Dr. Stein's street had been built when elegant Washingtonians either walked or rode in carriages. Now, the street was narrowed by the parked cars that lined both sides to the point that there was barely room for one lane of traffic.

"Turn your face away. Quick."

But October must not have understood him, because instead of looking away, she glanced toward him and said, "What?" just as the police car rolled past them.

The cops slammed on their brakes and threw the car into reverse, the engine roaring as they backed up. The alley light at the end of the bar flashed on, shining a spotlight at a ninety-degree angle to catch Tobie square in the eyes.

"Shit." He grabbed her hand. "*Run.*"

14

They raced to the end of the block, the police cruiser roaring in reverse beside them. A woman's voice boomed over the car's loudspeaker, "This is the police. Stop where you are and put your hands up."

"This way," hissed Jax, dragging October around the corner.

A long block of rowhouses reared up before them, hemming them in on both sides. Tires squealing, engine revving, the police cruiser plowed backward into the intersection.

"We can't outrun them!" shouted October.

Jax laughed. "No. But we can outsmart them."

Without breaking stride, he leaped sideways to bring down his right foot, hard, on the bumper of the Beamer parked beside them. The Beamer's alarm rumbled to life, horn honking, lights flashing. Two cars down, he did the same thing to a Jag, then a Mercedes, then a Lexus. One car alarm set off the next until the entire street was filled with flashing headlights and wailing sirens and the monotonous, maddening *beep-beep-beep* of car horns.

"Didn't you just draw *more* attention to us?" she asked, sprinting beside him.

"Watch."

Windows went up. Doors banged. Someone shouted. Irate car owners spilled into the street just as, red and blue beacons pulsing, the police cruiser wheeled in a clumsy turn and roared after them.

The policewoman rolled down her window and roared, "Get the hell out of my way!"

But the cops were now going the wrong way up a one-way street. The driver of a Hummer lumbering down the narrow street toward them stood on his brakes. The cops went into a skid, the cruiser coming to shuddering halt just inches from the Hummer's heavy grill.

The doors of the cop car flew open. The policewoman screamed at the Hummer driver, "Get that fucking tank out of my way!"

Her partner hit the pavement at a run, shouting, "*Freeze! Police!*"

"Shit," said October with a gasp.

They darted down the nearest side street. But at the third house on the block, Jax whispered, "Here," and pulled her into the shadows of a low hedge bordering the narrow front yard. The smell of wet leaves and damp earth rose up around them. Crouching beside her, he put his hands on her shoulders and said, "No matter what happens, I want you to stay down."

"Me? Where are you going?"

She was breathing so heavily, he could feel the shudders ripping through her. Yanking off his peacoat, he draped it around her shoulders. "The cops are looking for a man in a navy coat running away with a woman. I'm just a guy in a cream sweater going for a walk to see what all the commotion is about."

"But . . ."

He touched her cheek. "Watch for me. I'll be back with the car."

Pushing up, he thrust his hands in his pockets, turned, and walked calmly back the way they had come. He'd almost reached the last house on the block when the beefy policeman, gun in hand, came tearing around the corner and skidded to a halt, his head swiveling as he looked up and down the empty block.

"Hey, you," he said to Jax. "I'm looking for a young woman in sweats and a guy in a dark jacket. You seen them?"

Jax rubbed the back of his neck and screwed up his face as if in thought. "Yeah, actually. I think they ran across the street and then went that way."

"Thanks," shouted the policeman, hitching up his holster as he trotted off in the direction Jax pointed.

"Glad to help, officer," Jax called after him.

Jax cast a quick glance at the mayhem still engulfing the next street. The driver of the Hummer—a small blond woman in a pink hoodie—was having a really, really hard time backing up under the angry glare of the policewoman.

Smiling faintly, he kept walking, then doubled back around the block to his car.

By the time he pulled up beside the low hedge, the rain had started up again. He rolled down his window and said, "We need to get you a *hijab* or something."

She slid into the seat beside him, bringing with her the scent of the rain and a sprinkling of crushed, dead leaves. When she reached for the seat belt, he noticed she was shaking. "Are you kidding? After that, I think I want a burqa."

Somewhere in the Pyrenees: Saturday 3 February 4:00 A.M. local time

Noah Bosch awoke with a start of panic.

He stared wildly about, his heart pounding with terror as

he searched the frigid, dimly lit railway carriage for what had awakened him. The world outside the swaying train was a black void, the windows reflecting the interior of the coach back at him.

The carriage was old and smelled strongly of the toilet at the front of the car. Some half dozen passengers dozed in the high-backed, worn seats, their bodies swaying rhythmically with the motion of the train. *Clickety-clack, clickety-clack.*

Leaning closer to the window, Noah felt the cold emanating from the glass. They were passing through a small village, a collection of dark, silent stone houses that were there and then gone. A shrill whistle echoed back from the engine at the front of the train, and he thought that might have been what penetrated his sleep to jerk him awake.

He'd been dreaming about a woman named Julie, a girl with straight brown hair and a freckled nose and a laugh that never failed to bring a smile to his heart. Once, she had believed in him, had believed in whatever story he was following, believed he had what it took to be the next Woodward or Bernstein.

But Woodward and Bernstein had belonged to another era. And their paper hadn't fired them.

"Carl Bernstein's wife left him, too," Julie had told him, pausing in the doorway to look back at him.

"That's because he was cheating on her. I'm not cheating on you, Julie," he'd told her.

And then she'd put her arms around his neck and kissed his lips and whispered, "No. But I've been cheating on you, Noah."

He ran the pad of his thumb across his lower lip, now, remembering that kiss. It irked him that he still wanted her, still missed her. She'd left him for a sportscaster. A CNN reporter would have been bad enough. But a jock?

At the click of a latch, he jerked his head up. He watched,

his breath quickening, as the door to the malodorous toilet opened. A squat woman with a massive bosom and iron gray hair emerged and waddled back to her seat. Noah took a deep breath and let it out slowly, willing himself to relax.

He'd bought a ticket from Davos to Zurich, then he'd leaped off at a station too small to invest in video surveillance equipment. He'd doubled back on himself, train hopping from one small village to the next, until catching the overnight train to Madrid. Surely no one could have followed him? But he kept remembering the look in that bullnecked Secret Service agent's eyes as he stared at Noah across the width of the snowy, crowded street in Davos.

Noah's source had warned him they had one of their own in the Vice President's Secret Service detail. Which meant they now knew about Noah—if they hadn't already.

The problem was, Noah didn't have all the information he needed about *them*. That's why he was on his way to Madrid, to try to talk to a biblical scholar named José Antonio Zapatero Sanchez. Zapatero had retired to the small village of Medinaceli, to the northeast of the capital. Noah hoped like hell the Spaniard had the information he needed.

Because while Noah might not know enough about the dominionists' plans to stop them, he knew more than enough to get himself killed.

15

Lulled by the warm purr of Jax's powerful engine, Tobie didn't realize she was falling asleep until she awoke to find herself staring at a dark stretch of water framed by bare branches. A forest of tall masts rocked gently back and forth against a black sky; the scent of damp earth and pines filled the air. The sign on a nearby unpretentious two-story clapboard building read WASHINGTON SAILING MARINA.

She sat up with a start. "Where are we?"

Jax pushed open his door. "Daingerfield Island Park. It's upriver from Alexandria, near Reagan National Airport. I thought you could use someplace more comfortable to sleep than my car. You don't get seasick, do you?"

She scrambled after him, staggering as a cold, sharp wind slammed into her. "We're taking a boat?"

"Not taking it. Just hiding on it." He hauled the gym bag out of his trunk and nodded toward the rows of gleaming wood and fiberglass hulls. "The ketch-rigged Hallberg-Rassy at the end of the second dock."

She stared out over the rows of expensive sailboats. The Hallberg-Rassy was a good forty-five to fifty feet long, with a sleek hull and tall, bare masts that rocked back and forth against the dark waters of the river. "Wow. I'm impressed."

He laughed and turned toward the docks. "Don't be. It belongs to a friend."

Holding her wind-whipped hair with both hands, she fell into step beside him, their footfalls on the weathered planking echoing hollowly in the dark stillness. "You don't think he'll mind that you're hiding a wanted fugitive on his property?"

"You're not technically 'wanted.' You're just a 'person of interest,' remember?"

"Tell that to the cops who chased us," she said dryly.

"And no—he'll understand."

She studied Jax's lean, high-boned profile. The Hallberg-Rassy had to be worth several hundred thousand. "He must be a good friend to let you use his boat."

"He is."

Suddenly, she understood. "It's one of your stepfathers, isn't it?"

Jax laughed. "The second." Jax's mother, Sophie Talbot, was a famous Washington, D.C., socialite and hostess who had managed to rack up eight marriages during the course of her colorful career. Only her first husband—Jax's father—had been a penniless nobody. His successors had included a secretary of defense, a Supreme Court justice, and several senators. And Jax had managed to remain on surprisingly good terms with most—although not quite all—of them.

Tobie let her gaze drift over the dark expanse of water stretching from the tree-covered promontory to the lights of the city on the opposite bank. "Talk about hiding in plain sight."

"Hopefully, it won't be for long," said Jax, although they both knew the truth: that if they couldn't figure out who was after her, and why, she could spend the rest of her life on the run.

Or die young.

Jax stood in the doorway to the sailboat's forward cabin, one shoulder propped against the frame, his gaze on the woman who slept the deep sleep of exhaustion beneath the down coverlet. He could hear the gentle rhythm of her breathing, see the faint twitches that told him her dreams were not restful.

He had her safe, now. But how long could he keep her that way? He pushed away from the hatch to go pull his laptop from his duffel bag. Seated on the padded built-in bench beside the galley, his computer on the table before him, he began a systematic search of what was publicly available on Special Agent Mark Kowalski.

From all appearances, the guy was a model citizen. Coached Little League. Taught Sunday school at his local church. He was also quite the rising star at the Bureau. Jax found several newspaper articles praising his participation in various FBI operations, including one feature with a photo of Kowalski standing beside the head of the Criminal Investigative Division, Duane Davenport.

Frowning, Jax reached for one of the throwaway cell phones he'd tossed in his gym bag before leaving the house. He'd learned long ago the value of keeping a supply of unlisted, prepaid phones on hand for those occasions when he wanted to be certain Big Brother wasn't listening to his conversations or tracking his location. Still skimming through a series of articles on the FBI, he put in a call to Matt von Moltke. Matt was the head of Division Thirteen, the dead-end career-wrecker to which the CIA transferred incurable loose cannons like Jax when they refused to mend their ways.

A groggy Matt answered on the seventh ring. "Hello?"

"Hey, Matt. Jax here."

There was a moment's silence during which Jax imagined Matt squinting first at his bedside clock, then at the blank caller ID on his phone. "Jax? What the hell kind of trouble you got yourself into this time?"

"You didn't watch the ten-o'clock news?"

"No." Matt yawned loudly. "What did I miss?"

"The FBI is trying to kill October Guinness."

"They *what*?"

Jax gave him a succinct recap of the night's events. "We need a list of the artifacts October was brought in to view and copies of the sketches she was doing when the hit took place."

"That might not be easy to get. The FBI will have taken over the investigation."

"I thought we were all one big happy family these days. Post–9/11 interagency cooperation and all that."

Matt huffed a soft laugh. "Yeah, right."

"We also need everything there is to know about this guy Kowalski."

"I'll see what I can do." Matt paused. "Keep her safe, Jax."

"I will."

Closing the phone, Jax went topside. The rain had eased off, leaving the night cold and clear and damp. He stood with his hands wrapped around the wet rail, his gaze on the dark, gently heaving waters of the river.

He stood that way for a long time, running through everything October had told him and trying to make sense of it. He knew enough about remote viewing to know that even a viewer as talented as October could be wrong. Sometimes she accessed the wrong site—or the right site at the wrong time. Sometimes she veered away from the intended target to something more interesting nearby. And then there were the times when the information she accessed was correct, but her interpretation of that information was wrong.

He kept thinking something like that must have happened this time. Or maybe the recent unexpected death of the Vice President had somehow bled into her viewing of the Mesopotamian artifacts, convincing her of a link that wasn't there. Except . . .

Except that two—maybe three—people were already dead.

Would someone really be willing to kill and kill again, simply to keep his possession of a stolen artifact a secret? In Jax's experience, people with money didn't go to prison—at least, not unless they somehow pissed off lots of other important people with money. Prisons were for the guy who stole twenty bucks from the corner grocery store or who sold cocaine in the blocks. Not for the defense contractor who defrauded the government of billions or the banker who fleeced his customers or the high-rolling collector who bought 4,000-year-old carvings of questionable provenance.

So why the killing spree? And why the determined manhunt? What did those two unidentified men standing beside some deep but unknown lake have to hide? Jax suspected it was a hell of a lot more important than an ancient inscribed tablet or gold Sumerian necklace.

The problem was, all Jax and October knew about the two nameless men at this point was that they were superrich, that they had a connection to some mysterious ancient artifact, and they controlled at least one FBI agent.

That, and that they obviously possessed the power and connections to pluck a manuscript from the museums of Iraq in the middle of a full-scale military invasion.

Duane Davenport rolled his black Mercury sedan in close to the curb. He kept the engine running against the cold, his gaze narrowing as he studied the neat redbrick rowhouse across the street. The place was built right on the water in one of the choicest areas of Old Alexandria. Davenport had heard that the CIA agent who owned the place had inherited it from his grandfather, the late esteemed Senator Winston, a staunchly conservative, God-fearing man who'd be rolling in his grave if he knew what his grandson was up to.

Davenport turned his head and punched down the window as the wiry form of Special Agent Mark Kowalski separated from the knot of men hovering in the shadows near the corner and walked up to the Mercury. A blast of frigid air scented by the nearby river rolled into the car's artificially heated interior. "What have you got?"

Kowalski rested his forearms on the door frame and hunched over so he could keep his voice low. "The cabby says he drove a girl fitting Guinness's description here just after eight. The girl claimed she'd lost her purse, and a guy came out and paid her fare. Our records show the house belongs to one Jax Alexander."

Davenport nodded. He already knew this. "So what's Alexander have to say for himself?"

"He ain't here. According to the neighbors, he lives alone." Kowalski rubbed the back of his hand against his nose. "You heard he's CIA?"

"I heard." Davenport drummed his fingertips against the leather-wrapped steering wheel. "Guinness worked with the CIA last fall, didn't she?"

"They're refusing to confirm that."

"Well they would, wouldn't they?" He nodded to the silent house across the street. "Take a look. See what you can find, then wire it."

"Do we wait for a warrant?"

"Negative." A warrant would be easy enough to obtain, but would take time. And time was the one thing Davenport didn't have. "Every minute that girl's out there increases the threat to the operation."

Kowalski gave a ringing laugh. "Are you kidding? She's a nutcase. What do you think she's gonna do? She didn't have a clue what she was seeing."

Davenport eased the Mercury into gear. "Maybe. But I don't intend to give her the chance to figure it out."

16

The sky was just beginning to lighten to a cold, bleak day when the train lurched to a halt in the Madrid station.

Rubbing the sleep from his eyes, Noah shivered and pulled the straps of his backpack over his shoulders. Outside the station, the city was just coming awake, the streets cold and gray in the feeble winter light. Pushing his way into a café across from the station, he ordered bread and hot chocolate, and sat down to mull over his transportation options.

He figured he probably had enough credit left on one of his cards to rent a car. But Noah knew from previous experience that car companies had a nasty habit of putting a hold on a big chunk of a guy's available credit and not releasing it for a week or more. If that happened, then Noah would be stranded in Europe, unable to buy a plane ticket home. Better to take the train out to Zapatero's village, he decided.

Of course, that was assuming that José Antonio Zapatero Sanchez was actually in Medinaceli at the moment—and that he'd agree to talk to Noah.

Hastily paying his check, Noah found a *locutorio*, or public telephone center, punched in Zapatero's number at his allotted machine, and waited breathlessly while he listened to the phone ring and ring.

On the fifth ring, a man picked up and said querulously, "*Dígame.*"

"Professor Zapatero?"

"*Sí.*"

Noah let out his breath in a relieved sigh. "This is Noah Bosch. I'm a journalist with *The Washington Post*. Dr. Salah Araji gave me your name and number and suggested I call you."

It was all a blatant lie. Not only had the *Post* terminated Noah's employment, but Dr. Araji had refused to have anything to do with anyone since the U.S. invasion of Iraq.

There was a pause. Professor Zapatero said, "*Sí?*"

"I'd like to come talk to you today, if I may?"

"*Por qué?*" Why?

Noah hesitated. In his experience, mentioning the Babylonian Codex was a surefire way of ending a conversation. He said vaguely, "I'd like to interview you for an article I'm doing on early Christian manuscripts from Mesopotamia and the Levant. I understand that's your area of expertise."

"*Sí.*"

Noah glanced at his watch. How long did it take to get to Medinaceli? "I'm in Madrid now. I could be at your house by, say, one o'clock?"

There was a long silence. Noah was afraid the Spaniard was going to say no. He heard a woman's voice in the background. Then Professor Zapatero said, "Make it three," and hung up.

Duane Davenport was drifting off to sleep when he heard his phone vibrate against his nightstand. He glanced at the number and quickly slipped from his bed.

Sarah didn't stir.

He waited until he'd reached the downstairs den before he hit RETURN CALL.

Laura Brockman answered immediately. "I thought you could use some good news. Bosch just called Professor Zapatero."

"Son of a bitch," said Davenport. "He called Zapatero? How much does this little shit know?"

"It doesn't matter," said Brockman. "By tonight he'll be dead."

17

Leo Carlyle racked his barbell and sat up, shaking the sweat from his eyes. The drone of the private jet's engines was a steady, familiar hum that vibrated through him pleasantly. Pushing to his feet, he grabbed a towel and went to stare out the nearest window at the puffy white clouds spreading out far below him.

They'd left Davos at nine that morning, bound for D.C. He planned only a brief stop to touch base with a few key players, then it would be on to Idaho.

Leo owned houses in a dozen different cities around the world, from Zurich to D.C. to Rio. But the sprawling log lodge overlooking Lake Coeur d'Alene remained his favorite. It would be good to get home.

He downed a bottle of mineral water and then, using his jet's secure phone, put in a call to his assistant, Casper Nordstrom.

Nordstrom picked up on the second ring. "Yes, sir?"

"Lunch is confirmed?" Leo asked, swiping his face with the towel.

"Yes, sir. At the K Street House."

"Good. And the other matter? How is that progressing?"

"Our friends in the Bureau still haven't managed to track the source of the leak to the journalist."

Leo frowned. "Perhaps they don't understand the urgency of the situation."

There was a pause. "I'll see that they are reminded."

Leo tossed the towel aside. "And my globe-trotting wife? Any idea where she is?"

"She's flying in from Thailand this morning."

"Thailand? What the hell was she doing there?"

"Visiting a refuge for young girls rescued from the sex-slave trade."

Leo *humphed* derisively. It was the new fashion—conspicuous benevolence. But Leo's current wife—a thirty-one-year-old former Miss Colorado named A.J.—sometimes took the fad a little too seriously. "Tell her that if she can fit it into her busy schedule, it would be nice if she could join me in Idaho."

"Yes, sir."

Leo glanced at his watch. "We should be on the ground in a few hours. Have the car waiting."

"It's already at the airport, sir."

Leo tossed the phone after the towel and went to take a shower.

18

Tobie awoke to find a pale hint of dawn glowing through an overhead skylight. She lay still, trying to remember where she was, trying to push away the lingering wisps of a haunting dream. But the images persisted, of a ruby-eyed snake and a golden menorah that melted slowly into an ancient cross. With a sudden rush, memory flooded back, and she shivered.

She could hear Jax moving around nearby. Throwing aside the quilt, she went to stand in the narrow passage that led to the main cabin or saloon. He was just pulling a sweater over his head. From the looks of things, he'd spent the night on the built-in bench beside the galley.

"When are you meeting Matt?" she asked.

"Seven." He fished one of the cell phones from his gym bag and tossed it to her. "Here. Just don't call anyone you know. By now the FBI will be monitoring the lines of every-

one from your next-door neighbor to your favorite kinder-
garten teacher."

She shoved the phone into the big kangaroo pocket of her
sweatshirt. "So why even bother giving it to me?"

"I've programmed it with the number of the throwaway
phone I'm using. If you need to move, call me." He slipped
his Beretta from the holster he wore at the small of his back
and set it on the table. "Insurance."

She eyed the gun with misgivings. "You do remember I'm
a lousy shot."

"Like I could forget?" He turned toward the ladder. "When
this is all over, remind me to take you to a shooting range."

"The Navy already tried to teach me to shoot, remember?
It didn't work."

But he just laughed.

After he'd gone, she hauled out paper and pen and tried
to reconstruct the drawings of her viewings. But she found
herself too restless to settle. Finally, she pushed up from the
bench and prowled the confines of her hideaway.

The sailboats of Tobie's experience had all been dinghies or
small Colgates. In comparison, the Hallberg-Rassy was huge.
A comfortable cabin paneled in gleaming teak with its own en
suite bath took up the entire bow. Then came the main cabin
with its miniature teak and brass galley tucked in beside the
ladder leading up to the cockpit, and a roomy living area complete with a teak table and built-in padded benches. Beyond
that, a short hall led past a chart station and the engine room
with an adjacent compartment for the backup generator. A
small head and a second cabin occupied the stern.

She thought about going topside for some fresh air, then decided that would be a bad idea. By now her picture would be
plastered across every newspaper and TV station in the area.
She suspected the hood of Jax's sweatshirt pulled up over her
hair wouldn't exactly qualify as an effective disguise.

Turning away from the ladder, she went to settle on the bench again and forced herself to relax.

Focus.

Reaching again for the paper, she sketched the climate-controlled room and its carefully preserved racks of ancient manuscripts; the sprawling lodge with its towering stands of fir and pine and the expanse of water spreading out before it; the private jet and the men who'd stood beside it. She made notes, too, of every fleeting impression, every nuance and vague symbol she could recall.

Most people thought a remote viewing session must be similar to staring through a distant portal or maybe watching a movie in your head. But it wasn't like that at all. The information came to her in flashes and was typically disjointed—vague impressions; sensations of light and heat and smell—even taste. It's why she tended to use expressions such as, "It feels like . . ." or "I get the impression of . . ." as she groped to coalesce the bits and pieces of information exploding in her mind into a coherent image. Sometimes she succeeded.

Sometimes she didn't.

When it came to making sense of the strange images of snow and snakes and water that had been coming to her when Kowalski burst through the viewing room's door, Tobie was hopelessly confused.

Frustrated, she pushed aside her notebook and reached for Jax's computer. Opening an Internet browser, she hesitated for a moment. Then she typed in "Davos + Vice President Bill Hamilton" and hit SEARCH.

The sun was just clearing the tops of the bare branches of the cherry trees rimming the Tidal Basin when Jax met Matt von Moltke on the path beside the Inlet Bridge.

A giant of a man with wild hair and a flowing, silver-laced

beard, Matt had been stuck in Division Thirteen for more than twenty years, ever since he'd kicked up a fuss about the U.S. training and funding of death squads in El Salvador. Ironically, the situation had suited him just fine, since the guys in Division Thirteen were pretty much left to their own devices—until the Company needed them to do something no one else wanted to touch.

"I had to call in a couple of favors," he said, passing Jax a bulging manila folder, "but I got the preliminary crime-scene report. Everything from October's first viewing session is there. But the recordings of the entire second session have been erased and whatever sketches she was doing are gone."

"Kowalski obviously cleaned everything up before he called the cops." Jax flipped open the folder and cast a quick glance through the crime-scene report, pausing at a photo of Captain Peter Abrams, his shirtfront ripped and sodden with dark blood. "How's Abrams?"

"Alive. Barely."

"Has he regained consciousness?"

"Not yet."

"That may be just as well for the moment."

Matt nodded. "Colonel McClintock got the Navy to station a couple of guards in Abrams's room. The FBI is kicking up a fuss—they want their own guys in there. But so far the Navy's managed to hold firm."

"They damned well better, if they want Abrams to have a chance."

"Yeah. But how do you tell the Navy they can't trust the FBI? McClintock's fit to be tied that he can't come up here and help deal with things himself." They turned to walk along the water's edge, Matt's leg dragging badly in the cold. A close encounter with a Bouncing Betty on a muddy jungle path in the Mekong Delta had left him with an ungainly gait, but he never let it slow him down. He said, "The FBI knows October showed up at your house last night."

"That didn't take long."

"They're pretty stirred up over there. You know what they're like when they lose one of their own. They even called the DCI at home to ask for your file."

"And?" Jax and Gordon Chandler—the director of Central Intelligence, or DCI—had a long feud going back to the days when Chandler had been the United States ambassador to Colombia and an irate Jax had coldcocked the son of a bitch in the middle of a diplomatic dinner party.

"Duane Davenport—that's the head of the CID—wants to see you ASAP."

Jax grunted. As head of the FBI's Criminal Investigative Division, Davenport might be expected to involve himself in the inquiry into the death of one of his agents. But Jax was remembering that smiling photograph of Davenport with Special Agent Mark Kowalski. "What can you tell me about this guy Kowalski?"

"Not a lot. He's been with the Bureau about fifteen years. Started out as a cop in Jersey, same as Davenport. No unusual displays of wealth or other ill-gotten gains. He's divorced. The wife got the kids and the house. He recently bought a smaller place in Arlington. He seems wholesome enough, if a trifle hyper-religious. He's a regular at the Bureau's prayer breakfasts and in the Promise Movement. That sort of thing. I'm gonna run everything we got through the GIS."

Jax lowered his chin to hide a smile. The GIS—the global information sifter—was the Company's latest toy: an incredibly powerful computer program designed to sift through and correlate unbelievable quantities of disparate information. But so far, Jax hadn't been impressed. "Go ahead and give it a try."

"I keep telling you, that thing's amazing."

"Right."

Matt reached into his pocket and pulled out a folded sheet of paper. "This came in just as I was leaving. It's a copy of the list of antiquities Agent Cox had selected for Tobie to view." He paused. "There's no manuscript on it."

"What?" Jax scanned through the list. Statues, cuneiform cylinders, vases, a necklace, a gold dagger . . . no manuscript. "You're sure this is the final list?"

"She had it in her hand when she was killed."

"Someone could have switched it."

Matt shook his head. "Not a chance. She'd given copies to the other members of her team. And you're not going to convince me they're all in on this."

"No," agreed Jax.

Matt rubbed a hand down over his wild beard. "How's October holding up?"

"Okay. You've heard what they're saying about her psychiatric discharge. Somebody obviously has access to her military records."

They'd reached the FDR Memorial, with its red granite walls and trickling waterfalls. Matt swung to face him. "There's one more thing you might find interesting: an antiquities dealer by the name of Gabriel Sinclair was found floating beside the dock of his house in the Hamptons this morning."

"Chilly weather for a swim."

"He was wearing silk pajamas."

Jax stared off across the Tidal Basin, the blue water reflecting the bare branches of the cherry trees and the clear cold sky above. "I knew Sinclair. He isn't just any antiquities dealer. He's probably the biggest dealer in ancient Mediterranean artifacts in the country—if not the world."

"The timing is certainly interesting." Matt buttoned the

top of his jacket against the wind. "I'll keep digging. See what turns up. We can meet at the cathedral amphitheater at seven tonight." He started to turn away, then paused to look back and say, "And go see Davenport. Otherwise they're gonna put out an APB on you."

19

Rearing high above the Rio Jalón on a barren, windswept mesa, the crumbling stone battlements of Medinaceli rose pale and stark against a gunmetal gray sky.

As the commuter train chugged into the station, Noah Bosch stood at the top of the passenger car's steps and stared at the steep, narrow road winding up the side of the mesa. No one had told him there was an Old Medinaceli and a New Medinaceli, and that the train stopped in the modern settlement that had grown up along the Madrid to Zaragosa highway far below the ancient village.

Stepping off the train, he approached the stout woman behind the ticket counter. "*Pardon*," he said, his fractured Spanish painful even to his own ears. "Is there a bus up to the old village? Or maybe a taxi?"

"No," she said and turned away.

Noah shouldered his backpack and glanced at his watch.

It was already ten to three. "*Shit*," he whispered, and took off at a steady jog.

The day was cold, the wind brisk. But after a couple of steep kilometers, he was hot, the straps of his pack digging into his shoulders, his breath coming painful and labored. *When the hell did I get so out of shape?* he wondered, blowing hard. He'd turned out for cross-country in high school, even run a couple of marathons in college. Yet here he was, wheezing like a fifty-year-old chain-smoker.

The whine of a car's engine brought his head around. Turning, he spotted a blue Citroen laboring up the hill toward him and hopefully stuck out his thumb.

The Citroen whipped past him, the young woman at the wheel not even glancing in his direction.

"Thanks," Noah shouted after her.

By the time he reached the top and collapsed against the base of what looked like a crumbling old city gate, his face was streaked with sweat and dust, and he had a stitch in his side.

It was also twenty past three.

"You are late," said a voice behind him in lightly accented English.

Glancing around, Noah found himself staring at an elderly gentleman with a darkly weathered, heavily lined face and an elegant white mustache and goatee. Small but lithe, he was wearing a wool cap, rugged brown trousers held up by leather suspenders, and an old canvas jacket that hung open.

He held a wind-ruffled bouquet of snowdrops in one hand.

Noah slid off the stone platform. "Professor Zapatero?"

The old man inclined his head. "*Sí.*" He nodded to the wind-worn structure rising beside them. "I wonder, do you know that's a Roman triumphal arch you are leaning against?"

Noah twisted around to stare up at it. "Roman? Here?"

Zapatero gave a soft chuckle. "Oh, yes. It was the Romans who built Medinaceli's first walls. It's difficult to dig anywhere in the village without hitting the remains of their villas and their temples and their synagogues. Or the remains of their successors, the Moors. The Moors extended the walls, you see, and built their own houses and their mosques and a castle. But then the city fell to the Reconquista, and the synagogues and mosques all disappeared, to be replaced with churches and monasteries and convents."

The old man's eyes crinkled and he made a tsking sound with his tongue. "And you, you are standing there thinking, *I have come all this way to talk to this crazy old man about the early Christians of Mesopotamia, and listen to him, he's giving me a history lesson about some half-dead village.* It doesn't occur to you, does it, that there's a reason I'm telling you all this?"

Noah shook his head. "I don't understand."

"Come," said the Spaniard, and turned away, leaving Noah to follow or not, as he chose.

20

The massive concrete pile of the J. Edgar Hoover FBI building
took up an imposing stretch of Pennsylvania Avenue between Ninth and Tenth Streets. Built in the Brutalist style
of the sixties and seventies, it had harshly repetitive angular
geometrics and a blocky construction that made it look like
a fortress. *Or a prison,* thought Jax, going through the heavy
security.

He was met by a slim, attractive woman with long blond
hair and a Glock 26 on her hip who led him to Duane Davenport's comfortable offices overlooking Pennsylvania
Avenue. The assistant director—or AD, as the head of the
Bureau's Criminal Investigative Division was called—was
seated at his desk. He had his dark head and massive shoulders bent over something he was writing and said curtly,
"One moment," without bothering to look up or apologize.
It was a not-so-subtle way of impressing Jax with the AD's
power and authority.

Jax smiled.

He wandered the AD's office, his gaze taking in the large, ornately framed photograph of Davenport with a smiling former president Robert Randolph. Beside it hung a similar photograph of Davenport with Secretary of State Forest Quincy. Personally, Jax thought the newly inaugurated president was making a mistake, keeping his predecessor's appointment, but then, Jax had never been fond of either Randolph or his band of thugs.

If Davenport had had his picture taken with the *new* president, he hadn't bothered to get it framed yet.

The AD finished whatever he'd been writing and looked up. "I expected you in my office an hour ago," he snapped.

"Really?"

The other man's face darkened perceptibly. "I want to know, when was the last time you saw October Guinness?"

Jax met the other man's icy stare with a bland smile. "I think you already know the answer to that question."

Davenport stretched back in his black leather executive chair, his attention seemingly all for the pen he twirled around and around at the tips of his fingers. He was a handsome man, tall and fit and accustomed to dominating other men with his size and his looks and the force of his own sense of superiority. "I want to hear it from you."

"All right." Although he hadn't been invited to do so, Jax very deliberately repositioned one of the straight-backed chairs facing the desk and sat down. "She came to my house last night. She'd lost her purse and she needed me to pay off her cab. So I lent her a couple hundred dollars and drove her to the Omni Shoreham."

"You expect us to believe she got a room there? There's absolutely no record of it."

"I don't care what you believe. I'm just telling you what happened."

Davenport sat forward with a jerk and tossed the pen onto the tooled leather surface of his desk. "I've heard about you, Alexander. You have a bad reputation as a smartass. A loose cannon who likes to play by his own rules."

Jax let his eyes crinkle with amusement. "In my business, that's not necessarily a bad thing."

Davenport didn't smile back. "What did Miss Guinness tell you she planned to do?"

"Ensign. Ensign Guinness."

Davenport's lips tightened. "What did *Ensign* Guinness say she was going to do?"

"I didn't ask."

"It's my understanding you and Guinness are friends."

"We've worked together a couple of times, yes."

"Tell me about her."

"You know why Agent Cox brought her here?"

Davenport huffed a contemptuous laugh. He obviously wasn't a fan of remote viewing. "I know."

"Then you know she's very good at what she does."

"She was given a fucking psychiatric discharge from the Navy."

"She's not crazy," Jax said evenly, "if that's what you're implying."

"But she's not exactly normal, either, wouldn't you say?"

Jax showed his teeth in a smile. "Define *normal*."

Davenport pushed to his feet and went to stand at the window overlooking the famous avenue below. "You know what happened at the Warton Office Park last night?"

"I know what your agent says happened."

Davenport glanced back at him. "You have reason to doubt him?"

"Let's just say I disagree with some of his conclusions."

Davenport pursed his lips in thought. "Did Guinness tell you about the shooting?"

Again, Jax chose his words with care. He was walking a dangerous, narrow line. For all he knew, Davenport could be up to his bulging biceps in last night's shootings. Then again, the guy might simply be a colossal jerk. And if Davenport *wasn't* involved, then Jax had to be careful not to say anything that could end up making October look worse, should she ever find herself facing murder charges.

"No," said Jax. "The first I heard about it was from the morning news."

"You don't find that strange? That your friend told you nothing?"

Jax shrugged. "You forget what I do for a living. It was fairly obvious something had happened to frighten her badly. But I didn't press her for an explanation and she didn't give me one."

Davenport leaned back against the window, his arms crossed over his chest. "I'm curious: where exactly did you spend last night—after you dropped Guinness at the Omni?"

Jax smiled. "Had your men watching my house, did you?"

"Just answer the question."

"I went to visit an old friend—and no, I'm not going to give you her name," Jax added when Davenport opened his mouth to ask just that.

"You're familiar with the phrase 'obstruction of justice'?"

Jax glanced very deliberately at his watch and pushed to his feet. "I'll leave my lawyer's address with your assistant."

Davenport snorted in derision. "If you hear from Guinness again, you're to contact this office immediately. Is that clear?"

"Got it."

"Special Agent Brockman will see you out."

Jax swung away. But at the door he paused to glance back and say, "I'm curious about something: Kowalski told reporters he discovered the shooting when he came back from getting everyone burgers. Is that right?"

"Yes. Why?"

"Did he happen to say what October ordered?"

Davenport frowned. "A burger, like everybody else. Why?"

"You're sure?"

"Of course I'm sure. What the hell difference does it make?"

Jax studied the other man's tightly held jaw and narrowed eyes. "October is a vegetarian."

Davenport blinked. "You're right," he said without missing a beat. "Now that you mention it, I think Kowalski did say she asked for a salad."

And that, thought Jax as he turned away, told them exactly what they needed to know about AD Duane Davenport.

Wordlessly, he followed Agent Brockman through the maze of corridors and out into the weak winter sunshine.

Like October, he was about to become a fugitive.

21

The Spaniard led Noah along the *paseo* **that ran at the outer** base of Medinaceli's crumbling town walls. Noah had no idea where they were going, or why.

He followed anyway.

"I take it you're here because of the Babylonian Codex," said Zapatero, striding along with the easy, loping gate of a lifelong hiker.

"Not just the codex," said Noah, struggling to keep up. The wind blowing up from the valley was like a cold battle-axe, the long grass beside them brown and dead, the ancient, weathered stone houses of the village looming above them to cast crenellated shadows across the dusty path. Noah kept close to the old wall.

The Spaniard glanced back, his dark eyes glinting with amusement. "Not only? What else, then?"

Noah gave a rueful smile. "Okay—you're right. I'm interested in the codex."

Zapatero made a derisive clicking noise with his tongue. "You Americans. Why have you all become so fascinated with the end of the world?"

Noah tripped over a stone that had tumbled onto the path from the wall above. "It's true then, what I've heard? That the codex is an early copy of the Apocalypse of St. John?"

"Not just an early copy; it is the *earliest* text we have, predating the other known texts by half a century or more. It also includes of a number of verses that were subsequently omitted from the later known texts. It is not unusual for early manuscripts to show subtle differences in wording. But the codex goes beyond that."

"So what exactly do these newly discovered verses say?"

Rather than answer, Zapatero squinted off across the gentle hills spreading out below them, where acres and acres of windmills spun furiously, giant towers of electricity-generating steel such as Don Quixote could never have imagined. "You know, of course, that the Revelation of St. John is only one example of what is known as apocalyptic writing?"

"I've heard there were others. But most have been lost, right?"

"Many, yes. But not all. Apocalyptic writing was enormously popular several thousand years ago, and not just in Jewish circles. The Sibylline Oracles, the Qumran War Scroll, the Apocalypses of Ezra and Baruch, the ancient teachings of Zoroaster . . . there were many such 'apocalyptic' writings floating around the Mediterranean at the time, although most are now known only to scholars."

"Yes," said Noah. "But they're not particularly similar to each other, are they?"

"Quite similar, actually. Parts of the War Scroll sound so much like the Apocalypse of John that when you read it, you find you must keep reminding yourself you are not reading the

Bible. The imagery in both books is very much in the tradition of Jewish apocalyptic literature: horns and beasts, angels and demons, seals and cups—these are all symbols we meet again and again in the works of the period. You see, writers had a different attitude toward originality in those days. They saw nothing wrong with borrowing passages from other authors."

"Like the Old Testament story of the Great Flood," said Noah. "That was adapted from an earlier Mesopotamian myth, wasn't it?"

Zapatero nodded. "Many of the Old Testament stories were borrowed from the Sumerians and the Babylonians. The writers of apocalyptic literature took a similar approach. As far as they were concerned, they were all working in a similar tradition with a similar purpose: to address the mystery of evil and explain it."

Noah studied the Spaniard's lined, sun-darkened profile. "And they explained it as a product of demonic forces?"

"Essentially, yes. But were they attempting to predict the end of the world?" Zapatero pressed his lips into a thin line and shrugged. "Probably not. You must remember that the word *apocalypse* did not originally mean 'the end of the world.' It meant only 'to reveal what is hidden'—which is why the Apocalypse of John is also known as the Book of Revelation."

"So how old is Revelation?"

"As we know it, the book was probably given its final form around the year A.D. 100. But its origins are murky—very murky. In all likelihood it is a compilation of several earlier works, which were themselves taken from the Talmud and the writings of the Zoroastrians, the Egyptians, and the Canaanites. The vision of the beast rising from the sea is a good example; it is a very obvious adaptation of the vision of the four beasts rising from the sea in Daniel, which itself echoes earlier works."

"But the verses weren't copied verbatim, right? They were reframed and reworked?"

"Yes, but the seams where they were joined are still visible to trained scholars. Chapters Four through Eleven of Revelation are generally considered the earliest, while Chapters Twelve through Twenty-two were added decades later. Only Chapters One through Three and a few verses of Chapters Twenty and Twenty-two can with any confidence be identified as securely Christian."

"So where do the previously unknown verses fall?"

"Between what we now know as Chapters Four and Five. Essentially, they form an entire lost chapter."

Noah felt his pulse begin to quicken with anticipation. By now, they had reached the narrow tip of the plateau, where the town walls fell away and the remains of a ruined castle rose before them at the far edge of a barren field. Only two of the castle's towers had survived, one round, one square. The wind was stronger here, buffeting his ears and carrying the scent of wood smoke.

He stared across the rough field in confusion, "Why are we here?"

Zapatero led the way across the dead grass. "Once, this was an Arab castle; then, the seat of the dukes of Medinaceli. Now . . ." A spasm of what looked like pain crossed his features. "Now, it serves the village as a cemetery."

"As a—" Noah broke off as he followed Zapatero through a narrow arched door in the castle wall. Inside, the castle lay open to the cold gray sky. All that remained was a rough field of windblown grass surrounded by crumbling walls and crowded with row after row of weathered tombstones and simple crosses.

He understood, now, the snowdrops Zapatero clutched in one hand.

Feeling awkward and out of place, he watched as the

Spaniard went to rest his simple bouquet against a black granite tombstone in the newer corner of the cemetery. Zapatero made a quick sign of the cross and bowed his head.

Noah ducked back outside. Swinging his pack off his shoulders, he rubbed his aching neck and drew in a deep breath.

There was not another soul in sight, the houses of the sleepy village lying perhaps a quarter mile in the distance, so that he suddenly felt oddly isolated and exposed. As he stared out over what he'd first dismissed as an empty field, his eyes began to pick out the stone foundations of vanished buildings lying buried in the long, windblown grass. Medinaceli had obviously once been a much larger place than it now was. He remembered that it was to the Duke of Medinaceli that Christopher Columbus had come, seeking financing for his voyage to the New World. For some reason, the thought made him shiver.

Zapatero joined him after a few moments. "My wife," he said simply.

They cut across the field in silence, following a rutted lane that led back to the closely packed houses and narrow, winding streets of the village. As the golden sandstone walls of the ancient houses closed in around them, Noah said, "The lost chapter of the Babylonian Codex: what does it say?"

"The references are predictably obscure. But what is particularly fascinating is that one of the verses matches an inscription found on a mosaic here in Medinaceli."

"*Here?*"

Zapatero's eyes crinkled in a smile as he watched a hawk soar high above the red tiled roofs and pointed church spires of the village. "Many mosaics have been found here. One of the largest was discovered in front of the ducal palace when the plaza mayor was repaved a few years ago. It is difficult to do much digging around here without running into one."

"But . . . why would an inscription from a lost chapter of Revelation have been used in an isolated outpost of the Roman Empire?"

"I'll show you."

"You'll *show* me?"

Smiling faintly, Zapatero turned down a passage so narrow that Noah had to fall back and follow behind, squeezing between houses so old their walls bulged out, almost touching overhead. At its end, the passage opened onto a small plaza framed on three sides by ancient stone houses. On the fourth side rose a crumbling, shuttered church.

A blue Citroen stood parked beneath the plaza's sole scraggly olive tree.

Following Noah's glare, Zapatero said, "Ah my daughter is home," and pushed open the heavy, worn door of the three-story medieval house that stood at the corner, its lower walls built of massive square-cut stone blocks pierced by small, barred windows. "Please, come in."

They entered a soaring, high-ceilinged room, longer than it was wide, with dark beams and quarry-tiled floors and heavy dark wood furniture that looked stark and monastic against the room's plastered, whitewashed walls. A roaring fire burned on a rugged stone hearth at one end of the room beside wide, shallow steps with tiled risers leading to the floors above. The air was heavy with the scent of beeswax and wood smoke and old stone.

Noah glanced around the room. "You have a copy of the codex here?"

"In a manner of speaking."

"What does that mean?"

Smiling faintly, Zapatero took off his wool cap and hung it on a peg beside the door. He left on his coat. "Would you like me to take your pack?"

"That's okay. I'm good." All of Noah's notes and his

laptop were in that backpack; he never let it out of his sight. "But—"

He broke off as a door opened behind him and a woman's voice said, "There you are, Papa."

Noah turned. It was the girl from the Citroen.

A slender woman with delicate features and long, straight brown hair who reminded him of Julia, she stood in a doorway that led to what looked like a book-lined study. She pulled the door closed behind her and gave Noah a wry smile. "It's you, is it?"

Zapatero looked from one to the other. "You've met?"

"Not exactly." She went to lift a coat from the row of plain pegs and opened the front door. "I'm off to get some bread. I won't be long."

Noah stared after her in bemusement.

"This way," said Zapatero.

Increasingly puzzled, Noah adjusted the weight of his pack and followed the Spaniard through a tall set of French doors that opened onto a broad flagstoned terrace. It was only then that he realized the house lay at the edge of the village, backing right onto the town walls. The terrace looked out over a sloping garden hemmed in on two sides by high, irregularly coursed stone walls. In the summer one might sit here and sip sangria while staring out over the broad Sorian plain. But now, in winter, the rugged tables and chairs were covered, the massive terra-cotta pots empty, the long, sloping garden brown and shriveled by a cold wind.

They walked down a set of broad, shallow steps, toward a curious low-roofed building that stood at the edge of the garden, its golden stone walls worn and darkened by wind and time. Large, square blocks of worked stone formed its lower courses up to perhaps four or five feet; above that, the stones were more irregular, as if the building had at some point been repaired or rebuilt. There were no windows, only a low, narrow door fashioned of stout, iron-banded planks set into a horseshoe-shaped arch.

"That's a curious-looking garden shed," said Noah.

Zapatero gave a soft laugh. "That 'garden shed' is one of the oldest existing buildings here in Medinaceli. It's been rebuilt several times over the years, but my daughter has discovered evidence that suggests it was once used as a synagogue. She's a noted archaeologist in her own right, you know. She says it may have continued in use as late as the twelfth century. Then the Christians conquered this part of Spain, and all those adhering to the Jewish or Muslim faiths were either forcibly converted, driven out, or killed. Their holy places were destroyed or converted to other uses—in this case, first a barn, then a storeroom."

"So how old is it?"

"As far as we can tell, the original structure dates to the time of the emperor Claudius. But there is a mosaic—" Zapatero broke off as the sound of a ringing phone drifted down the slope from the house behind them. "Excuse me," he said, turning back. "I won't be but a moment."

He took the steps to the terrace at an easy lope that belied his age, while Noah stayed where he was, his gaze going back to the ancient stone synagogue. Through the open door, the Spaniard's voice carried on the cold air. "Hello?"

There was a moment's pause, then, "Hello? Who is this? Is anyone there?"

Noah swung around, seized by a sudden, awful certainty. *"No! Get off the phone!"* he shouted, and began to run, just as the house before him erupted in a roaring explosion of flame and death.

22

Easing his BMW out onto Pennsylvania Avenue, Jax kept one eye on his rearview mirror.

Davenport had given him a chance to turn October in to the FBI, and Jax hadn't taken it. He could think of only one reason Davenport had let him walk out a free man: he was planning to let Jax lead him to October.

Jax wove deliberately in and out of the morning traffic, watching for a tail. He even circled around the block a few times, just to be sure.

He was not being followed.

Careless, he thought, heading south toward Alexandria. Davenport should have put someone on his ass, just to make it look good. The absence of an official shadow told Jax his friends at the FBI had used the time he spent in Davenport's office to mount a tracking device on his car.

Turning onto his own street, Jax slowed, his gaze scanning the parked cars scattered up and down the block. A white van idling near the corner immediately drew his attention.

They probably thought they were blending into the neighborhood just fine, with their colorful magnetic sign proudly proclaiming THE MERRY MAIDS: FRIENDLY, FAST, AND EFFICIENT. *We clean your house so you don't have to!* But apart from the van's giveaway tinted windows and improbable bristling of antennae, they'd parked in front of a house Jax knew had a live-in Guatemalan housekeeper.

Smiling faintly, he pulled into his carport, seemingly oblivious to the FBI agent in coveralls pretending to trim the hedge across the street. Crossing in front of his car, Jax let his keys drop. Cursing loudly for effect, he stooped to retrieve them and felt beneath the front fenders until he located the little black box of the FBI's tracking device.

He left it in place.

Maliciously whistling the endless, maddening refrain of Beethoven's Ninth, he entered the house through the kitchen. Since his friends in the van couldn't have been sure how long Jax had planned to be out the previous night, they wouldn't have taken the time needed to hardwire their snooping equipment. Which meant they'd had to get creative and find ways to hide a bunch of transmitters.

He strolled slowly through the house. To anyone watching, he would look relaxed, oblivious. In truth, he was anything but. Kitchens were always easy to bug—just stick a microphone and video camera with a wide-angle lens under the refrigerator. He spotted it right away and turned to hide his smile.

Bookcases were another great spot, as long as the target was the kind of guy who bought his books by the yard and never looked at them again after the room was "done." Walking into his living room, Jax cast a casual eye over his shelves as if searching for a book to read. He soon spotted the intruder: a hardcover copy of Ayn Rand's *The Fountainhead* with a tiny lens in its spine. *Cute,* thought Jax. Selecting a nearby volume at random, he tucked it under his arm and turned toward the entry.

Still whistling, he stooped to gather the mail that had fallen just inside the front door slot and spotted another small lens, about the diameter of a pencil and connected by a fiber-optic cable to a transmitter fastened beneath the hall console.

Resisting the urge to give the FBI surveillance team in the van the finger, Jax took the stairs to the second floor two at a time. He retrieved a black leather bag from his closet and tossed in a change of clothes. Then he carried the bag into the bathroom and closed the door.

Bathrooms weren't easy places to bug—too many hard, flat surfaces. But Jax went over it carefully, just to be certain. Satisfied, he reached beneath the frame of a wide, full-length mirror that hung opposite the sink and released the catch. Sliding the mirror to one side, he revealed a custom-built compartment stocked with everything from a Heckler and Koch MP7 and a collection of machine pistols to false IDs and various disguises.

He worked quickly, selecting a driver's license and credit cards issued in the name of James Anderson. He took a stack of twenty-dollar bills, reconsidered, and added another stack. A lock-pick set and a transmitter detector went in the bag next; a couple of black cylinders a bit larger than a roll of quarters went in his pocket. Conscious of the empty holster at the small of his back, he snapped a loaded cartridge into his backup Beretta. Then he added a Walther PPK and FN Five-Seven to the bag.

He had a feeling things were about to get ugly.

Davenport was preparing for a meeting with the secretary of the interior when Kowalski called from the surveillance van.

"The subject has arrived at the house," said Kowalski.

Davenport glanced at his watch. "Alone?"

"Affirmative."

"What's he doing now?"

"He's in the bathroom." There was a pause. "He's been in there a long time. I'm not sure what he's up to."

Davenport snorted. "What do you think he's doing in there?" He tossed a file in his soft leather briefcase and zipped it closed. "I want two teams on the asshole's tail the instant he leaves the house."

"Not a problem," said Kowalski. Davenport could hear the sound of the van's passenger door being drawn back and Kowalski's feet hitting the pavement. "The guy doesn't have a clue we're watching him."

Clipping his phone back onto his belt, Davenport turned to find Agent Brockman leaning against his door, her arms crossed at her chest, a sardonic smile lifting the edges of her lips. He said, "What the fuck are you smirking about?"

She pushed away from the door. "Did you know that the National Park Service has a policy of recording the license plate numbers of any cars left overnight in a national park?"

"No, I didn't. Is there a reason I should care?"

"I think you might. You see, the Agency's computers interface with the Park Service. Which is how we know that last night, Jax Alexander's car was parked at Daingerfield Island."

Davenport swung his briefcase off the desk and frowned. "What the hell?"

"Daingerfield Island is the site of the Washington Sailing Marina. I crosschecked the names of the marina's boat owners against Alexander's file."

"And?"

"Ted Thornton keeps a fifty-foot Hallberg-Rassy at the marina. Now, it just so happens that Thornton was married to Mr. Alexander's mother when he was a kid. I already contacted the ranger in charge of the area. He says a man and a woman were seen going aboard the Hallberg-Rassy late last night. The man left at dawn, but the woman is still there." She paused. "I have a two-man team standing by, ready for your order."

Davenport clapped her on the shoulder and planted a kiss on her cheek. "Brockman, you're a genius." He swung away. "You know what to do."

She called after him, "Is now a good time to talk about that promotion?"

He laughed. "No."

23

Noah felt a wave of heat and pressure slam into him, knocking him off his feet.

He rolled onto his stomach, face pressed into the dead grass, arms wrapped protectively around his head. Broken glass and charred bits of wood rained down around him, ripped at his sleeves, thumped against his back. He lay flat, lungs laboring to suck in air, ears ringing. When he finally dared to raise his head, it was to peer at a strange, silent world of billowing smoke and dust.

He pushed to his feet, trembling badly. From what he could see, the blast had blown out the house's doors and windows. But the solid eighteen-inch-thick stone walls had contained most of the explosion. He could see flames licking through the gaping windows. Smell the stench of charred flesh.

He took one shaky step, two, toward the stairs leading up to the terrace and the house, then staggered to a halt. There was nothing he could do. Anyone who'd been inside that house was dead.

Noah should have been dead.

His chest jerking with each breath, he whirled back around, searching the high-walled yard for a way out. Stumbling on the uneven ground, he staggered to the plank door of the old synagogue and tried the handle.

Locked.

He rammed his shoulder against the solid panels. Rattled the latch. Slammed his palms so hard they stung.

Useless.

Shuddering now with fear and delayed reaction, he spun around. *Don't panic. Don't panic,* he kept telling himself.

His gaze fell on what looked like a rickety gate set into the nearby stone wall and half hidden by a tangle of vines. Clawing the brown stems aside, he grasped the rusty iron latch with trembling hands and felt it give.

"Thank God," he whispered, struggling against the matt of thick stems. He managed to drag the gate inward over the stony ground perhaps a foot and a half. Then it stopped, wedged tight.

Taking off his pack, he squeezed through the narrow opening to find himself in a dirt lane that curved around toward the village's old Arab gate. Through the gate's pointed arch he could see the bleak, open Sorian plain.

No one was in sight.

He stood for a moment, his back pressed against the cold, rough stone of the wall. His legs were shaking so badly he could barely stand up.

Hunching over, he braced his hands on his knees, drew the sweet, cold air into his lungs. It surprised him that he could hear no sirens or alarms, no shouting. Then he realized he couldn't hear anything, just the constant, maddening ringing in his head.

Swiping his forearm across his face, he pushed away from the wall, shouldered his pack, and began to run.

24

Seated cross-legged in the sailboat's main cabin with Jax's computer balanced in her lap, Tobie skimmed rapidly through the reports on Vice President Bill Hamilton's death. She discovered Jax was right: a preliminary autopsy had concluded that Hamilton died of a heart attack.

Frowning, she flipped through articles on the World Economic Forum in Davos. The images of narrow snow-filled streets lined with steep-roofed chalets felt familiar. But was that because she'd seen them in her viewing, or because she remembered them from the nonstop TV coverage of Hamilton's sudden death?

She couldn't say.

She found herself staring at a photograph that had been taken just moments before the Vice President's death, as he paused to speak to a man outside the frosted oriel window of a small restaurant. The caption beneath the photograph identified the man as journalist Noah Bosch.

Noah.

A coincidence? Maybe. Maybe not.

Tobie studied the grainy image. The man looked to be in his late twenties or early thirties. Lean and fine-featured, he reminded her of a young John Lennon, with his wire-framed glasses and earnest expression.

She typed in "Noah Bosch" and hit SEARCH.

Jax's computer made a strange whirling noise and froze.

"Oh, no. Not *now*," she wailed.

Tobie had a bad reputation—well deserved—for interfering with or destroying any electronics that came within a certain radius of her body. Her sister liked to say she was radioactive; her brother refused to let her walk through the door of his apartment or ride in his Mercedes. DVD players, the fuel-injection systems of cars, Bluetooth headsets—all were at risk. But PCs seemed to be particularly vulnerable. She hit CONTROL-ALT-DELETE and prayed.

Nothing.

She hit it again and breathed a sigh of relief as the laptop hummed back to life.

The search engine pulled up literally hundreds of articles with Bosch's byline. He'd written an entire series on something called "dominionism," whose titles she skimmed past rapidly. But at the bottom of the third page she came across an article that made her breath catch.

Early Christian Treasures Stolen from Iraq.

Clicking on the link, she found herself staring at a photograph of a large Syrian Cross, cast in gold and studded with precious stones. A paragraph halfway down the page leaped out at her.

Noah Bosch had written, "According to Father Saverius Adel, an Assyrian priest formerly of Dora, Baghdad, now staying at the Holyland Franciscan Monastery in Washington, D.C., one of the most precious items lost in the chaos of the invasion was an ancient papyrus known as the Babylonian Codex. Recently discovered buried in an early Christian church in a village near the ruins of Babylon about an hour's drive south of Baghdad, the book is believed to date back to the first or second century A.D. 'Early analysis of the text suggests it may be an alternate version of one of the books of the New Testament,' says Adel, 'and may even prove to predate the canonical text.'"

Trembling now with excitement, Tobie was just typing "Babylonian Codex" into the search engine when she heard a strange squeak, followed by a barely perceptible thump, as if something soft had knocked against the sailboat's stern.

Her gaze flew to the hatch at the top of the ladder leading to the cockpit. She'd left it unlocked.

The computer slid off her lap. Surging to her feet, she scrambled up the ladder to secure the sliding door's latch with trembling fingers. But she knew she'd bought herself only an extra minute, maybe two.

She was trapped.

Jax noticed the black Crown Victoria when he was on the Capital Beltway, headed west.

The Crown Vic was being careful not to stay too close. But then, it didn't need to, thanks to the tracking device silently beeping beneath Jax's right fender. As he turned onto Route 123, he spotted the second Crown Victoria, also black. There were two men in each car.

They weren't going to be easy to lose.

Pulling into the massive shopping complex known as Tysons Corner, he parked near Macy's and entered the mall. He did not glance behind him or give any indication he knew he was being followed.

He bought Tobie a new pair of jeans and a navy turtleneck at a small boutique on the piazza, seemingly oblivious to the big, dark-headed guy with a strong jawline who loitered just outside. If the guy had a partner, he was more discreet.

Leaving the boutique with a large shopping bag, Jax turned toward the nearest anchor store and headed up to lingerie on the third floor. There were few things more obvious than a male FBI agent in a lingerie department.

Politely declining the sales clerk's offer of assistance, Jax cut between a densely packed rack of lacy black bras trimmed with satin ribbons and a row of red silk nightgowns with plunging necklines and thigh-high slits. Glancing back, he saw the dark-headed guy draw up at the edge of the lingerie department as if he'd slammed into some kind of dangerous force field.

Beyond him, looking equally uncomfortable, hovered a wiry, sandy-haired agent Jax recognized as Mark Kowalski.

Their partners had obviously stayed with the Crown Vics.

Jax pushed deeper into the racks of seductive little wisps of nothings. The FBI agents nodded to each other and split up, Kowalski staying near the top of the escalators while his darker companion swung around the perimeter in a wide arc to take up a position at the opposite end of the department.

Both stood with their shoulders hunched, their gazes darting left and right, as if in terror that someone they knew might see them here.

Jax eyed a nearby display of cream silk teddies trimmed with black lace. Nice. Lifting one of the teddies off the rack, he scanned the nearby aisles, assessing his fellow shoppers. There was a slim woman in a camel-hair coat pushing a baby in a stroller. Beyond her, an older woman was eyeing what Jax's Irish grandmother liked to call "foundation garments." And then there was the twenty-something girl in a fluffy white jacket who had a mouth full of chewing gum and a rope tattooed around her neck.

Jax studied her more closely. She was wearing a short

denim skirt and black tights with silver studded black ankle boots. A matching silver stud glinted in her left nostril and a silver hoop pierced her right eyebrow. Her short red hair stuck out from her head in artfully gelled spikes. Her lipstick was purple, her skin deathly pale—except for the tip of her nose, which was red. She kept sniffing as if she had a cold. Or did cocaine.

Perfect.

"Excuse me," he said with an easy smile as he walked up to her. "I'm wondering if you could help me?"

She turned her head to look at him, her brows drawing together in suspicion, her jaw working her gum hard. "Whatcha need?"

He nodded toward a distant rack of terry cloth robes, beyond which Kowalski had taken up his stand. "I'd like to play a joke on my friend there. He wants to buy his wife something for her birthday but he's too embarrassed to come in here. I'll give you fifty bucks if you'll go ask him if he thinks your boyfriend would like this teddy."

The girl's eyes widened. "Are you for real?"

Jax held out a fifty-dollar bill and the teddy. "The money's real enough."

She sniffed, her native caution obviously at war with her desire for the money. "That's all I gotta do?"

"That's it."

She took the teddy—and the money—and gave him a saucy smile. "You got it."

Jax watched from behind a rack of knit pajamas as she sauntered up to the FBI agent, gum smacking loudly.

"Hey, dude," she said. "Help me out here?"

Kowalski startled and looked behind him.

"Yeah, I'm talking to you," she said. Planting herself in front of him, she held the teddy up under his nose. "You think my boyfriend would like this?"

Jax didn't stay to watch. Hunkering low, he slipped out through the nearby children's department. The last thing he heard was the girl's triumphant voice, saying, "Dude! What is it with you? If I can go into the plumbing department at Home Depot, why should this place freak you out?"

25

Standing just inside the mall's entrance, Jax scanned the parking lot.

He could see one of the black Crown Victorias idling two aisles over and three cars down from where he'd left the BMW. The second FBI vehicle was nowhere in sight; if the teams were following procedure, it would be parked on the far side of the mall, its driver no doubt yawning as he watched the stationary little bleep coming from the tracking device on Jax's car.

Stripping off his peacoat, Jax shoved it into his shopping bag. FBI agents were like cops: if they were looking for a bare-headed guy in a dark jacket, they tended not to pay attention to guys in pale sweaters with baseball caps.

Pulling the Washington Nationals cap he'd bought from a vender in the mall's piazza low on his forehead, he pushed through the heavy glass doors.

The sun might be shining, but the wind was brisk and strong. Ducking his head as if in response, he strode quickly up the lane behind the waiting Crown Vic. As he passed the idling black car, he could see the FBI agent sitting behind the wheel, his gaze fixed on Jax's car, his head tipped to one side as he cradled a cell phone against his shoulder.

Keeping his face turned away, Jax eased one of the black cardboard cylinders from his pocket. He waited until he was just past the white Audi parked on the far side of the Crown Vic, then swerved right. Pulling the cylinder's pin, he tossed the canister over the Audi's white hood as if throwing away a crumpled cigarette pack.

A smoke grenade charged with hexachlorethane, the canister went off with a loud *boom* that sent a massive cloud of foul black smoke billowing up and out. The Audi's burglar alarm went off, its horn going *beep beep* as the smoke whooshed out, rapidly obliterating visibility for a good twenty to thirty feet.

Shit. This time, the last thing he wanted was a damned alarm.

Quickly tossing the second cylinder, he cut through the aisles of parked cars and backtracked to his BMW. Throwing up a crooked arm to protect his nose and mouth from the spreading smoke, he felt beneath his wheel well until he found the FBI's tracking device. His eyes were stinging. He could hear sirens and shouting as the mall cops descended on the scene. But the smoke was too thick for Jax to see them.

Detaching the tracking device, he transferred the FBI's little black transmitter to the sleek silver Mercedes S-Class parked beside him.

Then he slid behind the BMW's wheel, eased the convertible into reverse, and drove off.

Davenport was leaving his meeting when the second call came through from Kowalski.

"We lost him."

"What the fuck?" snapped Davenport, ducking into the

backseat of his waiting car. "How the hell did that happen?"

"He went into Tysons Corner. Me and Welch followed him, but he gave us the slip."

"I thought you said he had no idea we were watching him? What about Mundy and Jackson?"

"Jackson lost sight of the jerk's car when he set off a smoke grenade. Mundy was waiting on the other side of the mall, watching the GPS signal. But it didn't move." There was a pause. "The son of a bitch found the tracking device and stuck it on another car. He was gone before we knew what had happened."

"Put out an APB on the asshole. I want him brought in. Now."

"I thought we wanted him loose so he could lead us to the girl?"

Davenport nodded to his driver, who pulled away from the curb. "The girl is being taken care of."

Her heart pounding hard, Tobie backed away from the cockpit hatch.

Over the gentle lapping of waves against the hull, she caught a strange brushing sound, as if someone were climbing the ladder at the stern. Then came the scuff of footsteps in the cockpit overhead.

Whirling back to the saloon, she scrambled to grab Jax's gun off the table. Holding the Beretta in one shaking hand, she tried to rack it, only to discover the slide was so stiff she could barely get it to shift.

"Oh, God, no," she whispered. "Come on."

Spinning back toward the hatch, she saw a shadow darken the door's smoked Plexiglas window. As she watched, the latch began to lift.

Gritting her teeth, she transferred the 9mm to her left hand, grasped the slide with her right, and yanked. The slide eased back and a round entered the chamber with a satisfying *click*.

Holding the Beretta in a two-handed grip, she aimed the muzzle at the cockpit hatch. The handle jiggled a second time, then stilled, as if the men above had realized it was locked.

A silence fell, so intense she could hear her own breathing. Then, through the thinly curtained windows that ran along the top of the saloon, she saw a shadow.

One of the men was slipping down the side deck, toward the bow.

For an instant, she couldn't think what he meant to do. Then she remembered the skylight hatch in the ceiling of the forward cabin.

Her gaze jerked back to the cockpit hatch. One of the shadows was still there, no doubt to make certain she didn't slip out while his friend broke in through the forward cabin.

Still clutching the Beretta, she backed toward the narrow hall that led from the main saloon to the aft cabin. She'd just reached the door to the engine room when she heard the *pop* of the hatch in the forward cabin being forced, followed by the thump of a man's weight hitting the berth beneath it.

They were inside.

By now, the blood was pounding through her veins so hard her hands were tingling. Peering around the corner to the saloon, she saw a darkly clothed figure with a nasty-looking silenced Glock materialize in the doorway from the forward cabin.

Tobie aimed at his chest and pulled the trigger, twice. One of the brass instruments mounted on the wall near his head shattered in an explosion of glass and metal.

Shit.

With a curse, the guy jerked back and fired off four shots in quick succession as Tobie ducked behind the engine room. She could hear the bullets thumping into the bulk-head beside her.

"FBI. Nobody needs to get hurt," called the man in an amazingly calm, clear voice. "Just throw down your weapon and come out."

"Fuck you," shouted Tobie, and fired off another three rounds in the general direction of his voice.

"*Mason?*" shouted the guy in the cockpit overhead, slamming his foot against the hatch.

She heard the wood of the door splinter. Shifting her angle, she fired a couple of rounds up through the deck and heard a yelp.

"Son of a bitch! What the hell is going on down there, Mason? Take her out!"

Tobie sucked in a deep, frightened breath . . . and smelled gasoline.

Looking down, she saw a pool of liquid leaking out from beneath the engine room's door and running across the deck. One of the slugs must have penetrated the bulkhead and ripped through the generator's fuel supply.

Backing quickly into the aft cabin, she leaped up on the bed, unlatched the skylight hatch above it, and jumped down again. She figured that what she was about to do would either save her life or kill her. But at this point, she was going to die anyway. Holding the Beretta's muzzle in the gasoline puddle, she closed her eyes and pulled the trigger.

She'd been afraid the gasoline would go up in a giant whoosh. Instead, it caught fire with a soft blue flame that flickered, then slowly began to spread across the floor.

She didn't stay to watch.

Scrambling back onto the bed, she levered herself up through the aft skylight hatch. She could see the dark back of the asshole in the cockpit. He was still kicking at the latch and hadn't heard her. She fired off a quick round in his direction and then dove off the stern into the wind-whipped gray waters of the Potomac.

She plunged deep, her body screaming in shock as the icy river closed around her. Arcing up, she broke the surface almost at once, gulping in air and shuddering with fear and insipient hypothermia.

By now, flames were leaping out of the aft hatch. Sucking in a quick breath, she dove again, deep, just as the sailboat exploded in a huge, percussive *whoomp*.

26

Jax could see the oily smoke roiling into the sky even before he parked the four-door gray Toyota sedan behind the marina's clubhouse.

He had rented the Toyota under the name of James Anderson. Mr. Anderson had graying hair and a mustache, and he wore a cheap suit that seriously offended Jax's sensibilities. His only consolation was the knowledge that no one he knew would recognize him if they saw him.

Closing the car door with a quiet snap, he watched the red and blue lights of the emergency vehicles splash across the clubhouse walls and bounce off the surrounding trees. He counted two fire engines, an ambulance, and a half dozen police cars. But it was the coroner's van that drew and held his attention, his footsteps echoing dully in his ears as he walked out on the dock.

A half-grown kid in a navy-and-white-striped jersey dashed past. Jax reached out and snagged his arm. "What happened?"

"The Hallberg-Rassy just blew up!" said the kid, practically trembling with excitement.

Jax nodded to the black body bag being wheeled toward them on a gurney. "Who—" His voice cracked and he had to try again. "Who got killed?"

"I don't know. They're both burned pretty bad."

"Both?" Jax stared at the blackened, submerged wreck of the sailboat, and felt his phone begin to vibrate in his pocket.

He dug it out. Only two people had this number: Matt and October. He flipped open the cheap phone with a hand that was not quite steady. "Hello?"

"Jax?"

"*October.*" He squeezed his eyes shut and let out a soft laugh. "Where the hell are you?"

"Listen, Jax . . . I—I'm sorry, but I'm afraid I kinda blew up your ex-stepdad's boat."

Madrid, Spain: Saturday 3 February 6:05 P.M. local time

Noah was still trembling.

Three hours later, and he was *still* trembling. Some ballsy investigative reporter he turned out to be.

Afraid to surface at the train station in case it was being watched, he'd caught a ride back to Madrid with a family of Germans who'd stopped in Medinaceli to have their picture taken in front of the village's famous triumphal arch. Now, his hands shaking and his ears still ringing, he set his laptop on the table of a coffee shop near the plaza mayor and started looking for Wi-Fi service.

Logging on, he went straight to his Hotmail account.

He'd set up the account several months ago, when his source had first contacted him. He didn't know who she was. He didn't even know if she really was a "she," although she called herself Linda. She had refused to give him any personal details about herself. All he knew was that the information she provided him was always—*always*—spot-on.

At first, when he was writing his *Who Really Runs the World* series for the *Post*, she'd tantalized him with brief messages. Like, "Have you looked into who paid for Senator So-and-So's latest trip to Uganda?" or, "Here's a copy of the 'Common Agreement as a Core Group'; think your readers would be interested to hear that elected members of Congress and banking execs are forming themselves into secret cells based on the organizational models of the Mafia and terrorist groups?"

Her tips had led him to places he never would have gone, like to the "K Street House," where members of Congress were given subsidized lodgings in exchange for their participation in "Spiritual Warfare"; to the Christian Embassy; and to the Council on National Policy.

And then had come that memorable afternoon in early January, when he'd logged on to his Hotmail account and found her terse, two-sentence message: *They're planning to kill the new administration. Right after the inauguration.*

He'd written back at once. *Who is 'they'? How do you know this? How and when will this happen?*

It had been an agonizing five days before she got back to him. *Don't ask how I know about it. But it's real. I just don't know where or how.*

He'd written back, *Can you find out?*

A week later, she answered. *It has something to do with the Babylonian Codex.*

He wrote back, *The WHAT???*

Her response had been swift, terse, contemptuous. *And you call yourself a reporter?*

In the two weeks that followed, he'd learned everything there was to know about the Babylonian Codex—which was, basically, not much. He'd even run an article on the theft of Iraqi antiquities in the *Post*, hoping to smoke something out.

But he never did figure out what the hell the codex had to do with anything.

Then, three days ago, a new message had popped up in his Hotmail account. *They're going to kill the VP in Davos.*

That's when Noah stormed into his editor's office, ranting and raving about a plot by slimy corporate robber barons in cahoots with religious fanatics to take over the country.

She'd told him he was fired.

Now, when Noah opened up his Hotmail account, he found a message from Linda waiting for him.

I told you they were going to kill Hamilton! Why didn't you STOP it??? You didn't even write about it!!!

He typed back, *I tried. The Post fired me and Hamilton laughed at me. No one will publish this story without something to back it up. I need PROOF.*

To his surprise, her response was almost instantaneous. *What do you need?*

He wrote, *How exactly did they kill Hamilton?*

He waited.

A few minutes later, she answered. *I can't get you that.*

He typed, *What can you get me?*

He waited an hour. Two.

Her response never came.

27

Jax found October hiding under the cover of a small sailboat berthed at the outer dock. She was soaking wet and so cold she was turning blue. But she took one look at him as she crawled out from beneath the blue canvas and went off into a peal of laughter. "Why do you look like an aging version of Magnum, P.I.?"

"Very funny." He threw his arm across her shoulders and puller her close. "Pretend like you're hugging me and keep your head down, okay? There are cops crawling all over the place."

Wrapping her arm around his waist, she snuggled her face into his chest as they crossed the parking lot. "I can't believe that cell phone didn't fall out of my pocket when I dived in the water."

"I can't believe it still worked." He opened the passenger door of the Toyota for her. "Hurry. You're going beyond blue to gray."

She drew up short. "What happened to your BMW?"

"The Toyota goes with the mustache. It's called a disguise." He gave her an evil grin. "Wait until you see what I got for you."

They drove to a diner about five miles up the river. Jax ordered hot coffee while Tobie went to change into the clothes he'd brought her.

She was gone a long time.

When she finally reappeared, she'd been transformed into a Muslim fundamentalist, complete with a long-sleeved tunic over her new turtleneck and jeans, and a white headscarf that completely hid her hair and did strange, unexpected things to the shape of her face.

"Wow," he said, staring at her. "I can't believe how different that thing makes you look."

She slipped into the booth opposite him. "I can't believe you bought me a *hijab*."

"It was your idea."

"It was?"

"Actually, I think you wanted a burqa."

She tipped her head to one side, her eyebrows drawing together in a frown as she studied his gray hair and salt-and-pepper mustache. "I guess I should be thankful you didn't bring me a blue wig and a granny dress."

"I got those, too. Along with a walker."

She stared at him. "That's a joke, right?"

"No." Jax pushed the steaming coffee toward her. "Drink."

She wrapped her hands around the cup, but she didn't drink it. "What I don't understand is, how did those guys even find me?"

"It's not hard when you've got the head of the FBI's Criminal Investigative Division on your side."

"When you've *what*?"

He gave her a quick rundown of his meetings with Matt and Duane Davenport.

"Jesus," she whispered. "Who are we dealing with here?"

"I'm not sure." He drew the paper Matt had given him from his pocket and slid it across the table toward her. "Elaine Cox had the list of antiquities you were brought here to RV in her hand when the police found her. There's no manuscript of any kind on it."

"*What?*" October snatched up the list in disbelief. She stared at it a moment, then raised her gaze to his, her eyes dark and huge. "This doesn't make any sense. If the manuscript wasn't even on the list, then why send someone to kill me?"

"I've been thinking about that. The only explanation that makes any sense is that whoever has the manuscript also has something else that *is* on the list."

"I don't get it."

Jax leaned forward, his forearms laid along the tabletop, his fingers laced together. "You told me once that a remote viewer will sometimes be drawn away from the intended target to something else nearby—something that's more powerful."

"Y-yes. But—"

"That could be what happened here. Remember what Dr. Stein was telling us? About the rumors that certain rich, powerful collectors had put in advance orders for the exact antiquities they wanted stolen from Iraq?" Jax tapped the sheet of paper between them. "There might be a dozen artifacts on this list, but I bet you'd find that they're in the hands of no more than six or eight collectors. Very rich men with their own private galleries containing Mesopotamian art."

"And manuscripts," said October softly. "So what are you suggesting? That some gazillionaire put out an order for a few select artifacts from the Baghdad Museum, including the papyrus I saw? Then he hears the Art Crimes Team is bringing in a remote viewer, and that one or more of the items in his private gallery might have made the final cut and are on the list, so he gets his man in the FBI to send one of his agents to watch the viewing and take me out if it looks like I'm getting a little too close for comfort?"

"Which you did."

"Which I did." She was silent a moment, her fingers trailing up and down the sides of her mug. He noticed the color was starting to come back to her cheeks. She said, "I was reading about Davos this morning, before my visitors arrived."

He frowned. "And?"

"One of the articles had a picture of Vice President Hamilton talking to a *Washington Post* reporter just minutes before he was killed. It was the reporter's name that caught my eye. Noah. Noah Bosch. So I looked him up. Just last week he wrote an article about early Christian treasures stolen from Iraq, and one of the items he mentioned was an ancient papyrus that had been discovered buried under an old church near Babylon." She paused. "That can't be a coincidence."

Jax stared at her. In spite of himself, he felt a chill run up his spine. *How did she know these things?* But all he said was, "What papyrus?"

"According to an Assyrian priest Bosch interviewed at the Franciscan Monastery here in D.C., it's an older version of one of the books of the New Testament."

"An *older* version?"

"That's what he said." She dropped her voice and leaned forward, as if afraid someone might overhear. "This still doesn't make any sense. What could some Bible verses have to do with the assassination of the vice president of the United States?"

Rather than answer, he nodded toward her still full cup.

"Drink up. I want to make a visit to the *Washington Post*."

She reached for the check. "We can go now."

He beat her to it. "Uh-uh. *Hijab* or no *hijab*, I'm not going to risk taking you into a room full of reporters who spend their lives following the news. Someone might recognize you."

"But—"

"No buts." He dropped a ten-dollar bill on the table. "If you want to do something, go talk to this Assyrian priest. What the hell is an Assyrian priest, anyway?"

"I don't have a clue."

Duane Davenport paused in the hallway outside the coroner's office, his hands clenching into fists at his side. The air was thick with the stink of antiseptic and the pervasive, ineradicable odor of death.

"I'm sorry," said Special Agent Brockman. "They were good men."

He turned on his heel to walk rapidly toward the exit. "Three agents," he snapped. "We've now lost three agents because of that bitch." It didn't matter that Agent Cox had died at Davenport's own orders; her death was as much October Guinness's fault as the two men whose charred bodies he'd just seen rolled into refrigerator drawers.

"We're still searching the river," said Brockman, keeping pace with him. "It's possible she died in the explosion."

"I don't think so. It's like she's a witch or something." He slapped open the door to the parking lot and stood for a moment, sucking the clean, cold air into his lungs. "We've grossly underestimated this woman. Twice now. We've been acting like we're dealing with some dim-witted crackpot, only she's shown us that she's anything but."

Brockman started to say something, then pressed her lips together.

Davenport stepped off the curb, his suit jacket flaring open to reveal the Glock in his shoulder holster. "Think about it. The minute Guinness realized we were out to get her, she basically had two choices: run as far and as fast as she could, or stay and try to figure out who we are and what we're up to. Nine hundred and ninety-nine out of a thousand people would have run. She didn't."

"'Even Satan disguises himself as an angel of light,'"quoted Brockman.

Nodding, Davenport strode rapidly toward their car, "Get me the recordings of those remote viewing sessions she was doing for Cox. If we're going to get this witch, we need to know exactly what we're dealing with—and what she knows."

28

An unobtrusive structure with redbrick and white trim, the K Street House had served for forty-five years as a place where like-minded men—from defense contractors and religious leaders to corporate lobbyists and members of Congress—could meet in a quiet, private atmosphere to discuss strategies and plot their next moves. To this end it boasted several private dining rooms, a superb kitchen, and a bar that was always open.

And it was all funded by tax-deductible contributions.

Leo Carlyle sat at his favorite chair beside a window overlooking the street, an appetizer of pâté de foie gras and toast on the table before him. Also at the table were Warren Patterson, affectionately known as "America's Minister"; Dick King, the new CEO of Keefe Corporation; and Ross Cole, an insurance company executive who personally pocketed one out of every ten dollars paid to his company for health insurance. They were just four of those who called themselves the Apostles, a select group of bold men who were willing to go further—and faster—than any of God's servants had yet dared to reach.

Carlyle took a slow sip of his champagne. "Things are going along well, gentlemen." He nodded to Patterson. "Time to up the rhetoric on the need to retake the Seventh Mountain."

Patterson's famous green eyes sparkled. "I have a broadcast scheduled for tonight. I think you're going to like it."

Dick King, the bullet-headed CEO of Keefe, swallowed a mouthful of rare prime beef and said, "Who's the scapegoat going to be?"

Carlyle smiled. "A true scum of the earth. A militant atheist lawyer who's not only a member of the Council for Secular Humanism, but who also does pro bono work for the ACLU."

"Sounds perfect," said Ross Cole.

Patterson glanced at his watch. "What time is our 'Satanic Leader' scheduled to address the nation?"

"Now." Leo pointed the remote at the giant TVs hanging suspended in opposite corners of the room.

The Latin features of Daniel Pizarro, the newly elected president of the United States, filled the screen.

"Over the past thirty years," said Pizarro, his face drawn and serious, "the American dream has been stood on its head. The statistics are frightening. In 1982, the wealthiest four hundred individuals in this country held an average of six hundred and four million dollars each, if converted to today's dollars. But today, right now, the top four hundred people in the United States own an average of three point nine *billion* dollars each. That's more than one and a half trillion dollars all together. Ten percent of the entire gross domestic product of the United States is now in the hands of just *four hundred* people. The top one percent of Americans controls more wealth than the bottom ninety percent *combined*.

"This is wrong. Today, in this country, the superrich are getting richer while everyone else is getting poorer. The hardworking citizen who labors for his wages pays a higher tax rate than the idle rich who let their money work for them.

"Now, some people will tell you the government has no business interfering in any of this. Well, they're wrong. Government is not here just to protect you from the thief with the gun who wants to steal your wallet. A government should also prevent its citizens from being robbed by the insurance companies and the banks and the energy companies who cheat and defraud their fellow citizens and pollute our great country in an ugly, unchecked scramble for profits.

"For the past thirty years government has abdicated that responsibility. They have allowed lobbyists to pressure Congress into scrapping the regulations that once kept us safe, which is why we're in the sorry mess we're in today. Well, I'm here to tell you: no longer. Not on my watch."

Leo Carlyle pointed the remote at the screens and zapped the newly inaugurated President Pizarro into oblivion.

"My God! The guy's a fucking communist," exclaimed Ross, leaning back in his chair.

"What do you expect?" said King. "He might call himself a Catholic, but his mother was a Jew."

"Since when are Catholics any better than Jews?" said Patterson, and the rest of the men at the table laughed.

"Not to worry, gentlemen," said Leo. "Four more days, and the nightmare will be over."

29

Forty-five minutes later, Jax walked into the offices of the *Washington Post* on Fifteenth Street and handed one of the receptionists a set of very real looking Homeland Security credentials bearing the name James Anderson. Jax knew a guy named Ernie DeMoss in Adams Morgan who did even better work than the CIA.

"I'd like to see Noah Bosch," said Jax, smoothing his graying mustache.

The receptionist—a chubby-cheeked redhead with freckles and a name tag that read TERRANCE—cleared his throat. "Do you mind if I ask why?"

Jax put on his best glower. "Sorry. It's official business."

Terrance swallowed with enough force to bob his Adam's apple up and down. "Excuse me," he said and groped for the phone.

After a furtive, whispered conversation, he said, "This way," and led Jax to a glass office at the back of the newsroom.

A slim, fifty-to-sixtyish woman in a black silk jacket and cream shell rose from behind the desk. "I'm Kelly Brian, head of the Metro desk," she said, her hand outstretched. She had an attractive, gently aging face framed by sleek gray hair. But Jax had no doubt that beneath that deceptive smile, she was as hard as nails. She couldn't have reached this office otherwise.

"Please, have a seat," she said. "I understand you're looking for Noah Bosch."

"That's right." Rather than take the chair indicated, he shifted his weight into a widespread stance and clasped his hands behind his back.

She raised one eyebrow. "I take it you're here because of the photograph of Noah with the Vice President in Davos?"

When Jax simply stared at her expectantly, she cleared her throat and said, "I don't know what Noah was doing in Davos. But I can assure you that he wasn't on assignment for us."

"Bosch doesn't work for you anymore?"

"Not since last week."

"You fired him?"

She gave a wry smile. "Let's just say, Noah and the paper had a parting of the ways."

"Why?"

"Why?"

"That's right. Why."

She sank into her chair, her palms resting flat on the surface of her desk. "I should tell you that our personnel actions are confidential. Then you'll get a warrant and our lawyers will get involved . . . so let's just cut to the chase, shall we? I don't think it's any secret that times are difficult for newspapers all across the country. Because our hometown happens to also be the nation's capital, our circulation remains strong. But we still need each and every one of our reporters to generate a steady stream of printable stories."

"And Bosch wasn't doing that?"

"Don't get me wrong; Noah is a real hustler. He's done some excellent work in the past. But about three months ago I assigned him to do a series we called 'Who's Really Running the World?'"

"What was his answer?"

"The usual suspects. The Trilateral Commission. The Rand Corporation. The Bilderberg Group."

"Doesn't exactly sound like news."

"Maybe not to you. But to many of our readers, the discovery that there is basically a revolving door between Wall Street and the Treasury, or that former presidents—who still receive CIA briefings—are sitting on the boards of huge conglomerates that invest heavily in everything from the defense industry to oil . . . Well, that's pretty alarming stuff. Especially these days."

Jax kept his face stern. "You say Bosch began this series three months ago?"

She nodded. "Right after the election. President Pizarro won on a promise to rein in the corporate bandits and shut down the tax havens that are costing American taxpayers one hundred billion dollars a year. Bring back the regulations that once kept us safe from everything from poisoned drinking water to irresponsible financial bubbles. There's a groundswell of anger in this country."

"And you decided to ride it?"

Her chin lifted a notch. "We're a newspaper. Our job is to inform. And the fact is, there's a lot of misinformation floating around out there. A lot of fear. And it's being fed, deliberately."

"You mean, by those who have something to lose if President Pizarro succeeds?"

"In a word? Yes. The kind of people who can afford private islands don't let go of their advantages without a fight.

And they have the money to buy newspaper chains and television networks."

"Not to mention politicians."

"Especially politicians. And pulpits."

"Pulpits?"

"Pulpits. Part of it's a neat synergy of interests. The superrich don't want any kind of international regulations or controls that will get in the way of their ability to shelter their money and exploit people, while the hysterical fringe sees any kind of international body as the first step on the road to Armageddon."

"Ah. The Antichrist."

"You got it. There's also a bizarre strain of what we call free-market fundamentalism involved. Part of it's a holdover from the days of the Cold War, when any attempt to regulate or even refine capitalism was seen as akin to godlessness. But there's also a strong element of old-fashioned Calvinism. The idea that the rich are wealthy because God has blessed them, while the poor are poor because God doesn't like them—or is punishing them because they're evil."

"Whatever happened to 'It's easier for a camel to pass through the eye of a needle than for a rich man to enter the Kingdom of Heaven'?"

"One must assume they don't read that part of the Gospels."

Jax said, "So you weren't happy with the work Bosch did on this series?"

"On the contrary. At one point we thought he was positioning himself for a Pulitzer. But then he became positively obsessed with the dominionists. He just couldn't let it go."

"The whats?"

"The dominionists." She tilted her head to one side. "I'm not surprised you haven't heard of them; very few people have. They make it a point to fly under the radar. And 'do-minionist' is not a name they typically use themselves. Basi-cally, they're a loose coalition of politically active religious radicals who believe that the United States should be gov-erned exclusively by biblical law."

For a moment, Jax was convinced he hadn't heard her right. "You don't mean as a theocracy?"

"Yes. Or, as some would say, a theonomy."

Jax huffed a soft laugh.

She did not smile. "They're actually not a very funny group of people. They're deadly serious. And they're very closely aligned with some of the key people in the financial industry and the military-industrial complex. At first, Noah turned in a riveting new series of articles that we ran through most of December. But then he started going off the deep end."

"In what way?"

"He was making wild accusations about certain very pow-erful, influential men. We weren't getting anything we could print."

"What kind of wild accusations are we talking about? Against whom?"

She gave him what he was coming to think of as her Mona Lisa smile. "Nothing I care to repeat."

Jax gave her his Homeland Security scowl. "Who were his sources?"

"Never anyone who was willing to be named. That was the problem."

On the wall behind her hung a framed copy of the *Post*'s 1974 front page announcing the resignation of President Nixon. Jax nodded toward it. "If I remember correctly, it was anonymous sources that helped break the Watergate story."

She kept her gaze on his face. "That was over thirty years ago. Times have changed. The American people have changed."

"Have we? Or is it just American newspapers that have changed?"

"Now that's an unexpected comment coming from someone with Homeland Security."

Jax pulled out a notebook and tried to look officious. "Can you tell me how to contact Mr. Bosch?"

She shook her head. "Sorry. His wife kept the apartment when the marriage broke up and I don't know where Noah went. He said he was planning to write a book on the Council on National Policy. But whether that's what he's actually doing or not, I couldn't say."

"The Council on National Policy?" said Jax, looking up from his notebook. "What's that?"

Kelly Brian stood with her hands pressed flat against the surface of her desk and leaned forward to give him one of her damnable smiles. "Look it up."

Surrounded by gently rolling wooded parkland, the Franciscan Monastery of Mount St. Sepulchre lay in a residential neighborhood in northeast Washington, D.C.

Tobie went first to the library, where she printed out a copy of Noah Bosch's article that she read again in a cab on the way to Mount St. Sepulchre. Asking the driver to return for her in an hour, she paid off the taxi in the U-shaped drive that lay just inside the monastery's massive gates, her head falling back as she stared up at the century-old church beside her. Built in the style of a Byzantine cross, its walls gleamed golden in the winter sunshine.

"I'm afraid you've just missed the tour," said a heavily accented voice behind her. "But if you hurry, you can probably catch up with them in the cloister walk."

She turned to find herself being addressed by a burly monk in a dark brown habit cinched at the waist with a crude rope. He was big and broad shouldered, with a broken nose and hazel eyes and a head of curly golden-brown hair. "Actually," she said, walking toward him, "I'm looking for Father Saverius Adel. My name is Yasmina Khalil."

The monk spread his arms wide and laughed. "I am Father Saverius. How may I help you?"

Davenport was at his desk, his laptop running the video of October Guinness's last remote viewing session, when the call came through from the monk at the Franciscan monastery.

Brother Basil's voice was hushed. Strained. "You said you wanted to know if Father Saverius received any visitors."

Davenport sat forward with a jerk. "That's right."

"Well, there's a young woman here to see him right now."

"A young woman?" Davenport snapped his fingers at Brockman to get her attention. "What does she look like?"

"She appears to be an Iraqi Muslim. She's wearing a headscarf."

Davenport frowned. It didn't sound like Guinness. Then again, she might be wearing a disguise. "How tall is she?"

"Not tall. And slight."

Davenport glanced at his watch. "Thank you, Brother. I'll send someone right away."

"I'll go," said Brockman as he pushed to his feet.

"No. Send Kowalski and Welch. You and I need to take a trip up to Bethesda."

30

It wasn't until Tobie looked into the monk's dark, puzzled eyes that she remembered she was disguised as a Muslim fundamentalist. *Not one of your better ideas, Jax,* she thought.

"You're Iraqi?" Father Saverius asked her in Arabic.

"Originally, yes," she said, answering him in the same language. They turned to walk along the Rosary Portico, a vast red-tiled cloister walk that stretched around the perimeter of the garden. "My professor at George Washington suggested I talk to you. I'm doing a paper on the theft of ancient Christian manuscripts from Iraq." She'd practiced the lie several times in the taxi, to make sure she could deliver it without stumbling. She'd never been very good at making things up.

"You sound like a Gulf Arab."

She gave a startled half laugh. "Probably because I lived in Dubai and Qatar as a child." That part was actually the truth. As the daughter of a Navy officer and the stepdaughter of a petroleum engineer, Tobie had grown up in a dozen different countries and she'd learned the language of each of them.

"I must admit," she said, their footsteps on the arched

walkway a soft cadence in the stillness of the garden. "I'm not entirely clear on what an Assyrian priest is. You're not a Franciscan, are you?"

"The Franciscans have been generous in offering me a refuge here, but I am not of their order, no. I am a member of the Holy Apostolic Assyrian Church of the East. The Assyrian Church traces its origins to the ancient Mesopotamian See of Seleucia-Ctesiphon, which was founded by St. Thomas the Apostle himself."

"It's that old?"

"It is indeed. We are among the oldest Christians in the world. Like Christ, our native language is Aramaic. For two thousand years we lived and prospered in the land of our origin. Just ten years ago, there were one and a half million of us in Iraq. But now . . ." He spread his arms wide, then let them fall to his side again. "Today, there are no more than three or four hundred thousand of us left in our homeland."

"Perhaps one day all Iraqis—Christian and Jew, Sunni and Shiite—will be able to go home and live again in peace," she said quietly.

"Perhaps."

They walked along in silence, the repetitive arches and alternating spiraled columns of the portico throwing bands of sunlight and shadow across the portico's paving. After a moment, he said, "Most Americans don't even know that such things as Arab Christians exist. They think of Christianity as *their* religion, something intrinsically Western. Something born of Western traditions and Western culture. They forget that Christianity was born and nurtured in the Middle East, just as Jesus was born in Palestine. From there his disciples spread across the Levant and Asia Minor, then west to North Africa and east to Mesopotamia, Persia, and India. You have only to look at the names of the early church fathers to understand the Middle Eastern roots of Christianity: Clement of Alexandria was an Egyptian. St. Augustine was a Berber from what is now Algeria. Ignatius of Antioch lived in ancient Syria."

"I knew that Alexandria and Antioch were important early Christian centers. But I didn't realize ancient Iraq was one, too."

"It was one of the most important. There was a large, very old Jewish community in Babylon—just as there were Jewish communities throughout the Mediterranean world. It was to these Jewish communities that the first apostles carried their teachings."

"The Syrian cross," said Tobie, turning toward him. "The one that looks like a Jewish menorah combined with a Christian crucifix. That's what it comes from?"

He nodded. "It symbolizes the blending of the Jewish tradition with the new Christian teachings. You must remember that the first Christians were Jews. They were even called Christian Jews. They believed that Jesus was the Messiah, but they also continued to observe Mosaic Law. In fact, there was quite an argument in the early days as to whether or not gentiles could even *be* Christians. There were many who opposed the Apostle Paul's teaching that non-Jews could become Christians without also becoming Jewish—in other words, without being circumsized or observing Mosaic law."

Tobie was starting to feel out of her depth. "I'm afraid I don't know much about the first centuries of Christianity."

"Not many do, even when they are raised Christian. They often assume the tenets of their faith have always been the same. In truth, there were many different teachings and interpretations competing with each other during those first centuries. Some Christian leaders preached that Jesus was the son of God, while others thought he was a prophet. There were even some who completely rejected the Old Testament—who believed that Christianity was a new religion and should be cut loose from its primitive Judaic roots. They even had their own gospel."

She looked at him in surprise. "How many different gospels were there, originally?"

"Dozens—although most are now known only from fragments. You see, in the first years after Jesus's death, the early Christians relied on what is known as the Sacred Oral Tradition—stories of what Jesus had said and done, passed from one believer to the next. It's these oral traditions that were later written down as gospels and dialogues and logia, and expanded and explained by various treatises."

"Which is why they differ—because everything was oral at first?"

"Exactly. Scholars argue as to when these various works were first committed to paper. Most were probably in circulation by A.D. 150. But it wasn't until the Council of Nicaea—three hundred years after the death of Jesus—that the leaders of the church got together and decided on a uniform doctrine. They determined what Christians should believe and which books would be accepted as part of the New Testament. The books they included became known as the *canon*. Those they rejected were called *apocryphal*."

"And everyone agreed?"

"Hardly. But by then the church had the power of the Roman state behind it. Heretics who persisted in believing anything that deviated from the orthodoxy were treated the same way as pagans who refused to convert: they were either exiled or put to death."

"You don't hear much about that part of early church history."

Father Saverius's eyes crinkled in amusement. "No, indeed. I'm afraid the number of Christians martyred for their faith pales to insignificance compared to the thousands of pagans and heretics thrown to the lions or burned alive."

Tobie's gaze narrowed against the winter sunlight as she studied the ancient catacomb symbols that decorated the walls of the portico. "So what happened to the gospels and other writings that didn't make it into the official New Testament?"

"They were ordered destroyed. Burned—along with the plays, poems, histories, and philosophical treatises of the 'pagan' Greco-Roman world. You've heard of the Gospel of St. Thomas?"

"It was found in Egypt, wasn't it? At Nag Hammadi?"

Saverius nodded. "Some Egyptian farmers dug up a sealed earthenware jar that contained a dozen ancient codices dating back to the second century. One of the codices turned out to be a complete Gospel of St. Thomas, which was previously known only through fragments. The Gospel of St. Thomas was written for a school of Christians who—like the Assyrian Church—claimed Thomas the Apostle as their founder. But when the four canonical gospels—Matthew, Mark, Luke, and John—were defined as the only acceptable gospels, the Gospel of St. Thomas was ordered destroyed. The copy found at Nag Hammadi probably came from the library of the nearby monastery of St. Pachomius. The monks buried it when the possession of such works was labeled a heresy punishable by death."

"When was it written?"

"That is difficult to say. The text found at Nag Hammadi was in Coptic—an ancient Egyptian language written in the Greek alphabet. It was probably copied around A.D. 340. Earlier Greek fragments are much older, dating back to the second century. The original was probably composed somewhere between A.D. 50 and 100."

"So it's very early."

"Oh, yes. Perhaps the earliest of them all."

"How exactly does the Gospel of St. Thomas differ from the others?"

"It's written as a logia—a series of sayings—rather than as a narrative. But theologically, the differences are mainly eschatological."

"Escha—" she shook her head. "What's that?"

"Eschatology. The end of the world. Armageddon. Revelation."

Tobie felt a sudden, inexplicable chill run down her spine.

Saverius said, "The Gospel of John speaks of a future eschaton, where Jesus will return in triumph to overthrow the rulers of the world."

"What did St. Thomas believe?"

"That the end of the world had already begun."

"Well, I guess he got that wrong."

Saverius laughed. "I don't know. It's all relative, isn't it? He also believed that the resurrection of man would be spiritual rather than a literal, bodily raising of the dead."

"So the papyrus discovered near the ruins of Babylon was a copy of the Gospel of St. Thomas?"

"Actually there were several papyri found together. And yes, one was a copy of the Gospel of St. Thomas—the oldest copy known, and written in Greek. Early reports dated it back to the beginning of the second century."

Tobie felt her heartbeat accelerate. "And the others?"

"By far the most significant was a copy of Revelation. Dr. Salah Araji—the professor who was studying the papyri— called it the Babylonian Codex."

"But if the Babylonian Codex is just a copy of Revelation, why is it significant?"

"For several reasons. The earliest previously discovered copy was the Chester Beatty Book of Revelation, which dates to about A.D. 250—and that is only a fragment of Chapters Nine through Seventeen. The Babylonian Codex is much older. But more importantly, it differs significantly from the canonical version."

"Differs? In what way?"

A yellow cab turned in through the monastery's arched gate. They watched it roll to a stop in the elongated turn-around drive, and they walked toward it. It seemed hard to believe that an hour had passed.

Father Saverius said, "Unfortunately, the codex was discovered late in 2001—during the course of some restoration work on a village church that had been damaged by U.S. bombing during the first Gulf War. Dr. Araji was still working on the translation when the United States attacked again in 2003 and the codex was stolen. He was never able to publish his findings."

Another car was pulling into the monastery: a black Suburban with tinted windows that parked on the far side of the turnaround. Tobie watched it warily. She said, "This Dr. Araji you mentioned—the Iraqi scholar who was working on the codex—is it possible to contact him?"

Father Saverius breathed out a long, pained sigh. "I'm afraid not. His mother, wife, and three children were all killed in an attack. Needless to say, it devastated him. He has cut off all contact with everyone."

"Is he still alive?"

"Last I heard. But he's refusing to have anything to do with Western scholars until all foreign troops are withdrawn from the country. As I understand it, he devotes most of his time these days to organizing a movement calling for reparations payments."

"That's not going to get very far."

"No," Saverius agreed.

The taxi driver, a short, fleshy man with the dark features of a Pakistani or Indian, had gotten out of his car and was walking toward them. He'd left the door of the cab open and the engine running in a not-so-subtle hint.

Tobie glanced toward the Suburban. It had parked, but no

one was getting out. *Shit*, she thought. *Shit, shit shit*. The wind fluttered her headscarf and she put up a hand to steady it. "Thank you so much for your help, Father."

"My pleasure." He gave a small, old-fashioned bow and swung away.

"Ready, Miss?" said the taxi driver.

Glancing across the neat garden at the center of the turn-around, she saw the front doors of the black Suburban fly open. Two men in gray business suits, white shirts, and ties hopped out. One was big and dark, the other sandy-haired and lithe.

It was Mark Kowalski.

31

Rather than rely on Wikipedia's entry on the Council on National Policy, Jax went to see one of his former stepfathers, Benjamin Rosenthal.

Once a national security advisor under Clinton, Rosenthal was now a professor of political science at Georgetown University. A stoop-shouldered, hopelessly nonathletic man with thin gray hair badly in need of a trim, he had black-framed glasses and a basset-hound face that was all sagging jowls.

"The Council on National Policy is a very powerful and very determined group of individuals," he told Jax as they walked together across the campus. "It was formed during the early years of the Reagan administration. They call themselves an educational foundation for tax purposes, but it's essentially just a networking group that brings together wealthy donors with ultra-right-wing activists. They meet three times a year to strategize ways to achieve what they call their shared goals."

"Which are?"

"Minimalizing government regulation of banking and

commerce. Gutting environmental protection laws and workers' safety regulations. Getting rid of the minimum wage. You name it—if it stops the rich from getting richer, they're usually against it. They're big on funding for the military industrial complex. And of course they're heavy on what they call traditional Western values, which basically translates into the law of the land circa 500 B.C. in Jerusalem."

"In other words, they're dominionists."

"Not all of them. But many of them, yes. Cornell University's Center for Religion, Ethics, and Social Policy has a project they call Theocracy Watch. They've named the Council as a leading force in the dominionist movement."

"Why have I never heard of it?"

"Because they do their best to keep themselves out of the limelight. They're like the Fellowship—or as it's often called, the Family: they made a deliberate decision to 'submerge,' as their leaders put it. Their meetings are closed and their membership list is a closely guarded secret."

"So who's on it?"

Rosenthal grinned. "Ex-Watergate burglars. Ex-Iran-Contra guys. Retired generals. Lots of politicians of the same stripe. A bunch of scarily dogmatic billionaires—mainly from the defense and oil industries, with a few manufacturers and retailers and financiers thrown in. Lots of fundamentalist preachers."

"Which ones?"

"Just about every one you see on TV or on the best-seller lists."

Jax stared off toward the river. "So why are these guys called 'dominionists'?"

"It comes from a passage in Genesis. 'And God said, Let us make man in our image, after our likeness: and let them have dominion over the fish of the sea, and over the fowl of the air, and over the cattle, and over all the earth, and over every creeping thing that creepeth upon the earth.' "

Jax shook his head. "I don't get it. How do they take a biblical passage about fish and cows and turn it into a godly mandate to take over the United States and impose biblical law on everyone—whether we want it or not?"

"Because they've convinced themselves that's God's plan, and they're arrogant enough to believe that He has chosen them to implement it."

"Now that's scary."

"The implications are even scarier. Since dominionists think they're doing God's work, that means that if you stand against them—or even just disagree with them—then as far as they're concerned, you're disagreeing with God. And if you disagree with God, then you're obviously on the side of Satan."

"How long has the movement been around?"

"The Family first arose in the thirties, in opposition to the New Deal and labor unions. But the movement was given a real impetus in the 1970s when a man named Rousas J. Rushdoony started what he called Reconstructionism. He wrote a big, nasty book called *The Institutes of Biblical Law*, in which he argued that the United States—all societies, in fact—must be governed by Old Testament law."

"Must?"

"Must. According to Rushdoony, when God gave his followers dominion over all the earth, it came with an injunction that requires them to subdue all nonbelievers in preparation for the return of the Messiah."

"Subdue? How?"

"Any way they can. The guys who came after Rushdoony have been more subtle. They toned down his rhetoric, got rid of the most overt racism and—unlike Rushdoony—they don't usually talk openly about stoning homosexuals and adulterers.

But if you look at the various dominionist groups—the New Wave Reformation, the New Apostolic Reformation, Joel's Army, the Spiritual Warriors moment, the Prayer Networks—you'll see Rushdoony's influence. What we're talking about is really a reactionary, radical political movement that has cloaked itself in religion but is very serious about taking control of our government and institutions."

"*Stoning adulterers?*"

"It's in the Old Testament." Rosenthal pushed his glasses back up onto the bridge of his nose. "Traditionally, evangelicals believed in the idea that salvation comes from faith in Jesus Christ. The emphasis was on repentance and the conversion of individual souls; when they talked about the Kingdom of God, they were talking about something spiritual."

" 'My kingdom is not of this world,' " quoted Jax softly.

"Exactly. Well, the dominionists have basically thrown all that stuff out the window. They teach that salvation can only be achieved by setting up a literal, *physical* kingdom of God on earth, and that's what they're determined to do. Their role models are guys like Machiavelli, Stalin, Hitler, Mao, Polpot. Even Genghis Khan and the Mafia."

"They don't actually say that, do they?"

"They do indeed. Don't get me wrong—they obviously don't share Stalin or Mao's *political* philosophies. But they do admire their techniques, and they study them. We look at Hitler and Stalin and see mass murderers—the ultimate in evil manipulation and coercion. But the dominionists look at those guys and see a genius for organizing, and a model for inspiring followers and working by stealth. They even call their prayer groups *cells*."

"Cells?"

"Cells. They go on and on about how much they love America and how they're fighting for freedom. But the truth is, they hate America—or at any rate, the America that really exists. And while they talk a lot about liberty, what they really want is to be free to impose their views on everyone else. It's basically totalitarianism, dressed up in religious trappings."

They walked along in silence. After a moment, Rosenthal said, "Why are you asking me all this, Jax?"

"You know I can't tell you that, sir."

Rosenthal pressed his lips together and nodded in understanding. "The former president was a dominionist, you know."

"Randolph?"

"Randolph. They played a huge part in his election, and he repaid them handsomely. Take a good, hard look at the appointments he made and you'll see that almost every one of them was a dominionist. I warned President Pizarro before he was inaugurated that he needs to work quickly to get these people out of the federal government—especially the military. But you know Pizarro. He's being so careful not to do anything that could in any way be perceived as partisan. He doesn't understand that these guys don't believe in compromise. As far as the dominionists are concerned, if you're not with them one hundred percent, then you're an enemy of God. They genuinely believe that Pizarro is evil."

"Because he doesn't want to see this country turned into a theocracy?"

"That, and because he's a half-Jewish Catholic whose parents immigrated from Mexico. The dominionists might have buried Rushdoony's racism, but it's still there. A lot of them believe in the demon seed theory."

"The what?"

"The belief that white Anglo-Saxon Christians are descended from Adam through Abel, while everyone else is descended from Cain and Satan via Eve's little misadventure with the serpent."

"But . . . that's just nasty."

"That doesn't mean people don't believe it."

Jax squinted up at the winter sun. "You say the dominionists are powerful in the military. What about the FBI?"

"The military, the FBI, the CIA, the Secret Service, Homeland Security. You name it. They've had eight years to burrow in deep. And make no mistake about it, these people's first allegiance isn't to this country. It's to their vision of the way they think this country *should* be."

"If there were a plot to overthrow the new administration, would these guys support it?"

Rosenthal's face sagged. "*My God*, Jax. What are you saying?"

"Nothing you can repeat."

Rosenthal stared off across the quadrangle. After a moment, he said, "There's someone up in Olney, Maryland, you need to talk to. A Major Richard Kjos. He's retired now, but he used to be a Lutheran pastor in the Air Force until the dominionist influence got so bad he couldn't stand it anymore and got out. He's dedicated his life since then to exposing their agenda. He knows far more about them than I do. I'll give him a call. Tell him you'd like to meet him."

Jax turned their steps to where he had left the rented Toyota. "I can understand how a few crazies might believe in this stuff. But military men? Government officials? Is it really possible?"

"I imagine most sane Germans said the same thing back in 1933."

Jax smiled. "You've heard of Godwin's Law, haven't you? The minute you bring Hitler or the Nazis into a political discussion, you're supposed to lose all credibility."

Rosenthal didn't smile. "Make no mistake about it, Jax: as someone who lost family members in the Holocaust, nothing infuriates me more than the baseless or exaggerated comparisons that have become far too common these days. But there is also a very real danger in arbitrarily shutting down all discussion that could legitimately use such an important lesson from history to help us understand our own times. You see, it seems to me that Godwin's Law is based on a fallacious assumption: that nothing like Hitler or the Nazis can ever happen again—or at least, that such a thing could never happen here, in the United States. It's a dangerous fantasy— as if we're too pure, too good, too *God blessed*. We're not. No one is."

"Still . . . it's hard to think of it happening here."

"You know what Sinclair Lewis said, don't you?"

They paused beside Jax's rented Toyota. "No—what?"

"He said, 'When fascism comes to America, it will be wrapped in the flag and carrying a cross." Rosenthal put his hand on Jax's shoulder. "Go see Major Kjos."

32

Tobie's gaze met Mark Kowalski's across the wide loop of drive-
way. "Shit," she whispered and started to run toward the
taxi.

Kowalski and his companion reached under their coats.

"Look out!" she shouted to the taxi driver. "Get down!"

The *boom* of the FBI men's big Glocks shattered the monastery's silence. She heard the taxi driver let out a startled
cry. Glancing over her shoulder, she saw him go down, his
left leg blooming scarlet.

"Oh, God, no," she said on a frightened exhalation of breath.

Lunging through the open door of the taxi, she slid behind
the wheel. Fumbled with the gearshift. Threw the car into
drive and hit the gas.

The taxi—an old Buick—lurched forward, the door slamming shut as she careened through the monastery gates. Ignoring the stop sign at the end of the wide drive, she veered
right onto the cross street, tires squealing. The driver of a
silver Mercedes sedan stood on his brakes and laid on his
horn as she fishtailed in front of him. She threw a quick
glance in her rearview mirror. No sign of them.

Yet.

The taxi drove like a mushy old boat. She tore down the tree-lined street. Her breath was coming in frightened pants and she was shaking so hard she had to grip the wheel until her knuckles ached. She figured she had at most one or two minutes before the bad guys scrambled into their car and came roaring after her.

Along with the rest of the FBI and every cop in the district, she reminded herself. If she was going to lose them, she had to do it now.

A road opened up to her right in the heavily wooded, hilly parkland that lay just past the monastery. She swung into it, the taxi's bald tires skidding in leaf mold and mud. The lane was narrow, little more than a roughly paved track that curved down a hill through winter-bared trees and shrubs. Too late, she realized that what she'd turned on wasn't a road at all but a drive that curled around to a parking lot at the rear of the monastery. Beyond that she could see a couple of abandoned greenhouses at the base of the hill, then a field.

There was no way out.

Shit, shit, shit.

Plowing through the trees, she slid around a long, sloping curve and spotted what looked like an abandoned caretaker's cottage or shed, built into the side of the hill and close to the lane. She spun the wheel to the right, cutting in tight beside the old clapboard structure. Her left front fender caught a wheelbarrow and she heard the crunch of metal, the crash of breaking glass as she took out a headlight.

Slamming on the brakes, she slid to a stop in the lee of the weathered building. She waited, trembling, her gaze fixed on the rearview mirror. She could hear the Suburban's powerful engine gunning around the wooded curve. She waited until the big SUV's shiny black hood appeared around the edge of the barn.

Then she threw the taxi into reverse and hit the gas, hard.

The taxi screamed backward. She rammed into the Suburban broadside, the force of the impact sending the big car
careening off the road.

The SUV slithered sideways down the barren hillside,
cocked at a crazy angle. Then it toppled, filling the air with
the tearing crush of metal and the shattering of glass as it
tumbled over and over.

Tobie rammed the taxi into drive and took off without
looking back.

She was heading toward Michigan Avenue when she
heard the explosion. Glancing in her rearview mirror, she
saw a billowing cloud of black smoke roiling up against the
cold sky.

She kept going.

Jax was parked on a narrow street near Georgetown, where
he and Tobie had agreed to rendezvous, when a battered
wreck of a taxi clanged up behind him and screeched to a
stop.

One front fender was crumpled, its headlight smashed; the
entire back end was caved in to the point he wondered how
the wheels managed to turn. As he watched, the rear bumper
fell off with a clatter.

October slid out from behind the wheel.

He went to meet her. "What the hell happened to you?"
he said.

She shoved the hair out of her face with a shaky hand. Her
hijab had slid down and was wrapped around her neck like a
scarf. "They found me."

"You okay?"

She leaned back against the side of the taxi and nodded.
"They shot the cabdriver in the leg. I hope he's going to be
okay."

Jax walked around the cab and let out a low whistle. "You really did a job on the poor guy's taxi."

She pushed away from the Buick and gave him a long, hard look through narrowed eyes. "You've got a lot of nerve to talk. How many cars have I seen *you* wreck?"

He laughed. "I don't think I ever demolished a taxicab." From the distance came the wail of a siren. He caught her arm and pulled her toward the Toyota. "Come on. Let's get out of here."

They took I-95 North, into Maryland. As they drove, Tobie gave Jax a quick rundown on what the Assyrian priest had told her about the Babylonian Codex, while Jax filled her in on Noah Bosch and the dominionists.

At the end of it, he said, "It's beginning to sound like you nailed it. I don't know what the hell a bunch of ancient Iraqi artifacts or a biblical manuscript can possibly have to do with the assassination of Vice President Bill Hamilton, but it's pretty obvious they're all linked." He frowned. "Somehow."

"So what's these guys' next step?" said Tobie. "Kill President Pizarro?"

Jax thought about it a moment, then shook his head. "What does that gain them? The Speaker of the House is Canadian, and the president pro tempore of the Senate is from Pizarro's own party."

"Maybe they think that with Hamilton and Pizarro dead, they can force a new election."

"Maybe. But there's no guarantee the results of a new election would be any more to their liking. Whatever they're plotting, I can't see them leaving the end to chance."

She twisted around in her seat to face him. "What if they think they can influence the selection of the new vice president? Get someone in the number two slot who's more to

their liking—or who's under their control—and *then* kill
Pizarro?"

"I suppose that's possible." Jax took the exit at Calverton
and turned toward the northwest. "We need to find out exactly who we're dealing with. Fast."

Major Kjos met them in the book-lined study of his century-
old farmhouse on the outskirts of Olney. He was a trim,
rosy-cheeked man of medium height, with Viking-blue eyes
behind wire-framed bifocals and a shock of thick blond hair
just beginning to fade to white.

"Come in, come in. Have a seat," he said, indicating a
worn chesterfield sofa facing an enormous fireplace. A roaring fire chased away the winter's chill. "Dr. Rosenthal tells
me you have some questions about dominionism." His eyes
crinkled into a smile. "He also tells me I'm not to ask you
any questions—not even your names."

"We appreciate your agreeing to see us on such short
notice," said Jax as he settled beside Tobie on the sofa.

"Someone needs to be paying attention to these people."
The retired Lutheran chaplain sank into an old mission
rocker beside the hearth. "They've been flying under the
radar for far too long."

Jax rested his forearms on his knees and leaned forward.
"Rosenthal says dominionism has become a powerful force
within the U.S. military. Is that true?"

"It's worse in some branches than in others. But yes, it's
become a serious cause for concern. Fervent, intolerant religious beliefs and nuclear bombs are a dangerous combination." Kjos folded his hands together and rested them on his
lap. "Are you familiar with Mikey Weinstein?"

Jax shook his head.

"He's a former JAG officer who once served in the White
House under President Reagan. He had two kids at the Air

Force Academy in Colorado Springs, and he became so alarmed when he realized what was going on there that he started the Military Religious Freedom Foundation. It's dedicated to helping American service men and women fight back against what has effectively become a pervasive, coercive atmosphere of proselytizing in our armed forces."

"How bad is it?"

"When you've got a deputy undersecretary of defense for intelligence at the Pentagon going around the country giving speeches to churches and saying that the U.S. military is recruiting a spiritual army of warriors for God's kingdom, it's pretty damn bad."

"He really said that?"

"I'm afraid so."

Tobie said, "But that's just one man."

"I wish he were the only one. A few years ago one of these outfits made a video in which they had flag rank officers—that's generals and admirals—standing in uniform *in the Pentagon* talking about exercising biblical leadership to raise up a 'godly' military. They should have been court-martialed. Instead, they were promoted. We've had officers riffed from the military because they didn't attend prayer breakfasts; soldiers serving in Iraq disciplined by their sergeants because they refused to join in imprecatory prayers with their squadrons before launching attacks on Iraqi villages. In just a few years, the Foundation has collected thousands of complaints from service people stationed all around the world."

"You mean, from non-Christians in the military?"

"Actually, no. Ninety-six percent of the complaints come from Christians. About three quarters of those are traditional protestants—Lutherans, Methodists, Episcopalians, and Presbyterians; the rest are Catholics. You see, this isn't a Christian-Jewish-Muslim issue, or a Republican-Democrat issue. This is about a concerted effort being made by people who basically have no respect for either our institutions or anyone who doesn't conform to their ideology. Essentially, we're talking about the American version of the Taliban. If we let them take over our military and government . . ." Kjos blew out a long, worried breath. "Well, let's just say that as far as I'm concerned, this is more of a threat to the United States than al-Qa'ida ever could be. The real danger of the twenty-first century is fundamentalism, and it doesn't matter which holy book these fanatics are clutching. When you're talking about people who are intolerant—who think *they* have a monopoly on truth and goodness—everyone else is the enemy."

Jax glanced at Tobie, but said nothing.

Kjos peeled his glasses off his face and began polishing them with a handkerchief he pulled from his back pocket. "I know it sounds like something from a bad thriller—scary theocons infiltrating the government and military as part of a plan to take over the country. Which is probably why no one can believe it's actually happening."

"It's a bit of a leap, isn't it?" said Jax. "To accuse people who talk about wanting this country to be more 'godly' of actually plotting to take over the government?"

Kjos settled his glasses back on his face. "Have you read the Book of Revelation?"

"No," she admitted.

"Yes," said Jax.

Kjos smiled. "It's a strange, beautiful, and very misunderstood book. In the early centuries of the church, a number of bishops argued against including it in the canon because of the difficulty of interpreting its symbolism and its potential for abuse. Martin Luther found the portrayal of God in Revelation so horrible that he didn't think it belonged in the Bible, and even John Calvin was of much the same opinion. It presents a very Manichaean, dualistic division of the world into good and evil, where everyone is either an agent of God or a tool of Satan. It also contains a strange portrait of Jesus—not as the Lamb of Peace but as an almost primitive sky god."

Jax said, "I thought Manichaeism was denounced as heretical in the early years of the church."

"It was. But it never really went away. And now it's been grafted onto this strange, retrograde warrior cult of aggressive nationalism and masculinity. These people don't want any part of the Lord of peace or the Jesus of the Gospels. Basically, they worship Jesus as some kind of divinely anointed Rambo. To listen to them, you'd think the Bible is like a cafeteria from which they can pick and choose what they want. They ignore the Sermon on the Mount and the passages where Jesus talks about compassion and condemns worldly wealth, and focus on their own bizarre, bloody interpretation of Revelation—and the most violent parts of the Old Testament, of course."

Tobie leaned forward. "But why is Revelation so important?"

"Probably because it's so mystical that it lends itself to being twisted to mean virtually anything you want it to mean. These people will tell you they believe the Bible should be read literally. But for some reason when it comes to Revelation, that approach breaks down. I mean, they don't believe a *literal* beast is going to appear at the end of the world—they think the beast is a symbol for someone else. Two hundred years ago a lot of people thought the beast was Napoleon. Sixty years ago, it was Hitler. Then the communists."

"Or the Catholic Church," said Jax.

Kjos nodded. "The Catholic Church is a perennial favorite. Now it's more often the UN or Muslims. There's always *someone* who can be labeled the Other, the enemy. Listen to their rhetoric; it's very militaristic. They talk about spiritual warfare and prayer warriors. They march and blow trumpets. Give the graduates of their schools real swords."

"But it's all just . . . symbolism, isn't it?"

"Is it? What about the Bible Boot Camps, where they give their kids paramilitary training? I'd say that's a little more than symbolic. They talk about raising up a 'Joshua Generation' to take over the world *by force*. The focus is very much on violence and revenge. The problem is, when you tell people they've been chosen by God and everyone they don't like is going to hell, it feeds their feelings of superiority. It sanctifies their hatred and rage, and gives them a sense of purpose—in this case, taking over the United States and using it as a platform from which to cleanse the world of evil."

Kjos pushed to his feet and went to pull a book from one of his shelves. "Ever hear of a guy named Warren Patterson?"

"Yes," said Jax.

"No," said Tobie.

Kjos held out the slim blue volume. "His megachurch is just outside Baltimore. Trinity Hills. His last book sold over thirty million copies. Think about that. *Thirty million.* He has his own TV network, his own university. An oil refinery in Texas. Even a few diamond mines in Africa. The man started out as a used-car salesman. Now he's worth something like half a billion dollars, and what he's selling is a vision of churches, states, and corporations forming partnerships to pave the way for Christ's return. It's like a blueprint for revolution by stealth."

"What's the book called?" asked Tobie, reaching for it.

"*Faith Multipliers.*"

She took the book in her hands and flipped it over. The entire back cover was taken up by a photograph of a smiling, white-haired man with a handsome tanned face and brilliant green eyes.

"What is it?" Jax asked, watching her. "What's wrong?"

"That's him."

"You know him?" said Kjos.

She looked up, her gaze meeting Jax's. "I've *seen* him," she said, choosing her words carefully.

33

Duane Davenport and Special Agent Brockman stood side by side, unspeaking, as they rode the elevator up to the ICU at the National Naval Medical Center in Bethesda. Last Davenport had heard, Captain Peter Abrams was still in a coma. But after watching the tapes, Davenport had decided not to wait to see if the Lord planned to take Abrams naturally.

They found two guards standing in the corridor outside Abrams's door: a naval lieutenant and a chief petty officer. Both men wore holstered sidearms.

Davenport flashed his FBI badge and went to brush past them into the room.

The lieutenant stepped into his path. "I'm sorry, sir. No one is allowed into the Captain's room except for naval medical staff. And even then, one of us goes in with them."

Davenport drew up short, his nostrils flaring with indignation. "Do you have any idea who I am?"

"No, sir."

"Duane Davenport. Head of the FBI Criminal Investigative Division." Davenport jerked his head toward the bed. "This man is the only witness to the murder of an FBI agent."

The lieutenant stood with his hands behind his back, his stare stony. "Sir, I have orders that no one goes in this room except for medical staff."

Davenport leaned toward him, his jaw tight, his voice ugly. "Believe me, it won't be good for your career if I have to go over your head to the Center Commander."

The asshole didn't even blink. "I'm sorry, sir, but I'm afraid you'll find that not even Admiral Donateli can authorize your entry. My orders come from the office of the chief of Naval Operations."

Davenport forced himself to swallow a welling of rage. It might be difficult, but there were ways. "I'll be back," he told the lieutenant and swung away.

"Do we know anyone in the office of the chief of Naval Operations?" Brockman asked as they walked back down the hall.

"We must," he said.

He was reaching for his phone when the call came through from the D.C. police, telling him that Kowalski and Welsh were dead.

34

"So which one is he?" Jax asked, turning the rented sedan out onto the highway and heading toward Baltimore. "The one with the house on the lake?"

October shook her head. "The other one. The guy with the Gulfstream." She flipped through the copy of *Faith Multipliers* that Kjos had given them. "If I remember the jargon from my basic training days, a 'force multiplier' is a factor that dramatically increases the combat effectiveness of a military force. These guys really like using military terms, don't they?"

"I don't think it's a coincidence." He glanced in the rearview mirror. Nothing. "Patterson is obviously pretty good at multiplying. His megachurch boasts a congregation of something like thirty thousand."

She turned the book over to stare again at the handsome, smiling man on the back cover. "I've never understood how some of these guys become so huge. Why them and not—say—Pastor Kjos?"

"Part of it's what they say—they seem to have perfected the technique of making people feel good about themselves.

But it's also because of the way they say it. They're very charismatic people with hypnotic voices and delivery styles. For some it's natural, but the techniques can also be learned. They've basically taken the old revival-tent formula and augmented it with some advanced neuroscientific studies on trance induction and state generation. There's a guy in California who's made a fortune out of showing other churches how to increase their donations by eighty percent, mainly by using carefully staged lighting and sound effects."

"Praise the Lord and pass the collection plate."

"Exactly." Jax flipped open his phone and put in a call to Matt.

"This isn't a good idea," said Matt quietly.

Jax said, "One quick question: Is our Irish friend still looking into a certain diamond-mine owner?"

There was a pause. "He is."

"Have him meet us in the parking lot in half an hour."

Jax closed his phone and handed it to October. "Here; yank the battery, would you? We'll toss it in the trash as soon as we stop."

She fiddled with the battery unit, looking for the lock. "Who's 'our Irish friend'?"

"Sean O'Reilly. MI6."

She looked up in surprise. "The British are investigating Warren Patterson?"

"They are indeed. I first heard about Patterson when he was mixed up in some ugly things that were going on in Latin America. But lately he seems to have moved on from funding death squads in El Salvador and Guatemala, and shifted his focus to Africa. He's gotten very buddy-buddy with the head nasties of places like Uganda and Sierra Leone. A little assassination here, a little regime change there—you get the idea."

"Nice."

"It gets better. He has a special affinity for strong men who can promise to grant him mining leases, especially for gold and diamonds. He caught MI6's attention when his name surfaced as part of a failed coup involving British mercenaries in Equatorial Guinea."

"Good Lord."

Jax pulled off at the next exit. "I don't think the good Lord has anything to do with it."

She stared up at the three massive white crosses crowning the far hill and frowned. "Where exactly are we going?"

"To church." He turned into the rest stop at the base of the slope. "But first Mildred needs to put on her Sunday go-to-meetin' clothes."

She groaned. "Not the gray wig and the walker!"

Jax grinned. "Unless you'd rather show up at a fundamentalist church dressed as a *Muslim* fundamentalist?"

Sean O'Reilly proved to be a short, leprechaun-like Irishman from Belfast, with wavy dark hair and a sharp-featured face and dancing gray eyes. Dressed in a very proper suit with a white shirt and conservative tie, he was waiting for them beside a stand of oaks, their branches etched starkly against the cold late-afternoon sky.

"Matt tells me you're interested in our man Warren," he said, shoving his hands in the pockets of his slacks and hunching his shoulders against the wind. "What's up?"

"We're still trying to figure that out," said Jax. "How's the investigation coming?"

"It's going nowhere fast." O'Reilly shivered. "These guys have a lot in common with Scientology and the Moonies; only the deep pockets are allowed into the inner circle, and they know how to keep their mouths shut. I'm winding things up and heading back to London tomorrow. You're lucky you caught me."

Jax stared across the sea of cars toward Trinity Hills's massive, limestone-sheathed sanctuary. The setting sun threw long shadows across the parklike grounds and lit up the compound's white walls with a golden glow.

In addition to the sanctuary, he could see a bookstore, a fitness complex, a theater, an office building, and a large, glassed-in bus stop with a sign that read, SHUTTLE TO TRINITY HILLS UNIVERSITY CAMPUS. The church itself looked more like an auditorium or a municipal building than a place of worship. There was no steeple, no spire, no bell tower, no religious icons of any kind except for the three stark, giant crosses that towered over everything from the top of the hill.

"This place is huge," said October, leaning over her walker. Even with the wig and some skillfully applied makeup, she didn't make a particularly convincing old lady. The posture and attitude were all wrong. She was hopeless when it came to going undercover.

O'Reilly led them across the crowded parking lot. "The sanctuary seats eight thousand, which means it's twice the size of the theater in Hollywood where they hold the Academy Awards. Patterson built it three years ago for a hundred million. Cash."

"Wow."

"It caused quite a stir at the time. Even motivated one of the local senators to launch an inquiry into the church's finances. The senator insisted the inquiry wasn't against the separation of church and state because it had nothing to do with the church's doctrine and everything to do with its tax situation, but of course our man Patterson denounced the whole thing as an attack on religious freedom and property rights."

"So what happened?"

"The senator uncovered some real gems—like Patterson's habit of staying in five-thousnd-dollar-a-night presidential suites, and the twenty-five thousand the church had just spent on a marble-topped commode for his toilet. But churches don't need to file financial statements or even keep records. Which means that while hundreds of millions of dollars pour through here every year, there is literally no accounting of where any of it goes."

October said, "The senator gave up?"

O'Reilly scratched beside his nose. "Actually, he died."

Jax said, "Plane crash?" A lot of politicians and journalists who'd asked uncomfortable questions—or governmental aides who'd made noises about testifying—had been dying in small plane crashes lately.

O'Reilly shook his head. "Heart attack. Quite a shock it was, too; the senator was only forty-eight and had no history of heart problems."

Jax and October exchanged glances.

They had reached the broad sweep of concrete before the sanctuary itself. Strains of organ music and voices lifted in song drifted through the closed doors. O'Reilly said, "Ever watch Warren Patterson work a crowd?"

"No."

He reached for the long polished-brass handle of one of the arena's massive doors. "Then you're in for a real experience."

They entered a vast, cavernous space, dark except for the flashes of white and yellow strobe lights that pulsed at a steady beat across rows and rows of shining, upturned faces. Rather than sit on hard wooden pews, the thousands of faithful lounged comfortably in individual upholstered seats that rose in a semicircle of theaterlike tiers so that everyone had a good line of sight. Their gazes were trained not on an altar but on a central stage, where a chorus of young women in filmy pastel chiffon dresses locked arms and swayed back and forth, their voices raised in joyous song. Three huge 18-

by 32-foot high-definition LED screens mounted strategically around the auditorium—it was hard to think of this place as a church—displayed the words of the hymn for the faithful, complete with a bouncing little ball to help them sing along. "*Jesus, lead your warriors into battle.*"

An impressive sound system picked up the voices and the sepulchral dirge of the organ and doubled it back at them, until the entire auditorium throbbed with sound and light and pulsating joy. Then a muffled boom rose from the stage, and the audience—it was hard to think of them as a congregation—gasped in delight. Fog rose from beneath the platform, catching the yellow and white lights in an eerie evocation of heaven or hell—Jax wasn't sure which. The music and mist spiraled up, the lights flashing faster and faster in a rising crescendo that came to a sudden, crashing halt.

The lights went out. A spotlight cut through the darkness, illuminating the tall, broad-shouldered figure of the man now standing at the pulpit.

"*Praise the Lord,*" shouted Patterson.

Thousands of rapturous voices answered him. "Praise the Lord!"

Jax leaned forward to whisper to O'Reilly, "We need to know where Warren Patterson and his jet were at seven o'clock last night. Is there any way you can look that up?"

From his pulpit, Patterson spoke, the clear, hypnotic cadences of his voice echoing around the auditorium. "In the Bible, God left us a message that is loud and clear. He tells us that it is our mission to take dominion of all the earth. Our mission and our duty. Now, this isn't going to be easy. The agents of the devil don't give up easily. It's gonna take strategy and its gonna take war. But make no mistake: the time has come for God to triumph. *Hallelujah!*"

The faithful shouted back, "*Hallelujah!*"

O'Reilly said, "I don't need to look into it. He was here."

October cast the Irishman a quick, incredulous glance. "You're sure?"

"Positive. I watched him preach last night myself. He did his God the Warrior routine to a packed house and then came back at dawn this morning and delivered it again."

From his pulpit, Warren Patterson said, "More than thirty-five years ago now, God gave a vision to three godly men: Loren Cunningham, Bill Bright, and Francis Schaeffer. God told these men that it's our duty as His soldiers to reclaim what God calls the Seven Mountains. You see, the Seven Mountains are the gates or the portals if you will, to God's Kingdom."

He held up his fingers, counting each off in turn. "First, there's the Mountain of Education, because God wants his children to be taught the truth of His creation, not fed satanic lies by the ungodly. Second, there's the Mountain of Media. We've all seen the lies the so-called mainstream media can spin. We must take over the media, so that truth can be interpreted for the faithful rather than twisted by the agents of evil the way it is now.

He held up another finger. "The Mountain of Arts and Entertainment. Think about how much time we all spend watching TV, and you'll realize how important it is that the media be controlled by men who enforce God's values. Fourth, the Mountain of Religion, so that God's people can finally worship Him in joy and truth, the way He meant them to. The Sixth Mountain is the Family, where women and children must be shown how to live as God intended rather than being left to pursue their own wicked, selfish desires, thus bringing a curse to all to come."

October said, "Does he mean what I think he means?"

O'Reilly said, "Yes."

"The Mountain of Business," continued Patterson, holding

up six fingers, "Where men should build for the glory of God rather than for the Prince of Darkness. And, rising above all, the Mountain of Government. Because it is government that controls all the other mountains. And who sits at the top of this mountain? Right now, it's the Prince of Darkness himself. But the time has come for bold men to retake the Mountain of Government for the Lord. The time has come for those who do not truly follow Christ to be cast out, not just from our government but from our land. Cast out, or destroyed."

Again, October's gaze met Jax's.

"Now, some people might say, Oooh, Patterson; that sounds a bit like totalitarianism. Well, yes. It's true: You see, the servants of the Lord are going to have some work to do, cleaning the temple and smiting the agents of the devil and destroying the spirit of the antichrist that now dominates the earth—"

"God help us," whispered Jax. "These people are essentially declaring a holy war on the rest of humanity."

"—but as the Lord foretold in Revelation, the days have come. Already the Lord has sent a great rising of the sea at New Orleans, when the waters that flowed through the reeds of life like the ruby-eyed serpent killed all before them." Warren Patterson's voice rolled across the vast auditorium. "And when they receded, all was turned to dust. And now, the Lord tells us, the sun shall be cut in half like the moon."

O'Reilly whispered, "I don't know about you, but I don't remember reading that anywhere in Revelation."

"It's from the codex," said October, her gaze fixed on the tall, ramrod-straight man behind the pulpit.

O'Reilly threw her a quick, puzzled look. "What codex?"

Duane Davenport was driving back to D.C., the emergency light on his Mercury flashing, when the call came through from Casper Nordstrom.

The assistant's voice was soft and smooth, with a dangerous edge—like a dagger hidden beneath a silk sheath. "According to my latest tally, you've lost five FBI agents in less than twenty-four hours. What exactly is going on, Duane?"

Davenport exchanged a quick glance with Brockman. "We've encountered some difficulties cleaning up a few loose ends. But it's nothing we can't handle."

"I hope you're not going to tell me one of your loose ends is October Guinness. Can't your people handle one little witch?"

Davenport set his jaw. "She has help."

There was a pause. Nordstrom said, "What kind of help are we talking about?"

"The CIA agent she worked with in the past. But now that we understand the situation, we can make adjustments."

"See that you do," said Nordstrom, and hung up.

35

Dusk was falling by the time Jax turned the rented sedan onto
I-95 and headed back toward D.C.

October sat beside him in silence, her arms hugging her
chest, her face troubled. She'd yanked off the gray wig and
tossed it on the backseat, wiped the makeup off her face,
then simply shoved her hair up under Jax's Nationals baseball cap. It made her look absurdly young and vulnerable.

"None of this makes any sense," she said at last, as he
idled in bumper-to-bumper rush-hour traffic on the beltway.
"I *saw* him. I'm sure of it. He had his fancy private jet parked
right there, beside that lake. It's obvious he knows about the
codex—he was *quoting* from it. And you heard him—he did
everything but come out and declare war on the Constitution. Yet O'Reilly says he never left Maryland?"

"If you want, I can ask Matt to check the jet's flight records, just to be sure. But it's not like O'Reilly to get something like this wrong."

"I don't know . . . ." She scrubbed a hand across her forehead. "Maybe I'm the one who's wrong. Maybe Patterson
just looks like the guy I saw."

Jax threw her a quick, troubled glance. He was the one who was always challenging the reliability of remote viewing, the one who laughingly called it a bunch of "New Age woo-woo nonsense." Only now that she was questioning her own results, losing confidence in her own skills, he found himself, oddly, driven to defend her against herself.

He said, "You told me once that remote viewers can unintentionally slip in time—that you'll be tasked with viewing a target in the present but be drawn to a different time that's somehow more significant, or at least more intense. Or that sometimes a part of what you're seeing can be from the past even if most of it is in the present—as if one time somehow bleeds into the other."

She turned her head to look at him, but said nothing.

"Well," he prompted. "Couldn't that be what happened?"

"I suppose." She didn't sound convinced. "It's just . . ." She let out her breath in a huff. "First we find out the manuscript I saw wasn't anything I was actually tasked to view. Now we're told the guy I think I saw couldn't have been where I saw him. Maybe I just . . . had a miss. It happens. No remote viewer is ever one hundred percent accurate. There's a reason the Army and CIA got out of the remote viewing business back in the nineties. It's just . . . not reliable."

"Right. And because you had a complete miss, a bunch of seriously scary bad guys have spent the last twenty-four hours trying to kill you."

A ghost of a smile touched her lips. "And here I thought you're the one who doesn't believe in remote viewing."

"I don't." He pulled off at the next exit. "Which is why I've been trying to come up with a way to figure out who the other guy you saw is."

At that she laughed out loud. "Well, that makes a lot of sense." The smile faded. "And exactly how do you propose to accomplish this feat?"

Jax turned across the Francis Scott Key Bridge. "I've been thinking about what Dr. Stein said—that the theft of the major Iraqi artifacts was probably coordinated and planned in advance."

"Yeah, but . . . how does that help us?"

"Think about it. If it's true, then whoever organized the theft knows the name of the collector who put in a request for the Babylonian Codex."

"But someone like that would go through an intermediary, wouldn't he? I didn't think the rich did anything for themselves."

"They don't. But how many major collectors do you suppose we're talking about in this business? I suspect whoever coordinated the thefts knows exactly who his customers are."

"Okay. So some übershady antiquities dealer out there knows who ordered the Babylonian Codex. But we don't have a clue who this übershady dealer is. And even if we did, why would he give us the name of one of his best customers?"

Jax turned onto M Street and slowed, looking for a place to park. It was a trendy shopping area lined with quaint restaurants and high-end boutiques and, halfway down the block, a certain little bow-fronted shop painted a discreet hunter green. As usual, parking was a nightmare. He said, "You've never met my mother, have you?"

"No." There was a pause, after which October added diplomatically. "I've heard of her."

Jax smiled. "Her fourth husband—" He broke off. "Or maybe it was her fifth? Anyway, he was into old jewelry. As in gold Parthian earrings and Etruscan garnet necklaces."

Her eyes went wide. "You mean you can buy that kind of stuff?"

"You can buy anything these days. And I do mean *anything.*" He'd reached the end of the block without finding a place to park; he swore softly and swung back around. "Needless to say, he didn't last long. But he left my mother with a passion for two-thousand-year-old ornaments that all her subsequent husbands have slavishly labored to indulge."

They were coming back up on the little bow-windowed gallery. A tasteful, gold-lettered sign proclaimed, THE TREASURE CHEST. Beside the door, a smaller sign read, SPECIALIZING IN THE ANCIENT CULTURES OF THE MEDITERRANEAN AND BEYOND. MADELEINE LIVINGSTON, PROPRIETOR. ANTIQUITIES BOUGHT AND SOLD. APPRAISALS. COLLECTION CONSULTATIONS.

A black-and-white sign propped up in the window read CLOSED. Inside, the lights were dimmed to a golden glow, but Jax could see the shadow of a woman moving around in the back of the shop.

October said, "Let me guess: this is where Mom gets her geegaws?"

"A lot of them."

"So you—what? Think Madeleine Livingston here is the mastermind behind the theft of the century?"

"No. I suspect that honor goes to a Brit by the name of Gabriel Sinclair. Picture a cross between Yves St. Laurent and Elton John, and you'll have a handle on Gabriel."

"So why aren't we going to see Gabriel?"

"Because Gabriel was found floating off the end of his dock in the Hamptons this morning." Jax swooped in at the mouth of the alley that ran along the rear of the shops, hit the emergency flashers, and hopped out. "Just keep driving around the block. I'll be back in a few minutes."

She shouted something after him, but Jax was already trotting down the dark, rubbish-strewn alley.

36

Madeleine Livingston had installed a Medeco M3 high-security lock on the gallery's alley door. The Medeco was the gold standard for door locks; they even used the suckers at the White House. Their claim to fame was a very clever little sliding mechanism. Only problem was, the mechanism could be bypassed with a piece of wire inserted into the keyway. Then all it took was a modified screwdriver and a little bump and, hey presto, you were in.

Closing the door quietly behind him, Jax found himself in a storage area stuffed with piles of boxes and packing crates. Exotic chords plucked from a sitar played over the sound system, an evocative melody that whispered of distant lands and ages past. Pausing behind an archway curtained in hunter green velvet, Jax watched as a tall, impossibly thin woman dressed all in black bent over a large wooden packing crate, scattering curls of fine wood shavings. Her impeccably coifed blond pageboy swung forward, hiding her face.

He thought, at first, that Madeleine Livingston was unpacking the crate. Then she straightened, her hair settling to reveal an elegant, fine-boned face, as she reached for what looked like a painted wooden Egyptian mummy mask, vintage first or second century, and began wrapping it.

"Big order," said Jax, stepping from behind the curtain. "Or are you planning to relocate?"

She swung to face him with a gasp, one bony, heavily beringed hand fluttering up to clutch the heavy agate necklace that hung around her neck. (Parthian, second century, Jax figured.) Her smooth, unlined face made her appear to be in her forties, although he suspected she'd had a bit of help in that department, so that sixties was more accurate. "You startled me," she said, her South African accent still strong despite the thirty-odd years she'd been in business in Georgetown. "How did you get in? The gallery is closed."

"Yes."

She took a step toward the ornate Baroque-looking desk that stood in a corner. If she had a panic button, that's where it would be.

"Don't," he warned.

She drew up sharply, her chest lifting with a quickly indrawn breath. "What do you want?"

"Just some information."

"Oh? And who are you?"

"Homeland Security." He held up his fake credentials. At this rate he was going to wear the damned thing out.

She raised one meticulously arced eyebrow. Christ, she was a cool one. "Do I know you? You look familiar."

He had, in fact, accompanied his mother on one or two of her browsing expeditions. But he hadn't been sporting salt-and-pepper hair and a walrus mustache at the time. She was obviously very good at remembering her customers.

He said, "On April 8, 2003, on the day the United States forces invading Iraq reached Baghdad, the last of the staff that had been working feverishly to protect the collections of the National Museum and National Library were forced to flee. Over the next two days, in a scene that must have been reminiscent of the looting of Rome by the barbarians or the sacking of Constantinople by the crusaders, the most exquisite treasures of ancient Mesopotamia were stripped from their cases to disappear forever into the shadows of the international antiquities market."

She turned back to her crate and resumed wrapping the mummy mask. Only a careful observer would notice that her hands were shaking. "I don't deal in stolen goods," she said evenly. "We provide provenance on everything we sell. My customers have my complete assurances that I have performed due diligence on all of my merchandise. To the best of our knowledge none of the items in our gallery has been illegally obtained from any excavation, monument, or collection."

"To the best of your knowledge," said Jax dryly. In the background, the sitar played on, joined by men's voices ululating strange unknowable harmonies. He let his gaze travel over the tastefully displayed glass-fronted cases full of sandstone reliefs, of votive statues and fertility goddesses and bronze shields from millennia long past. "And those thirty Etruscan vases you were forced to buy back and return to the Italians a few years ago when a customer discovered the latest addition to his collection had been lifted from a Roman museum and in a rare fit of conscience informed the authorities?"

Her jaw hardened in indignation. "We were misled by the seller."

Jax smiled. "Pesky things, those excavation numbers they write on artifacts."

He wandered the gallery, pausing to admire a particularly fine early Christian Coptic textile some eight inches square depicting the Sacred Horseman. Fifth century A.D., proclaimed the tag: $1,750. He said, "I've been thinking about the Iraqi National Museum theft; about how it could have been done. Oh, not the random looting of the second day, when the poor of the neighborhood decided to join in the free-for-all. I'm talking about the initial break-in. The careful removal of the museum's finest, most coveted artifacts.

"You see, I remember those days leading up to the war on Iraq. It was obvious to anyone who was paying attention that the invasion was coming. Now, if I were an unscrupulous dealer in antiquities with lots of wealthy customers I knew weren't overly concerned about assurances of due diligence and the like, I might have seen that as a golden opportunity."

"This is ridiculous." She gave up all pretext of packing. "How could anyone imagine pulling off a theft of that nature in the middle of a war?"

"Ah, but you see, the invasion provided the perfect cover. Not only that, it also emptied the museum of its staff and guards, and got rid of all those nasty Iraqi soldiers and customs officials who normally guard the borders and tend to get irate when people try to steal their patrimony." He bent to study a three-inch-high Egyptian Bronze Horus falcon, circa 680 B.C.: $3,800. "Now, if I were said unscrupulous dealer, my first move would be to approach one of the mega-corporations that were poised to rake in billions by providing the kind of logistical support the Army used to do for itself. Outfits like Halliburton or Keefe Corporation that got those big, juicy no-bid contracts. Just think of all those trucks carrying supplies into Iraq and then deadheading back to Kuwait—you know, rolling into Baghdad loaded but coming out empty."

She stood very still, her arms crossed at her chest, her head thrown back. "You overestimate me if you think I'm capable of coordinating something of that magnitude."

"Oh, I don't think you did. I think the mastermind behind the whole operation was Gabriel Sinclair, working in ca-

hoots with someone like Adelaide Meyer, who was CEO of
Keefe at the time. I hear Adelaide had a thing for ancient bas
reliefs, so I suspect she and Gabriel had a longstanding . . .
friendship. And her connections to the dirtier guys in our revered former president's administration and the upper brass
of the military were enviable."

Madeleine Livingston's nostrils flared. But she said nothing.

"I suspect it was the guys at Keefe Corporation who saw
that the top brass ignored the pleas of the world's scholars
to send troops to guard the museum and library. It would
be Keefe that arranged all that cumbersome but oh-so-
necessary paperwork. And it was probably Keefe—working
through a subsidiary called Global Tactical Solutions, which
is basically a bunch of mercenaries and thugs for hire—that
organized the commandos who went in, secured the perimeter while the battle for Baghdad was still raging, and then
preceded to 'liberate' the priceless treasures of Iraq. Gabriel's role would have been to guide them in what to take—and
of course to arrange for the buyers to receive the loot after
it was ferried out of Iraq in the back of those supposedly
empty Keefe Corporation trucks."

He swept one hand in a wide arc, taking in shelves of ancient marble and glass, wood and stone, pottery and metal.
"This is just the low end of the market. The really valuable
stuff never appears on gallery floors or websites; it's sold
privately, to carefully selected buyers."

She was silent for a moment. When she spoke, her voice
was low and steady. "What do you want from me?"

"A name. One of the items stolen from Baghdad was a
very early text of the Apocalypse of John called the Babylonian Codex. I don't know if it came from the museum or the
library. But I do know it wasn't taken by chance or on spec.
Some collector put in a very specific order for it. I want to
know who that collector is."

"I don't know. I know what my own particular clients received, but that's all. I told you, I didn't coordinate this."

"No. Gabriel coordinated everything. And now Gabriel is dead."

Her face had gone slack, so that she suddenly looked much older than she had before. "He's not the only one," she said softly. "I heard this morning that a dealer in Seattle was found strangled in his bed."

He walked up to her. "Tell me. Who ordered the Babylonian Codex?"

She shook her head, her eyes wide with fear. "I told you, I don't know. I really don't."

"Okay. I can accept that." Jax reached inside his coat and unfolded Elaine Cox's list of twelve of the most precious of Iraq's tens of thousands of missing artifacts. "But you know the antiquities market. You regularly attend every major auction from New York to London to Basel; you know whose representatives bid on what. You have an international clientele and advise customers on enhancing their collections. So you can look at this list and tell me who ordered—or is likely to have ordered—the various items on it. Just the Americans," he added. "I don't think the individual I'm looking for is from overseas."

"I can't give you that! The names of clients are held in the strictest confidence. If it were to become known that I—"

"It won't become known."

She gave him a twisted smile. "And of course I believe you."

"Look, I know better than to appeal to your sense of patriotism—"

Her eyes flashed anger. It was amazing the things that did—and did not—raise her ire. "I'll have you know I have been an American citizen for twenty-five years."

"—so I'll appeal to your sense of self-preservation instead. The guy I'm looking for thinks he's on a mission from

God. As far as he's concerned, he's one of the new Chosen Ones, which means he thinks he has a license to lie and steal and cheat and kill and do whatever he wants, as long as he can convince himself it's in the service of the Lord. Ever read the Old Testament?"

"I'm Jewish."

"Good. Then you know all about King David and King Solomon and their proclivity for breaking every commandment ever carved in stone. But they went down in history as the good guys anyway, because as far as the scribes writing their history were concerned, they were the Chosen Ones. They had a covenant with God, which was like a 'Get Out of Hell Free' card. Well, the guy I'm after thinks the Jews broke that covenant when they crucified Jesus—"

"Actually, it was the Romans who—"

"Technicality. Doesn't matter to these guys. They'll tell you that when the Jews turned away from the Messiah, they lost their spot. There's a new covenant now, and these guys think it's with them. And before they're done, they're going to make David and Solomon look like a couple of choirboys."

"You're just trying to scare me."

"Really? I'd have said the death of Gabriel and your friend in Seattle already did that."

Her chin lifted a notch. She was one tough cookie. "These deals all went through years ago. Why would I be in danger now?"

"Because we're suddenly getting close to them."

"Them?"

"Them. Which means they're getting rid of anyone who might give them away. If you're smart—and I know you are—you'll tell me what I need to nail these guys. I'm not talking about you having to appear in court someday. All I need is a little information and then you can go away and hide until this is all over."

She set her jaw, hard, and reached for the list. "Give me that."

She studied it for a moment, frowning. Jax handed her a pen.

She drew a line through the first item on the list, a massive, four-and-a-half-thousand-year-old carving of a bull that had once adorned a temple built by the King of Ur. "This I know went to a collector in Hong Kong." She circled the next piece, an eighth-century-B.C. ivory plaque inlaid with lapis and carnelian and gold. "There are two possible American buyers for this one: a Texas oilman named Buddy Gibson and a Silicon Valley IT billionaire named Carson Henderson."

The third item, again, was crossed out. "That would have gone to Hong Kong, too." She circled the fourth, the golden dagger from Ur. "This is probably in the collection of Aaron Leibowitz, in New York." She crossed out the fifth and sixth pieces, too. "Russia," she said simply.

An unpleasant smile transformed her face as she circled the next item, a gold bracelet studded with lapis lazuli, and wrote beside it. "Senator Talbot."

Senator Richard Talbot was Jax's latest stepfather. "I didn't think he had that kind of money," said Jax.

"You'd be surprised . . ." She paused a beat, then added, "Mr. Alexander."

He gave a startled laugh.

She circled the next artifact. "The Inanna Vase would have gone to Leo Carlyle. He would never have allowed anyone else to get it." She crossed out two more items. Beside the next, she wrote simply, "Randolph."

"As in, former president Randolph?"

"Who do you think?" Circling the final item—an exquisitely preserved, life-sized marble statue of Athena from the second century before Christ, she wrote four names—

an arms manufacturer, an investment banker, a hedge fund manager, and the owner of a chain of very successful drug stores. "This last one is difficult. I know the bidding was intense, but I never learned who won."

Jax took the annotated list and slipped it back into his pocket. "What about something like a rare, second-century copy of Revelation? Which of these men are likely to have put in an advance order for that?"

She gave him a tight smile. "I could give you dozens of names—everything from private universities with fat endowments and an elastic moral code to corporate titans who act as if they have the connections to get into heaven no matter how many lives they destroy."

Jax shook his head. "I'm only interested in the men whose names you just gave me."

"Ah," she said, her mouth turning downward in a thoughtful frown. "In that case, it would probably be—"

The quiet *snick* of a pistol being racked jerked Jax's attention to the curtained archway at the rear of the gallery.

"I suppose I should thank you for opening that Medeco lock for us," said the man who stood there.

37

The man was dressed in black slacks with a black turtleneck and a black watch cap, and he held a Ruger Mark II suppressed .22 caliber pistol in an easy, professional grip.

The MkII was an assassin's gun, popular with the CIA and Special Forces types because the suppressor was built right into the thick barrel. The small caliber meant the guns were reliably effective only with a well-placed head shot at close range. But what one lost in firepower one gained in stealth, for only a suppressed .22 was truly silent. Yes, a 9mm or a .45 could be suppressed, but even with subsonic ammo they were still far from "silent"—unless you called the sound of a big, unabridged dictionary smashing to the floor quiet.

One look at the Ruger told Jax all he needed to know.

"Get down!" he shouted, lunging at Madeleine Livingston. He pushed her behind the big packing crate and dived behind the nearest display case just as the assassin in the archway squeezed off three rounds.

The first two bullets thumped into the crate, the only sound the impact of lead against wood and the tinkle of the ejected shell casings hitting the floor. The third round was aimed at Jax. But the caliber was too light to do more than crack the laminated glass of the case in a spiderweblike pattern.

Madeleine screamed, her hands coming up to bracket her head, her body jerking with each suppressed shot as if she'd been hit.

Scrambling up into a crouch, Jax was reaching for his Beretta when a second guy appeared in the archway—a big redhead packing some serious heat: a .357 Magnum Colt Python.

"Shit," swore Jax, throwing himself flat.

The big redhead squeezed off a round that punched straight through the display case, shattering both sides, and raining glass and pulverized stone on Jax's head and shoulders.

Her eyes wide with terror, Madeleine bolted for the front door.

Jax yelled. "Stay down!" Still lying flat, he aimed his Beretta through the case and fired five rounds at the guy with the big Colt.

Jax's rounds hit home. The redhead staggered back, the Colt blazing wildly. One bullet ricocheted off a brick wall; another shattered a towering display case of Bronze Age shields and stone battle-axes and obsidian knives hafted to restored shafts.

But even as he fired, Jax saw the assassin with the Ruger pivot and send a bullet high into Madeleine's back. Gasping in shock and pain, she spun around, her blond pageboy flying out around her head, her mouth slack.

Two more rounds punched through her forehead.

Then, lithe and quick, the assassin dove through the curtained archway just as Jax landed two more rounds in the redhead's chest.

The redhead fell backward, his shirt shiny with dark red blood.

Breathing heavily, Jax stayed where he was. He had no way of knowing if he'd killed the guy with the .357 Colt or not. He heard the alley door slam open, felt the cold bite of night air blowing in through the storeroom. The assassin obviously wanted Jax to think he'd fled.

Jax wasn't that trusting.

He pushed to his feet, crossing cautiously to where the redhead lay sprawled in a spreading puddle of blood. Jax kicked the Colt away from the man's hand, sending the revolver spinning across the floor.

Then his gaze lifted to the green velvet curtain shifting heavily in the icy wind.

Reaching into the shattered wall case beside him, Jax grabbed one of the Bronze Age shields. The shield had obviously been extensively restored, with the original bronze conical dome reinforced with a backing of heavy oak. Slipping his left hand into the inner grip, he thrust the shield through the curtain—

And heard the *ping-ping-ping* of the .22's suppressed rounds hitting the ancient metal.

With a roar, Jax charged through the curtain, slamming the shield up into the assassin's face. The two men went down hard, grappling together, rolling over and over. Their flailing bodies caught the green curtain and yanked it down in billowing, blinding folds.

Battling free, Jax lost his grip on his Beretta and crashed back against the shattered display case. Staggering up, the assassin lunged at him. Jax closed his fist around the shaft of one of the ancient obsidian daggers and brought it up to plunge it deep into the assassin's heart.

For an unsettling moment, the guy's startled, confused

gray eyes met Jax's. Then his eyes slid back in his head and he toppled over.

Sitting up on his heels, Jax took a deep breath, the hand he brought up to wipe across his upper lip not quite steady. Then he pushed to his feet and went to see if Madeleine Livingston still lived.

38

Leo Carlyle cradled the ancient alabaster vase in both hands,
his fingertips skimming over the cool stone. Beneath his
touch, the outlines of the carved procession of sheep and
oxen, of worshippers bearing fruit and grains, still felt crisp
despite the passing of the millennia.

There'd been a time when he'd seen such pieces as mere
commodities; blue-chip investments to be bought and sold
for financial gain. But with knowledge had come passion,
and with passion, joy. He'd read once that the psychological
basis of all collecting was sensual pleasure, that Sigmund
Freud himself had possessed more than two thousand artifacts from the days of Rome and Greece and the kingdoms
of Egypt.

Freud had been a Jew. Yet rather than collect the heritage
of his own kind, he had found his delight in the works of
the ancient pagans. So perhaps it was not so strange after
all that Leo, who had taken Jesus Christ as his personal lord

and savior, should find his greatest delight in the possession of the relics of the early enemies of Judea—the Babylonians and Egyptians, the Hittites and the Assyrians.

Once, five thousand years ago, the vase in his hands had graced the palace of a mighty Mesopotamian king. Known as the Inanna Vase, its concentric bands of carving depicted the sacred marriage of the pagan goddess Inanna, known to later generations as Ishtar. Now, the Mesopotamian king who'd prized this vessel lay long dead, his civilization destroyed, his false gods and goddesses long forsaken.

Smiling at the thought, Leo settled the vase in its specially designed case and closed the glass door. The case stood on a plinth, one of many scattered the length of what he jokingly called his Thieves Gallery, for although he had paid handsomely for its contents there was nothing here to which he held clear title. More glass cases lined the walls. In an adjoining room, its environment even more carefully controlled than this one, Leo kept his collection of manuscripts.

In contrast to the profane, sensual world of his Thieves Gallery, Carlyle's manuscript collection was a sacred undertaking devoted entirely to the early works of the church fathers, from Clement of Rome and Ignatius of Antioch to Ambrose of Milan and Augustine of Hippo. Most precious of all was one crumbling papyrus whose secrets had been preserved for centuries by the sands of Mesopotamia. Now, the time was almost right for its truths to be revealed.

He moved to stand before it for a moment. So deceptively common, it was, the black ink of its ancient lettering fading against the yellowed fibers of the ancient reeds that formed its pages. Yet it held him entranced by the power of its holy presence and its promise of a glorious future.

Smiling again, he turned and left the private gallery, securing the concealed entrance behind him.

Emerging into his library, he took a call from his assistant, Casper Nordstrom. "Yes?"

"You asked for an update," said Nordstrom. "They still don't have the girl." He paused. "I'm not convinced Davenport is telling us everything."

Leo went to look out the plate-glass window behind his desk. The night was clear, a full moon throwing a silvery pathway across the frozen surface of the lake. The window was triple glazed, yet the cold still came off the glass in waves. "Do we need to do something about him?"

"No. He knows they fucked up. I think in the end he can handle it."

"Keep me informed," said Leo. "We have three days to get this mess cleaned up."

His gaze still on the lake, Leo reached for one of the hand-rolled Montecristos always kept fresh for him, wherever he might be in the world. He was clipping off the end when the sound of his study door opening brought his head around. A.J. stood in the doorway, her tall, willowy figure clad in clingy red silk, her long fair hair tumbling in artfully tousled waves around her tanned shoulders. "I told you not to disturb me," he said coldly.

The faint smile on her lips never slipped. "The Senator has been here for twenty minutes. I know you own him, but it might be a good idea to put in an appearance."

Leo flicked open his silver Tiffany's lighter. "Careful, dear. Your snark is showing. Is that wise?"

She stood quite still. Daily workouts with her own personal trainer kept her body slim and sinuous, while, thanks to the wonders of Botox, the delicate flesh beside her eyes still showed smooth and unlined. But she was becoming tiresome. Apart from her globe-trotting benevolence and bleeding heart tendencies, she wanted children of her own, and she couldn't seem to understand why Leo had no desire to add to the expensive brood he'd already accumulated. But then, intelligence wasn't one of the attributes that tended to attract Leo to a woman.

"I'm just worried about you," she said breathily. "You've been working so hard lately."

Leo lit his cigar and blew out a stream of fragrant smoke. "I'll be there in a moment."

She gave him a wide beauty-queen smile and left.

He stared after her, thoughtful. When this was all over, she would have to go. He puffed on his cigar again, contemplating the pleasures of shopping for her replacement. In his experience, women found power and wealth tremendous aphrodisiacs. Leo already had plenty of both.

He was about to have a whole lot more.

39

By the time Jax met up with October, they were forty-five minutes late for their meeting with Matt.

Emergency vehicles were already descending on the block, their flashing red and blue lights cutting through the night as she slid over so he could drive. "What the hell—"

"Madeleine Livingston is dead." Easing out into traffic, he gave Tobie a terse explanation of all that had happened.

"What exactly are these guys doing?" she asked. "Killing any antiquities dealers who might be able to implicate them?"

"Looks like it. Here." He handed her the annotated list of artifacts and big-league collectors. "There's a netbook with 3G service in the bag on the backseat."

"A PC?" she said in a strange voice as she twisted around to rummage through the bag. "I don't get along with PCs very well."

"Just look these guys up and see if you recognize anyone."

As they sped up Wisconsin Avenue, she typed their rogue's gallery of names into Google, one after another. "What a bunch of assholes," she said as she flipped through images of Gibson, Henderson, and Liebowitz; all turned out to be busts. "Just think of the good someone could do with even a fraction of these guys' money. The rain forests you could preserve. The medical research you could fund. The schools you could build in Africa. And what do they spend it on? Boats and planes and the destruction of the world's archaeological sites."

He gave a soft laugh. "You might not have noticed, but people with altruistic impulses don't usually become gazillionaires."

"Obviously not. But you'd think—" She sat forward suddenly. "Got him."

"Who?"

She turned the screen toward him. "Leo Carlyle. Ever hear of him? It says he's in finance."

Jax glanced at the image of a stocky, dark-haired man with a neatly trimmed beard and piercing blue eyes. "Yeah, I've heard of him. The guy perfected the art of moving money from one country to the next to avoid paying taxes on it."

She pecked away at the keyboard. "This says he has five kids, ranging in age from eight to twenty-eight, all from his first two wives. None at all by his current and third wife, A.J., a former Miss Colorado." October paused to look at a picture of A.J., a tall, willowy blond with a heart-shaped face and a surprisingly sweet smile. "Pretty."

"What's the A.J. stand for?"

"It doesn't say. But listen to this: 'Among Leo Carlyle's many holdings are a London town house overlooking Hyde Park, a villa in the South of France, a penthouse overlooking Central Park in New York, a sprawling ranch outside of Wichita Falls, Texas, and a rustic, twenty-five-thousand-

square-foot lodge on Lake Coeur d'Alene in northern
Idaho.' "

"Idaho, huh? Any pictures?"

"I'm looking." She paused. "Damn."

"What's the matter?"

"It just froze. Hang on." She fiddled with it for a few minutes, then said, "Aha. That's the house."

"You're sure?"

"Yes."

He turned onto Massachusetts Avenue. "See? Your viewing wasn't a miss. It was just a little off target."

"A *little*?" She looked at Elaine Cox's list again. "My target's the present location of the Inanna Vase, and I veer off
to an early biblical codex? I think I'd call that more than
'a little' off target. And God only knows what date I was
seeing."

The soaring, illuminated towers of the National Cathedral
appeared above the trees. Jax swooped in close to the curb
and hit the brakes. "It doesn't matter. The important thing is
that we now know at least two of the key players in this. We
know they killed the Vice President. We know they're planning to take over the government of the United States and
turn it into a biblical theocracy. They've been saying they
were going to do this for the last fifty years, only no one's
been listening. Now they're ready to make their move. Killing Hamilton was the first step."

Their gazes met and held. October said, "The question is,
What's next?"

Tobie thrust her hands deep into the pockets of Jax's peacoat, her breath billowing out around her in a white cloud as
they followed the dark, winding lane that led to the amphitheater. Occasional widely spaced streetlamps cast pools of
golden light over the winter-browned grass and brought out

a sparkle like scattered diamonds on the icy blacktop. The combination of darkness, plummeting temperatures and a stiff wind had driven most of the lingering tourists off the Cathedral's exposed promontory; they were alone.

Turning onto a path that cut through the low plantings of redbud and viburnum, they could see the bulky figure of a man perched on the edge of one of the open-air theater's stone-banked terraces. He had his shoulders hunched, his head sunk low against the wind. At the sight of Jax and Tobie, he stood up and stomped his feet. "*Damn* but it's cold out here."

Jax grinned. "This was your idea." They turned to walk along the sweeping arc of sandstone and grass, toward the steps that led down to the stage area. "Anything come up?"

"You mean apart from the fact you've been named as a person of interest by the FBI and I had to use some very rusty evasive skills on my way here to make sure no one was following *me*?" Matt ran a hand down over his wild, bushy beard. "Well, let's see: I looked into your Noah Bosch. It's as if he's dropped off the face of the earth. No one knows where he is."

"He's probably dead. But try putting his name on the watch list, just in case."

"On the what?" said Tobie.

"The watch list. Any time Bosch's name comes up in an e-mail or cell-phone conversation or any of the other electronic communications the NSA gobbles up, Matt'll hear about it."

Tobie stared at him. "You mean our government does that?"

"That's right. Land of the free and home of the watched. It's supposed to make you feel safe."

"It doesn't. It just makes me feel . . . watched."

Matt chuckled. "So what exactly have you two fugitives

from justice been up to? And what the hell does any of this have to do with Trinity Hills and Warren Patterson?"

Jax gave him a quick summary of everything they'd learned so far.

At the end of it, Matt let out a low whistle. "Leo Carlyle and Warren Patterson? Man, they don't come much more powerful than those guys. And the problem is, everything we've got so far is hearsay and supposition and dead men's tales. We got nothing that'll stick. If I try going to the DCI with this, he'll laugh me out of his office."

Tobie said, "I don't get it. These guys talk openly about throwing out the Constitution and instituting a 'godly dominion.' How do they get away with that?"

"Because until these loony birds actually *do* something, it's all legal. And yeah, I know they're working to plant their people in everything from the military to the Justice Department and the FBI. But this is a free country. They've got that right."

"But they're using our tolerance to overthrow everything this country was founded on and institute their intolerance!"

"Until they do something—"

"But they did! They killed the Vice President. And that was just the beginning."

Matt blew out a long, hard breath. "The thing of it is, Tobie, we can't prove any of this. Right now, the best doctors in the country are saying Bill Hamilton had a heart attack."

"But—" she began, then broke off.

Matt was right. This was exactly the kind of situation that had caused all the intel agencies to eventually move away from remote viewing. Apart from the fact that RV results were often difficult to interpret or just flat-out wrong, even when a viewer was spot-on, there was simply no way to prove it. Over the course of the past twelve hours she'd found herself doubting the results of her own viewing; how could she expect anyone else to believe it?

She glanced at Jax. "You're being very quiet."

He gazed across the amphitheater's natural hollow to the dark, bare branches of the surrounding wood of beech and oak. "I've got an idea."

Matt and Tobie said together, "What?"

He swung to face them. "I want October to do another remote viewing."

Tobie stared at him. "You *what*?"

He turned to Matt. "You've seen it done before, right? If I write down the target, can you do the tasking?"

"Me?" said Matt. "But—"

"No buts." Jax glanced at his watch. "I've got a nasty feeling we're running out of time."

40

They rented a room at an aging motel in Anacostia, just off Good Hope Road.

The unit was small, the two double beds taking up most of the floor space. A spindly sign featuring a tipping martini glass with a crooked olive hung above the bar across the street, its red neon light filling the room with a lurid glow. Jax took one step through the door, wrinkled his nose, and said, "Is this place going to work?"

October peeled off the peacoat and baseball cap and tossed them on one of the beige chenille-covered beds. "As long as they've got hot water." She reached for the bag of deli sandwiches they'd picked up on the way. "Just let me eat something and warm up, and we can start."

While she took a steamy shower, Jax tore a sheet from the large notepad they'd bought for October's sketches. He wrote the target in big black letters, folded the page over and over, and thrust it into the manila envelope they'd also purchased.

Matt sat on the end of one of the beds and watched him warily. "So what's the target?"

Jax sealed the envelope's flap. "You know I can't tell you that."

"It's been a long time since I've seen this done, Jax. Maybe it'd be better if you did the tasking."

"I can't. I'm the one who picked the target, remember? If I'm even in the same room with October while she's doing the viewing, there's a chance I'll influence her. The only way we can be sure she's actually on target is if you two are the only ones in the room and you're both totally blind to the target."

"Where you gonna go?"

Jax looked up as the old pipes thumped and they heard October turn off the shower. "The bathroom."

The bathroom was steamy and warm and close.

Jax put down the lid on the toilet and tried to get comfortable. From the next room came the sound of Matt clearing his throat as October settled down to relax into her deep meditative state. He'd seen her go through her routine before, sitting quietly, eyes closed, breathing slowed. It didn't take her long.

"I'm ready," she said after a few minutes.

Jax heard Matt clear his throat again. "Okay, Tobie. The target is written down in this envelope here. Just tell me what you see."

There was a pause, during which Jax became aware of the sound of his own breathing. She said, "I get the impression of something black, like a black box. Only there's no lid. Just . . . seams."

Jax sat forward with a start.

She said, "It's connected by a thin rope to another object that's round, like a cylinder. The cylinder is black, too."

"Okay," said Matt. "What else can you tell me?"

"The box is rectangular. Longer than it is wide, but not very thick." There was a pause, during which he knew she had begun to sketch. "I don't think it's a rope. It's a wire."

"All right, Tobie," said Matt, although Jax could tell from the puzzlement in his voice that he didn't have a clue what she was seeing. "Back up a bit so you can describe it better. How big is it?"

"It's pretty small. The rectangular part is maybe four by six inches. It's made small deliberately, to be hidden. The other part is supposed to fit in your hand. It's not quite twice the size of a can of tomato paste."

"Okay. Can you, um, maybe tell me what this black box is made out of?"

"It's smooth and hard, like a plastic. But that's just the outside casing."

There was a pause during which Jax could picture Matt fumbling for something to say. It was all Jax could do to stay in the darkened room, his hands folded together and tapping against his clenched lips to keep from calling out the string of questions he wanted Matt to ask.

Matt said, "Can you describe what's inside the box and cylinder?"

"I get the impression of batteries. The box part sends the energy it generates along the wire to the cylinder part."

"Can you see inside the cylinder?"

Another pause. "It's different. I get the impression here of a bunch of little boards. Like this." There was silence while she worked on her sketches. She said, "I think they're like circuit boards. Then there's this cone-shaped thing that fills the diameter of the cylinder. It looks sort of like a tiny version of those disk antennas you see for satellite TVs. And there's this protruding thing in the center."

Jax wanted to groan. October was a gifted linguist and a phenomenal remote viewer; but her knowledge of engineering and mechanics and electronics obviously left much to be desired.

Matt said, "Is there anything else you can tell me about this . . . thing?"

"I get the feeling it's a weapon. There's a button on the cylinder part that you press, and this beamlike thing comes out. Only it's not exactly a beam, it's like a frequency. That's it. An electrical frequency."

"An electrical frequency? What kind?"

"I don't know. It's like . . . it feels like a . . . a microwave. That's what I keep getting. Microwave."

"Shit," whispered Jax, one hand cupped over his mouth.

In the other room, Matt said, "Anything else, Tobie?"

"No. That's about it."

Jax went to stand in the doorway to the bedroom. Matt was sitting in the room's only chair—a straight-backed uncomfortable thing with an orange Naugahyde seat. October was cross-legged on the bed, a scattering of sketches around her. Jax walked over to pick them up.

Her knowledge of electronics and engineering might be limited, but she was very competent at drawing what she saw. He studied the sketches with a growing sense of disquiet. He'd seen something like this before, only on a much larger scale. A much, much larger scale.

Someone had obviously discovered how to make it portable.

"The target," said Matt. "What was it?"

Handing October the sketches, Jax retrieved the envelope from the top of the dresser and held it out. After a moment's hesitation, Matt took it and tore it open.

"Well, I'll be damned," he whispered.

"What?" said October, scrambling off the bed to peer over Matt's shoulder at the paper.

Jax had written: *The device or substance used to provoke Bill Hamilton's heart attack.*

41

"But . . . I don't understand," said Tobie, her gaze going back to the scattered drawings. "What is it?"

Matt reached for her sketch of the device's inner workings. "It looks to me like some kind of a microwave weapon." He pointed to the rectangular part of the device. "This part here is basically a lithium battery pack. It generates a current that runs along here—" He traced the drawing of the wire to the cylinder. "I'm guessing this is an RF capacitor. The electric current flows through this magnetic chamber to this output antenna, that then generates a pulse of energy."

"You mean, like a Taser?"

"Sort of," said Jax. "Except that what this does is take the frequency and modify it."

Tobie looked from one man to the other. "Modify it into what?"

It was Jax who answered. "A frequency that stops the heart."

She said, "Is that possible?"

Matt combed his fingers through his beard, his dark brown eyes troubled. "Theoretically. The body is like anything else that generates energy—it forms an electrical current. Hit the heart with the right frequency and it'll freeze up."

She sank down on the edge of the bed. "And that would show up in an autopsy as a heart attack?"

"Basically, yes," said Jax. "The United States has already developed and deployed microwave weapons, but they're huge—big enough that they need to be mounted on a Hummer. Our guys have used them in Iraq."

"That's scary," said Tobie.

Matt tapped the paper in his hand. "Not as scary as this. This isn't designed for crowd control. It's designed to kill. Up close and personal, with a very narrow beam. One carefully selected victim."

"The perfect assassin's weapon," said Jax.

"Pretty much."

Jax went to pull back the curtains from the window overlooking the pavement below. The red neon martini glass across the street blinked on and off, on and off, a steady rhythmic pulse. After a moment, he said, "This isn't a military weapon. It's designed for covert action."

Matt chewed the inside of his lip. "I've sure as hell never seen it."

Jax looked over his shoulder at him. "That doesn't mean we don't have it."

The two men's gazes met and held.

Tobie looked from one to the other. "Holy shit. What are you saying? That the bad guys have people in the CIA, too?"

"I don't believe it," said Matt.

Jax took a deep breath. "Believe it, Matt. These people have spent the last forty years burrowing deep into their so-called seven mountains. They're the perfect subversives: they look like us and sound like us, but they sure as hell don't think like us. Everything we hold most dear is what they want to destroy."

Matt stooped to gather Tobie's sketches together with hands that were not quite steady. "Tomorrow morning I'm taking these in to our technical services guys and asking them." He turned toward the door. "I'll meet you at nine o'clock at the Jefferson Memorial and tell you what I've found."

"Matt? Just—" Jax broke off.

Matt paused with a hand on the knob to look back at him. "Just—what?"

"Just be careful."

Madrid, Spain: Sunday 4 February 2:05 A.M. local time

Noah sat at the small table beneath the window of his room in a rickety old hotel near the plaza mayor. He'd been up half the night compulsively checking his Hotmail account every five minutes.

Nothing.

Heavy-limbed and bleary-eyed with exhaustion, he glanced at his watch, swore under his breath, and staggered to his feet, determined to go to bed. He was just about to close down when his laptop's e-mail program went *ding*.

Hastily dragging out the chair again, he hunched forward and opened his inbox.

Linda's message was tense. Terse. *I have information I can give you if you're willing to meet me.*

Noah rubbed the heels of his palms against his gritty eyes in disbelief. For months he'd been trying to cajole her into talking to him face-to-face. But she had steadfastly refused to meet him.

He typed, *You're willing to meet me? Where? When?* He stopped himself from adding, Why now?

The response came back a minute later. *Monday morning. Nine o'clock. Marrakech. Can you make it?*

Morocco? If he took the train to Algeciras first thing in the morning and then caught a ferry to Tangier, he could be in Marrakech by Monday morning without having to face all the risks of exposure that would come with flying. He wondered what in God's name she had to give him that required meeting him in person—and in Morocco of all places. But he was too afraid of spooking her to ask for details or explanations.

He typed, *I can make it. Where in Marrakech?*

She answered, *Dar Si Said.*

What the hell is that? he wondered. But he typed, *I'll be there. How will I recognize you?*

I'll recognize you. There was a pause. Then: *You're not afraid to meet me?*

He stared at the screen, his heart pounding.

He typed, *Should I be?*

The answer was a long time in coming. He'd about decided to give up and go to bed when her final message of the night came through.

The information I have to give you could get you killed.

42

Early the next morning, Matt walked Tobie's sketches across to the Technical Services Division of the CIA's sprawling Langley complex. He was careful to take photocopies rather than the originals because all visitors to the TSD were heavily monitored; he could take paper *in*, but he couldn't bring it out again.

The TSD was basically the CIA version of James Bond's Q. If an agent needed a poisoned-dart pen or a specially equipped motorcycle, these were the guys who built it. But the thing most people didn't understand about the TSD was that the geeks who worked there puttered away in relative isolation from one another. In the intelligence community, the fewer people who knew about a dirty project, the better.

So finding out whether or not Tobie's nasty little weapon had come out of the TSD was not going to be easy. The geek Matt was coming to see—a hulking black guy from Atlanta named Bailey Frye—was the go-to techie for batteries and power supplies. Matt sometimes suspected Frye slept in his lab, since the guy was always there. His Aladdin's cave was one of about a hundred such labs that opened off long corridors like the cells of a high-tech honeycomb.

"Hey, Matt. Long time no see," said Frye, his thick, plastic-framed glasses sliding down his nose as he buzzed Matt in through the lab's security system. "Things've been pretty quiet over at Division Thirteen lately, huh?"

"A bit."

Frye's lab, maybe fifteen by twenty feet, was lined with sleek gray metal cabinets outfitted with combination locks. But the center of the room was taken up by two big wooden tables with non-conductive butcher block-type tops covered with an array of miniature saws and specialized Dremels and bits of wire scattered amid partially dismantled motors and battery packs.

At one end of the nearest table sat what looked like a see-through miniature helicopter.

"What the hell is that?" said Matt, hunkering down to get a better look at it.

Frye grinned. "Something you didn't see. It's a remote-control helicopter made completely out of Lexan. Pretty neat, huh? The battery pack is so quiet even a bat would have a hard time hearing it, yet it's powerful enough not only to fly the bird but to also run this little TV camera here"—he pointed to a tiny lens mounted underneath—"*and* a super-sensitive multidirectional microphone. There's no infrared signature, and it has the radar cross-section of a Bic pen."

"Man, that's something, all right," crooned Matt.

Frye's grin widened.

Matt pushed to his feet and pulled Tobie's drawings from his pocket. "I got something I need your help with, Bailey," he said, holding out the pages. "Have you ever seen something like this?"

"*Jesus H. Christ.*" Frye's hands clenched on the rough drawings. "Where the hell did you get these?"

"So you have seen it before."

Frye used one thick finger to push his heavy glasses back up onto the bridge of his nose. "Seen it? I made the battery packs. One of the guys down the hall came to me maybe eighteen months ago and said he needed a power supply that would fit into a coat pocket and deliver a specified kind of voltage at such and such a cycle. I gave him what he wanted, but he came back a week later and said it hadn't worked. Turned out his specs were wrong. He'd underestimated the power-supply requirement."

"You know what this thing does?"

"Yeah. Vince—that's the guy who built it—was like a kid. He was practically giggling, he was that proud of it. Once I revamped the power supply, he gave me a demonstration. Took me out to a friend's farm and killed a fricking goat with it." He flipped through the drawings to Tobie's schematic of the cylinder portion of the device. "One push of this button, and it shoots a pulse of energy. Bam. Stopped that poor billy goat's ticker, just like that. Vince called it the MLFI—microwave life-form interrupter." Frye gave a quiet laugh that shook his big frame. "Pretty sick, huh? More like life-form *terminator,* if you ask me."

"You know who he built it for?"

"Come on, Matt; you know I couldn't tell you that even if I knew—which I don't. Vince said the guys who came to him were looking for a way to eliminate some activists causing problems for our pet dictators in the Middle East. Regime change in Africa. That kind of shit. A way to kill that would look completely natural." Frye gave another one of his silent, shaking laughs. "Now every time anyone over there dies of a heart attack, I think, *hmmm.*"

"How many battery packs did you make?"

"Five."

"So there's five of those suckers floating around out there?"

"I guess." Frye paused for a moment, the smile fading from his face, his eyes troubled.

"What is it?" Matt asked.

"About a week after Vince zapped that goat, he died in a one-car wreck down near Mount Vernon. Brakes failed. Maybe I been around you spooks for too long, but . . . Well, let's just say it didn't sit right with me." Frye nodded to Tobie's drawings. "Where'd you get those?"

"You don't want to know." Matt went to pass them through Frye's shredder and stood watching until the last fragment curled and fell into the receptacle. "Ever tell anyone else that you knew what Vince was working on?"

"Nope."

"Good. Don't."

43

A thick fog hung over the heaving waters of the straits, reducing the fading daylight to an eerie glow.

Noah stood at the rail, the collar of his coat turned up against the spray picked up from the curling bow waves. Shoving his hands deeper into his pockets, he found himself wondering how the hell he had ended up here, on a rusty ferry halfway between Spain and North Africa, on his way to a dangerous rendezvous with a shadowy, mysterious figure.

In the beginning it had all been about the story, about a journalist's overwhelming drive to be the first with the most sensational filing. It was still about the story, about every reporter's endless quest to snare a career-making Pulitzer Prize. But somewhere along the line, Noah knew that his ingrained obsession with story placement and deadlines and competition had merged with the recognition of an urgent need to protect his country from a danger no one else even seemed to realize was there.

And now?

He breathed the cold, salty air deep into his lungs. Now, his own life was on the line. There was no turning back. He had to find a way to break this story before the shadowy figures behind it killed him.

It was as simple as that.

Washington, D.C.: Sunday 4 February
10:00 A.M. local time

By ten o'clock, thick clouds were closing in on the city to cast long shadows across the classical white marble columns of the Thomas Jefferson Memorial. The wind had a sharp bite to it that warned of coming snow

And Matt still hadn't shown up.

"Think something happened to him?" asked Tobie. She had her hair tucked up under a navy watch cap and had wrapped a big bulky scarf around the lower part of her face. But she was still nervous about being spotted.

Jax smoothed his fake mustache. "Something may have come up. Or he could have been followed." He didn't exactly sound convinced.

"We can't stay here much longer. The guards will notice us."

"Pretend you're reading the inscriptions." Jax tipped back his head, his gaze following the great man's words engraved in marble along the walls surrounding the giant bronze statue. "Did you know that Jefferson considered his authorship of the Virginia Act for Establishing Religious Freedom a more important achievement than serving two terms as president of the United States?"

"No. But it doesn't surprise me." She turned to look out over the windblown mall. From here she could see across the

Tidal Basin to the Washington Monument and, beyond that, the White House. Still no sign of Matt. "I imagine Jefferson must be rolling in his grave about now."

"Spinning like a top."

It was another ten minutes before Matt came running up the monument's long steps, his bad leg dragging, his breathing heavy.

"Thank God," said Tobie, going to meet him.

He bent over, his hands on his knees as he fought to draw in air. "Man, am I out of shape." He sucked in another deep breath and straightened to gasp out, "Walk with me."

They turned to walk along the top of the monument's steps, away from the thin huddle of determined tourists.

"I talked to a guy in the Technical Services Division. He says the device Tobie saw was manufactured there eighteen months ago. It's called the MLFI—microwave life-form interrupter. And get this: they made five of them."

"Any idea who for?" Jax asked.

Matt shook his head. "The minute I start looking into that, I'm gonna draw way more attention than I want to at the moment, and I'll never find out anyway. The important thing is, we know Hamilton was killed, we know how, and we know that the guys who did it have some pretty high-level contacts in the Agency."

Tobie said, "So we've got enough for you to go to the DCI, right?"

Matt swiped the sleeve of his coat across his sweat-slicked forehead. "I thought about that. Then I realized it's the stupidest thing I could do."

Tobie shook her head, not understanding. "But . . . why? You said the guy in TSD admitted he made the device."

"Yeah. But you gotta understand that what he told me was off the record. He just designed the battery pack. The only reason he knows the specs of the entire device is because

Vince—the geek who built it—was too proud to keep quiet about it." Matt paused. "And Vince died in a car wreck just a couple of days after he turned the device in. I looked at the police report. It was no accident."

Tobie thrust her hands deeper into her pockets and stared off across wind-whipped gray water. "I still don't understand why we can't take this to Chandler."

Jax had grown unusually solemn. He said, "It's because you think Chandler might have links to the dominionists, too. That's it, isn't it? Funny, I always knew the guy was a grade-A asshole. But I never pegged him for a traitor."

Matt said, "The thing is, I don't think these guys see what they're doing as un-American. They think they're just following God's plan. Watering the tree of liberty with the blood of patriots and all that. I'm not saying Chandler *is* involved, but I know he's got ties to both the Council and the Fellowship. Randolph appointed him, remember?"

Tobie said, "So why don't we send what we have to the press?"

Jax gave a soft laugh. "Because no respectable news agency would touch this."

Matt nodded. "Jax is right. The American public has been conditioned to laugh at conspiracy theories—or at least ones that involve their own government or white Anglo-Saxons. They're perfectly willing to believe all kinds of crazy nonsense as long as it's somebody like the Libyans or the Russians doing the conspiring. But this? Tin foil hat land."

Tobie said, "Jeez. Don't they read history?"

"No," Matt and Jax answered in unison.

"So we do *nothing*?"

"No," said Matt. "What we do is, we find more proof. I went to put Noah Bosch's name on the Watch List like you asked, and guess what? It was already there."

Jax's eyes narrowed. "Reporting to whom?"

"Davenport. And there was a hit. He surfaced in Madrid yesterday."

"Madrid?" Jax and Tobie looked at each other. "What the hell is he doing in Madrid?"

"Not a clue." Matt reached into his pocket and came out with a folded orange Post-It note. "I got his wife's name and address, if you want to try talking to her. She works for the Park Service at Arlington Cemetery."

"I thought they were divorced?" said Tobie.

"Separated. She's shacking up with some sports reporter." Jax said, "That's got to hurt."

"Could be why Bosch has dropped out of sight."

Jax shook his head. "I might believe that if it weren't for one thing."

"What?"

"He's got Duane Davenport looking for him." Jax hesitated. "If Chandler is in any way involved with these guys, you know they're going to be watching you."

Matt nodded. "Somebody followed me from Langley. I lost them by taking three cabs and cutting through the Kennedy Center and then the Watergate. But I'm thinking they're closing in on us, Jax. And every time we meet, we're taking a big chance."

Jax tucked Julie Bosch's information into his pocket. "Set up a Gmail account. I'll be babyloniancodex1. You be babyloniancodex2."

Matt frowned. "It's risky."

Jax shrugged. "It's a risk we'll have to take."

44

They found Julie Bosch at the visitors center of Arlington Cemetery, tapping away at a computer while a wan-faced teen with dark curly hair waited solemnly.

"Here it is," said Julie. "Your brother is in Section 60." She jotted the lot and grid numbers on a slip of paper and handed it to the kid with a sympathetic smile. "Take Roosevelt Drive past Section 7 and turn right on McClellan."

As the young man moved away, she turned to Jax and Tobie. "May I help you?"

Jax laid James Anderson's Homeland Security credentials on the counter before her. "We need to talk to you about Noah."

All the animation drained from Julie Bosch's face. She cast a quick glance around and leaned forward to say quietly. "This isn't a good time. We're very busy and—"

"Take a break," said Jax. "Now."

They walked through a sea of white marble tombstones. Hundreds of thousands of them, sweeping in undulating, green-swathed phalanxes over the gently rolling hills. The temperature was plummeting, the clouds above heavy with the promise of snow. Tobie kept her hands buried deep in the pockets of the peacoat and let Jax do most of the talking.

"We're looking for your husband. Noah Bosch."

Julie Bosch drew in a deep breath that flared her nostrils and widened her eyes. She was a slim woman in her late twenties, with creamy skin, soft brown eyes, and delicate features that quivered slightly, as if with fear. "We're separated," she said in a tight voice that hinted at origins below the Mason-Dixon Line. South Carolina; perhaps Charleston.

"But you haven't been separated for long, have you?"

"No."

Tobie saw Jax swallow a spurt of impatience. He said, "You have no idea where he is?"

"No."

"Any idea why he might be in Spain?"

"Spain?" She shook her head, her soft brown hair brushing the tops of her shoulders. "No. I'm sorry, but I really can't help you." She started to turn back toward the visitors center. "Now if you'll excuse me—"

"Not so fast," said Jax, reaching out to snag her arm. "You do know what Noah was working on when he lost his job at the *Post*, don't you?"

"Yes." She threw another of her quick, frightened glances around, as if the inhabitants of those rows and rows of silent graves might be listening. "He was obsessed with the dominionist influence here in D.C. He was always ranting and raving about their involvement in everything from the death squads in Latin America to the big push to bomb Iran. I kept telling him he was committing the journalistic version of suicide. Those people have become way too strong to touch. Just to acknowledge they exist is stupid." She blew out an angry breath "But of course he never listened to me."

"So he talked to you about his research?"

"Are you kidding? He was always trying to tell me what kind of chicken to buy and where to get my prescriptions filled. Just because this company or that was owned by a dominionist."

"You didn't listen to him?"

"Huh. Name me a corporation that isn't run by sycophants and crooks of some stripe or the other." She swung her arm toward the monument-bedecked capital across the river. "Just like all those fine senators and representatives. They're nothing more than a bunch of whores. They're supposed to be representing the people. But the truth is, most of them are in bed with the insurance companies and the banks and the military contractors. Everyone with any sense knows it. But do people care? No."

"Noah cared?" asked Tobie.

Julie swung her head to look at her. "Noah was an idiot. He had this stupid vision of a country that was actually governed by the people and for the people, rather than by a bunch of plutocrats who rake in billions while the rest of us slave away, struggling just to keep our heads above water."

Tobie gave a wry smile. "An idealist."

"Yeah. Like I said, an idiot."

Jax said, "Did he ever talk about something called the Babylonian Codex?"

Julie Bosch laughed. "He drove me nuts with that thing. He was convinced the dominionists were using this so-called lost chapter"—she curled her fingers into mocking air quotes—"as a blueprint for their final push to take over the country. Assassinate first the vice president, then the president. It was the craziest thing I ever heard him come up with."

Tobie caught her breath, her gaze flying to meet Jax's.

He said, "Did Noah know what the lost chapter said?"

"Of course not! There was some guy in Iraq who was

working on translating it before the war. But he supposedly refuses to talk to anyone whose country participated in the invasion." Her brows drew together in a frown. "Maybe that's what Noah is doing in Spain. Maybe someone there knows about his precious 'secret chapter.'"

"Spain participated in the 2003 invasion of Iraq," said Jax. "They only pulled out after their right-wing government fell."

She shrugged. "I don't know then. It's all so stupid. As if anyone would actually try to take over the country and run it according to their interpretation of divine law."

"You mean, like the Taliban did in Afghanistan?"

"This isn't Afghanistan!"

"Yet the vice president did actually die two days ago," Tobie pointed out.

Julie Bosch gave an exasperated huff. "Yeah. Of a heart attack. Right in front of everyone. Nobody *killed* him."

Jax threw Tobie a warning look. "Do you have any idea where Noah was getting his information?"

Julie shrugged. "He had some source. He was always hush-hush about her. But the truth is, I don't think he knew who she was himself."

"She?" said Jax.

"He thought it was a woman, although he never knew for sure. She only communicated with him through e-mail."

Jax said, "Did he ever tell you anything about her? Anything at all?"

Julie thought for a moment, then shook her head. "Not really. He used to call her Linda."

"Linda?"

"That's what she called herself. Linda Lovelace. You know, from that 1970s porn flick that prompted Woodward and Bernstein to call their source Deep Throat. Personally,

I thought it was kinda sick. I mean, who names themselves after a porn star?"

They drew up at the top of a rise. From here they could look out over Arlington's acres and acres of dead soldiers, sweeping nearly up to the massive walls of the Pentagon. For some reason, the proximity of the two suddenly struck Tobie as creepy.

Julie said, "There really is nothing else I can tell you."

Tobie studied her soft, haunted eyes. "Did you know Noah was in Davos two days ago?"

"You mean when Bill Hamilton—" Julie broke off. She took a step back, then another. "I don't want to know about this," she said, her voice rising in near hysteria only to fall to a strained whisper as her instinctive caution reasserted itself. "I don't know anything about this. You hear me? Anything."

And with that, she turned and fled.

Jax and Tobie sat at a corner booth in the shadowy recesses of a pizzeria in Clarendon. The place was a study in clichés: red and white checked tablecloths, vino bottles covered with melted wax, travel posters of Tuscany and Sicily framed in rustic wood and hung above faux-stone wainscoting. But a real wood fire blazed up hot and bright on the hearth, the warmth slowly thawing frozen fingers and toes.

Jax took a long, slow swallow of his red wine. "We've been wondering what in the hell the Babylonian Codex had to do with all of this. Now we know."

Tobie shook her head. "How can anyone take a lost chapter of a book written nearly two thousand years ago and interpret it as a godly authorization to kill the administration of the United States?"

"If you're deluded enough to think you have a mandate from heaven to impose some warped version of your religion on everyone else, I can see believing that God wrote down his instructions and then kept them hidden for a couple of millennia until it was time for you to act on it."

"Somehow, I can't see good old St. John scribbling away in his cave on Patmos composing verses about zapping Vice President Hamilton's heart with a microwave weapon at Davos."

Jax laughed. "No. But that's the nice thing about Revelation. It's so convoluted and symbolic you can make it say just about anything you want it to."

Tobie said, "We need to get our hands on that chapter."

"True. Only, how exactly do you propose we do that?"

She watched him take another sip of his wine. Sometimes he was so calm and cool she wanted to shake him. She leaned forward. "We know where it is, right? At Carlyle's lodge in Idaho. All we need to do is break in and steal it."

Jax laughed again.

She glared at him. "What's so funny about that? You break in to places all the time."

He paused while their waitress—a perky little blond who looked about sixteen—dumped a steaming hot mushroom and spinach pizza and two plates in the middle of their table. "Enjoy!" she chirped and flitted away.

"Well," said Tobie. "Why not?"

"Because someone like Carlyle is going to have his antiquities collection protected by a museum-level security system and private guards, that's why not. Unless you can remote view the floor plan and a dozen other very important details, we'd be walking into a high-security facility completely blind. Never a good idea."

"Okay," she said, digesting this. "So maybe we can't get our hands on the codex itself. But he would have made digital copies of it, right? Isn't that the way they translate these things? They work off high quality photographs rather than the originals. So we steal the photos. They're probably on a disk."

Jax lifted a steaming slice of pizza and put it on the plate in front of her. "Here; eat. You never eat."

"I eat all the time. Just not when I'm tense."

"So have some wine, relax, and then eat." He took a piece for himself. "If I'd known you weren't going to eat, I'd have ordered pepperoni."

"This is better for you than pepperoni."

"Right. Like pizza is good for me? Between the oil and the cheese, it's a lost cause."

"The digital copies of the codex," she said again. "We could steal them. Couldn't we?"

"Maybe. If we knew where they were. Which we don't." He took a bite of pizza, chewed, and swallowed. "Carlyle probably has the images stored with the original. As far as he's concerned, it's pretty sensitive stuff, right? Seems to me that if we want to find out what those lost verses say, we need to go to the paleographer who first translated them." Jax looked up from his pizza. "What was his name?"

"Dr. Salah Araji. But he doesn't talk to Americans, remember? Apart from which, he doesn't have the codex anymore. Carlyle stole it."

Jax reached for another slice of pizza. "Carlyle stole the codex from the National Museum. But Dr. Araji wouldn't have been working from the original either. He'd have made digital copies, too. And I bet he still has them."

Tobie felt her stomach give an unpleasant lurch. She was glad she hadn't eaten any of the pizza. "But Araji is still in Iraq."

"So? We go to Iraq."

She stared at him. "*Are you nuts?*"

"No."

"We can't go to Iraq!"

Jax swallowed a mouthful of pizza. "Trust me, it's a hell of a lot easier to go to Iraq than to break into Carlyle's compound."

She sucked in a deep, quick breath. "I . . . uh . . . I really don't fancy the idea of going back to Iraq. The last time was not . . . fun."

He drained his wineglass. "I hear things are great there now. Hardly any suicide bombings. And the number of IED incidents is way down."

"Oh, that's so encouraging." She leaned forward. "I still have nightmares about that place. I don't even like hearing the name of it. I swore I'd never go anywhere near it again. Ever. In this life or the next."

"You know what they say: it's better to face your fears than to run away from them."

"Not when your fears are getting killed in a war zone!"

"It's not like we're going into combat."

"The entire country is a battlefield!" She raked her hair out of her face, her mind racing. "There's no way I can get there, remember? Davenport will have put my name on every watch list in existence."

Jax reached for his wineglass and smiled at her over the brim. "I wasn't planning to fly commercial. I think I can get us a ride with a friend."

She flopped back against the high, padded booth. "Not Bubba again."

"What's wrong with Bubba?"

"Nothing. I just . . . um . . . I don't have a passport. They require visas in Iraq these days, you know—unless you're part of the occupation. And then there's all those checkpoints and—"

"Not a problem. I know a guy who can fix all that. His

name is Ernie DeMoss, and he does great work." Jax pushed to his feet. "Bring what's left of the pizza. You might decide you're hungry later."

"Hungry? On my way to Iraq?" She reached for her wine and downed it all in one long pull. "I think I'm going to be sick."

45

Tobie's new passport——complete with an "official" visa for Iraq——took just over an hour.

Tracking down the current whereabouts of Dr. Salah Araji was a little more difficult. It involved a string of delicate phone calls and some covert back-and-forth e-mailing with Matt to elicit the information that the scholar had abandoned Baghdad after the death of his family and returned to his native village not far from the ruins of ancient Babylon. He spent his days as a volunteer toiling to save the devastated site and his nights hunched over a computer writing long, impassioned articles that no one in the corporate media was willing to publish.

And he steadfastly refused to have anything to do with anyone whose native language was English.

"This doesn't sound promising," Tobie said as they drove toward an obscure airfield in northern Virginia. "I think we're wasting our time."

"You just don't want to go to Iraq."

"Of course I don't want to go to Iraq. No one who's sane wants to go to Iraq."

By the time they reached the small airstrip outside Lees-burg, the sun had completely disappeared behind heavy clouds and the first flakes of snow were beginning to fall.

They found Bubba Dupuis hunkered down beside the near wheel of a plain white Gulfstream G550 with absolutely no identifying markings. He was a big, fleshy Cajun with a badly receding hairline and a salt and pepper ponytail that hung halfway down his back. Last time Tobie saw him, he'd been sporting a drooping mustache. But that was gone now, replaced by swooping sideburns right out of the old Wild West. He wore torn jeans stuffed into biker boots and a red hooded sweatshirt under a denim jacket. Straightening, he stood with his fingertips tucked into the pockets of his jeans and a grin splitting his face as he watched Jax climb out of the gray Toyota. "What's the matter, Jax? You finally wreck that cute little German sports car of yours?"

"Not yet."

"I don't get it. How come you manage to wreck every car you drive except your own?"

"I don't."

"You do," said Tobie and Bubba in unison.

Bubba laughed and came to enfold her in a big bear hug. "I hear you been havin' a hard time of it."

It struck Tobie as a stupendous understatement. But all she said was, "I was doing okay until Jax decided he wanted to take a little side trip to Iraq."

Bubba laughed again. "Y'all are lucky you caught me when you did. If I hadn't had a lousy flat tire I'd'a been outta here hours ago." He squinted into the thickening snow. "We better get goin' if we want to beat this storm."

"Exactly where in Iraq are you headed?"

"Najaf. That's about a hundred miles south of Baghdad."

"That'll work," said Jax.

As they settled into the jet's plush leather seats, Bubba

secured the door and intoned, "Thank you for flying Bubba Air. Remember that your seat cushions are not flotation devices, so if we have to ditch in the water, you're shit out of luck. And if you die, we can't be sued because we don't exist."

"Thanks, Bubba," said Tobie. "That helped a lot."

Bubba grinned. "Service with a smile, that's our motto."

Once, he had been a marine pilot. But an aversion to taking orders had ended his military career prematurely. Now, he called himself a contract pilot, although "soldier of fortune" might have been more accurate. For the last four months he'd been flying mysterious cargo and passengers in and out of Iraq for the CIA.

"At least we're going someplace warm," he said, sliding into the pilot's seat. "Did Jax tell you about the time he made me land on an ice lake in Kazakhstan?"

Jax took the copilot's seat and reached for the headphones. "She doesn't need to hear this, Bubba."

"Yes she does," said Tobie. "What were you doing in Kazakhstan?"

"Lake Balkhash. It's just over the border from the Uygar Autonomous Region in China."

"The what?"

"You know; the Uygars. Chinese Muslims. Jax was breaking some Uygar dissidents out of prison in Urumqi. So there I am, parked out on this friggin' frozen lake, when Jax and a couple of Uygars come riding up on shaggy ponies with half the Chinese army chasing them."

"It wasn't half the Chinese army," said Jax.

"Never let a few facts get in the way of a good story." Bubba tapped his controls. "That's weird. Everything just sorta froze up. Only time I ever saw that happen was the last time I flew y'all."

Tobie quietly went to sit at the back of the plane.

"Huh. Weird and weirder. Everything's okay again." He glanced back at Tobie. "Buckle up tight; we're ready to rock 'n' roll."

She put her head down between her knees and groaned.

The two men walked along Pennsylvania Avenue. The headlights of the cars swishing past stabbed the gathering gloom to reflect off the falling snow.

The younger man, his straight blond hair ruffled by the icy wind, said, "Mr. Carlyle has some concerns."

"We're closing in on the girl," said Davenport. "It won't be long now."

"Good. Nevertheless, we have decided the cleanup needs to be expanded."

Davenport cast his companion a quick, sideways glance. "To whom?"

Casper Nordstrom swept his hair back in a fastidious gesture. "Dr. Salah Araji."

"Who?"

"The Iraqi paleographer who published the first reports on the codex. He has knowledge which might prove awkward."

"He's in fucking Iraq."

Nordstrom drew up outside the Department of Justice. "Are you saying you can't handle it?"

"No. I can contact some guys at GTS." GTS, like Blackwater, was a private security company that supplied the Defense Department with mercenaries. "It's just . . . Why?"

"Mr. Carlyle didn't ask for your understanding. Only your cooperation."

"He's got it," snapped Davenport.

"Good. See to it."

Davenport was standing on the corner watching Nordstrom's slim form disappear into the snow-filled gloom, when Agent Laura Brockman came up to stand beside him.

"Problem?" she said.

"A new target. Only, this one's in fucking Iraq. Which is going to mean farming it out to some GTS guys."

Brockman said, "I can go. Make sure the job gets done right."

"No. I have another mission for you." He started across the avenue. "You do have a passport, don't you?"

"I do," she said, stepping off the curb beside him. "Several. Where am I going?"

"Morocco."

46

Before they landed in Najaf, Jax used Bubba's satellite phone to make arrangements with a friend at the embassy's CIA station to send a car and driver to meet them at the airport.

Bubba gave a loud snort as he banked into a curve and circled around toward the runway. "Guy must not know you well. Otherwise he'd have more sense than to lend you his car."

Jax grinned. "Why do you think he's sending a driver?"

The city of Najaf stretched out below them, a huddle of flat-topped concrete and stone-fronted buildings blasted by sandstorms and three decades of nearly continuous warfare, murderous economic sanctions, and bombings. At its center rose the great golden dome of the Imam Ali Shrine, one of the most sacred Shi'ite holy places in the world. Beyond that stretched the Wadi as-Salam, the Valley of Peace, the largest cemetery in existence.

According to legend, Najaf was, like Jerusalem and

Mecca, one of the portals to heaven, which meant that a lot of people wanted to be buried there. To accommodate the steady stream of pilgrims—and corpses—the Iraqis had built a gleaming new terminal of glass and steel.

"Okay," said October, peering out the window at the lines of jets from Syria and Lebanon, Pakistan and the Gulf. "That's not what I expected."

"I told you," said Jax. "Now that we're pulling out our troops, things are getting better."

October grunted.

Bubba dropped out of the sky and touched down on the dusty runway of Forward Operating Base Endeavor, which was separated from the civilian airport by a barbed wire fence. Bristling rows of Apache and Blackhawk helicopters, Humvees, Bradleys, and M–1 Abrams tanks stretched across the desert.

October put her head down between her knees again. "I think I'm hyperventilating."

Jax clapped her on the shoulder on his way to unlatch the door. "You're going to be just great."

Jax's friend at the embassy had sent a top-of-the-line Range Rover, all gleaming champagne metal and tan leather seats. A slim, wiry Iraqi named Tareq al-Mukhtar leaned against the side of the SUV smoking a cigarette. According to Jax's contact at the Embassy, Tareq had been a mineral engineer with a degree from the Colorado School of Mines. Now, he earned a living however he could.

"Joe says I'm not to let you touch the steering wheel," said Tareq, an ironic smile lifting the edges of his thick dark mustache as he blew out a final stream of smoke and ground his cigarette butt under his heel. "He says the last time he lent you a car, in Cairo, you brought it back looking like a lump of Swiss cheese."

"That wasn't my fault," said Jax.

Behind them, Bubba snickered. But all he said was, "If y'all want a ride home, you gotta be back here by one. I got a schedule to keep."

Tobie said, "If you leave me here to die, Bubba, I'll never talk to you again."

Bubba laughed. "One o'clock. Be here."

They hurtled north beside the blue waters of the Euphrates, cruising along at a horn-blaring, vision-blurring 120 mph. "The faster you go, the better chance you have of getting there," Tareq told them, stomping on the gas.

Tobie—who'd elected to sit in the backseat—cast an eye over the jumble of cardboard boxes and red plastic cans that half filled the rear. "What's all this stuff?"

Tareq glanced back at her and grinned.

"Uh . . . goats," warned Jax.

Without letting up on the gas, Tareq swerved around a herd of dusty brown and white goats that had strayed out into the road. Over the squeal of tires, he said, "The jerry cans are insurance. If you're driving any distance in Iraq, you learn to take your own gasoline with you. Thanks to Halliburton and Keefe, the supply lines are a mess."

"And the box of what looks like wine?"

"The finest Côtes du Rhône, flown in direct from France this morning, just for the ambassador. He's very particular about his wine."

"Nice to be the ambassador," said Jax.

Tobie said, "Not to Iraq."

They hurtled on through the flat, open landscape. Nearer the river stood date palm groves and wide fields of vegetables and barley greening under the strengthening sun. But to the west stretched a vast, windswept desert, harsh and deadly.

"Have you ever been to Babylon?" asked Tareq, lighting

another of his foul-smelling Turkish cigarettes and exhaling a stream of blue smoke through his nostrils.

"My dad brought me here when I was really little," said Tobie. "But my memories are kinda blurry. I remember being disappointed because I expected the Hanging Gardens to still be there. And the Tower of Babel looked nothing like the picture in my Illustrated Children's Bible."

"Believe me, it looks even worse now." Tareq rolled down his window, letting in a deafening blast of desert air. "The American forces turned Babylon into Camp Alpha."

"They *what*?"

"That's right. They took one of the greatest archaeological sites in the world and converted it into a military base. They brought in bulldozers and leveled the 'hilltops'—which were really the unexcavated parts of the old city—to make parking lots and helicopter pads. They drove their tanks over the Processional Way and smashed the ancient paving. They pounded stakes into the fragile tops of four-thousand-year-old walls so they could string their concertina wire, and ripped deep, wide trenches through the heart of the city center. Then they filled their sandbags with the archaeological material because it was just lying around, easy to pick up."

Tobie shook her head. "I don't understand. Why would anyone do something so . . . unforgivably barbaric?"

Tareq took a deep drag on his cigarette. "They claim it was to 'protect' the site."

Jax huffed a soft laugh. "Sorta like 'We had to destroy the village in order to save it'?"

"Pretty much." Tareq ground out his cigarette. "Me, I think it was deliberate. You don't destroy one of the Wonders of the Ancient World by accident."

Tobie looked from one to the other. "So why did they do it?"

Jax said, "Religiously inspired revenge for the Babylonian Captivity described in the Old Testament was probably part of it. Or maybe cultural jealousy—a desire to wipe out all evidence that the Iraqis were once the most highly advanced civilization in the world. Then again, it could be because according to certain Christian fundamentalists, the Antichrist will arise in Babylon."

"Revelation again," said Tobie.

Jax nodded. "We just can't seem to get away from it, can we?"

Marrakech, Morocco: Monday 5 February
6:45 A.M. local time

The first rays of the rising sun were just breaking over the Atlas Mountains when Noah's train pulled into Marrakech. As his *petit taxi* sped toward the mighty gates that guarded the medina, the golden light hit the *pisé* walls of the city's medieval ramparts, turning them from a warm ochre to a vivid burnt orange.

It was a place of magic, Marrakech. Of magic and mystery, of towering intricately carved minarets and tangled souks scented with all the spices of the ancient silk route—cinnamon and cloves, frankincense and myrrh. They wove through narrow winding streets, past crowded markets selling reed baskets and hammered brass plates and sticky pastries sweetened with honey.

Then his taxi drew up at the mouth of a dark passage and the driver said in French, "From here, you must walk."

"Walk?" said Noah, fumbling for his wallet.

The driver made a sweeping motion with a knifelike hand. "Walk."

Paying off the taxi, Noah hugged his backpack close and cast a quick glance around. Two ragged boys skipping along the gutter stopped to stare at him and laugh. He felt conspicuously out of place and, as he plunged into the shadowy, cavernlike alleyway, more than a little afraid.

47

The ruins of the once mighty city of Babylon rose before them on the banks of the Euphrates River, its crumbling walls and silent tells softened by the morning mist. Once, 3,700 years ago, this had been the largest city in the world, a vast metropolis of temples and palaces, libraries and markets, theaters and public parks. Now it was all but deserted, home only to a handful of Iraqi soldiers in dusty camouflage and burgundy berets, and a few determined volunteers desperately trying to limit the effects of the destruction wrought by the latest band of conquerors.

Tareq parked the Range Rover in the shade of a grove of date palms, where a boy of about twelve dressed in a ragged brown sweater pulled over a white dishdasha was selling *chai* and *kufta*—tea and a kind of spiced meatball on skewers—from a stand fashioned of crudely lashed poles roofed with dried reeds.

"He says Dr. Araji is working on what they call the Eighth Trench," said Tareq, munching on *kufta* as they walked up the dusty road toward the site. "In the religious section of the city. The boy says you don't want to go anywhere near the professor when he's working on the American trenches."

"Sounds promising," said Tobie, squinting up at the black Apache helicopter that hovered above them like a malevolent insect, its blades beating the morning air with an ominous-sounding *whomp-whomp*. She'd thought at first it was a U.S. Army chopper, but it wasn't. It was a transport, the Circle K logo on the tail identifying it as a Keefe Corporation asset.

Tareq, too, watched the helicopter fly off toward the landing pad in the distance, but said nothing. The so-called private security forces, or mercenaries, had a reputation for being even more trigger-happy than the regular troops. And they were essentially accountable to no one.

"So," said Jax, rubbing his hands together as if in anticipation. "Where is this despoiled religious section?"

Tareq grinned. "This way."

They found Dr. Salah Araji standing at the top of a loose mound of sand mixed with smashed bricks and pottery shards. He had a clipboard in one hand and wore a fierce scowl that pulled down the corners of his mouth and drew his eyebrows together into a knotted V.

"I'm going to go take a look at the Ishtar Gate and smoke a cigarette," said Tareq.

"Coward."

Tareq smiled and sauntered away.

"Let me do the talking," Jax whispered as they walked toward the professor.

Tobie said, "I always do."

"No you don't." He raised his voice and shouted, "*Marhabah*." Hello.

The Iraqi turned toward them, his scowl deepening. He was a stocky man of medium height, probably somewhere in his late forties or fifties, with several days' worth of gray stubble covering his craggy face. "Where are you from?" he demanded in Arabic.

"France," said Jax without missing a beat.

"You're a liar. You're Americans," said Araji, turning away.

Jax laughed. "How did you know?"

"You're dressed like Americans. You even walk like Americans." He nodded to the great gash before them, a gaping trench some ten feet wide and six feet deep that extended for nearly 500 yards across the ancient site. "See this? You did this." He kicked at the broken artifacts that littered the earth at his feet. "See that glazed brick? It has an inscription. It says 'I, Nebuchadnezzar, built this.' You? You destroyed it."

Jax and Tobie exchanged glances.

Dr. Araji rolled on. "Just digging this trench was enough of an abomination. But then you went off and left it open, exposed to the wind and the rain. Now the sides are starting to collapse, doing even more damage to the site."

"I agree with you," said Tobie. "It's sickening."

Jax hissed at her.

Tobie ignored him. "It's also a violation of the Hague Convention. The people who did this ought to be tried as war criminals."

Araji stared at her a moment, wide-eyed. Then he laughed and swung away to slide down the mound of rubble. "What do you want?"

They scrambled after him. "We want to know about the extra verses you discovered in the Babylonian Codex. What they say."

"Really? And why should I tell you that?"

Tobie threw Jax a panicked look.

He said, "There are people in the United States who believe the Book of Revelation is a literal description of what is going to happen at the end of the world. And now they've convinced themselves the newly discovered verses in the Babylonian Codex are like secret instructions left just for them."

Araji continued walking. "Telling them what?"

"We don't know. We think they have a plan to take over the U.S. government. That's why we need your help."

Araji drew up at the base of the pile of rubble left by the American bulldozers. "Do you know something?" he said, switching unexpectedly to flawless English. "A few years ago, a *National Geographic* team came in here and conducted DNA tests on today's Iraqis so they could compare them to the bones of the ancient Babylonians. You know what they found?" He thumped his chest. "We are the descendents of the people who built this."

He spread his arms in a wide sweep that took in the towering ramparts, the walls of glazed brick decorated with relief sculptures of lions and serpents. "Look around you. Five thousand years ago, my ancestors created the world's first cities. The world's first government. Once, we had a bicameral legislature with an elected leader. Hard to believe, isn't it? A democracy that existed five millennia before the world ever heard of the United States! Yet it's true. Then came many years of war, and in order to better protect themselves the people made the role of the leader permanent. After that, it wasn't long before the kings became hereditary. But it didn't really buy them safety. Invaders came, and in time the desert covered our cities."

He let his arms fall back to his sides, his voice dropping. "All great empires eventually fall. Perhaps it is your turn, now." He smiled. "Didn't last too long, did you?"

"Dr. Araji—" Jax began.

The professor cut him off. "No. You tell me some crazy religious fanatics are planning to take over your country? You know what I say to you? Good! I hope they do to your country what you have done to mine. Lay waste your cities. Burn your libraries. Poison your soil and water. Rape your women. Kill your—" His voice broke, and he had to stop and swallow before he could continue. "Kill your children."

"I think they're the same people," said Tobie quietly.

He swung to face her. "What is that supposed to mean?"

"It means that these people have been directing U.S. foreign policy for years, from the shadows. They're the ones who pushed for the invasion of Iraq and manufactured the 'evidence' that was used to sell the war to the American people. They're the ones who turned the ancient ruins of Babylon into a military camp, so that they could destroy it in some kind of crazy act of revenge for Nebuchadnezzar's destruction of Jerusalem. And they're the ones who helped organize the looting of the National Museum and Library, so that they could get their hands on the codex."

Araji's face had gone ashen.

"Please," said Tobie. "If you want revenge for this"—she swung her hand in a wide arc that took in the cracked walls, the collapsed temples—"give us the verses of the lost chapter."

48

Dr. Araji scrubbed a trembling hand over his haggard face. "I wish I could help you, but I can't. I don't have it anymore."

Jax said, "But you must have made digital copies. Photographs. The notes from your translations—"

"All were lost when the archives were burned. And my personal copies were destroyed just two weeks later. A band of contractors—from Keefe—broke into my house. Machine-gunned my wife and children. Set fire to our home. Afterward, they said 'sorry'. They said they got the address wrong. Sorry."

Jax glanced at October and knew she was thinking the same thing he was—that the brutal murder of Araji's family and the destruction of his house was no accident.

She said, "Can you remember any of the verses?"

"Remember?" The Iraqi gave a soft laugh that held no joy or amusement, only bitter anguish and regret. "Sometimes I can't even remember my wife's smile, or the smell of my children's hair when I'd hold them close. The years before the war have become a blur."

"Perhaps you sent parts of it to a fellow scholar?"

This time, Araji's smile held genuine amusement. "You don't know much about paleographers, do you? We're a very jealous, possessive lot, I'm afraid. Our careers depend on our publication record, which means that until our final papers are presented, we're very careful to keep our discoveries to ourselves. I published an article describing the discovery of the codex and the existence of the lost verses, but not their contents. Do you realize that parts of the Dead Sea Scrolls are still unknown? And they were found back in the forties. Is it some big conspiracy to keep their contents secret? No. It's simple, professional jealousy."

A rattle of falling stones drew Jax's attention to two men approaching along the berm of sand and shattered artifacts. They were dressed in khakis and carrying Heckler and Koch machine guns. But they weren't soldiers: their black baseball caps with the Circle K logo marked them as contractors, probably from the Apache they'd seen landing.

Araji was saying, "A colleague of mine in Spain did talk me into sending him one of the verses."

Jax was only half listening. He didn't like the way the contractors were carrying their weapons. Not casually slung over their shoulders, but with their hands on the grips, muzzles pointing down, fingers inside the trigger guards.

October said, "Spain?"

Araji nodded. "A biblical scholar named José Zapatero, from Medinaceli. A brilliant man, but far too ready to share everything he knows with anyone who asks." Again, that ghost of a smile. "Afterwards, I wondered what possessed me."

As Jax watched, the two men split, fanning out as if to position themselves at a 45 degree angle.

Jax said, "I think we've got trouble," just as the two contractors brought up their weapons.

"Get down!" Jax yelled, reaching for his Beretta as he threw himself flat.

He sighted on the nearest contractor, a big muscle-bound grunt with a jaw like a tugboat, and pulled the trigger three times in rapid succession. *Bam. Bam. Bam.* The asshole went down—just as Jax heard the *rat-tat-tat* of an HK.

He swung the Beretta to the second contractor and nailed the guy right between the eyes. Then he put two more rounds in the sonofabitch's chest before he fell.

Jax lay prone, his gun held at the ready, his breath coming hard and fast as he scanned the ruined walls and littered dirt, looking for more bad guys. Nothing. From the distance came the pounding of running feet, the sound of excited voices speaking Arabic.

He turned his head to where October crouched in the lee of a wall. "You okay?"

She nodded, her throat working hard as she swallowed.

Then he glanced over to where Dr. Araji had been standing. He lay flat on his back, his chest a pulpy red mess, his eyes open wide and sightless. "Damn."

The running footsteps were coming closer. Jax caught October's hand and pulled her up. "Let's get out of here."

He grabbed the assault rifle from the nearest contractor and saw it was an MP5 N, a variant manufactured for United States SEALS. *Interesting*, he thought, tossing the strap over his shoulder and taking the guy's canvas ammo bag, heavy with extra magazines.

"You think that wasn't the end of it?" said October, watching him.

"I think it's a long way back to Najaf." He took off toward the Range Rover at a run. "Where the hell is Tareq?"

49

Tareq was already throwing the Range Rover into reverse when they made it back to the palm grove.

They scrambled inside and hauled ass down the highway. Tareq kept the accelerator floored, weaving around stray camels, battered civilian cars packed with women and children, donkeys loaded with vegetables.

"Who do you think those guys were sent to kill?" October asked, looking over her shoulder. "Us, or Araji?"

"Araji," said Jax. "They took him out first." He sat in the backseat, the Heckler and Koch in his hands. "But now they know we're here."

October glanced at Tareq. "How much farther?"

"Thirty kilometers."

"Shit." They'd reached a desolate stretch of road, where the few scattered villages were only blasted hulls, their houses' walls scorched by fire and pockmarked by bullet holes and broken gaps left by tanks and RPG fire.

Jax said, "They're cleaning up every loose end they can think of. First Gabriel Sinclair and Madeleine Livingston. Now Dr. Araji."

"Do you think they know about Zapatero in Medinaceli?"

Jax turned his head to eye a dun-colored Hummer that was speeding up on their ass, fast. "Maybe. Maybe not. But they know Bosch was in Madrid. They may figure it out."

"We need to get to him first."

"Ah . . . Tareq . . ." said Jax, just as the Hummer accelerated hard and slammed into the back of the Range Rover.

The impact sent them careening wildly across the road and shattered the back window. "*Y'allah*," shouted Tareq, tires squealing as he brought the SUV under control again and floored it.

Jax swore, "Son of a bitch." Tossing the HK over his shoulder, he clambered into the rear. "Try to hold it steady!" he shouted as he whipped out his Beretta.

"Steady? *Habibi*, have you seen this road?" Tareq demanded. "Abrams tanks and pavement are not a good combination."

Steadying the Beretta as best he could, Jax aimed at the head of the Hummer's driver and squeezed the trigger.

The bullet bounced off the windshield, leaving a little pockmark.

"Shit. It's got bulletproof glass!"

"Why aren't you using the damned machine gun?" October demanded, climbing into the backseat.

"Because this is a hell of a lot more accurate." Shifting his aim, he put a couple of rounds into the grill and saw sparks as the bullets ricocheted off into the desert.

"Jesus Christ. The damn thing is armored, too. Who are these guys?"

"Keefe," she said quietly.

Jax met her gaze. Six months before, the CEO of Keefe had tried to have her killed.

"Look out!" she shouted.

Whipping around, Jax saw a man's head and shoulders appear above the Hummer's sunroof.

Jax brought up the HK and nailed the asshole.

Tobie cheered.

Tareq shouted, "Now what do we do?"

Jax kept a sharp eye on the Hummer. "I'm thinking, I'm thinking."

Tobie ripped into the nearest case of wine. "Give me your pocketknife."

"What?"

"Your pocketknife," she said, hauling out one of the vintage bottles.

Jax laughed. "October, you are a genius."

"I don't like the sound of this," said Tareq, watching them in the rearview mirror. "*Y'allah,*" he yelped as Jax used his pocket knife to punch in the cork. "The ambassador's wine!"

Jax said, "You can console the ambassador with the thought that all this bouncing around wouldn't have been good for it anyway."

"Right. As if—*Y'allah,*" Tareq yelped again as Tobie emptied the wine onto the backseat's floorboards. "Now what are you doing? *The car!*"

"Front passenger window," October warned.

Jax brought up the HK and sprayed the contractor who was trying to maneuver an RPG launcher out the window.

October reached for the nearest jerry can.

"You're spilling it," Jax warned as she splashed gasoline into the now-empty wine bottle.

"Oh? Like this is easy? Find me something to shove into the top."

Jax took his pocketknife, cut a slit down the back of the leather seat, and handed her a wad of stuffing.

"*Y'allah!*" cried Tareq. "What are you *doing*? You are destroying Joe's car!"

"Just give me your lighter, okay? And drive."

October handed Jax the Molotov cocktail. "Here. I'm not lighting it. I'm afraid I'll blow up the whole car."

"No!" shouted Tareq.

Jax handed it back to her. "Make some more, first."

She grabbed another handful of stuffing. "Here they come again," she warned as the Hummer accelerated toward them.

Lifting the HK, Jax emptied an entire magazine onto the Hummer's windscreen, just to make sure they didn't get any ideas. The glass didn't break, but thirty rounds did a pretty effective job of covering the bulletproof glass with lots of little splats and dings.

"What are they doing now?" October asked, her attention all for the half dozen bottles of wine she was emptying onto the floorboards. The Range Rover smelled like an unholy alliance between a vintage wine cave and a wrecked oil tanker.

"Sitting tight, but keeping close on our asses. I just hope they don't get the bright idea to call in some helicopter gunships."

"Hush. You'll give them the idea."

"Right. How can I do that?"

"Studies have shown that thoughts are energy. You send your thoughts out into the ether and someone can easily pick up on them without realizing where the idea came from."

"Stop it with the woo-woo, okay? Just focus on the Molotov cocktails."

They hurtled across the desert at a good 140 mph. A couple of times the Hummer tried to edge up beside them. But Tareq set the Range Rover careening back and forth across the road, forcing them back. The Hummer had the advantage of being built like a tank, but its maneuverability was lousy.

"Okay," said Jax as soon as October had five bottles lined up. "Slow down a bit, Tareq."

Tareq eased up on the gas. The Hummer immediately pulled up within five or six feet of them.

Jax lit the first two Molotov cocktails, then handed October the lighter. "You're going to have to light the rest, whether you like it or not."

"*Y'allah!*" screeched Tareq.

Jax bounced the first bottle off the windshield, which was not what he was aiming for. The second one missed completely, smashing into sparks on the road. The third and fourth landed right against the grill.

The Hummer might be armored, but its engine still needed air, which meant that the plates behind the grill were baffled. As the burning gasoline splashed up into the engine block, it set fire to wires and vacuum hoses. Black smoke poured out from beneath the hood. The Hummer's expensive little computer melted.

The Hummer coasted to a stop.

"All right!" shouted Tareq, punching the air with his fist as he floored the accelerator.

Jax slumped back against the side window, the HK still cradled in his arms. "Let's get out of here before they call in hel—"

But October put her fingers against his lips and said, "Hush."

50

Noah sat on a low wall overlooking the pavilion at the center of the Andalusian garden of Dar Si Said. Once, this had been the grand palace of a vizier, who'd covered its walls with intricate plaster friezes and *zellij* tilework, and surrounded its shady courtyards with graceful arcades that echoed with the soothing trickle of fountains.

Noah had been sitting here for almost an hour.

He cast a quick glance around. The museum was nearly deserted. The only Westerners he could see were a young Danish couple in jeans and heavy sweaters, and an elderly Frenchman who gave Noah a quizzical look as he passed in and out of the museum's succession of rooms.

Noah had been sitting there long enough that it had occurred to him he was probably a fool for coming. What if he was being set up? What if he'd been lured here so that he could be killed?

He stood quickly, breathless with a sudden terror. Then

it occurred to him that anyone intending to lure him to his death would have picked a more desolate rendezvous—or a very crowded one.

He sat down again.

A Moroccan woman dressed in an elegant cream wool kaftan topped with a filmy silk *mansourya* came to sit on the far side of the nearest fluted column. Most Moroccan women wore a *hijab*, or headscarf, but not the veil. Yet this woman had covered the lower half of her face so that only her eyes showed.

"Don't look at me," she said in an undervoice roughened by fear.

He glanced quickly away again, but not before he saw that her eyes were blue and that a stray lock of flaxen hair peeked from beneath her headscarf. Somehow, her fear reassured him. If she was afraid of *him*, then surely he had no reason to fear *her*?

"So you really are a woman," he said, before he could stop himself. "I did wonder."

At that, she gave a soft laugh. "What were you expecting? An old man with nicotine-stained fingers and a raspy cough?"

Her voice, like her eyes, was young. He tried to place her accent but couldn't. It was mainstream USA.

"I didn't know what to expect," he said, although that was only partially true. He knew how he'd always pictured her: dark and voluptuous, a prettier, more sophisticated version of the famous porn star of the seventies. Instead, she was tall and thin and very fair. Beautiful, but not voluptuous. Refined and elegant rather than earthy or sensual.

She said, "Did you wonder why I wanted you to meet me in Morocco?"

"Yes. Although not as much as I wondered, *Why now? Why meet me now, after all these months?*"

"Because we're running out of time."

She shifted her weight to reach into the cream leather bag she carried slung over one shoulder. "You said no newspaper would print your story without proof. What if you had an example of the device used to provoke Bill Hamilton's heart attack? Would that be enough proof?"

"You have it?" he said incredulously.

"No. But I know someone who does." She handed him a photograph.

He found himself holding a picture of a man. Clean shaven and fresh faced, perhaps twenty-five or twenty-six years old, his light brown hair cut short, his white dress shirt worn rolled up at the sleeves. In the picture, he was standing in the door of a grass hut beside two naked Africans, and he was smiling.

"His name is Michael Hawkins," she said. "He used to work for Warren Patterson Ministries in Sierra Leone. But for the past eight months he's been hiding here, in Morocco, at a ruined casbah called Telouet, in the High Atlases. He's living with a family that sells rugs to the few tourists who make it that far south."

Noah turned to gape at her, completely forgetting she'd warned him not to look directly at her. "Eight months ago there was governmental upheaval in Sierra Leone after the previous strongman died unexpectedly. Of a heart attack."

"Most unexpectedly."

"How do you know this guy Hawkins?"

She colored faintly. "Let's just say we're old friends." She paused. "It's not an easy place to get to—you'll need to either rent a car or take a *grand taxi*." The *petits taxis* like Noah had caught from the train station were only for the city; for longer hauls across country Moroccans used what they called a *grand taxi,* usually bigger—and older.

"You'll also have to work to convince him to talk to you,"

she said. "But this may help." She pulled the ring off her little finger and held it out to him. "Well, take it."

It was a simple ring of worked silver inlaid with black enamel in a pattern similar to the stylized geometric carvings on the arch above their heads.

She said, "If you show Michael this ring, he'll know you come from me and that he can trust you. But you're the one who's going to have to convince him to give you what you need."

She pushed to her feet, then looked back in surprise when he put out a hand, stopping her.

Noah said, "When you first came, you said we're running out of time. They're going to move against the President next, aren't they? When? You do know when, don't you? Tell me."

But all she said was, "Soon." And then she left him there, with the silver-and-enamel ring cradled in the palm of his hand.

51

Bubba was supervising the loading of a stack of mysterious wooden crates into the Gulfstream's cargo hold when Tareq pulled up at the edge of the runway. The big Cajun turned away from the jet, his eyes widening as he took in the Range Rover's smashed rear end, the slashed leather seats, the wine-splashed, gasoline-soaked interior.

"Jesus H. Christ," he said, peering through a window. "What the hell did you do to this thing, Jax?"

Tareq punched down his window. "Get them away from here. Quickly. Before they wreck what's left of the car."

"Come on. It could have been worse," said Jax, closing the passenger door with infinite care.

"Next time you want to borrow a car, go see the Kurds or something," said Tareq, tires squealing as he floored the accelerator and took off.

"Thank you," October called after him.

"I don't think that'll help," said Jax. He turned to Bubba. "How soon can we be out of here?"

"Ten minutes." Bubba's smile faded. "Why?"

"Well . . . we might be getting some company."

"Holy shit." Bubba took off for his cockpit at a lumbering trot. "We're outta here *now.*"

Jax waited until they were airborne before telling Bubba they needed to make a little stop in Spain.

"Spain!" bellowed Bubba. "I'm supposed to be on my way to Berlin! Do you have any idea what's in my cargo hold?"

"No. What is it?"

"You don't want to know."

"We shouldn't be long. I think there's a small airport outside of Soria where you can land."

"Soria? Where the hell you going?"

"A place called Medinaceli."

52

Noah took a *grand taxi* out of the city toward the southwest, climbing up into the towering peaks and fertile valleys of the High Atlas Mountains. As they rose higher and higher, the road narrowed into a series of hairpin turns cut through a stony, barren landscape. Earth-colored *pisé* hamlets, far flung and half deserted, clung to the high slopes or huddled in wadis beside trickling streams. By the time they climbed to the Tizi-n-Tichka Pass, a cold wind was buffeting the ancient Mercedes and Noah could see icy streaks of snow lying in the shadows at the edge of the road. He realized too late that he was plunging blithely into a wild, primitive, sparsely inhabited land. And he felt it again, that shameful, sick fear that brought a sheen of sweat to his face and clenched his gut.

On the far side of the pass, his driver turned off onto a bleak, deserted road that dropped down a steep valley to the casbah of Telouet. Once, this had been the grand residence of el-Glaoui, the pasha of Marrakech. But then el-Glaoui had made the mistake of supporting the French in their war against the king. When the French pulled out, el-Glaoui and his family were exiled, their lands seized, their gracious, fortified palaces left to crumble. Now, Telouet was little more than a huddle of humble houses sheltered behind the shattered towers and red-toned high walls of the ruined casbah.

Opening the car door, Noah staggered as the brisk cold wind hit him in the face. The driver, a Berber by the name of Mustapha, pointed to his watch in warning; they would need to leave within the hour if they wanted to make it back to Marrakech before nightfall. Noah certainly had no desire to be stranded in the wilds of the Atlases after dark.

Winding around the side of the casbah's soaring red walls, Noah followed a dusty track to the hamlet itself, a huddle of small shops and high-windowed houses with thick *pisé*—rammed earth—walls and flat brush roofs. He was just wondering how the hell he was supposed to find Michael Hawkins if the man chose not to be found when he spotted the American missionary seated in a slice of sunshine at one of the battered white metal tables in front of a combination rustic café and rug shop that faced the road.

Gone were the preppy chinos and pressed white dress shirt of the smiling young man in Linda's photograph. In their place, Hawkins wore the striped handwoven *djellaba* of the Berbers, with a pointed hood he had pushed back off his head. He was sipping a cup of *chai* and watching Noah's approach through narrowed eyes.

Stepping up onto the flagstoned terrace, Noah set Linda's silver-and-enamel ring on the rusty surface of the table before the young missionary. "A mutual friend said to give you this."

Hawkins stared at the ring. He made no move to pick it up. After a moment, he raised his gaze to Noah's face. "What do you want?"

"Information. I'm a journalist."

Hawkins laughed. He took one more sip of his *chai,* grimaced, then pushed to his feet and walked off down the road toward the casbah.

Noah scooped up the ring and shoved it back into his pocket as he followed. "I understand you were a missionary in Sierra Leone," Noah said, trotting to catch up with him.

Hawkins cast him a quick glance but kept walking, his boots kicking up little eddies of dust as he cut across the heaps of crumbling rubble. After a half century of neglect, much of the palace was collapsing into rusty red mounds of dissolving brick and fragmented stone. "And if I was?" he asked after a moment.

"I want to know what happened to the former president of Sierra Leone."

Wordlessly, Hawkins ducked through a low doorway.

After a moment's hesitation, Noah followed him.

He found himself in an ancient courtyard of worn earth-colored walls and sagging arcades, still miraculously standing against the elements. Hawkins was already disappearing down a shadowy passage. Noah plunged after him.

"How much do you know about Warren Patterson?" Hawkins asked without looking back.

Noah said, "I know he's been a leading member of the radical religious right for years."

Hawkins gave a soft laugh. "That's one way to put it. Before Patterson, most churches were either apolitical or dedicated to social work. They tended to focus on the part of the gospels where Jesus says stuff like, 'Come, you who are blessed of My Father, inherit the kingdom prepared for you from the foundation of the world. For I was hungry, and you gave me food; I was thirsty, and you gave me drink; I was a stranger, and you invited me in; naked, and you clothed me; I was sick, and you visited me; I was in prison, and you came to me.'"

"So what happened?"

"Warren Patterson happened. He's probably the most successful—and wealthy—televangelist in history. He started a religious television network—Ministry Broadcasting Network, or MBN—using money donated to his church. On the surface that seems okay because his network was running a lot of Christian programming. Only it started making so much money that it could no longer be part of his 'nonprofit' ministry. So Patterson had the ministry sell MBN to him, personally, for almost nothing. And then he took the company public and made several hundred million dollars from the sale of the stock."

The passage they were following erupted suddenly into a vast, stunningly well-preserved reception room with Andalusian-style engraved stuccowork and a painted wooden ceiling that took Noah's breath away. It was a moment before he could say, "Is that legal?"

Hawkins swung to face him. Here, in this frigid, abandoned Arabian-nights setting, he looked more like a Berber warrior than a Christian missionary. "Legal? What does legality have to do with it? The only thing that matters is that no one in the Justice Department has the balls to go after a certified 'man of God' like Patterson. So Patterson was free to take his hundreds of millions and look around for some investments."

"And he looked at Sierra Leone? Why Sierra Leone?"

"Because it's one of the richest countries in Africa—or rather, it should be. The problem is, all that mineral wealth goes to one man: the president. Up until six months ago, that was a guy named Jeffrey Koboto. Imagine your typical African dictator on steroids, and you've got President

Koboto: torture, extortion, extrajudicial killings, systematic rapes, child soldiers—you name it, he was into it. Things got so bad the UN slapped sanctions on him, and the U.S. went along with them. So Koboto went to Patterson."

"I don't get it. Why?"

"Patterson and his buddies have a long history of snuggling up to dictators. The dictators let the evangelists come in and set up missions—with the force of a very nasty state behind them. In return, Patterson and his friends have the connections to get the U.S. government to ignore things like UN sanctions or give them huge arms packages. So Koboto announces that—thanks to Patterson—he and his countrymen are all saved for Jesus, and Patterson convinces the State Department that Koboto is really a misunderstood nice guy so they ought to lift the sanctions. Then Patterson and his buddies get a huge diamond mining concession from Koboto as a way of saying thank you."

"Who are Patterson's buddies?" Noah asked sharply.

"Keefe Corporation and Carlyle Enterprises. The three of them formed a company in the Cayman Islands they call Kingdom Mining."

"That's sick. How do you come into all this?"

"I was part of the window dressing. Koboto dedicated Sierra Leone to Jesus, and I was sent in to help coordinate the missions to convert the natives." A muscle went into convulsions along Hawkins's jawline.

"And?" prompted Noah.

The missionary went to stand before one of the vacant windows, its broken wrought-iron lights silhouetted against the barren landscape beyond. He sucked in a deep breath that lifted his chest. "It's . . . it's a strange, twisted version of Christianity they're pushing in Africa these days. This is not your grandmother's gospels. It's heavy into demons and witches and warriors, and it's gotten all twisted up with the native-African religious beliefs into something that is truly ugly. I've seen little kids—sweet, innocent things no more than four or five years old—branded as witches by their village pastor and driven off into the jungles to die. Sometimes they're killed outright, either by the other villagers or by their own parents. We're talking about thousands of children, all across Africa, being killed in the name of Jesus. It's . . . horrific."

"Good God. Why?"

"Because the best way to unite people behind you is to give them a common enemy—an 'other' to hate and fear."

"*Their own children?*"

Hawkins shrugged. "It works."

"Patterson did nothing to stop it?"

"Patterson believes in witches and demons himself. They're in the Bible. Besides, by that point, Patterson had problems of his own. You see, once Koboto got the State Department to lift the sanctions, he started making noises about taking away Patterson's diamond mines and giving them to some Israeli outfit that was offering to sell him arms. So Patterson hooked up with Koboto's nephew and arranged to have Koboto killed."

"How do you know about this?"

Hawkins kept his gaze on the scene outside the window. A dusty Land Rover had driven up and disgorged two tourists. They were wearing *djellaba* similar to Hawkins's over their frayed jeans and had camera bags thrown over their shoulders. Hawkins said, "I was there. I saw it happen. I saw how they did it."

Noah felt his blood thrum with excitement. "So how did they do it? How did they kill him?"

Hawkins shook his head and swung away from the window.

Noah followed him through another low door, onto a terrace that looked out over the ruined bulk of the casbah and the harsh stony valley beyond. Noah said, "Koboto had a heart attack, right? He was forty-six years old and healthy, then he suddenly dropped dead. I heard they even had an autopsy done in France, to prove it wasn't just another of your typical African coups. The autopsy showed nothing suspicious, just like with Vice President Bill Hamilton. You have heard about that, haven't you?"

"I've heard."

"I was in Davos when it happened. Standing right there, no more than a dozen feet away. I didn't see a thing. You've got to tell me: *How are they doing this?*"

Hawkins turned his face into the wind. His voice was a whisper. "If I tell you, they'll kill me."

Noah cast a significant look around, taking in the dusty red, windswept slopes and crude huddle of houses. "Are you kidding? They're looking to kill you right now and you know it. That's why you're hiding here, in the middle of nowhere. Because you're afraid they'll kill you for what you know. Don't you understand? Telling me, now—helping me bring these guys down—is the only chance you've got."

Hawkins gave him a long, hard look. "Why should I trust you?"

"Because the woman who gave me the ring trusts me."

The missionary set his jaw, hard. But after a moment, he seemed to come to some kind of a decision. "I've got something to show you."

Noah followed Hawkins down a set of worn steps that curved around to come out on the far side of the casbah. There, a row of three houses with earthen walls and high windows framed with ancient wood faced onto the ruined palace. Ducking through one of the low doorways, Hawkins emerged a moment later carrying something small and dark. "Here," he said, handing it Noah. "Take it."

Noah found himself holding a black rectangular box connected by a wire to a small cylinder. He stared at it. "What the hell is it?"

Hawkins shook his head. "I don't know. All I know is, don't press that button and point it at anyone you don't want to die."

Noah turned the strange device over in his hands. Carefully. "How did you get it?"

"After they killed Koboto, they gave it to me to get rid of. Can you believe that? Like I was one of them. They just took it for granted I'd have no problem with the fact they murdered a man."

"Sounds to me like if anyone ever deserved to be eliminated, it's this Koboto character."

"You'd think. Except, believe me, the nephew makes Koboto look like Mother Teresa. It wasn't Koboto's crimes that got him killed. It was all that money. As far as Patterson is concerned, he and his cronies can do anything they want. Anything. It doesn't matter how vile it is as long as they're doing God's work—or what they convince themselves is God's work. They lie, steal, kill—just like David and Solomon. Because, you see, as far as they're concerned, they're the new Chosen Ones, which means they're held to a different standard of accountability."

Noah glanced up at him. "You don't believe that?"

Hawkins shook his head. "Seems to me if God were going to work through people, he'd hold them to a *higher* standard of accountability than everyone else. Not a lower one."

"So you took this device and ran?"

Hawkins drew in a breath that raised his chest and nodded. "Why here?"

He shrugged. "It's where I ended up. The Berbers are an incredibly hospitable people. They don't judge me. They don't try to proselytize me. I've learned a lot from them." He gave a wry smile. "And I can repay them by helping them sell their rugs. I was a marketing major in college, you know."

Noah held up the deadly device. "Can I have this?"

Hawkins put up both hands, palms facing forward, as if holding Noah at bay. "Please. Take it." He squinted up at the westering sun. "If you're planning to make it back to Marrakech before nightfall, you should get going."

They turned to walk along the base of the casbah's towering walls, toward where Noah had left his *grand taxi*. They could see the two tourists farther up the hill, near the café/rug shop. One of them, a woman, had the hood of her *djellaba* thrown back, revealing long, straight blond hair.

Noah stared at her.

Hawkins said, "You will write about this? Get the story published?"

Noah glanced at him. "Can I quote you on any of this?"

Hawkins drew up sharply, the heels of his boots scraping across the small stones in the path as he pivoted to face Noah. "God, no."

"But without you as a source—"

"No." Hawkins nodded to the strange device in Noah's hands. "You have the weapon. It's enough. Or at least, it'll have to be enough. I can't—"

He broke off. Following his gaze, Noah saw the blond woman reach into her camera bag and come up with a machine pistol.

53

"Jesus Christ!" Noah shouted, diving behind the low earthen wall beside them just as the two "tourists" opened fire. Looking back, he saw Hawkins throw up his hands and stagger, jerking again and again as the bullets ripped into him. Then he went down hard.

Noah didn't want to look at what the spray of bullets had done to the missionary's head and chest. Choking back a sob, he hunkered low, bending almost double as he ran along what smelled like a goat pen. Reaching the backs of the houses, he darted out into the road and saw the dusty old *grand taxi* barreling toward him.

Noah waved his arms frantically. The driver hit the brakes and threw open the passenger door. Noah dove in just as the Moroccan gunned the accelerator again.

They peeled off, stones flying, the door swinging shut as Noah struggled to right himself. A round of machine-gun fire chewed into the side of the Mercedes, shattering the window of Noah's door and sending glass flying.

"Y'allah!" shouted the driver, roaring up the hillside.

Jerking the seat belt down across his chest, Noah threw a

quick glance behind. Through the dust he could see the two killers running for their Land Rover. He realized he was still holding the cylinder of Hawkins's strange weapon clenched in one hand, the rectangular piece dangling by the wire. Sitting forward he swung his pack off his back and brought it into his lap. He was shaking so badly he had a hard time opening the zipper so he could shove the contraption inside.

They tore up the narrow, twisting road, tires squealing on the turns, engine laboring hard as the incline steepened. Piles of sun-blasted red boulders reared up on their left, the other side of the road falling away in a sickening plunge Noah tried not to think about.

"*Haihum jayyeen*," said the driver, his eyes on the rearview mirror. "*Meen hummeh?*" He threw a quick glance at Noah. "*Meen inta?*"

Noah shrugged his shoulders helplessly, not understanding. Slewing around in the seat, he saw the Land Rover come roaring up behind them. His heart felt as if it were wedged up in his throat. As he watched, the woman leaned out the passenger window, her blond hair flying in the wind, and sprayed them with another round of machine-gun fire.

Noah yelped and ducked low. He could hear the bullets pinging into the metal, glass flying as first one, then another window blew out.

"Can't you go any faster?" he shouted over the wind rushing in through the broken windows.

The driver—a plump, middle-aged man with a dark, sweat-sheened face and thick, gray-streaked mustache—gripped the steering wheel with both hands, his knuckles white. "My taxi," he kept repeating over and over. "Look what they are doing to my taxi."

Accelerating into a hairpin curve, he sent the big old Mercedes careening around the switchback, rear end fishtailing, just as the woman in the Land Rover opened fire again.

Bullets ripped the upholstery, shattered the dashboard. Noah felt a warm spray hit his face and knew it was blood. The big Mercedes spun out of control.

"Mustapha!" Noah screamed.

The taxi slammed sideways into the rocky cliff face. The impact sent the heavy car airborne. Noah had a weird sense of moving in slow motion, his world narrowing down to a tunnel-like vision of red rocks and barren scrub viewed through a cracked windshield as the car tilted sideways and kept going. It was as if they flew through a strange, dust-swirled, silent void, the old Mercedes executing a graceful pirouette through space.

Then the car slammed down on its roof and skittered sideways along the road, the impact tearing through Noah's body, stealing his breath and sending up a billowing cloud of dust.

He gasped in agony, fighting hard to draw air into his empty lungs. He realized he was hanging upside down and clawed frantically at the seat belt that held him suspended. Releasing the catch, he curled into a ball as he landed on the roof. Pain exploded in his shoulder, reverberated through his body.

Only then did he glance over at Mustapha. The driver was dead, his eyes open wide, one side of his head gone.

"Oh, my God," sobbed Noah.

He could smell the hot engine, the reek of spilled gasoline. In a panic, he grabbed his backpack and squeezed through the broken window of his mangled door. His backpack caught on a jagged piece of metal and he yanked it free. Kicking away from the taxi, he skittered backward across the rutted road—

Just as the car exploded in a giant fireball.

54

Jax and Tobie rented a little two-door Seat Ibiza in Soria.

Bubba leaned against the car. "I'll give y'all until seven o'clock. Then I'm outta here."

"Eight," said Jax, sliding behind the wheel.

Bubba glanced at Tobie. "Seven thirty. But don't be late."

"Yes, Mother."

They drove across a high, windswept plateau of winter-browned, shrub-covered hills. "You think this is what Noah Bosch was doing in Spain?" Tobie asked, staring across the undulating stone-strewn fields to the flat-topped mesa crowned by Medinaceli's medieval walls. "Coming to see Zapatero?"

"Seems reasonable, doesn't it?"

"I wonder who his source was. Someone close to Patterson, you think? Or Carlyle?"

Jax turned off onto the narrow road winding up to the top of the plateau. "Patterson and Carlyle are just the two men we know about. I suspect there are a good half dozen billionaire nutcases up to their Armani-clad necks in this scheme. Pizarro is threatening to derail their little gravy train. They're not going to just roll over and give up their privileges without a fight."

She stared out the window at bleak hillsides covered with windmills. "Duane Davenport knew Bosch was in Spain. I wonder if they got him?"

"Probably," said Jax.

They parked the Seat in the shadow of the crumbling ducal palace overlooking the village's vast plaza mayor. Like the narrow medieval streets through which they'd passed, the plaza was deserted, the ancient, golden-hued stone buildings fronting the square standing quiet and forlorn in the last rays of the cold winter sunshine. When Tobie closed her car door, the sound echoed around the vast space.

"Wow. Where is everyone?"

"Dead," said Jax. "Or living in Madrid."

They found a little old woman in black sitting in a battered, straight-backed wooden chair beneath the age-worn arcade that ran along one side of the plaza. She gave them directions to Señor Zapatero's house, her eyes narrowed as if with a secret knowledge she had no intention of sharing.

"Something has happened," Tobie said as, following the woman's directions, they took the crooked lane that opened off the far end of the plaza.

"Why do you say that?" Jax demanded, his head falling back to scan the silent stone facades and moss-covered tile roofs.

"There's something she wasn't telling us."

Jax brought his gaze back to Tobie's face. "What is this? More woo-woo mind reading?"

"No." She squeezed through a narrow passage that opened up into a smaller plaza centered around a crumbling, shuttered old church. "It's women's intuition. It's all a matter of—"

She broke off. The house opposite the church was a black-ened shell.

"Shit," whispered Jax.

Stepping up to the gaping, blackened doorway, they found a young woman on the far side of the fire-blasted room hun-kered down beside what looked like the charred remains of an ancient trunk. She was sifting through the rubble, occa-sionally pausing to put something into the small plastic box she held.

"Excuse me," said Jax, slipping easily into Spanish. "We're looking for José Zapatero."

"He's dead," said the woman, her attention all for her task. "There was an explosion."

Tobie drew in a quick breath scented with ash and burnt wood. "Oh, God. I'm so sorry."

Jax said, "You're Zapatero's daughter?"

"That's right. Antonia." She looked up, her shoulder-length brown hair falling into her eyes. She brushed it back with one hand, leaving a streak of soot across her forehead. Her face was wan, her eyes red and swollen. "Who are you?"

Jax surprised Tobie by telling the woman the truth. "We're with United States intelligence."

"Is that so?" Antonia didn't sound terribly impressed—or convinced. "And what does any of this"—she swept her hand in a wide arc that took in the shattered windows and blackened walls—"have to do with the United States?"

"Are you familiar with the Babylonian Codex?"

She pushed to her feet, the contents of the small plastic box rattling in her hand. "I'm a classical archaeologist. Of course I know about the codex." She glanced from Jax to Tobie, then back.

"What?" prompted Jax when Antonia looked at him ex-pectantly.

"You have identification?"

He handed her James Anderson's Homeland Security credentials.

She studied it thoughtfully for a moment, then tossed it back to him. "These could easily be fake. How would I know?"

"Actually, they are fake," said Jax, pocketing the badge and ID. "My real name is Jax Alexander and I work for the CIA, not Homeland Security." He nodded toward the scorched walls. "I think this explosion was the work of rogue FBI agents."

She gave short, incredulous laugh. "If that were true, why would you tell me?"

"Because I'm getting desperate," he said. "Because Vice President Hamilton's death wasn't natural; it was murder. And because his death is part of a plan to overturn the results of the last election. The guys behind it are a bunch of financiers and industrialists in league with some loony fundamentalists who believe they have a God-given mandate to prepare the world for the Second Coming."

It sounded so incredible that Tobie expected the woman to laugh again. Instead, she said, "I have heard of this movement. Although I must admit, I find it difficult to understand."

"Have you ever heard of a journalist named Noah Bosch?"

"Actually, yes. He came to see my father yesterday. They were together when the bomb went off."

Tobie said, "So he's dead?"

Zapatero's daughter shook her head. "If he is, his body has not been found."

Jax and Tobie exchanged a quick glance.

Antonia set aside the small plastic box and dusted her hands on the seat of her jeans. "What precisely has any of this to do with either my father or the Babylonian Codex?"

"We think these men have decided that the lost chapter from the codex is their own private blueprint for action."

"That is the most preposterous thing I've ever heard. Have they never actually *read* the Revelation of John? It says quite clearly at the very beginning of the first chapter that these are things which must come 'shortly' to pass. Then John says it again, in verse three: 'the time is at hand.' And as if that weren't enough, God says once more in 22:10: 'The time is at hand.'"

Tobie looked at Jax. "I didn't know that. Did you know that?"

He shook his head.

Antonia said, "The early Christians were convinced Jesus would return soon—as in, in their very own lifetimes. They had this idea that since one person—Jesus—had already been raised from the dead, that the rest of them couldn't be far behind. In fact, there was a serious crisis in the early church when some of the first followers of the Messiah began dying and He still hadn't returned. Anyone who reads Revelation and thinks he's reading something that was meant to serve as a prophesy of the end times two thousand years in the future needs to learn more about the origins of his faith."

Tobie said, "But if it's not meant as a prophesy about the end of the world, then what is it?"

"Basically, it's religious poetry, inspired by earlier Jewish prophets and the cosmic myths current in the Mediterranean at the time. The author of Revelation—or perhaps one should more accurately say the 'authors'—were interpreting their own times for the followers of Jesus. It's all about giving moral support to Christians at a time of persecution, and providing consolation for the dismal fate of humanity in general. Its central message is very simple, which is why it has resonated so powerfully through the ages."

"What's the message?"

"That in the struggle of good against evil, God is not neutral." Antonia gave a wry smile. "Of course, do you think anyone has ever read Revelation and identified themselves as being on the side of the forces of evil? Men are always saintly heroes in their own minds—even when they're committing murder. Somehow they find a way to convince themselves they have a 'good' reason for what they're doing."

Tobie said, "So the 'beast' in Revelation was really meant to be—what? Rome?"

"Definitely. So is the Great Whore. So is Babylon; they were all standard code words at the time for Rome—because the Roman state was the Christians' enemy." Antonia reached for the small plastic box she'd set aside. "And the famous scary 'mark of the beast' without which 'no one can buy or sell unless he bears it'?" She plucked a small disk from the box and tossed it at Jax.

He caught it easily and rubbed the surface with his thumb. It was a coin. A Roman coin, now covered in soot.

"Virtually all Roman coins circulating at that time carried the image of the emperor, which certain Jews and early Christians considered a violation of the strict interpretation of the commandment against images. You literally couldn't buy or sell without the 'mark of the beast.'"

Tobie looked up. "And the number 666?"

"Probably referred to Nero. The ancients had a system known as 'gematria,' in which every letter had a specific corresponding number. If you added up the numbers of the letters in a man's name, you'd get a numeric value. Nero's name written in Aramaic has the value of 666. If you write his name in Latin, the value comes up 616. Which is probably why some of the earliest copies of Revelation assign to the beast a different number: 616."

"What number appears in the Babylonian Codex?"

"The number 616."

Tobie studied the other woman's pale, drawn face. "So you've seen the codex?"

Antonia shook her head. "One verse only. What I know of the rest I know from my father's conversations with Dr. Araji."

"Given that he hadn't published his translation yet, I'm surprised Dr. Araji shared any of it with you," said Jax.

Antonia said, "Let me show you why."

55

Noah scrambled backward, his heavy pack clutched one-handed against his chest, the heat of the fire from the burning car scorching his face.

Fine, loose stones ripped at his palm. He was trembling uncontrollably, his breath coming in noisy, wheezy gasps. He kept propelling himself backward on one hand, pushing his butt along the ground, his heels digging into the dirt, his gaze mesmerized by the inferno before him.

The road here was narrow, cutting into the rocky red cliff. The Mercedes had landed sideways across the road, blocking it completely. The flames and smoke and dust obscured all visibility. Right now, the homicidal maniacs in the Land Rover were probably thinking Noah had died in the crash. But when the flames died down, they'd see him.

Shuddering with terror, he pushed to his feet and spun around to take off up the road. The crackling, whooshing roar of the flames covered the patter of his footsteps in the dirt. He sprinted hard around the curve, then kept running, lungs gasping for air, legs reaching.

The rocky red hillside hid him from sight. But before him stretched the wide, barren, empty expanses of the High Atlases, the ochre tones of the stony earth turning fiery red beneath the slanting rays of the setting sun. Already he could feel the temperature plunging.

Soon, it would be dark.

Washington, D.C. Monday 5 February
11:10 A.M. local time

After working through the weekend, Duane Davenport was taking the morning off, staying home with the kids, who were out of school thanks to the snow. At noon, his wife, a nurse, would take over. He was helping his five-year-old daughter, Molly, push a giant ball of snow around the yard in preparation for making what Molly was calling "the bestest snowman I ever built," when the call came through from Agent Brockman.

He took it standing on the front porch, with the snow melting off his boots into little puddles that spread across the gray concrete. "This had better be important," he said, watching Molly struggle to heave the giant ball of packed snow by herself. "I'm busy."

"The Sierra Leone connection has been terminated," said Brockman, choosing her words carefully. The line was unsecured, and if there was one thing Davenport had learned in this business, it's that you never knew who might be listening. "There was an interesting development."

"Oh?"

"The Ark Builder was there, too."

Noah Bosch. "Well I'll be damned," said Davenport. "I assume you got him, too?"

"Probably. But it's inconclusive at this point. There was a car crash and the vehicle burned," she added by way of explanation. "But we got something even more valuable."

"What's that?"

"His Blackberry."

56

Antonia Zapatero led them outside to a flagged terrace and then down a shallow set of steps to a winter-browned garden enclosed on two sides by high stone walls. At the base of the garden stood a squat stone building, its ancient, honey-toned walls badly eroded and battered by time. Up to the height of about five feet, the walls were formed of large, carefully dressed sandstone blocks; above that, the stones became irregular, cruder, as if the structure had been rebuilt at some point. Its only opening appeared to be a weathered door set into a horseshoe arch.

"There used to be two windows," said Antonia, reaching into her pocket for a large iron key. "But they've been walled up. You can see traces of them, there." She pointed to just below where the courses of irregular stone began. "Once there was obviously a second story, as well; we've found remnants of steps that would have led up to the women's gallery, since women are not permitted to worship with the men."

"This was originally a synagogue?" said Jax.

She unlocked the door and thrust it open. "Yes. The original structure dates back to the time when Medinaceli was a Roman city. It survived as a synogogue through the Moslem period, up until the time of the Reconquista. Then it was abandoned. At some point the building collapsed. When it was rebuilt, the floor was covered with earth. Which was fortunate for us because those six inches of dirt helped to preserve this—"

She flipped a switch mounted on the rough wall, and a string of bare bulbs strung overhead blazed.

"My God," whispered Jax.

The old prayer hall was some eighteen to twenty feet long and perhaps a few feet narrower. A stone bench two feet high ran along three walls. Above that, traces of *mudéjar* plasterwork added during the age of the Moors still clung in places to the walls. But what instantly drew and held their attention was the vast mosaic that covered the floor.

A geometric border rendered in jewel-like tones of blue and green and ochre formed the outer edges of the mosaic. The same tones were used to fashion the mosaic's large centerpiece: a medallion encircling a large, rampant lion. Flanking the lion stood two shepherds. They faced each other across the central medallion, each bearing a lamb on his shoulders. A Latin inscription ran along the sides and top of the mosaic. But on the fourth side, along the base, flowed a vast blue sea teeming with fish. And along the top of the water slithered a long, sinuous serpent with a forked tongue and ruby-red eyes.

"The inscription," said Tobie, her voice cracking so that she had to swallow. "What does it say?"

Jax whispered to her, "What? A dozen languages and you don't know Latin?"

Antonia smiled, "It says, 'A Lion shall rise up, God's right hand, and on his shield shall be written, God's justice, God's judgment, God's glory.' "

Jax said. "That's from the Babylonian Codex?"

"Yes. It's why Dr. Araji sent the verse to my father. My father gave a paper on the synagogue at a conference shortly before the invasion of Iraq, and Araji came up afterwards and told him the inscription was from the Codex."

"I don't understand," said Tobie. "How old is this mosaic?"

"It dates to sometime in the first century A.D."

"But . . . you said this was a Jewish synagogue, right? Why are there shepherds?"

"The image of the shepherd with a lamb over his shoulders was actually a common Roman symbol for the virtue of philanthropy. Love of humanity was revered as an important part of Roman life; as Roman Jews, the people who built this synagogue would have absorbed that. It's like the fish—" She pointed to the teaming sea. "Fish were a standard symbol for abundance in the Roman world."

"And the ruby-eyed snake?" said Tobie.

"According to Dr. Araji, it also appears in the codex." She kicked off her shoes. "You can walk out on it, if you are careful."

Slipping off their shoes, they followed her out onto the ancient paving.

She said, "In the early years of the Christian movement, there was no distinction made between Jews and Christians. But the destruction of the temple in Jerusalem proved to be a turning point. After that, those who insisted that Jesus was the Messiah were expelled from the synagogues. It's one of the main things that led to the Christians having trouble with the Romans. You see, the Jews had a long-standing deal with the emperor, which made them exempt from participating in the Roman civic rituals. As long as the Christians were considered Jews, then they too were protected. But once they became separate, they lost that protection. The Roman thinking was, if Christians weren't actually Jews, then Christianity couldn't be seen as part of an ancient religion that needed to be respected; it was just a new—and dangerous—superstition. In general, the Romans were actually very tolerant of religious diversity. As far as they were concerned, you could believe anything you wanted—as long as you did your civic duty by participating in the rituals."

"So you're saying—what? That this mosaic dates from the period before the Christians were expelled from the synagogues? And that's why the inscription from the lost verses of Revelation is here?"

"Perhaps. Or perhaps the lost chapter from the codex was part of an earlier Jewish work that is now lost but that was still extant when this mosaic was made. Right now, we just don't know."

Tobie hunkered down beside one of the four medallions that formed part of the border design. There was one medallion in each corner, with each medallion framing a different object. This one contained a golden menorah—a standard Jewish menorah, not a Syrian cross. She pivoted to study the other three medallions: a shofar, a sword, and a shield.

"What do the objects in the outer medallions mean?" she asked.

"Dr. Araji said they are also drawn from the Babylonian Codex's lost chapter. But he refused to send us the other verses."

Tobie sucked in a deep breath of cold, dank air. "Do you know of anyone else Dr. Araji might have sent some verses to?"

"I'm sorry, no."

They walked back up to the house in silence. At the terrace, she said, "I'm sorry I couldn't have helped you more."

"We appreciate all the information you've been able to

give us," said Tobie. "And we apologize for intruding on you at the time of your loss."

"Here," said Jax, holding out the Roman coin he still had in his hand.

She shook her head. "Keep it."

He brushed his thumb across the face of the emperor it bore. "So who is he? Which emperor?"

She gave a crooked smile. "The beast himself. Nero."

57

Noah caught a ride on the back of a motor scooter with a skinny teenager heading back to Marrakech after a visit to his grandmother's farm.

The kid rode like a maniac, leaning into the hairpin turns and weaving in and out of traffic as the lights of the ancient city drew closer. Normally Noah would have been nervous, riding without a helmet, trusting his life to someone who obviously took his culture's fatalistic attitude toward life to an extreme. Instead, he had to bite his tongue to keep from urging the kid on faster and faster.

The boy dropped Noah just outside Bab Agnaou, one of the ornately carved medieval gates to the medina. Walking quickly through the dark streets, he found a coffee shop near the Dar Si Said. There, huddled at a table next to the room's small heater, he logged onto his Hotmail account and sent a furious email zipping through the ether to Linda Lovelace.

You set me up!

The answer came back just minutes later. *What are you talking about?*

Noah typed, *You almost got me killed! I was jumped. Michael Hawkins is dead, and so is my driver.*

There was a long pause. Then, *I had nothing to do with that, Noah. Either they followed you out there or they came for Michael and you just got in the way. I am sorry about Michael. He was a good man.*

Noah typed, *I don't believe you. I think you set me up.*

Her reply came zipping back. *Don't be a fool. If I'd wanted you dead, I could have had you killed this morning, in Marrakech.*

He thought about it a moment and realized she was right. He typed, *I'm sorry. It's been a bad day.* Which was, he figured, the epic understatement of his life.

She answered, *Did you get the device?*

Noah stared at the screen, a shiver running up his spine. So she knew about the strange, deadly device. Why hadn't she told him about it? He hesitated, his hands hovering over the keys. Then he typed, *No.* He realized that sounded kind of bald, so added, *Hawkins told me about it.*

She wrote, *Do you have enough to publish this story?*

No, he typed. *I need the lost verses from the Babylonian Codex. Can you get them for me?*

He sat there for a long time, staring at his small screen, refreshing constantly to make sure he was still connected. Half an hour later, when he was about to give up and go looking for a room for the night, her reply came through.

Meet me in London, tomorrow morning. St. Giles Cripplegate. Nine o'clock.

He sucked in a deep breath. He wanted desperately to ask, Why? Why do you want to meet me again, when you refused to meet me for so long? If you have the codex why didn't you give it to me today?

But even more than before, the fear of offending her, of driving her away, stopped him. He did a quick online search to be sure he could make it from Marrakech to London in time. It would mean flying, of course, but that was a risk he was going to have to take.

He typed, *I'll be there.*

It wasn't until much later, when Noah was getting ready to board his flight to Madrid and London, that he discovered the torn side pocket on his pack.

He stared at it for a moment in confusion, then remembered catching the pack on a jagged piece of the doorframe as he was scrambling out of the taxi. He tried to remember what he'd stashed in there. Extra batteries for his digital camera. A box of Imodium ID.

His Blackberry.

He'd yanked the battery before he left Davos, knowing that anyone with the right connections to the U.S. intelligence community could use the phone's GPS system to track him. He hadn't given it a thought since then.

He rooted through the rest of his pack, just to make certain he hadn't stuck it someplace else. But the Blackberry was gone.

He clutched the battered, dusty pack to his chest, aware that he was starting to hyperventilate again. He tried to tell himself it didn't matter, that the phone would have been incinerated along with the car.

But the loss nagged at him, like the phantom pains from a missing limb.

58

By the time they reached the airport on the outskirts of Soria, Bubba already had his engines running.

"Another thirty seconds and I'da been outta here," he said, slamming the door closed behind them.

"Aw, come on Bubba," said Tobie, carefully taking a seat far away from Bubba's instrument panel. "You wouldn't have left without us. Would you?"

"Yes," said Bubba and Jax together.

Jax waited until they were airborne, then put in a call to Matt. "Hey, Matt—you know that fancy new search engine you've been bragging about? Well, here's some stuff I want you to run through it, along with every angle you've got on Carlyle and Patterson and Davenport: lamb, lion, serpent, shepherd, sea, fish, shofar, cross, sword, shield."

"Slow down, slow down," said Matt. "What was that last bit?"

"Sword and shield," repeated Jax.

"What is this shit?"

"It's from the lost chapter of the Babylonian Codex."

"You finally got a copy of it?"

"One verse. Plus hints at what's in a few more. Put it all through the GIS and see what you come up with."

"I thought you didn't believe in the GIS?"

"I don't."

Matt chuckled. "Then you're not going to believe this: I've been running a few searches myself and came up with something interesting. At around noon today, A.J. Carlyle—that's the latest Mrs. Leo Carlyle, by the way—flew from Marrakech to London."

"So? I understand she's quite the world traveler."

"Yeah, but here's the interesting part: according to Air Moroc, Noah Bosch is as we speak also flying from Morocco to London."

"Bosch is still alive?" Jax was aware of October looking up at him.

"At the moment. But wait; there's more. An ex-Special Forces guy by the name of Jason Cavanaugh is flying out of Morocco later tonight, also headed for London. According to our records, this Cavanaugh guy now works for Keefe's little band of mercenaries."

"Shit. What the hell is going on?"

"I don't know. But whatever it is, it's going on in London."

Jax looked over at Bubba. "Any chance we can fly to Berlin via London?"

"Nope."

"But the fate of the universe may hang in the balance."

"Yeah? Well my contract is definitely hanging in the balance. I'm late getting this shit to Berlin as it is. I can maybe drop you in London after I make my delivery."

"But—"

Bubba grunted. "If you don't like the schedule, pick a different airline next time."

Jax blew out a long breath, stared out the window at the dark, cloud-filled sky, then put in a call to Sean O'Reilly. "Hey, O'Reilly—you back in London?"

There was a pause. O'Reilly said, "What do you want, Jax?"

"There's a woman who flew into London this afternoon by the name of A. J. Carlyle. Owns a big house overlooking Hyde Park. I need you to set up surveillance on her until I can get there."

"What, the CIA has a manpower shortage or something?"

"Let's just say the Company and I aren't exactly simpatico at the moment."

"Again?"

"I'll explain the whole situation when we get on the ground. We should be landing at about four o'clock tomorrow morning."

"Eight," corrected Bubba.

O'Reilly snorted. "I'm doing this why?"

Jax said, "Thailand. And then there's always those pictures of you doing the Highland fling in a kilt."

"Hey. You were there, too."

"Yeah. But I've got a better-looking ass."

O'Reilly laughed. "I'll have a car waiting for you at the airstrip."

59

Duane Davenport whistled as he strode through the bustling corridors of the J. Edgar Hoover Building.

By now they knew that Noah Bosch had not, in fact, died in a fiery car crash in the desolate mountains of Morocco. But that was okay, because the asshole would be dead soon enough.

Bosch's Blackberry had given them access to the journalist's Hotmail account. From that, they discovered the exact nature of the inside information his mysterious "source" had been feeding him. And they learned that she would be meeting Bosch at nine A.M. in St. Giles Cripplegate in London.

Davenport waited until he reached his office before putting in a call to Brockman. "Status?" he asked.

"Jason and I are booked on the next flight from Marrakech to London. We'll be there by tomorrow morning."

Davenport could hear the *click-click* of her boot heels as

she walked rapidly through the tiled airport terminal. He said, "Don't miss him this time, Brockman."

"We won't, sir." The boot heels went *click-click-click*. "Any luck yet tracing the identity of this lindalovelace1974?"

Davenport stared down at the snow-snarled traffic on Pennsylvania Avenue. He now knew exactly who Noah Bosch's source was, but the matter was delicate. Very delicate. He said, "We're still working on it. I'll keep you posted."

After he got off the phone with Brockman, he lingered for a moment, watching the red brake lights of the traffic below. Then, smiling faintly to himself, he put in a call to Casper Nordstrom.

"We need to talk. Now."

Coeur d'Alene Lake, Idaho: Monday 5 February
5:10 P.M. local time

Leo Carlyle stood at the edge of his snow-covered dock looking out over the frozen surface of the lake toward the jagged mountains on the opposite shore. The snows had come late that winter. When Patterson visited the compound in early January to finalize their God-directed response to the election, only the distant peaks had shown a dusting of snow, with the wind churning the open waters of the lake beneath a wolf-colored sky. Now, the ice extended out for nearly a mile.

"I'm sorry, sir," said Casper Nordstrom, standing behind him. The man had flown all the way out from D.C., just to tell Leo what he had to say in person.

Leo snorted. "No, you're not. You never liked her."

Nordstrom kept silent. There was no reason, now, to deny it.

The wind coming in off the ice was cruel, stinging Leo's face and rustling the boughs of the mighty firs on the slope behind him. He knew he and A.J. had been drifting apart—hell, he'd already decided it was time to move on. But who'd have thought the bitch would have the guts—or the brains—to betray him like this?

He felt a deep, powerful welling of anger, and turned to his assistant. "You say Davenport already has two people on their way to London to take care of this journalist?"

"Yes, sir."

Carlyle nodded and swung away from the lake. "Tell him to take care of her, too."

60

Tobie stared out the Gulfstream's window at the endless urban landscape sprawled beneath a cold gray sky. "Think there's any chance A. J. Carlyle could be Noah Bosch's source?"

"Nah," said Jax, coming to sit beside her. "I doubt she knows what Hubby is up to. Apart from which, even if she did, I can't see a woman like her caring."

Tobie swung her head to look at him. "What do you mean, 'a woman like her'? What's she like?"

"Beauty queen. Former Miss Colorado."

"Don't be a bigot," said Tobie. "Not all beauty queens are shallow, airheaded narcissists."

"No?"

"No. And if she's not his source, then what was she doing in Morocco?"

"Even if she is his source, what was she doing in Morocco? And what the hell are they both doing in London?"

" . . . with a killer after them?" added Tobie, her gaze drifting back to the neat pattern of streets and rooftops rushing toward them. "I wonder which one this guy Cavanaugh is here for."

Jax went to slip back into the copilot's seat. "Maybe both."

Noah stood at the front of the coffee shop, his gaze on the sandstone facade and soaring west tower of the church across the square.

The coffee shop was warm and sweetly scented with the aroma of freshly baked cinnamon buns. The morning had dawned overcast and misty, the bare trees in the square standing out dark and skeletal against a flat white sky. Surrounded by the ugly modern expanse of the Barbican, the medieval church of St. Giles Cripplegate looked forlorn and out of place, its gracefully arched windows and soaring buttresses a sad reminder of a lost age. The church stood isolated in the midst of a paved expanse of what Noah realized must once have been the old churchyard. Did they move the bodies, he wondered; or just pave right over them?

He'd been watching the church for twenty minutes now. But the only activity he'd seen was a stout matron in a blue wool coat and tightly permed gray hair who marched across the square and went in through the arched door at the base of the tall bell tower. She stayed for no more than five minutes and then came out again. Glancing at the date on his watch, he realized today was Shrove Tuesday.

Shifting his weight, he took a sip of his coffee and found it cold. He was just setting the cup aside when a black London cab pulled up at the edge of the square and a woman got out.

Noah watched her walk quickly along the side of the nave, toward the west front. She was tall and slender, wearing knee high black leather boots and a black cashmere coat. In place of the veil she'd adopted in Marrakech she wore a giant floppy hat and a pair of oversized sunglasses, but he knew it was her. She cast a nervous glance around, then ducked into the church.

Noah checked his watch. It was ten to nine.

He waited a few minutes, just to make certain no one was following her. Then he darted across the square and went in after her.

She was standing just to the left of the entrance, behind the last row of golden oak pews. She had her head tipped back, her gaze taking in the soaring wooden trusses of the ceiling, the clustered marble pillars that marched along the side aisles. At the sound of the door opening she turned, her body tensing. But at the sight of Noah, she visibly relaxed. She said, "You're early."

Noah sucked in a deep breath heavy with the scent of cold stone and incense and beeswax. "I was watching the church. I wanted to make sure you came alone."

"You don't trust me?"

"I only have your word for it that I wasn't set up in Telouet." He studied her face, but the hat threw dark shadows across her smooth-skinned, fine-boned features. He said, "I don't know who you are. I don't know why you're doing this. I'm not even sure why I'm here."

"You're here for the story." Her upper lip curled a bit when she said it, and he realized it was with contempt. For *him.*

Stung, he said, "So why are you here?"

"Me? I'm here to stop Carlyle."

"Why?"

She tightened her fist around the strap of the elegant little black Prada bag she carried. "Because if these people have their way, they'll destroy everything that makes America great. I don't want my children to grow up in a country run by a bunch of intolerant, religious fanatics who think people are poor because Jesus obviously hates them and untrammeled free-market capitalism is a divinely ordained economic system."

"That sounds really good. But why should I believe you?"

Again, that little curl of the lip. "Because, unlike you, I have nothing to gain and everything to lose by what I'm doing."

He felt a flush of anger heat his cheeks. "You think I haven't suffered because of this story?"

"This isn't just a *story*." She tilted her head to one side, as if the eyes behind those sunglasses were studying him and finding him somehow wanting. "I wonder: if you had a choice between saving your country and saving your story, which would you choose?"

"I don't see why I can't do both. The problem is, right now, I can't do either. This story is going nowhere. I have no proof of anything, and the one potential witness to part of the story I did have is now dead."

She drew in a hard breath that flared her delicate nostrils. "Tell me what you need. What will it take to get this out there?"

Noah cast a quick look down the length of the aisle toward the east window and lowered his voice. "You said they're using the lost verses from the Babylonian Codex as their blueprint. I need those verses."

"What are you willing to do to get them?"

Noah studied her beautiful, self-possessed face. *Who the hell was she?* Aloud, he said, "I don't understand."

She turned to walk slowly up the north aisle, Noah beside her, their footsteps echoing in the vast space. Her voice was little more than a whisper. "Leo Carlyle has been collecting Mesopotamian artifacts for the last fifteen years. The legitimate pieces that he buys on the open market are scattered throughout his various houses. But the illegal stuff—the antiquities he buys on the black market—are kept in his house on Coeur d'Alene Lake in Idaho. In a secret gallery that opens off the library."

"He has the Babylonian Codex there?" Noah asked sharply. More sharply than he'd intended.

"*Shh*," she cautioned, although there was no one around. "The manuscripts are kept in a special climate-controlled room off the main gallery. Just to the left of the door is a fireproof metal cabinet where he stores the digital copies of his manuscripts, along with their translations."

Noah stared at her. "How the hell do you know all of this?"

Reaching up, she took off her sunglasses and hat and shook out her long flaxen hair. "Because I'm his wife."

Jax found O'Reilly himself waiting at the edge of the runway, a white cloud of exhaust streaming from the rear of his sleek, dark blue Jag.

"Well, this is service," said Jax, opening the front door for October before sliding into the backseat himself.

O'Reilly threw the Jag into gear and hit the gas. "Your girl is moving. She left the house five minutes ago in a cab. I've got a couple of lads on her tail. She's headed toward St. Giles Cripplegate."

Jax filled O'Reilly in as they battled their way through morning London traffic. They were still on A 501 when a call came through from O'Reilly's lads: the target was nearing the Barbican.

"Why St. Giles Cripplegate?" said Jax.

"Can't imagine."

Ten minutes later, whipping around the corner onto Fore Street, O'Reilly swooped in close to the curb and killed the engine. A redhead with ruddy cheeks got out of the unmarked white van parked near the corner and walked toward them. O'Reilly punched down his window.

"She's in the church," said the agent. "About five minutes after she went in, a slim bloke in a torn tan canvas jacket and jeans went in after her. Neither one has come out."

Jax threw open his door. "That sounds like Bosch." He glanced back at O'Reilly, "You got a spare gun for October?"

O'Reilly pulled a Browning 9mm from the glove compartment and handed it to her. "What? You guys don't carry your own?"

"I should probably warn you I'm a lousy shot," she said, holding the gun awkwardly.

O'Reilly cast his eyes heavenward. "The Lord preserve us. Just be careful where you go pointing that thing, all right?" He slid out the car. "Come on. Let's go scoop up your compatriots before the bad guys get them."

61

A.J. Carlyle drew a thick sealed envelope from her Prada purse. "Here. This contains the key to the Idaho house, along with a sketch of the layout and all the access codes you'll need. I've also included a description of the compound's security equipment and guard schedule. There's a dog named Barracuda, but he shouldn't be a problem if you come prepared. I've explained it all in—"

"Hang on," said Noah, his hand tightening convulsively around the envelope. "What do you think I can do with this? I'm a journalist, not a thief!"

The pale white light from the high arched window above them streamed down across her flawless profile. "Surely you know someone—"

"No. What kind of company do you think I keep? It's your house; why don't you just sneak into this gallery and take the translation of the codex yourself?"

"Because the cabinet where he keeps the digital copies of his manuscripts and the translations is locked. It's a keyed lock, not a code pad, and as far as I know Leo has the only key. I've given you everything you need *except* that. If you can find someone who—" She broke off, her eyes widening, her chest jerking on a quickly indrawn breath as she looked around wildly. "What was that? Did you hear it?"

"Hear what?"

"There's someone else here."

"There can't be. I was watching the place before you came. You're probably just—"

And then Noah heard it, too. The quiet scuff of a sole against stone.

"Oh, my God," he whispered, just as the *pop-pop* of a suppressed pistol shattered the silence.

He dove between the two nearest pews. But A.J. Carlyle stood oddly rigid. Glancing back, he saw an expression of vague surprise come over her features. She took one awkward step, then staggered to her knees. As if in slow motion, she pitched forward onto her face. He could see a shiny black wetness sheeting her back.

Oh God, Oh God, he prayed, scrambling along the cold marble floor on his hands and knees. He was wedged in between the seat of one pew and the back of the next. Trapped.

Then he heard another *pop*, and the back of the pew beside his head exploded into splinters.

"Let me do the talking," Jax told October as they trotted across the paved square. The crumbling remnant of one of the old round barbicans from the vanished London city walls rose up incongruously beside them.

"If you don't mind," said O'Reilly, "this is my country, remember? I'll handle this." The Irishman pushed open the heavy wooden door at the base of the tower and then yelped as a spray of bullets chewed through wood and stone beside them. *"Bloody hell!"*

Dragging October with him, Jax dove sideways behind the ancient stone lintel. "Stay here and don't let anyone out," he told her, yanking his Beretta from the holster at the small of his back.

Quickly chambering a round, he glanced at O'Reilly, crouched down on the far side of the door.

Whipping out a Sig 226, O'Reilly yelled to his guys from the van. "Get around the back of the church! Now!" Then he met Jax's gaze and nodded.

The two men exploded into the church together, Jax lunging to one side, O'Reilly to the other. A big dude in a black leather jacket creeping down the right aisle swung his Glock toward them. O'Reilly's 9mm slugs caught the asshole square in the chest, the impact of the big bullets slamming the mercenary against the wall hard enough to leave a bloody smear as he slid down. The percussion of the blast contained within the thick stone walls was deafening.

They hunkered low behind the rear pews, their gazes sweeping the long, soaring nave. An eerie silence had fallen over the church. The cold, misty light streaming in through the clear high windows bathed the space in a white glow. The interior of the church was a study in contrasts, dark wooden ceiling and row after row of oaken pews standing out stark against the pale sandstone walls and marble floor.

His Beretta held at the ready, Jax crept up the side aisle, toward the altar. The air was thick with the smell of dank stone and old incense and freshly spilled blood. At the base of one of the marble columns he came upon the crumpled body of A.J. Carlyle.

From up near the chancel came the sound of a door being thrown open. A shaft of light streamed into the darkened nave.

"Shit," swore O'Reilly, charging up.

They heard a shout, followed by a burst of gunfire, the *crack* of a Glock answered by the boom of a .40 caliber pistol. Then a motor gunned. They heard a squeal of tires and more shots.

"Morgan? Cooper!" shouted O'Reilly, sprinting down the aisle.

He barged through the chancelry door, Jax right behind him.

The redhead from the van was down, dark blood streaming from his leg, with his partner hunkered beside him and trying desperately to stop the flow. "It was a woman! A fucking woman with long blond hair!"

"Did you see the car? Call it in, man!" Holstering his Sig, O'Reilly yanked out his phone and went to crouch beside his fallen man. "I need two ambulances! Quick."

Jax swiped the back of one hand across his forehead and turned back to the church.

Tobie was standing just inside the door at the base of the west tower. She had O'Reilly's Browning held in a steady, two-handed grip, its muzzle pressed into the back of Noah Bosch's skull.

Two hours later, Jax, October, and O'Reilly were sitting around the kitchen table of a safe house in Notting Hill.

O'Reilly said, "The dude with the Glock has been identified as Jason Cavanaugh. He flew in from Marrakech this morning."

"Thought so. Anyone on the flight manifest with him?"

"No one who booked their ticket at the same time." O'Reilly spread immigration photographs of six women across the table. "Recognize anyone?"

Jax scanned the faces of women old and young, fair and dark. He paused for a moment over the photo of a youngish woman with an unfashionable short dark pageboy, heavy glasses and big teeth. She looked vaguely familiar in some way. But he couldn't place her and shook his head. "Nope."

October said, "Does the press know about A.J. Carlyle?"

O'Reilly picked up the pictures and thrust them into a file.

"All they know is that an unidentified woman was shot in an apparent robbery in St. Giles Cripplegate."

"How's she doing?"

"She's in the ICU. It's still touch and go, but we've decided to let it out—quietly, of course—that she's dead. See what that turns up."

Jax pushed to his feet. "Shall we go talk to Mr. Noah Bosch?"

Special Agent Laura Brockman stood before the bathroom mirror. From the distance came the crackling announcement of a flight boarding being repeated in one unintelligible language after the other. Working quickly, she twisted her long blond hair up around the crown of her head and eased the black wig over it. The effect was not flattering.

Smiling, she slipped in a set of prosthetic upper teeth that gave her a bad overbite, then crowned it all off with a pair of really ugly plastic framed glasses. She smiled again at her reflection in the mirror and gave the pageboy wig one last twitch.

Then she shouldered her carry-on bag and went to catch her flight to D.C.

62

Noah perched nervously on the edge of a single bed covered in cheerful floral chintz.

The bedroom was decorated in what Julie used to call English-country-house chic: chintz balloon shade at the window, a dark Victorian dresser with a white marble top, a round bedside table covered with a cutwork scarf, a gently-aged bentwood chair. A disinterested observer coming upon the cozy nook at the top of the stairs might find it hard to believe Noah was a prisoner—unless they noticed the bars behind the chintz shade and the guard posted on the other side of the door.

He sat with his elbows on his knees, his hands clasped together and pressed against his lips. They'd searched him and taken his backpack and the envelope A. J. Carlyle had given him, but they hadn't hurt him. He kept telling himself he was safe. These people had saved his life, right?

But he didn't feel safe. He wondered if he'd ever feel safe again.

The sound of the door being unlocked brought his head up. Two of the people he'd encountered in the church—the

American guy and the girl who'd threatened to shoot him in the fucking head—came in and closed the door behind them.

The guy had Noah's backpack in his hands.

Noah straightened, but stayed where he was, his palms flattening against his thighs.

The American gave Noah a big smile that showed his teeth but did nothing to warm his cold blue eyes. "Hi there. I'm Jax Alexander." He nodded to the woman. "This is Ensign October Guinness." The girl went to lean against the cheerfully draped window, but the guy just stood there in a way Noah didn't like.

The guy said, "We know you've been investigating the dominionists. We know you were in Davos when the Vice President died. And we know you were in Spain when Zapatero was killed." He paused. "Being around you seems to be bad for other people's health, Mr. Bosch."

Noah stared at him. When he remained silent, Alexander pulled up the bentwood chair and sat directly in Noah's line of vision.

"What we don't know is what you were doing in Morocco." Alexander reached into Noah's backpack. "And where the *hell* did you get this?"

Noah found himself staring at the strange device given him by Michael Hawkins. He cleared his throat uncomfortably. But his voice was still a frightened croak. "Why should I trust you?"

"I'm not sure you have much of an option at this point, Mr. Bosch. How long do you think you'll last if we put you back out on the street? You seem to be very unpopular with someone."

Noah felt his stomach burn. For one, humiliating moment, he thought he might be sick.

Alexander exchanged glances with the woman. Unlike Alexander, she wasn't smiling. But she still managed to look a hell of a lot nicer—even if she had nearly made him crap his pants by putting a gun to his head.

She said, "Tell us, Noah."

Hunching forward, he let the story come tumbling out. It came in bits and pieces, with plenty of questions and back-tracking before it made much sense.

Alexander said, "You expect me to believe you had no idea you were dealing with Leo Carlyle's wife?"

Noah looked at him. "Why the hell would I lie about that at this point?"

Guinness drew from her pocket the envelope A.J. Carlyle had given him. The envelope had been opened. She said, "Why did Mrs. Carlyle give you this?"

Noah scrubbed one hand over his lower face. Christ, he needed a shave. And a bath. And clean clothes. He said, "That's where the Babylonian Codex is. In Idaho. She gave me the layout of the house and all the access codes and stuff."

Alexander said, "What did she think you were going to do with it?"

"She had some crazy idea I could break in and steal the digital copy of the codex." He tried to laugh, but it sounded weird even to his own ears.

He watched as Alexander turned his head and looked up to find the woman regarding him with a fixed expression.

"Oh, no you don't," Alexander told her. "Don't get any ideas."

She smiled. "Why not? You've got everything you need right here. What could possibly go wrong?"

"Something can always go wrong."

Half an hour later, Noah found himself whisked out of London to a small private airfield where a plain white Gulfstream waited. The pilot was some big, cranky Cajun who kept complaining about his "schedule" even as they were taxiing down the runway. Noah had a feeling they were taking him with them mainly because O'Reilly had said he didn't want to have to deal with "that bloody journalist" and no one seemed to know what else to do with him. Noah tried hard to hide his elation, but he doubted he succeeded. He was alive, and he was still on his story. Maybe there would be a Pulitzer Prize in his future after all.

"So," he said, going to sit across from his two rescuers once the jet was airborne over the Atlantic. "Turnabout is fair play, right?"

They looked at him questioningly.

Noah said, "I told you what I know. Now you tell me what you know. Right?"

"No," said Alexander. He had spread a bar towel on top of the built-in mahogany table that ran along one side of the jet's cabin and was in the process of cleaning his Beretta.

Noah was getting to the point of really disliking this guy. "Am I under arrest?"

The guy didn't even look up. "No."

"So as soon as we land, I'm free to go?"

"No."

"But . . . you can't just keep me against my will. That's like, kidnapping or something."

Alexander clicked the Beretta's slide back into place. "Yes."

Noah looked at the woman. "You're in—what? The Navy?"

"Yes."

Noah nodded toward Alexander. "Is he in the Navy, too?"

"No."

"So who's he with?"

"The federal government."

Noah had been a journalist long enough to knew what that meant. Everyone he'd ever met who said they were with the "federal government" was really with the CIA. "So the good guys know about this plot, right? It's just a matter of nailing these bastards?"

Alexander and Guinness exchanged guarded looks. Neither smiled, and Noah felt his earlier optimism begin to slip away.

"I think maybe we do need to tell him a little bit," she said.

"You may be right." Alexander slipped the Beretta back into its holster. "Ever shoot an assault rifle?"

Noah felt his heart slam up against his chest. "I've never shot a *gun*. Period."

Alexander slid off the bench. "Well, that may be about to change."

By the time the Gulfstream touched down at the icy airstrip on the shores of Lake Coeur d'Alene, Idaho, the winter sun had slipped low in the sky to throw a rich golden light over the snow-clad, tree-covered slopes.

Bubba and Jax had spent most of the flight from London calling in a lifetime of favors, pre-assembling everything from snowshoes and an M4 carbine to a tub of Ben and Jerry's ice cream and a neat little red-and-white MD 600 helicopter.

Tobie took one look at the chopper and groaned. "I don't understand why we can't just *drive* out to Carlyle's lodge."

"Because it's a long lake, and the estate is way down at the other end."

"So? We aren't planning to go in until midnight anyway."

"Yeah. But we might need to make a quick getaway." Jax threw open the cabin doors. "Don't worry; Bubba's a great helicopter pilot. He's only crashed three times."

"Twice," Bubba corrected him.

"You're forgetting Laos."

Bubba hitched up his tattered jeans. "That one doesn't count."

63

The photogenic young representative from Utah stared into the TV camera, her luminous dark eyes dewy with emotion. "I don't think this president is a real American. Listen to him! He's talking about joining with other countries to create international laws to restrict our freedoms. What is this? The New World Order? Americans need to be asking themselves, *Who does this man really answer to?* What is his agenda here? Frankly, I'm afraid for my country. I'm afraid—"

"Turn it off, Daniel," said Senator Savoie, a gin and tonic cradled in one hand. "Why torture yourself?"

President Pizarro pointed the remote at the screen and zapped the ostentatiously frightened politician into oblivion. "Jeez. Did you hear her? Next thing you know they'll be talking about black helicopters and stockpiling weapons in fortified bunkers."

Savoie settled deeper into his chair, his eyes crinkling into a smile. "What makes you think they're not already?"

Pizarro went to stand at the window overlooking the snow-filled gardens below. "I don't understand. Why can't they get it? We've entered a new era, when money and corporations move freely across national borders in a way that people and regulations can't. We've got to do something to control the disastrous trends of the last three decades, otherwise the entire world will end up being owned by a handful of corporations, and the rest of us are going to be reduced to the status of wage-earning serfs."

Savoie took a slow sip of his gin and tonic. "Careful, Daniel, or you're going to start sounding as crazy as they do."

Pizarro gave a rueful laugh and came to sit down opposite his friend. But he couldn't relax. "My wife, Pat, didn't want me to run for president. She's convinced they're going to try to kill me."

"They probably will," said Savoie, draining his glass. "At least once. We just need to make sure they don't succeed."

The two men sat on the snowy bleachers overlooking the ice-skating pond.

"You're certain A.J. is dead?" said Nordstrom.

"She's dead." Davenport watched a small girl out on the ice tilt back her head and go into a surprisingly professional spin. "We've had confirmation from two different associates in Scotland Yard. The incident is being kept quiet at the request of MI6."

"I don't like the sound of that."

Davenport shook his head. "It's nothing to worry about."

"And the reporter?"

"We're still dealing with the reporter."

"The way you're 'dealing' with the witch?"

Davenport tightened his jaw. "Neither one of them knows anything."

"You think."

"Even if they had the codex itself, they would never put the pieces together in time."

Nordstrom glanced at his watch. "Everything is in place for tomorrow?"

Davenport pushed to his feet. "By this time tomorrow night, the United States will have a godly man as president."

64

The night was clear, the northern sky a deep purple sparkled with an endless universe of stars.

Bubba flew low over the lake, the starlight throwing the chopper's shadow across the white snow as they hugged the shoreline. The quiet drone of the engine echoed off the steep, snow-blanketed slopes that rose beside them; the branches of the towering stands of fir and pine glistened white with a new-fallen snow. Looking out toward the middle of the lake, Tobie could see a black belt of open water edged by banks of white. But much of the lake was frozen over, the ice extending out for a good half mile from shore.

They passed in low over Carlyle's estate, a blast of frigid air filling the chopper's small cabin as Jax leaned out to study the compound. Built of rustic unpeeled logs and river-smoothed stones, the main house sat on a rise overlooking the frozen lake. They could see a pavilion down near the lakeshore and a guardhouse farther up the slope near the road, its steeply pitched roof thick with snow. Beyond that lay the runway Tobie had seen in her first remote viewing. They'd studied the compound on Google Earth, comparing

A.J.'s diagram with the layout in the satellite shots. It had all lined up perfectly.

"Looks good," said Noah Bosch, an M4 clutched awkwardly in his lap as he peered out the window.

Tobie didn't say anything. She was so nervous she was having a hard time breathing.

About a mile up the lakeshore, Bubba brought the chopper down on a broad snow-covered clearing before an empty estate with a For Sale sign out front.

"Just give us a holler if you need us," said Bubba, fishing a string of beef jerky out of his pocket and tearing off a mouthful. "I'll come pluck y'all off the end of the dock."

Jax threw open the doors. It was so cold that Tobie could feel the insides of her nostrils freeze as she drew in a quick breath. But her body was warm, almost hot, thanks to the insulated white reflective jumpsuits they wore. According to A.J. Carlyle's notes, the estate was protected by heat-activated infrared cameras; the suits would keep their body heat from escaping and setting off the alarms.

"Ready?" said Jax, shouldering a backpack.

She hopped out beside him. The truth was, she was scared half to death. But all she could say was, "Ready."

The night was unbelievably still, the only sound the soft exhalations of their breath and the squeaky crunch of the dry snow beneath their aluminum-and-Lytex snowshoes. They approached the compound from the frozen lake, the snow-draped mountains looming above them, silent and majestic. As they swung around a point, the lodge came into view.

"Look like what you saw?" Jax asked quietly.

"Yes."

He glanced over at her. "What's it like, to see in person something you've seen before, but only in your own mind?"

"Pretty weird, actually."

He huffed a soft laugh.

A long, empty pier stretched out into the iced-over lake. They leaned against its rough planking and unbuckled their snowshoes. "I just hope everybody's asleep," whispered Tobie, staring up at the dark windows of the sprawling lodge. The place was huge.

"If anything happens to me," Jax reminded her, "call Bubba and run like hell for this dock."

Tobie swallowed, hard. "Got it."

Their reflective suits white against the white of the snow, they crept up the hill to the lodge, to where a door opened off a small porch on the eastern wing.

The exhalation of her breath billowing white around her, Tobie watched as Jax slid the key A.J. had given Noah into the lock. It turned with a soft click. Jax gave the door a nudge, and it swung inward before them on well-oiled hinges.

He cast her a quick glance. *So far, so good.*

Slipping inside, they closed the door quietly behind them. They found themselves in a small mudroom that opened off the kitchen. Beside a rack of skis and poles in various sizes hung a security panel blinking red in the gloom. Jax punched in the four digit code A.J. had provided, and the light blinked from red to green.

"Huh," whispered Jax, as if surprised. "This may just work after all."

"Um . . . Barracuda," said Tobie as the shadow of a big black Doberman rose up, teeth bared in a low, menacing growl. Tobie held herself very, very still. "Nice Barracuda."

"Look what we brought you," said Jax, pulling the tub of Ben and Jerry's French Vanilla from his pack and prying off the lid. "Your favorite." He set the ice cream on the floor and nudged it toward the dog.

Barracuda growled again.

"It's not working," whispered Tobie, a bead of sweat rolling down her cheek.

"Maybe he's in the mood for chocolate?"

"We didn't bring chocolate!"

Barracuda took two steps toward them. Tobie stopped breathing. Then the dog's ears came up. His tail wagged, and he dropped his head to the ice cream.

"Slowly," mouthed Jax.

They skittered around the dog into a kitchen of rustic pine cabinets and very expensive industrial-size Viking appliances. As they cut across to the hall, Tobie slipped a Tazer from the holster on her belt and held it in a tight grip. She'd decided she really wasn't cut out for housebreaking. Her stomach hurt, and her hands were shaking, and she was having a hard time breathing.

Jax said, "Relax."

She glared at him.

Carlyle's library lay at the end of the hall. Slipping inside, they closed the door carefully behind them. The insulated curtains at the windows blanketed the room in almost total darkness, and they paused to don night-vision goggles. The room suddenly came into focus, all wood paneling and soft velvet and glass-eyed dead-animal heads mounted high on the walls.

"There," whispered Tobie. Crossing to the tall bookcase beside the hearth, she lifted the lid on a small carved wooden chest to reveal a recessed keypad. She punched in the three-digit code and a section of the bookcase swung slowly inward.

"Wow," she said softly. "That's neat."

A long gallery stretched before them, lined with glass-fronted cases.

"Look," whispered Jax. "It's the Inanna Vase."

Tobie studied the gleaming alabaster vessel. "That's what I was supposed to RV?"

"Yes."

They found the door to the manuscript chamber just beyond the vase. While Jax yanked off his gloves and went to hunker down in front of the locked metal cabinet, Tobie prowled the room.

It was much as she had seen it: the long table, the wall-mounted racks with their acrylic-encased manuscript pages. Unable to resist, she holstered her Taser and went to slide one of the mounts from its slot.

She found herself staring at an ancient sheet of papyrus, the reeds of the paper yellowed and faded, but the ink still amazingly dark and clear despite the passage of the centuries.

"Do you mind?" whispered Jax, switching on a penlight.

Slipping the manuscript back into its place, she went to hold the light for him.

"You need to teach me how to do this," she said, watching him work his pick in the lock.

He smiled as the tension wrench turned the cylinder with a little *click.* "First I need to teach you how to shoot." He eased the cabinet door open to reveal rows and rows of disks.

She started to skim through the titles, but Jax jerked the pack off his back and started dumping disks into it. "We take them all; we don't have time to be picky." Quickly shouldering the loaded pack, he closed the door to the cabinet and pushed to his feet. "Let's get the hell out of here."

But when they opened the door from the library to the hall, they could see a rectangle of light thrown across the floor from the kitchen.

"Shit," whispered Jax. "Somebody got hungry."

Tobie reached for her Taser. "Do we wait until they go away?"

Jax shook his head. "Too risky. They might decide to check on Barracuda and find the ice cream."

Creeping to the kitchen door, they could see a big, muscle-

bound guy dressed in camos and talking into the mike he
wore clipped onto his shoulder as he slathered mayonnaise
on six pieces of bread. "Okay, Corey; I got mayo, turkey,
ham, cheese, lettuce, and tomato. You want some pickles? I
think we may even have—" He swung around, saw Jax and
Tobie standing in the doorway, and yelled, "Intruders!" just
as Tobie zapped him with her Taser.

He went down hard, his body convulsing uncontrollably.

She stared at him in horror and dropped the Taser.

Jax was already sprinting across the kitchen toward the
door. "*Come on!*"

Bursting out the back door, they pelted down the slope
toward the lake. Behind them, Barracuda set up a ferocious,
belated barking.

"*Plan B!*" Jax yelled into his radio. "Now, Bubba. *Now!*"

A door at the far end of the house slammed open. Throwing a quick glance over her shoulder, Tobie saw a guy in
boxers and a T-shirt burst out onto the wide porch, a big gun
in his hands. "Oh, crap," she said, just as a spray of bullets
kicked up the snow around them.

Jax yanked out his Beretta and sent two or three slugs
thumping into the thick logs beside the guy's head.

The hero with the gun ducked for cover.

"Come on, Bubba," said Jax as they sprinted out onto the
dock.

Behind them, two guys with M16s roared over the crest of
the hill in an ATV, gunning hard through the snow.

"Bubba!"

The MD 600 swooped in over the frozen lake. Bubba
came in fast, bypassing the dock to take a sharp turn over the
ATV. The guys on the ATV took one look at those swooping
skids, cried, "Fuck!" and bailed off into the deep powder.
The empty ATV roared into a snowdrift and stalled.

Bubba wheeled and swung in low. Jax dove through the

open door while Noah hauled Tobie in behind him. A spray of bullets thumped into the dock and punched through the chopper's skin.

"Shit! We're outta here!" yelled Bubba, snow swirling around them as he kicked the MD 600 up. "Jesus H. Christ, Jax! You *always* do this to me. Can't you ever just *walk* out of a place?"

65

They waited until they were back in the Gulfstream and headed for D.C. before popping the disk neatly labeled "Babylonian Codex, translation" into Bosch's laptop.

Jax set the computer up on the jet's built-in mahogany table and flipped through the first verses. "Ha," he said. "Here it is. The lost chapter. Right between Chapter Four and what is now considered Chapter Five."

Tobie came to sit on the bench beside him, with Noah Bosch leaning over the table.

Jax read, "'And the angels said, behold the final days are fast approaching and it will come to past that the time of the world has ripened and the time for the harvest of the seeds of the evil ones and the good ones has come. And it shall be a time when inequity, and sin, and blasphemy, and wrong, and all manner of evil deeds increase, and when apostasy, wickedness, and uncleanness increase.'"

He paused for a moment, thoughtful.

Bosch said in an odd, hushed voice, "It sounds just like the Bible."

"That's because it all came out of the same literary tradition," said Jax.

Tobie leaned over Jax's shoulder and read the next verse. "'And it shall come to pass that the people dwelling in the nation of the Lord shall turn away from him, and they shall not perceive nor shall they hear, for they shall be given over to licentiousness. And they shall raise up cities of sin, Sodom and Gomorrah, and Babylon and Egypt, and they shall girt them with high walls and dwell there in darkness. And the Lord shall not be pleased.'"

"I guess you could interpret that to mean the United States today," said Bosch, frowning.

"Every age thinks they're drowning in licentiousness and inequity," said Jax. "Even the Victorians. Make that *especially* the Victorians."

Tobie kept reading. "'And He shall send a great rising of the sea as a warning, and many thunders and great lightnings shall cleave the sky. And the waters that flow through the reeds of life like a ruby-eyed serpent shall rise up—'" She broke off. "The ruby-eyed snake! There it is!"

"What?" Bosch looked from one to the other. "What ruby-eyed snake?"

"Never mind," said Jax, and took over reading again. "'A ruby-eyed serpent shall rise up and the sea with it, and then shall all the lakes and channels spill over. And the walls shall tumble down and the hills part, and the waters of wrath shall sweep over Sodom and Gomorrah, over Babylon and Egypt, killing all before them. And when they recede all shall be left as dust, and the sun shall be cut in half like the moon, and the moon shall not give her light.'"

"That's the part Patterson was quoting in his sermon the other night," said Tobie, sitting back with a soft thump. "But . . . I don't understand. What does it mean? How could anyone use this as a blueprint for anything?"

"Maybe it makes more sense as it goes along," said Jax. "Listen. 'But the people shall not heed the Lord's warning. And a bull shall come up out of the south, and that bull shall be red not white. And the wicked shall follow him as a new king, an evil-minded man, much-bloodied and given to wickedness, a dark and ominous prince whom all noble men despise, for he laid hands on the womb.' "

Bosch began to pace back and forth in the short aisle. "That line about 'much-bloodied' is interesting. I can see how the dominionists could interpret that as a reference to President Pizarro. Pizarro was a doctor before he went into politics, right? Plus you could say his parents 'came up out of the south'."

"Okay," said Jax. "I can see that. And then this next part would make sense, too: 'He shall reign a short time, but in those days there shall be all manner of evils.' If they assassinate him, Pizarro would certainly only 'reign a short time.' "

Tobie said, "He hasn't exactly had a chance to do 'all manner of evils.' "

"I guess that depends on your point of view," said Jax, and continued reading. " 'And he shall come declaring himself equal to God. But he shall prove that he is not, though with his words he shall promise to shore up the hills and calm the seas and restore life. And he shall lead men astray and gather lost men who have turned away from word of God.' "

Jax paused to look up, one eyebrow raised in silent inquiry. But Tobie and Bosch just shook their heads.

Jax said, "Here's the part from the mosaic in Medinaceli, 'And then a Lion shall rise up, God's right hand, and on his shield shall be written, *God's justice, God's judgment, God's glory.* And there shall come to pass before the final days a war that will throw the world into chaos and despair. A man who is a matricide shall come from the ends of the earth envisioning all manner of wickedness. And Beliar shall descend in the form of a man, a lawless king, slayer of his mother, who will persecute the fruits of the tree the

Twelve Apostles of the Beloved have nurtured. And he will claim to work for the glory of the Beloved and say, I am God, and after me there shall be no others. And the people of all lands shall believe him and venerate him, saying, *This is God.*' "

Jax frowned. "So who's this other guy supposed to be? Bill Hamilton? It can't be Carlyle. Beliar is another name for Satan, right?"

"Maybe they're both meant to be Pizarro," Tobie suggested.

"Could be," said Jax, although he didn't sound convinced.

"No, she's right," said Bosch. "Carlyle and Patterson could take that as more proof that the verses refer to Pizarro. Pizarro's mother died when he was born. So I guess in a sense you could say he killed his mother."

"In a sick, twisted kind of way."

"These people are sick and twisted," said Bosch. He nodded toward the laptop. "Go on."

Jax read, " 'And on the day of ashes, the Lion shall raise his mighty swords and he shall lead the first attack by the Sons of Light against the Sons of Darkness. And the Sons of Light shall banish darkness from the earth, and they shall go on shining until the age of darkness has come to an end. And the flame of God's sword shall devour the wicked before the altar of incense, and the fire shall consume their flesh. And the holy ones shall blow the seven trumpets of death with a sharp, clear blast, and the war javelins shall fly.' "

Tobie said, "Okay. I get that this part is about killing. But how? Where? *When?*"

Jax said, "Just listen. 'And the Lion shall say, Do not be afraid, and be strong in your hearts, for God goes with us to do battle against his enemies and the day shall be ours. Like the great reaper of souls you shall cut down and lay waste to the fallen, slaying wickedness without end. Take no prisoners, glorious ones, and despoil their women and slay their children. Fear not the evildoers, for you are God's chosen ones, and the Lord shall give you dominion over them so that all must bow before you.

"'And the Lion shall say, Take the earth for the Lord's glory and your reward shall be gold and silver and all that is precious.'"

Jax looked up.

Tobie stared at him. "That's it?"

"That's it. The next part starts what is now considered Chapter Five: 'And I saw in the right hand of him that sat on the throne a book . . .'"

Tobie was practically choking on a welling of frustration. "But . . . this doesn't tell us anything!"

Bosch came to sink down on one of the seats opposite the table. "Do you think Leo Carlyle is arrogant enough to identify himself with the lion in those verses?"

Tobie said, "I thought the lion was supposed to be Jesus?"

"Usually Jesus is referred to as the Lamb of God. It's only in Revelation that the 'Lion of God' seems to refer to Jesus. In the other parts of the Bible, the Lion of God is John the Baptist. That's one reason some scholars think big chunks of Revelation were actually written early in the first century about John the Baptist."

Jax swung the computer screen around so that it was facing the journalist. "So, does any of it make sense to you?"

Bosch read through the lost chapter again, then shook his head. "No."

Tobie raked her hair away from her face. "Send it to Matt. Maybe he can run it through that super computer program of his and come up with something."

"The GIS? I guess it won't hurt to try." Jax sent the entire chapter zipping off to Matt, then flipped back to stare at the strange, lost verses again. "It's all got to be in here. We're just not seeing it."

Bosch went to pull a bottle of mineral water from the refrigerator and twisted off the top. "We've figured out the 'who' part: it's the President. We know the 'what': his murder. And we know the 'why.' What we don't know is when, where, or how. Right?"

"Let me see it," said Tobie, tilting the screen toward her. The instant she touched it, the computer froze. "Shit."

"That's weird," said Jax, hitting control/alt/delete. It took him a good five minutes to get the translation back up again.

Tobie went to sit on the other side of the plane.

Bosch said, "A. J. Carlyle told me the timing of the assassination was very important because Leo was convinced it's foretold in the lost chapter. So there must be something—"

"*The day of ashes*," said Tobie suddenly.

The two guys turned to look at her. "What?"

"That's what it says, right? 'And on the day of ashes the Lion shall raise his mighty swords.'"

"Yes. But—"

"Today is Mardi Gras. Which means that tomorrow is—"

"Ash Wednesday," said Bosch.

Jax looked at his watch. "Actually, it's already Wednesday. It's nearly six A.M. in D.C." He returned to the computer and opened up a search engine. "So now the question is, where will the President be today? If we're lucky, he'll be having a nice, easy day at the White House."

Jax tapped at the keyboard for a minute, then said, "We're not lucky. The guy's got a ridiculous schedule planned. He's flying into New Orleans first thing in the morning to give a speech pledging the federal government to the rebuilding and protection of the city. Then he's flying over to Galveston to do the same thing there. And then it's back to D.C. to attend a concert at the Kennedy Center."

"So how do we know where they plan to hit him?" said Bosch. "It could be New Orleans, Galveston, or D.C."

"It's New Orleans," said Tobie.

Jax looked over at her. "And you get that from what?"

She pushed to her feet. "They're going off the first verses, where it talks about cities of sin." She reached for the computer.

Jax put out a hand, stopping her. "I'll read it. 'And He shall send a great rising of the sea as a warning, and many thunders and great lightnings shall cleave the sky. And the waters that flow through the reeds of life like a ruby-eyed serpent shall rise and the sea with it, and then shall all the lakes and the channels spill over. And the walls shall tumble down and the hills part, and the waters of wrath shall sweep over Sodom and Gomorrah, over Babylon and Egypt, killing all before them. And when they recede all shall be left as dust.' "

"See? They've decided the reference is to the flooding of the city. Remember how some people were saying the hurricane was God's vengeance on the city for its wicked ways?"

Bosch leaned over Jax's shoulder. "So what's this part about: 'and the sun shall be cut in half like the moon, and the moon shall not give her light'?"

Tobie said, "They're probably ignoring that part. These people ignore parts of the Bible all the time. If you can overlook 'Blessed are the peacemakers' and 'Thou shalt not kill,' you can skip over some obscure bits about the moon and the sun."

Bosch said, "Okay, so they're planning to kill Pizarro in New Orleans. But *how*?"

Jax flipped through the verses. "It must be in the part about the day of ashes. It says, 'The Lion shall raise his mighty swords' followed by a bunch of gobble goop. And then it says, 'The flame of God's sword shall devour the wicked before the altar of incense, and the fire shall consume their flesh. And the holy ones shall blow the seven trumpets of death with a clear, sharp blast, and the war javelins shall fly.'" Jax looked up from the computer screen, his face unusually solemn.

Tobie said, "This speech Pizarro is giving about pledging to rebuild New Orleans—where is he giving it?"

"Before the 'altar of incense,'" said Jax. "In St. Louis Cathedral."

"Oh, shit," said Bosch, reading over Jax's shoulder. "Senator Cyrus Savoie is going to be there, too."

She shook her head. "I don't understand. Why's that significant?"

"Savoie is the president pro tem of the Senate," said Jax. "Which means that with Representative Barnett ineligible to become president because of her Canadian birth, once Pizarro and Savoie are dead, the presidency would go to—"

"Secretary of State Quincy," whispered Tobie.

Bosch said, "And Quincy is a dominionist."

66

They landed in New Orleans to find the city wrapped in a cold morning mist and Colonel F. Scott McClintock waiting for them out on the wet tarmac. He had his right arm resting in a sling and was leaning against a white Louisiana State Police car.

"I got in touch with an old Army buddy of mine at the State Police," said the Colonel, pushing away from the car to help Jax haul a couple of garment bags and a cardboard box out the backseat. "He got us two troopers' uniforms and the official passes you'll need to get into the cathedral. But we'd better step on it. The President is scheduled to arrive in the French Quarter in forty-five minutes."

While October disappeared with her uniform into the Gulfsteam's bathroom, Jax quickly stripped off his shirt and yanked the heavy navy uniform off its hanger. "Were you able get some men into the cathedral to scan for explosives?"

McClintock shook his head. "My friend with the State Police tried to send a couple of troopers he trusts in there first thing this morning with sniffer dogs. The Secret Service guys wouldn't let them anywhere near the place. Insisted they'd already checked and everything was clear."

"That doesn't sound good."

"Nope. Matt tried to tell them we've got credible reports there's an attempt on the President's life planned for today. But of course he has nothing to back it up, and they told him the threats against Pizarro's life have been running at about fifty a day since the election."

"In other words, they just blew him off," said October, coming out of the bathroom and still tucking the hem of her uniform shirt into her trousers.

"Pretty much, yes. I think we can trust the state troopers who are down there. They've all been warned to be extra vigilant. But they're going to be watching the crowd, not the guys guarding the President. That'll be our job."

Noah Bosch, who'd been sitting stony faced, listening to them, pushed to his feet. "I'm coming, too—right?"

Jax buckled a duty belt around his waist. "You're staying here."

"What the hell are you talking about? I've been working on this story for *months*. You can't expect me to just sit here."

Jax studied the journalist's thin, earnest face. There was no denying the guy had been through hell the last few days. But the fact remained that Jax didn't really know Bosch, didn't know how far he could trust him, didn't know what he could depend on the man to do—or not to do.

He tossed his Beretta to Bubba. "Make sure he stays put."

Bubba caught the gun, his own face falling. "What? I'm not comin' either?"

Jax drew one of the state-issue Sig 220s from the box, chambered a round, and set the safety. "If we don't manage to stop these guys, you're going to need to fly out of here, fast." He cast a wry glance at Bosch. "Just think: you'll have the story of a lifetime, complete with the microwave device, the Babylonian Codex, and our dead bodies to back it up."

He slipped the Sig into the holster on his belt. "Of course, with Pizarro dead and the dominionists in power, you'll probably need to take it to some Canadian or British newspaper to get it into print."

A muscle jumped along the journalist's lean jaw. "You don't understand: this isn't about the story anymore. It quit being about the story a long time ago."

"Sorry," said Jax. He watched October tuck her hair up under her big Smoky-the-Bear hat, and turned to the Colonel. "Ready?"

"Ready."

At the door, Jax paused to look back at Bubba and say, "If he gives you any trouble, shoot him."

After they left, Noah prowled the Gulfstream's compact interior. It had begun to rain, a soft drip that pattered on the roof of the fuselage and ran down the windows in little streams.

Finally, after about ten minutes, he came to a decision. Turning to where the big Cajun lounged with his feet propped up and the Beretta in his lap, Noah said, "You ever shoot a man?"

Bubba sniffed. "Few times. Why you ask?"

It wasn't the answer Noah was hoping for, but he reached for his tattered tan jacket anyway. "Because I'm catching a taxi to that cathedral. If you want to stop me, you're going to have to shoot me."

It was 98 percent bluff, of course. But it worked.

The Cajun stared at him a moment, eyes wide. Then he dropped his boots to the floor with a thump and surged to his feet. "What you talkin' about? I'm coming with you!"

67

The fog was thicker near the river, drifting low over the tops of the tightly packed eighteenth-century brick townhouses of the Quarter. Strings of beads in purple, green, and gold dangled from wrought-iron balconies and glistened here and there in the gutters. The city looked like an aging, bedraggled party girl the morning after a wild binge.

Lights flashing, McClintock turned off Canal to find the Quarter's narrow streets filled with a surging crowd of locals hoping for a glimpse of the President mixed in with knots of half-drunk tourists left over from Mardi Gras.

"Somebody needs to tell these guys Mardi Gras is over," said McClintock, trying to bully his way through the mess. "Ash Wednesday's the day for repenting of your sins, not adding to them."

"Let us out," said Jax, throwing open the door. "We can make better time on foot."

October bailed out the other side, one hand clutching her wide-brimmed trooper hat to keep it from being knocked off.

"I'll find someplace to ditch the car and catch up with you," McClintock yelled after them.

"Now that we're here, what are we supposed to do?" said October as they pushed their way past the barricades that had been set up to block all vehicular traffic within a radius of several blocks of the cathedral.

"We need to think like terrorists," said Jax. "Crazy *American* terrorists." Reaching the corner of Decatur and St. Peter, he ran his gaze over the white, Spanish-style façade of the cathedral. Built facing the river, the centuries-old church looked out over the fenced gardens of Jackson Square. To the north and south of the vast square ran the long brick expanses of the Pontablo Apartments, their nineteenth-century iron lace balconies dripping with ferns and bougainvillea and plumbago. Two matching eighteenth-century municipal buildings known as the Cabildo and the Presbytere flanked the cathedral itself. Squinting through the mist, he could see government snipers positioned on their massive mansard roofs.

"I don't think they'll make their move out here," said October as they approached the cathedral's west front. "If they're following the codex, they'll believe he needs to die before the altar."

"'And the flame of God's sword shall devour the wicked before the altar of incense,'" he quoted softly. "The problem is, swords don't flame."

There were three arched entrance doors, flanked by corner turrets and crowned by a square central bell tower. Chartres Street, running between the cathedral and the iron fence of the square, had long ago been turned into a pedestrian mall. Now it was crowded with mobile command centers and dark unmarked security vehicles and throngs of sightseers. He said, "Is there another way into the building?"

"Nothing that's open to the public, although there's a door in the alley that runs between the church and the Presbytere. I think it leads to the sacristy."

Jax nodded. "That's the way the Secret Service will bring Pizarro in. They won't want to maneuver him through the crowds out here."

October eyed the mist-swirled entrance to the alley. "They could make a move there. It's close to the altar."

Jax shook his head. "They want Savoie, too, remember?"

Flashing their passes, they pushed through the last-minute crush at the entrance. The doors opened onto a tiled vestibule scented with incense and damp masonry. Inside, the cathedral was almost stark in its Renaissance simplicity, with a soaring barrel vault. Immediately below the painted ceiling stretched two high rows of clerestory windows, their untinted glass filling the interior with a soft glow. There were no transepts, just a long nave flanked by side aisles with small stained-glass windows. Above the side aisles ran deep galleries supported by rows of marble columns.

"That's where we need to be," said Jax quietly, nodding to the second floor galleries. "You take the south; I'll take the north."

"I don't know what I'm looking for," she whispered.

"Neither do I. But October—"

She swung around to look back at him questioningly.

"Be careful."

Twin spiral staircases, one for each gallery, rose within the corner turrets. Reaching the top of the worn stone steps, Jax found the north gallery empty except for a scattering of FBI people and, about halfway toward the apse, a TV news crew setting up to broadcast the President's speech live.

Peering over the stone banister, Jax stared down at the crowded rows of pews filling the nave below. At the eastern end rose the high altar, a gilded Rococo extravaganza at the top of a series of wide shallow steps carpeted in scarlet. Half a dozen thronelike chairs with pale silk coverings and carved wooden arms had been set up on either side of the chancel. Already, a number of dignitaries were milling about, taking their seats. Jax spotted a sumptuously vested cleric he assumed must be the archbishop, several women he didn't recognize, the mayor of the city, and the distinguished senior senator from Louisiana, Cyrus Savoie.

Glancing across the open space of the nave to the opposite aisle, Jax's gaze met October's. She shook her head. *Nothing.*

He looked at his watch. It was three minutes to eleven.

Despite the crowd, the cathedral was cold, a dank chill radiating off the old stones. Yet Jax was aware of a bead of sweat forming along his hairline, beneath his trooper's hat. Swiping the back of one navy sleeve across his forehead, he ran his gaze over the soaring columns of the altar, the lectern with its bulletproof shield.

If I were going to kill the President, he thought, *how would I do it?*

His attention shifted to the lattice screening that formed a section of the walls to either side of the chancel. "Shit," he whispered, just as a stirring of movement beneath the south gallery drew his gaze to the sacristy door.

The door flew open and President Pizarro, surrounded by dark-suited Secret Service agents, strode into the nave. The people in the pews surged to their feet, cheering and clapping enthusiastically, for Pizarro was young and newly elected and promised them a bright and different tomorrow. He was smiling, one hand raised in greeting, as Senator Savoie, leaning heavily on his cane, stepped forward to welcome the President.

A movement halfway down the north gallery caught Jax's attention. A young woman with long flaxen hair, her navy windbreaker splashed with the giant letters FBI across the back in bright yellow, was striding rapidly away from him, toward the east end.

It was only then, watching her, that he realized the gallery did not continue in an unbroken line all the way to the apse but was bisected near the sanctuary steps by a stout masonry wall a good three or four feet thick. Reaching the partition, the woman swung about to press her back against the solid protecting wall.

It was Special Agent Brockman.

He watched her tip her head to first one side, then the other, her hand going up to each ear in turn. And he realized suddenly what she was doing.

She was putting in earplugs.

"Stop her!" he shouted and started to run.

Pushing through the TV crew, he sent the cameraman flying. "Hey, watch it!" the guy yelled.

Jax kept going.

Deafened by her earplugs and focused on her task, Brockman didn't hear Jax's shout. Reaching into the pocket of her jacket, she drew out a small olive green plastic box with a plastic trigger and a metal wire. Jax knew instantly what it was: a detonator for a directional antipersonnel mine known as the Claymore in honor of the venerable Scottish swords of old. All she needed to do was flip the safety out of the way and squeeze the lever, and the altar below would turn into a fiery rain of death. *And the flame of God's sword shall devour the wicked* . . .

She was bringing the detonator up when Jax reached her. He saw the puzzlement on her face, then the flare of outrage as she recognized the man beneath the broad Louisiana State Trooper's hat.

"You!" she spat as he grabbed her wrist in his left hand. He wrenched it up, hard enough to break her hold on the detonator, and slammed his right fist into her face.

She staggered sideways, blood streaming from her nose, the detonator tumbling to their feet. Her eyes narrowing with determination, she lunged for it.

Jax threw himself on it, just as three FBI agents jumped him. "Keep him down! I'll get help," Brockman shouted, and took off running for the tower stairs to the ground floor.

Tobie was on the south gallery near the east end when she heard Jax's shout. She saw him grapple with the blond FBI agent, saw Jax go down, saw the woman jerk away to pelt down the length of the gallery and disappear into the corner turret.

"*Jax!*" Tobie cried, and took off after her.

The blond woman hit the vestibule first and was out the door before Tobie rounded the last tight spiral. She heard the FBI agent yell to the security people out front, "Get inside! They need your help! Incident on the north gallery!"

Tobie had to fight her way through the resultant stampede of police officers, plainclothesmen and Secret Service officers all rushing in the doors at once. By the time she burst down the steps, the blond FBI agent was already racing up the side of the square.

Tobie sprinted after her. They dodged silver-painted mimes on platforms, babies in strollers, sidewalk artists sheltering beneath colorful umbrellas. A tourist carrying a giant takeaway daiquiri cup staggered into Tobie's path. Tobie tripped over her and careened into a juggler to send his oranges flying.

The FBI agent was almost at the street. In another minute, she would be swallowed up by the crowds milling around the French Market.

Looking frantically around for help, Tobie spotted an unmarked black Crown Victoria parked pointing the wrong way on Decatur, across from the Café du Monde, the driver's door open against the curb. A man sat at the wheel.

"Stop that woman!" Tobie yelled as they pounded toward him. "She just tried to kill the President!"

The driver pushed to his feet. He was a big guy, dark and handsome. Reaching beneath his suit jacket, he drew a Glock from his shoulder holster, chambered a round, and calmly pumped four bullets into the blond FBI agent's chest.

The *crack-crack-crack-crack* of the gun sent tourists and sidewalk artists scrambling for cover, their screams echoing around the square.

The big bullets spun the woman around. Tobie saw the look of astonishment in her face as blood poured from her mouth and her eyes rolled back in her head.

"*Oh, my God*," said Tobie, dropping to her knees beside the woman's bloody body. She could hear the footsteps of the shooter approaching and looked up, furious. "Why did you—"

She broke off as he raised the muzzle of his gun to her face. "Thou shalt not suffer a witch to live," he said, his finger tightening on the trigger.

From half a block away, Noah Bosch shouted, "It's Duane Davenport! Look out!"

Davenport jerked the muzzle of his gun toward Bosch.

And Bubba Dupuis emptied Jax's Beretta into the FBI man's big body.

68

Noah sat in a hard, straight-backed chair, his elbows propped on the cold tabletop, his chin resting on his palms. He was so tired his mind was dull and his body ached for sleep. With him around the table in the frigid, windowless room were Jax Alexander, October Guinness, Bubba Dupuis, and Colonel McClintock. They'd been interrogated separately for hours by nameless, solemn-faced men in suits. Now they had been brought together.

They had been told nothing.

"Well," said Alexander, tipping back his chair so that it balanced on its rear legs. "At least we haven't been taken to some basement room and shot."

"Yet," muttered Bubba.

Noah supposed it was meant to be funny. But as far as he was concerned, these guys had a sick sense of humor.

A flurry of movement and voices in the hall drew everyone's attention. The door opened and Senator Savoie entered, leaning heavily on a cane. He was followed by some nameless suit carrying a cardboard box. Setting the box on the table, the suit nodded to the Senator and left.

"Ensign Guinness," said Savoie, glancing around the table, "gentlemen. What I am about to tell y'all is not to leave the confines of this room. If you speak of it to anyone, it will be categorically denied." He threw a long, penetrating stare at Noah. "Understood?"

"Why?" said Noah. "What is the government denying?"

"Everything."

McClintock raised one eyebrow. "And the two dead FBI agents?"

"Were unfortunately cut down in the crossfire of a local drug war."

"No one is going to believe that," said Guinness. "There were witnesses."

Savoie cleared his throat. "It's the oddest thing, but people tend to believe what they're told. In all the confusion, with bullets flying and everyone ducking for cover, who can say what actually happened?"

"I can," said Noah.

"Only if you want to lose all credibility. Even as we speak, Agents Davenport and Brockman are being hailed as fallen heroes on all the major cable news channels."

Guinness said, "That's just fundamentally wrong from so many different angles."

"This isn't about what's true or what's right; it's about what is necessary." Lifting the lid of the cardboard box, Savoie drew out the MLFI and nudged it toward the center of the table. "None of you has ever seen this. It doesn't exist. If you claim it exists, you will be ridiculed and discredited."

Alexander gave a soft laugh. "And the other four devices that are in circulation?"

Noah felt a chill run down his spine. There were *four more* of those suckers out there?

"We are endeavoring to track them down," said the Senator. "And identify the instances in which they may have been used in the past."

Guinness sat very still. "So you're saying—what? That Vice President Hamilton's 'heart attack' will remain just that? A heart attack?"

"That's right. Just as no information on the Claymore antipersonnel mines found hidden behind the latticework on either side of the cathedral's altar will be released to the public—although, obviously, a thorough investigation is already underway to identify the Secret Service agents involved in both incidents. The organization needs to do some serious housekeeping."

"It isn't just the Secret Service that's a problem," said Alexander. "The dominionists have positioned people in the military, the FBI, the CIA—"

Savoie cleared his throat again. "The President is not convinced things are that bad."

Alexander let his chair come forward with a *click*. "And you?"

Savoie met his gaze without blinking. "I am not the President."

Guinness said, "What about Patterson and Carlyle?"

Savoie turned to her. "At this point, we have no evidence against either one—or, in fact, against anyone. At least, not anything we can take to court."

"But . . . Carlyle has the Babylonian Codex and the Inanna Vase. If you got a search warrant and—"

"I seriously doubt a search of Carlyle's Coeur d'Alene compound would find anything." Savoie put the MLFI back in the box and carefully repositioned the lid. "By now the entire collection will have been moved."

Her face flushed with anger. "So you do nothing?"

"I didn't say that. A number of investigations will be launched. But the President has decided that the important thing right now is to unite the country."

"Behind a lie?" said Guinness.

"Behind the need to repair the ravages of the last thirty years." Savoie turned to October Guinness. "You have, of course, been cleared of any involvement in the deaths of Agent Elaine Cox and the night watchman. And I've been asked by the President to convey to all of you his sincere thanks for what you have done for your country."

"His *thanks*?" echoed Noah. "That's it?"

Savoie glanced toward him. "Under the circumstances, I'm afraid that's all that's possible. Although I have talked to my friends at the *Post*. You'll be happy to hear they're ready to name you as their new White House correspondent."

Noah drew a deep breath. Once, he would have killed for this kind of an appointment. Now, all he said was, "I'll think about it."

Savoie turned toward the door, the tip of his cane tap-tapping on the tiles. "Don't think about it for too long, Mr. Bosch. Refusing the position would be a grand gesture—but ultimately counterproductive."

Two weeks later, Jax stood beside a one-way mirror at the Algiers Naval Facility across the Mississippi River from the French Quarter. In the dimly lit, soundproof room on the other side of the glass sat October and Colonel McClintock. She had her eyes closed, her chest rising gently with each deep breath as she settled down into her Zone.

"That's good, Tobie," Jax heard the Colonel say. "Relax."

They had all come together to work with Dr. Elizabeth Stein in an effort to fulfill Elaine Cox's dream of using remote viewing to track down some of Iraq's missing antiquities. This would be October's first run against the artifacts since Elaine's death.

"Did you hear the news about Carlyle?" said Captain Peter Abrams.

Jax glanced at Abrams, who sat in a chair beside him. The captain's face was still pale and he had one arm in a sling, but he had insisted on being here.

"No," said Jax. "What?"

"Murder-suicide. This morning, in Paris. He was supposedly shot by his assistant, Casper Nordstrom, who then turned the gun on himself."

Jax grunted. It hadn't been twenty-four hours since the naked body of Warren Patterson had been discovered in Atlantic City, in the kind of cheap hotel where rooms rent by the hour. Heart attack, said the coroner. Another prominent dominionist, an insurance-industry magnate named Ross Cole, had disappeared off his yacht in the Gulf of Mexico and was presumed drowned.

"Who do you think is doing this?" asked Abrams. "Our guys?"

"It's possible. Although I'd be more willing to put my money on the dominionists themselves. Looks to me like they're eliminating anyone they think might have been compromised."

"In other words, they're still out there," said Abrams after a moment, his attention, like Jax's, on the scene on the other side of the glass. "Or at least some of them. Sometimes I feel like we're playing Whack-a-Mole."

"Pretty much, yeah."

On the other side of the glass, McClintock laid his hand on the paper on the table before him and said, "Okay, Tobie, focus on item number three seven nine four, and tell me what you see."

Beside Jax, Abrams said, "I thought you didn't believe in remote viewing?"

"I don't."

Abrams smiled. "Then why are you here?"

Jax kept his gaze on October. "Because I believe in her."

AUTHOR'S NOTE

Wondering what's real and what isn't? Here's a quick rundown, with sources for further reading.

• The government **remote viewing** programs, their history, and the various historical incidents described in this series are real. These programs, known as Grill Flame, Sun Streak, Center Lane, and Star Gate (among others), were officially terminated in 1995–96 and some of their relevant material declassified. For an entertaining look at the programs' history, we suggest *Men Who Stare at Goats,* by Jon Ronson (the book, not the movie).

• The remote viewing sessions described in this book are as accurate as we can make them within the confines of the story. For a more complete and authoritative analysis of the process, see Joseph McMoneagle's book *Mind Trek.*

• The **Babylonian Codex** is a figment of the author's imagination. The so-called lost chapter is actually a compilation of verses inspired by some of the numerous Jewish apocalyptic texts extant, including the Sibylline Oracles, translated by M. S. Terry; the Ascension of

Isaiah, translated by R. McL. Wilson and M. A. Knibb; the
Second Baruch and Enoch, translated by R. H. Charles;
The Apocalypse of Thomas, translated by M. R. Jones; and
the War Scroll (perhaps the most famous of the Dead Sea
Scrolls), translated by M. Wise, M. Abegg, E. Cook, F. G.
Martinez, and G. Vermes. For more on this tradition, see
James C. VanderKam, *The Jewish Apocalyptic Heritage
in Early Christianity*, and *The Apocalyptic Imagination:
An Introduction to Jewish Apocalyptic Literature*, by John
Joseph Collins.

• The **Book of Revelation,** also known as the Apocalypse
of St. John, is a cryptic, highly symbolic, and intensely con-
troversial book of the Bible. Its history as described to Jax
and Tobie by the various scholars follows current historical-
critical research. See, *Revelation*, by J. Massyngberde
Ford; *Cosmology and Eschatology in Jewish and Christian
Apocalyptism*, by Adela Yarbro Collins; *Jesus: Apocalyptic
Prophet of the New Millennium*, by Bart D. Ehrman; and
*The Apocalyptic Imagination: An Introduction to Jewish
Apocalyptic Literature*, by John Joseph Collins.

• The **dominionist movement** is both real and powerful.
Its adherents' aim is indeed to turn the United States into
a nation governed by their interpretation of biblical law.
Also real are Joel's Army, the Seven Mountains movement,
the New Wave Reformation, The New Apostolic Reformation, and the Joshua Generation. See especially Theocracy
Watch, a project run by Cornell University's Center for Religion, Ethics, and Social Policy, at www.theocracywatch.
org; *American Fascists: the Christian Right and the War
on America*, by Chris Hedges; *American Theocracy: The
Perils and Politics of Radical Religion, Oil, and Borrowed
Money in the 21st Century*, by Kevin Phillips; *Spiritual*

Warfare: The Politics of the Christian Right, by Sara Diamond, and *Roads to Dominion: Right-Wing Movements and Political Power in the United States*, also by Sara Diamond.

• **Rushdoony** and **Reconstructionism** are real. See Rousas J. Rushdoony's book, *The Institutes of Biblical Law*; and *Christian Reconstructionism*, by Gary North, Rushdoony's son-in-law. **The Family** or **the Fellowship** is real. See Jeff Sharlet's book, *The Family*. **The Council for National Policy** is real. Members past and present are said to include Jack Abramoff, Elsa Prince of the Blackwater Princes, James Dobson, Jerry Falwell, Gary North, Oliver North, Tim LaHaye, and Trent Lott. See www.policycounsel.org.

• **Mikey Weinstein** and **the Military Religious Freedom Foundation** are real. See www.militaryreligiousfreedom.org. For more on dominionists in the United States military, see Jeff Sharlet, "Jesus Killed Mohammed: The Crusade for a Christian Military," in *Harper Magazine*, May 2009. The former U.S. deputy undersecretary of Defense for Intelligence, Lt. General William G. Boykin, gained considerable notoriety for numerous speeches and interviews in which he disparaged Islam and cast the War on Terror in biblical terms.

• The widespread torture and murder of **African children accused by evangelical Christian pastors of being witches** is a very real problem. See *ABC NewsNightline* (abcnews.go.com/nightline), "Child Witches: Accused in the Name of Jesus," original air date May 21, 2009; *World News Network* (wn.com), "Children of Congo: From War to Witches," ICRC Interview, 11 parts, air dates not listed. Be warned, these images are haunting.

• For the **early days of Christianity**, see, among many others, *The Jews in the Time of Jesus: An Introduction*, by Stephen M. Wylen; and *Jews and Christians: The Parting of the Ways,* A.D. *70 to 135*, by James D. G. Dunn. For the **Assyrian Church**, see, *The Church of the East, an Illustrated History of Assyrian Christianity,* by Christoph Baumer; and *The Lost History of Christianity: The Thousand-Year Golden Age of the Church in the Middle East, Africa, and Asia—and How It Died*, by John Philip Jenkins.

• For more on the destruction of the archaeological site of **Babylon** by the United States military, see especially UNESCO's "Final Report on Damage Assessment in Babylon," available online at unesdoc.unesco.org/images/0018/001831/183134E.pdf. On **the theft of antiquities from Iraq**, see *Catastrophe! The Looting and Destruction of Iraq's Past*, by Geoff Emberling and Katheryn Hanson, editors, Oriental Institute, University of Chicago; and *Antiquities under Siege: Cultural Heritage Protection after the Iraq War*, by Lawrence Rothfield. The rumors that the thefts were preplanned and had some assistance are persistent, although little investigated. See among many others, "Professionals suspected in looting of museum," *International Herald Tribune*, 21 April 2003.

• For the **World Economic Forum** and the power of the "Davos men," see David Rothkopf's book *Superclass*: *The Global Power Elite and the World They Are Making*.

• The MLFI is a creation of the authors. However, the U.S. government has been actively investigating the development of **high-power microwave (HPM) weapons** for years. Persistent, credible reports suggest such experimental weapons were used in both the Gulf War and the War on Iraq. Microwave "crowd control" weapons have also been developed and deployed, although they are proving controversial since they are not exactly "nonlethal." All weapons of this nature developed so far are—to our knowledge—large. See "Details of US microwave-weapon tests revealed," *New Scientist*, 22 July 2005; "High Power Microwaves: Strategic and Operational Implications for warfare," by Colonel Eileen M. Walling, February 2000, at the Center for Strategy and Technology, Maxwell Air Force Base, Alabama; and "High-power microwave (HPM) E-Bomb," at global Security.org.

• There is no law requiring rangers to report the license plates of cars left overnight in national parks.